To Peggy with

A Grandma for Christmas

A novel by

Enjoy!

Sunny Serafino

"…life can change in a matter of hours by people who don't even know you…"
author unknown

ISBN: 978-1-60458-107-2

This book is a work of fiction. Names, characters and incidents are either the products of the author's imagination or are used fictitiously. Any resemblance to actual events, locals, or persons, living or dead, is entirely coincidental.

Introduction:

My books are an extension of myself. Each one requires new input, demands new efforts. Each one continues to fulfill my dreams. *A Grandma for Christmas* is a work of fiction but it touches many aspects of real lives, mine included.

Two women—as different as night and day, form an accidental and totally unknown alliance in the life of one precious child. The child is a child; the plot is unusual, devious at times, tense and uncertain but it continues to evolve until all the facts are known, all the questions are answered... or are they?

Acknowledgements and thanks:

No work is a single entity. A writer may think he or she works alone but input from many sources contributes to the final, finished product.

A simple thank you seems so inadequate to those of you who help me . All of you also know that it takes contributions of wisdom, expertise, time and talent, and that is what makes you very special to the work and to me personally.

Thanks go to—Dot Pansius who reads everything I write, over and over again and encourages me along the way, a very necessary and most welcome contribution—to Bette Crosby, a fellow author who has so much talent and has been in the wings for all my endeavors, sharing her confidence and support in this difficult but fulfilling endeavor called writing—to Sharon Gerdes and Bitsy Gillette who also share with me a valued measure of faith and who read and read and read the manuscript until it's a finished product—to Pat Lehane, Joe Tracy and Bob Morrissey, retired police officers who helped immensely in the areas I was so unprepared for—to Bill Rogers of Highlands Today—and to many more who stand in the wings with a hint when necessary, a word of encouragement and a pat on the back or a hug when needed.

I couldn't end my list of thanks without mentioning my darling husband, Lenny, who has encouraged and supported me from the very first word I etched onto paper. His steadfast confidence in my work, and me, even when I'm ready to give up, makes me feel almost a special as he claims I am. His love and support have kept me writing, fulfilling a life-long dream. I love him and I love what I do.

CHAPTER ONE

The journey of a 1,000 miles must begin with a single step.

Lau-tzu

Madison gripped the steering wheel, her knuckles white with tension. The road ahead became narrower and more twisted as she drove through the forested mountains. She was running away—a little scared maybe, but determined. *This time*, she thought, *this time I mean it.*

Her eyes blinked rapidly as the rain intensified. *If the temperature drops, I'll be skating on thin ice—literally,* she thought. She glanced at the dashboard clock. 2:04. The soup she'd forced herself to eat before leaving the city, sloshed uncomfortably in her stomach. At least she'd remembered to stock up on some groceries before leaving Philadelphia. A carton in the trunk held a whole roasted chicken, bread, butter, eggs, milk, cereal and coffee. She'd even thrown in her favorite cheese, some fancy crackers and a bottle of wine, not that she was celebrating anything. But on the other hand, maybe she should be celebrating. *Enough food to last a few days at the cottage; that's all I need. Peace and quiet and ...* She let her thoughts drift as she concentrated on the wet road ahead of her.

Visibility was getting worse every mile and she wiped a gloved hand across the windshield. *The temperature must be dropping,* she thought and taking one hand from the wheel, turned the radio on. Without taking her eyes from the road, she twisted the knob picking up one Christmas carol after another. The sentimental, familiar songs hardened her heart with every cheery word. This was Christmas Eve and she was alone—not that she hadn't been alone on past Christmas Eves or holidays, for that matter. Somehow past loneliness didn't seem as intense, not so painful; this loneliness was deeper; it cut into her heart like a knife going through soft cheese.

"Maybe it's the weather," she rationalized, then grimaced as she finally heard crackly static interrupted by garbled voices. A newscast. That's what she was looking for. She frowned as the reporter finished up local news and then said, "Now for the weather report. Sorry to tell you folks out there who are trying to get home for Christmas sometime tonight," his well-trained voice chirped, "but the weather front predicted to arrive early tomorrow morning has moved in faster than expected. Santa is going to have slow going tonight. Heavy snow and icy conditions are predicted within the next two hours for the entire upper north central counties of Pennsylvania. Expected accumulation is thought to be in the area of twelve to fourteen inches, perhaps more in higher elevations, and could even increase with the sudden fall in temperatures and rising winds. Driving is hazardous and getting worse. Better get '*over the river and through the woods to Grandmother's house,*' as soon as you can," he said with a singsong lilt.

The words to that song brought back vivid images. Childhood Christmases at her grandmother's house. Mysteriously the scent of gingerbread baking filled her nostrils. For a brief moment there was no wet, dark pavement in front of her, just the memory of a warm house and happy voices. "Just one cookie, Grandma. Please?" but she was warned, "You'll spoil your appetite." As if anything would keep them from filling their stomachs with turkey, stuffing, Aunt Alice's special 'smashed' potatoes. Even Brussels sprouts tasted good on Christmas Day. And the desserts! Madison felt her mouth water at the memories.

With an angry jerk she turned the radio off and now only the rhythmic thumping of the wiper blades broke the bleak silence. She was so alone!

Searching the growth along the side of the road to see if ice was forming on the branches, she muttered, "I've come too far now to turn back. Anyhow I've burned my bridges." *Well, not quite all of them, at least Jo knows where I'm going.* She smiled. Josephine Ignatia Petrillo—her best friend; the one she confided in, who knew all her secrets. The friend who shared in her triumphs, celebrating each new book with her and also her darkest moments when her life took one of her self-inflicted downturns and she needed a shoulder to cry on or someone to give her a well-deserved kick in the pants.

But Jo wasn't with her now and Madison drew in a deep breath and blew it through pursed lips. She pictured Jo, dark hair that refused to be contained by clips or scrungees, her natural dark skin always flawless and exotic looking. Tonight Jo was with her family, all eighteen of them. Madison knew what the crowded three-story house in Little Italy would be like, filled with relatives from great-grandparents to the newest baby, all accompanied by the smell of wonderful Italian dishes. She remembered the aroma of shrimp sauce and baccala and other traditional fish dishes that Madison had never heard of before. Then there were the wonderful desserts. Two years ago Jo had finally won her on-going battle to have Madison join them for the first time and after that it was a given that she would be with them for every Christmas Eve celebration. Last night when Madison had called her to tell her she was going away for a few days Jo had shouted into the telephone, "Dammit, you can't be alone on Christmas Eve."

She had had a difficult time convincing Jo that right now she needed to be alone. "This year is different, okay? I'll be with you next year. This year I'd be a wet blanket."

"Baloney. We'd cheer you up."

Madison agreed that might be possible but held her ground and now she was crawling along a narrow winding road in rain that was sure to turn to snow almost any time.

For a moment Madison shivered as if the cold outside had seeped into the car. She slowed for a curve. *Damn this weather!*

Her fingers gripped the steering wheel even more tightly as the rain turned to snow and the wipers brushed soft piles of white fluff to the sides of the windshield. She had to remind herself to breathe; her body was so tense.

Surely there would be somewhere she could pull off the road—maybe even get a cup of tea, see another human being. She sighed, rounded yet another curve and gasped. There up ahead was a glimmer of light and she sat taller, straining to see. A diner! Set back from the road, one lone car in front. Her grimace turned to a smile as she pulled her car next to the one in the parking lot. Taking her purse and hurrying through the snow to the steps, Madison thought, *See, things aren't all bad. I'll get through this. A hot cup of tea and then on to the cottage. I'll call Jo when I get there. I promised.* She pulled the glass door open and stepped into the welcome warmth.

CHAPTER TWO

...life can change in a matter of hours by people who don't even know you...

Author unknown

It was unusually dim inside the diner and a man stood at the cash register at the end of the counter nearest the door. "Well, about time you got here! Do you know it's Christmas Eve, for God's sake? Where the hell have you been?"

Madison stood rooted to the floor. She stared at the young man who slammed the drawer back into the cash register, glowered at her and reached for a jacket hanging behind him. She opened her mouth to speak when a small bundle of pink and blue ran to her, shouting, "Grandma you came. I knew you'd come. Mommy said so." Madison felt small arms clutch her legs and looked down into a cherubic face surrounded by dark curls. She looked from the tiny hopeful face to the young man, still behind the counter.

"Pretty dammed mean to leave the kid waitin' here all that time, is what I think. Waitin' for you. She was good. Not a peep. Kept tellin' me her grandma was comin' to get her. I kept givin' her milk and cookies. Have three kids myself. But it's Christmas Eve, lady. I gotta get home. Should' a been home an hour or more ago." He rattled his car keys. "Let's go."

"Wait," Madison stuttered. "I'm… I'm not this little girl's grandmother. I don't know who she is. I just stopped because I saw your lights and wanted a cup of tea."

"No tea, no coffee, no nothin'. No siree. I'm leaving, lady, and you're takin' the kid." He moved from behind the counter.

"I don't know this little girl," she said, bending down to look into wide blue eyes. "Who's your Mommy, honey? Who's your grandma?" Madison looked back at the young man. "How did she get here? Did someone just drop her off?"

"Look, lady. All I know is it was real crowded around two o'clock today. All the regulars celebratin' a little early. When the crowd left, there she was in a booth. All alone. Snowsuit, backpack and no one around. She keeps tellin' me she's waitin' for her grandma. You walk in. She yells "Grandma" and we're outta here. Let's get going. The snow is really comin' down now."

He stared into Madison's eyes. "I'm leavin'," he said nudging Madison towards the door, the little girl still holding onto the hem of Madison's jacket. "Get her backpack," he added, pointing to a purple denim backpack on the table in the first booth. "Let's go. I'm lockin' up."

"How can you be so cruel? Did you call the police? Someone has abandoned this child," Madison said, pulling the zipper on the child's jacket up under her tiny chin.

"She said she was waitin' for you." He stood by the door, his keys in his hand.

"Well she isn't waiting for me. I have no grandchildren. No children. You can't just abandon her here like this."

"I ain't abandonin' her. You're takin' her with you, Grandma, and I'm goin' home. Come on."

Madison turned her back to the surly young man and stooped down. She put her arm around the child. "Can you tell me who your mommy is, honey? What's her name?"

The child bobbed her head up and down. "Her name is Mommy."

Madison tried to smile. "Oh, I know but what do other people call her?"

The little girl lifted her shoulders and blinked her eyes. "Sometimes Missy and the mans call her Flower, but she's not really a Flower." The child put her fingers over her mouth and giggled.

Madison sighed. "Do you know where you live?"

Again the child shrugged. "Once we lived in a car but now we have a nice room."

Madison looked at the face of the owner of the diner. "Did you hear that? A homeless mother has abandoned her. Now what we have to do is find some authorities to take care of her."

"Lady I'm not findin' anyone. You wanna take over the search you go ahead. I gotta leave. It's getting' dark, I'm thirty minutes from home and it's snowin' like hell. Let's go. You want to call somebody, you do it."

Madison stood and picked up the child's backpack. She felt a small soft hand slip into hers and looked down into the angelic face again. The child looked a lot like her niece, Caitlin when she was younger and for a moment Madison felt her heart melt. Was it only last year, when she'd sought the help of a psychologist, that she'd been told some of her trouble stemmed from envying her sister's more normal lifestyle? Was that true? Madison pulled herself back to the present.

"Come on, honey. I'll help you find your grandmother."

Together the three left the diner, the young man turned a key in the lock and then hurried to his car. He paused, his hand on the door handle. "I gotta leave. You understand, don't you? They're waitin' for me."

The snow was driving hard now and both cars were covered with an inch of white fluff. Madison stooped and helped the child into the front seat, adjusted the seat belt and heard the catch snap. She walked around to the driver's side, noting the man still stood next to his car.

"You have a cell phone?" he said, his hand on the open car door.

"Yes."

"You can call someone, okay?"

"Yes."

"Sorry," he called softly through the snowy night. "I really gotta go."

"I understand," Madison said, although she really didn't. What had she done to deserve this? Was it fair that she was now saddled with someone else's child? Burdened with responsibility? All she wanted to do was get in out of the cold. Open that bottle of wine and unwind. Was that too much to ask? In fact, opening the wine sounded better and better. She wanted to be alone, which seemed surprising since all the way along this trip she'd bewailed the fact that she was always alone.

"Merry Christmas," the young man said ducking into his car.

"Merry Christmas," she called in automatic response.

Madison watched him back out, slipping and sliding onto the road. His taillights disappeared quickly into the gloom.

"Where are we going, Grandma?" the little girl asked as Madison slid behind the wheel.

"I'm going to try and find your real grandma, honey. I'm not your grandma."

"But Mommy said you would come and get me." She twisted in her restraint. "Mommy said you'd be there. To wait for you. And I did. And you came. I just knew it was you."

"Well, there must be some mistake but we'll work it out, okay?" She patted the back of the child's hand. "What's your name, dear?"

"Barbara Ann," she announced, "but everyone calls me Bitsy."

"Everyone?"

"Well," Bitsy said, "Mommy does. Missy does." She paused, then added, "and sometimes the mans do, too."

"What man?" Madison asked, a cold shiver crawling up her spine.

"All of them."

Madison sighed and started the car. With her right hand she pushed the heat up to high. "Let me see if I can get some help." Taking her cell phone from her purse she dialed 9-1-1 only to read "no service available" on the tiny screen.

"Oh, damn!"

"That's a bad word. Mommy says so."

Madison stemmed threatening tears. She didn't have time for crying now. Pulling out onto the road, she noticed the tracks made by the young man's car when he left the lot were almost obliterated and the snow was falling faster, adding marshmallow toppings to small bushes and along bare branches.

"Where are we going?" Bitsy asked.

"To a cottage. It's quite a long way and the road is pretty slippery but we'll be okay." Her assurance was hollow and she gripped the wheel even harder. "What a day," she mumbled.

"I like snow. It's pretty," Bitsy said.

"It makes pretty pictures but it's cold and scary sometimes."

"Scary things are make-believe," Bitsy said with worldly wisdom. "Mommy says so. It's silly to worry. She says that, too."

"How old are you, Bitsy?"

"I'm this many," she said and Madison turned to see four fingers raised. "But," she added, "I'll be five soon."

Madison thought the little girl looked younger. Maybe it was her size, she was very tiny, but then again what did she know about kids. "Do you have mittens or gloves?"

She shrugged. "Maybe in my backpack. Mommy put lots of things in there. It's heavy."

Madison glanced in the rear view mirror but couldn't see the backpack she'd thrown onto the back seat. She did, however, remember that it appeared to be stuffed pretty full.

"Why did you think I was your grandmother, Bitsy? Do I look like her?"

"I never saw my grandma before but you look just like Mommy said you would."

"Oh?"

"Yep. She said you would be pretty and have a nice smile and you would love me. I knew you were my grandma when you came into the restaurant," she added with authority.

Madison sighed. *What a predicament and now of all times,* she thought, straining to see through the increasing snow. *It's not like I don't have enough on my mind.* She glanced at the clock. If her cell phone didn't work, the towers were probably out of commission due to the weather. And at this time and place where would she find any help. "It's Christmas Eve, for God's sake," she muttered.

"I know," replied Bitsy. "Grandma, do you think Santa will find us? Maybe he'll get lost in the snow. Maybe he knows I'm not home anymore." From the corner of her eye, Madison saw the little girl's lower lip tremble.

"I'm sure he will, dear." *Now what? This poor baby is expecting Christmas and all she's got is me! No tree. No gifts. What was her mother thinking of!*

"Sometimes Christmas is different if you're not home, honey. Maybe this Christmas will be different."

"Mommy said you would love me," she repeated with a sniff.

Madison's heart curled into a tiny ball as if it was made of aluminum foil and some great hand had crunched it.

"Tell me, Bitsy. Does your mommy have any sisters? Brothers? Do you have cousins, aunts, uncles?"

"I don't think so. Mommy says she's never going back to Miss… Miss… I forget where."

"Is it a person you're trying to remember?"

"I don't think so."

Madison sighed. *If only I knew more about this child…or her family.* She stared ahead, concentrating on the road. Visibility was very poor now and her headlights poked two blurred holes in the raging snow they were pushing through.

After what seemed like an eternity, she saw the stone pillars that marked the driveway to the cottage. Turning with caution, as the road under the covering of snow was slippery and she'd fishtailed several times coming up and down hills along the way, she began the journey along the narrow lane.

For the past hour the drive had been tense and she'd had to concentrate on the road, keeping her own problems in abeyance. It worked for a while but after Bitsy fell asleep she couldn't keep the past from nagging her along the way.

"If only…" she'd started time and time again.

Finally, she saw the front of the cottage. *Cottage*, she thought. *More like the manor house on a fancy estate. Oh, well, that's part of the past, too. This is just a temporary stop.* She turned to look at Bitsy who was sleeping peacefully.

CHAPTER THREE

But our beginnings never know our ends...
Thomas Sterns Eliot

When she'd left the diner the young woman's heart had pounded crazily and her breathing was so labored she thought of nothing else but putting miles between her and the diner. Now she was numb, moving robotically, applying brake and gas, turning the wheel and making decisions as to what road to follow. There didn't seem to be any purpose for her journey and she didn't care.

Her body trembled but it wasn't from cold, it was... She sighed heavily. The young woman continued to drive along unfamiliar roads, her frozen fingers holding the steering wheel of the car in a death grip.

Lily Rose Smith hadn't had a great deal of good fortune during her twenty-four years of life. Born poor, she couldn't remember the number of places she'd live in, nor count the changes of school. At sixteen she'd left Mississippi and her struggling parents and four younger sisters. She headed north seeking anything that was better than fields under a cruel sun or hovels where there was little heat.

Over the years she'd worked in a dozen or more mills, crowded airless buildings that were smothering hot in the summer and bitter cold in winter. She'd sewed, operated a packing machine, stocked supplies and shipped heavy boxes. Once she'd even cleaned toilets in order to survive.

She felt a single tear slip down each cold cheek. "Working mills weren't all that bad compared to... But after I had my baby... I couldn't leave her all day.

Besides," she whined to herself, "the money was better. It was easier to disappear—blend in so's nobody took notice of you. Easier that way." She'd become accustomed to living in a very small world even if it was in the center of a huge city. All this space around her now frightened her.

Her mind wandered. Funny how she got to Philadelphia. She struggled to remember and a picture flashed into her mind. She saw the huge truck and the driver with a straggly black beard and arms covered with tattoos who'd given her a lift from Lexington. That was a rainy spring day five years ago. She never even knew his name but her short association with him was what led to her life in the City of Brotherly Love.

"Five years ago," she muttered, turning onto another anonymous, lonely road. "That was when I knew what Mama meant when she said, 'you do anything for your younguns, child. Anything." Lily counted Bitsy's birth as the only blessing in her short life. And now…

~ ~ ~

Two months ago, Lily knew something was wrong; she was losing weight but putting on inches. At first, she worried that she might be pregnant again, her belly stuck out so far, but she soon found out that wasn't true and while that was a relief, her discomfort and her worry continued to grow daily. She'd sit in her room, alone after Bitsy was asleep and puzzle over and over again. W*hat is the problem*? "Nighttime is such a worrisome time," she muttered, "when you got a true worry."

Late one night, after Bitsy was asleep, Lily tiptoed down the hallway to Missy's room. Missy was her only friend if you could call a six-foot tall, black hooker who wore a blonde wig, a friend. She was a good soul, though, watching Bitsy when Lily needed her to. She tapped tentatively on the scarred and nicked door.

"Who? Missy called.

"Me."

Missy opened the door. She still had her blonde wig on and wore a flowing caftan in iridescent colors. It accented her dark skin. "Drink?" she offered, lifting a glass half-filled with amber liquid.

"No, thanks. Got a minute?"

"Got nothing to do but…" she re-lifted the drink and took a big swallow. "Come on in. Where's the brat?"

"Sleeping," Lily said, stepping into a room much like hers except that this one was decorated with silver stars on dark walls and ceiling and the scent of incense permeated the air. Every surface, walls, tabletops and shelves, was crowded with statues, pictures and knick-knacks, most of them covered in glittery jewels.

"Sit," Missy said, pushing several velvet pillows aside. "What's up?"

"Me," Lily said, softly lowering herself to the ancient sofa. "I think there's somethin' wrong."

'Wrong? With you?"

"Yeah, I'm losin' weight, but look at my belly," she said raising the oversized tee shirt she wore. "Blowin' up like a balloon."

"Huh, losin' weight? Like that should be a problem?" Missy was skin and bones but she always saw herself as badly in need of a diet. Not that she cut back on the liquor. "That ain't fattenin'," she'd often said.

"I'm not tryin' to lose weight or anything. My belly is just gettin' bigger and bigger. God, I thought I was pregnant again but that ain't it."

"You sure?"

"Yeah. And, now when I climb the stairs I can't hardly breathe. I'm worried."

"Well, go to a doctor," Missy told her.

"Don't have insurance," Lily complained.

"There's free clinics, honey. Go there."

They talked for a few minutes and then Lily left and returned to her room. It was late but city sounds filtered through the lone window; the usual noises of the other tenants in the three-story rooming house with paper-thin walls seeped into her barren room. "I can't be sick," she muttered softly. "I have to take care of Bitsy." Tears slipped from her eyes and down her cheeks and she buried her head in her arms resting on the battered wooden table. Her straight black hair fell forward, covering her arms but not her sorrow. She was scared and where did a single mom, poor and alone go for help?

After another two weeks and more weight loss and even more difficulty breathing, Lily decided she might as well try for some free information and, after dropping Bitsy at Missy's, she boarded a bus to the clinic. She waited in the crowded, noisy waiting room for over two hours before she was ushered into a cubicle where a young man, with light brown skin and eyes as black as two chunks of licorice, began the examination. He poked and prodded, and asked question after question but after replying as best she could because his English was difficult to understand, she watched him clasp his hands behind his back and stare up at the ceiling for a moment.

"You must see Dr. Zinfanis," he said. "It is important."

"Can't. I don't have no insurance."

"I fix. I make appointment for you. Today."

"I can't..."

"It is necessary. Today," he added with authority.

Lily took the scrawled prescription he offered and returned to the waiting room as instructed. The messy room hadn't improved any and seemed even more crowded with pregnant women and children who wriggled and squirmed over the floor and any unoccupied furniture. Finally she was called to the window.

"You can see Dr. Zinfanis at two o'clock today. Here is the order and his address." The black woman behind the desk gave her a brief smile. "Good luck," she murmured, turning back to her computer screen.

Dr. Zinfanis' office was elegant compared to the clinic and after Lily checked in at the window and took a seat she shivered with apprehension. The wording on the door confused her. What was an oncologist? *Lord'a mercy, I can't pay for this kinda office,* she thought, paging through a magazine that appeared to have most of its pages.

Dr. Zinfanis looked incredibly young to have acquired all the diplomas and awards displayed in neat black frames on the walls in his office. He was tall, painfully thin and sandy haired. He wore a pristinely clean white coat and sat behind his desk reading the orders from the clinic. It seemed to Lily he took an awful long time going over the skimpy papers.

Finally he leaned back and looked at her intently. "I'm going to examine you now and then order some tests, blood work, an x-ray of your abdomen and chest, perhaps a CAT scan or MRI. We can schedule all that from this office. Then when we have the results we will know how to proceed."

"Doctor, I don't have no insurance."

"I understand. There are programs for help. We'll handle all that. Now," he said standing, "I'm going to have my nurse prepare you for my examination." He grinned at her. "Don't look so frightened."

"But, what do you think is wrong with me? I have a little girl... We don't have it so good," she said softly.

"No use guessing. I never do. Dr. ..." he looked at the notes from the clinic, "Dr. Singh was right to send you here. Wait until after the examination and see what tests are needed. When the tests come back, then we can talk about the diagnosis and prognosis."

The solemn sound of his voice and the big words added another measure of chill to her body.

Ten days later, after a visit to a lab for blood work, and a trip the hospital for x-rays and an MRI, which was about the scariest thing she'd ever done—like being put into a noisy coffin—she again sat in Dr. Zinfanis' examination room. Wearing a paper gown and shivering in the cold room, she waited for him.

When the doctor swung the door open he was smiling. He put the chart on the table and said, “How are you today?”

Lily grunted a greeting and felt her spirits lift a bit. At least *he* didn’t look worried.

“Just a few more pokes and then we’ll talk,” he said, helping her to lie back on the slippery paper sheet while the nurse covered her with a thin cotton sheet. When he asked her to sit up he turned and took the file. “Well, my friend, we have some problems here.”

CHAPTER FOUR

Only when we are no longer afraid do we begin to live.
Dorothy Thompson

When Madison stepped out of the car in front of the cottage, the snow was well over her ankles. Her sneakers, socks and the lower part of her tan cords sucked up the icy water like hungry sponges and she wished she'd worn the nice dry boots that were in the trunk of her car.

The cottage was dark and cold when Madison opened the front door. Although she'd been here dozens of times the interior suddenly felt foreign. Tentatively, she reached for the switch she knew was on the left wall in the foyer. When the overhead light came on she released a big sigh and then hurried to turn on a lamp next to one of the padded wing chairs near the fireplace. As she looked around quickly she was amazed at how big the room looked. She'd never noticed that before.

"Well, at least we got here safely. Thank you, Lord," she murmured and hurried back to her car and Bitsy.

She deposited Bitsy, still sound asleep, on the long sofa facing the fireplace and then made three more trips to the car getting everything in. The snow continued to fall but now the flakes were driven by a cruel wind almost horizontally across the clearing in front of the cottage.

Closing the door behind her and depositing her bag and briefcase on the foyer floor next to the box of food, she stripped her sodden socks and shoes from icy feet and pushed the suitcase into the living room. Bitsy still slept peacefully. Rummaging in her suitcase, she found her slippers and a pair of socks and put them both on, rubbing her feet to get feeling back.

Madison shivered in the cool room and remembered that the thermostat was on the wall in the west hallway leading to the master bedroom suite. She hurried across the room and pushed the arrow to heat, setting the temperature at 75°. She waited in the silence to hear the furnace in the cellar kick on. When she heard the soft humming she hurried back to the sleeping child. *Thank God the heat and electricity are left on, but then I know he always did that during the winter. The cable television and the phone are disconnected but we don't need those. Not for the few days we'll be here.*

Taking Bitsy's backpack, she sat on the opposite end of the sofa. Opening the Velcro sealed pockets and, unzipping the largest compartment, she began to pull the clothes out—tiny socks and panties, short-sleeved undershirts and flannel pajamas, a pink pair covered with white kittens and a purple pair with dancing bears. There were also neatly folded shirts, pants and sweaters and another pair of shoes, but no boots. In the very bottom of the bag, Madison found a small purple purse with red sequined letters. BAS. "Must be Bitsy's purse. Now at least I'll be able to ask her what her last name is. Why didn't I think of that before?" She sighed and looked over at the sleeping child still in her snowsuit. On her feet were Nike sneakers. She marveled at how much Bitsy's mother had managed to cram into the backpack.

When the backpack had been emptied, Madison searched through it one more time, hoping to find a note, an address, a telephone number, anything that would identify who Bitsy really was or, even more important, who her mother was, but there was nothing. "Damn her," she muttered, pushing the empty sack down next to the sofa.

"Are we there yet?" the child called, struggling to sit up, twin fists rubbing sleepy eyes.

"Oh, yes, honey," Madison said, hurrying to kneel at her side. "Here, let me get you out of those clothes. I've unpacked your things and I saw pretty pjs for you to put on."

Bitsy looked around in awe. The lights that Madison had put on glowed warmly in the large paneled room revealing open beams in the cathedral ceiling. Bitsy's eyes took in the fireplace and the floor to ceiling bookcases that took up two walls. "This is a pretty house, Grandma," she whispered. "It's so big. I like it."

"It is pretty, honey, not mine, though. We're just borrowing it for a few days."

Madison peeled the clothes from Bitsy's body and snuggled her into the pink pajamas. "Here, we'll leave your socks on because I didn't see any slippers."

"I don't have slippers anymore. They got too little for me."

"I'll bet you got too big for them," Madison said, smiling.

Bitsy grinned and nodded her head. "I'm getting big. Mommy said so. She even gave some of my clothes to the kids at my school."

"Oh," Madison said, eager to find out more about this abandoned angel. Did she detect a softening when Bitsy spoke—a southern accent maybe? "Where did you go to school?"

"It's in a church, on the way to the park. I'm going to real school next year. I only go to daycare sometimes—if Mommy has to work."

Madison's heart dropped. How many daycare centers were located in churches near parks in whatever town the mother and child had lived. "Where did you live, Bitsy? I mean what town or city?"

"Philadelphia," Bitsy said with a smug little grin acknowledging her pride in herself.

"Great," Madison said. *That would be like finding a needle in the proverbial haystack.* "I live in Philadelphia, too."

"I'm hungry."

Oh, damn, Madison thought, looking at the box of food. She had hoped she wouldn't have to deal with that tonight or at least until after they were settled.

"Well, honey, let me cover you with this afghan and you stay here warm and cozy. I'll unpack our food and see what I can make for you, okay?"

"No," Bitsy said, sliding from the sofa. "Mommy always lets me help with the grocery bags. She said I was big enough. I can help you, Grandma." She stood next to Madison and turned to look at the books.

"Wow. You sure have a lot of books. I love books. Mommy gave me two books today. Oh," she said frowning, her mouth forming a pout. "Mommy forgot them. They're still in her car." Tears filled her eyes.

Madison stooped down and cuddled the little girl to her chest. "That's okay, honey. We'll get more books."

"But, they were my Christmas presents. From Mommy."

Madison felt the child tremble in her arms." I don't know what to say," she whispered into the soft curls that brushed her cheek. She'd never felt as helpless as she did now and hugged the child to her. Bitsy, pulled back, pasted a smile on her face and said, "That's okay. Santa will bring me a surprise. He told me so when I sat on his lap."

CHAPTER FOUR

Only those who will risk going too far can possibly find out how far one can go.
T. S. Elliot

The car rattled with the thrust of the wind as Lily Rose drove along a narrow, snow-covered road. "A junker but it still goes," she murmured, fiddling with the knob for the heater but it only grumbled with an empty metallic groan and produced no heat. She remembered the day she got the car. *Kind of a trade*, she thought and folded her lips into a hard line. The man who gave the car to her assured her it was free and clear and suggested it might be better if she didn't get it fixed up. "I just bought four new tires and the brakes are okay. You just use it 'round town. Don't go travelin' too far," he said, patting her backside as he sauntered away. The car was several shades of blue, speckled with silvery spots where someone had tried to repair the many dents that pockmarked the exterior. Inside she'd covered the worn seats with some seat covers she found in a thrift store. They didn't fit very well and drooped and sagged in strange contours but the ownership made her feel important or at least gave her a sense of freedom. She remembered that feeling and wondered why she'd even thought of freedom at that particular time. It was before… She didn't use the car much and had never taken it more than four or five blocks from home and only when it was raining too hard to wait on the corner for a bus.

She sighed. When the doctor gave her the diagnosis and said she had very little time to live, she knew there was only one thing she really had to do. Find someone to take care of Bitsy. She panicked. She had few choices. Not trusting any friends she had, if she could really call them friends, and certainly reluctant to search for her parents, she knew she had to find a way to get someone, anyone kind and loving, to take care of her daughter.

For almost two weeks she thought of nothing else and nothing she thought of made any sense. *This is a kick in the ass*, she wailed silently. *I don't deserve this! Who will take care of my precious baby? The only livin' soul I ever had to love.* Her eyes were always red-rimmed and she told Bitsy time and time again she wasn't crying; that it must be allergies that made her eyes water so much. "Your eyes water and you sneeze a lot when you have allergies," she explained.

"But, what are 'lergies?"

"Oh, Bitsy. Don't ask so many questions. Allergies is stuff that makes your eyes watery and red."

When she was forced to rest going up the stairs to her third-floor room, and had to put the small bag of groceries she carried down twice before she reached their floor, she knew she was running out of time.

Lily told Missy about the doctor's report. Missy immediately volunteered to care for Bitsy. "After…" Missy began and then was unable to continue. Even her hard-hearted attitude melted when she thought of what lay ahead for her worried friend.

It was difficult for Lily to explain that she needed someone a bit more secure and, she added, "What would you do with a kid anyhow?" Missy nodded knowingly and then suggested wild ideas that Lily, even in her disturbed mental state, knew were too unrealistic to consider.

It was getting almost impossible for Lily to work and, she wondered, *how would it happen?* She always referred to her illness as 'it' rather than call it by the impossible name the doctor had given her. *Mesothelioma. What in God's green earth was that?*

Sometimes she banged her fist against the door or the table after Bitsy was asleep. Not hard enough to wake her baby but hard enough to hurt her hand and let her take her anger out on something. The doctor had suggested counseling but she didn't even consider it. How would she do all that and still make the plans she needed to. No, all her energy had to be focused on getting her baby settled before she… Her mood swung back and forth from self-pity because it just wasn't fair, to anger because… Well, she didn't know why she was angry or who to blame. Her anger grew with her desperation and was aimed at anyone and everyone, especially the doctors who had given her the dreadful news.

Actually, the solution came to her during one of her disturbed dreams; a woman with a beautiful face beckoned to her and she saw herself putting Bitsy into her welcoming arms.

On the morning after the dream, she then switched her scheming to *how* she was going to find this anonymous woman. *How?* What she needed was someone who would be a mother or, even better, a grandma, someone older, more settled, maybe even well off, to take Bitsy. With Bitsy tucked into the one narrow bed in her dreary rented room, Lily sat at the rickety table and thought and thought. How would that goal be possible? She really couldn't identify the moment when she thought of leaving her precious daughter in a public place to be found by the kind and loving person she dreamed of. But, she deliberated, not too public a place or the police would step in and that would mean foster care. No, she knew what that was like. She had to find just the right place.

The next morning, very early, she and Bitsy left the rented room. During the cold and lonely night, she had packed as much as she could into the backpack for Bitsy—the purple backpack with the yellow dancing bear. Bitsy's favorite color was purple.

Lily wore her best jacket over a thin turtleneck shirt and jeans. She took nothing for herself, just closed and locked the door, looked down the dingy hallway to Missy's door, then started down the long wooden flight of steps. There was no need to confide her plans in Missy. What could she do?

She didn't know what she was going to do after she left Bitsy… She had almost forgotten it was Christmas Eve and had to re-climb the stairs to get the two books she had purchased for Bitsy's present. She'd hidden a teddy bear in the trunk of the car before her baby awoke that morning. As she closed the trunk, the last thing she saw was two fuzzy paws holding a red satin heart.

Gasping for air, she helped Bitsy into the front seat of the old car and adjusted the seat belt. "Just for today you can sit in front with me. I want you right next to me, okay? Just this once."

Their first stop was for breakfast at a McDonald's on the outer limits of Philadelphia. Now Lily looked at every face, assessing what the chances were that this person or that one would be the right woman and how would she approach them, or should she? Her mind was clouded with indecisions. She knew what she had to do but how did she get there?

After breakfast and having no specific destination in mind, she took route Rt. 611 north. *Get out of town*, she thought, *where no one will know you. As if there's many folks who would know me anyhow.* She drove steadily, in a daze barely noting the countryside and small towns they passed through.

They stopped at a place called Easton for lunch at a Burger King and Lily read the two new books to the wide-eyed child. One was about kittens. Bitsy loved kittens and longed for one of her own. The second book played music when she opened it to read. In little tinkling sounds, *Santa Clause is Coming to Town* emerged into the crowded restaurant and the little girl's eyes widened and her hands clapped happily at the miracle of music coming from the pages of a book.

The books were Bitsy's Christmas gift. Now they're my goodbye gifts, Lily thought and wiped her eyes with the backs of her hands.

After lunch they took a busier highway west but soon got off on a country road that began to climb into the mountains. After that the roads became narrower and more winding and Lily didn't really care what numbers or names they had. They were just a means to put more distance between what she had left and where she was going on her quest to find the perfect woman to take care of her baby. But, as she drove she became less and less sure that she had chosen the right course. *Is there any other way?* She tried to take in a deep breath but couldn't. Her chest hurt. "Too late now," she murmured.

"Too late for what, Mommy?"

"Nothing, sweetheart. It ain't never too late for a body to do the right thing."

Later, she saw a diner ahead, right on the side of the road. It was stuck out in the middle of nowhere, but the parking lot was crowded; that was a good sign.

"We're stopping here, Bitsy. I'll get you a Coke."

Inside she heard friendly banter between the waitresses and patrons; calls of Merry Christmas and laughter filled the air. They all looked happy; they all looked as if they had friends and family, something Lily had never had.

Sliding Bitsy into the corner of a booth at the back of the diner, she ordered two small Cokes. When they came she carefully peeled the paper from one straw and stuck it into the plastic cup in front of Bitsy.

She took a tentative sip of her soda but it seems thick and so sticky she couldn't swallow.

"I have to go away for a little while, Bitsy. But," she said, cuddling her daughter to her. "There's a big surprise waitin' for you, right here." She smiled a grim smile. "Your grandma is coming to pick you up. All you have to do is wait for her."

The little girl looked into her mother's face. "But, I don't have a grandma."

"Yes, you do, sugar. You just never met up with her."

"When will you be back?" The child's blue eyes glistened with tears and her chin trembled.

Lily kissed the soft cheek and swallowed with difficulty. "As soon as I can, honey. You're such a good girl. I've had to leave you alone before. You..." Her voice clogged with emotion; she choked back tears and hugged the child to her. "Your grandma will love you, honey. Love you like nothin' you ever known. You'll know her soon as you set eyes on her. She'll be pretty and have a nice smile and love you and you'll love her too, sweetheart."

"But how will I know her?" The child's voice squeaked with her fear and tears slid down her petal soft cheeks.

"You'll know her, honey. She'll look just like a perfect grandma should look."

"Like the ones in books?"

"Even better. Oh, Bitsy it will be so good for you to have a brand new grandma. You'll always have an angel looking after you. It'll be exciting, like an adventure. Remember all the adventures we've had together?"

"Like the adventures in the books you read me?"

"Kind of like that, honey." Lily thumbed the tears from the child's cheeks and hugged her. Looking into the trusting blue eyes beneath the soft frown, Lily said. "I love you, Bitsy. I always will. You never, ever forget that, you hear?" She held the child's face in both her hands and kissed the soft cheeks, one at a time. "You be good, okay? Just wait here. Grandma will come, I promise." She held her shoulders stiff, her throat filled with a lump so large it made breathing even more difficult. *What am I promising? Is this the answer? Is it really too late to change my mind?* She twisted her cold hands beneath the table and felt that scary weakness sapping the strength in her body as it did so often now. *Do I have any other choice?*

She stood, took one last, longing look at her daughter, then turned quickly and went out the nearest door. But, before she drove away she took all her identification, even the pictures of Bitsy, from her wallet and tearing them to shreds she pushed them into the dumpster at the side of the diner. She didn't know exactly why she did that and she didn't dare look back.

The snow was getting heavier and still Lily Rose drove on. The roads were unfamiliar and she had no destination. Getting away was all she thought about; that and putting miles and miles between her and the diner. Her mind was clouded with confusion and she focused on only one thing, to do what she could for her baby daughter. The road was almost invisible and the rough countryside slipped by without her notice.

She pictured her baby, sitting patiently waiting for someone, anyone. Surely no one would leave a child alone on Christmas Eve. She slowed at an intersection, unsure of which way to turn.

She turned left, driving along a two-lane road that seemed to be a constant uphill grind. A sign indicated it was PA Rte. 742. At the top of the long hill the road leveled out and she looked out through the driving snow at what appeared to be a vast valley on either side of her. Suddenly the road began to turn downhill and a roadside sign indicated a series of curves ahead. Her arms stiffened. She was more comfortable in city traffic than she was out here where it was so lonely and empty.

She applied the brake and felt the car slide from side to side. "Good thing there ain't no traffic," she muttered, gripping the steering wheel even tighter. She glanced in the mirror to see if there were any cars behind her. Her eyes caught sight of the two books she'd read to Bitsy laying on the ledge beneath the rear window. Her Christmas gift! She'd forgotten them; she hadn't left them with Bitsy! And the teddy bear was still in the trunk. "No," she screamed. She had to go back. She had to. "I can't leave her," she said aloud, her voice tinny with fear. Her hands were fused to the wheel, her sight blurred by tears that flowed freely. "Oh, God forgive me— there's got to be some other way."

Braking and pulling on the wheel to make a U-turn, she felt the car slide around in a slow-motion circle. "Wait for me, Bitsy," she cried. "I'm coming back, sugar. Wait for me, little darling."

The rear fender hit one guardrail and spun in crazy circles on the snow-covered road. The car then hurtled across the road and struck the opposite guardrail. She heard the sound of metal on metal. With a strange sense of being an onlooker, she saw a gap in the rail, felt the car fly through the air. "Bitsy," she shrieked, as her head thrust forward, striking the windshield. Her neck hurt and suddenly it was dark.

She never felt the succession of trees the car crashed through as it careened down the mountainside, rolling over and over and ending up with the roof of the car buried in a narrow gully. Immediately, snow began to cover the vehicle and cast a hush over the scene. The landscape was silent. The two books that had rested on the back window ledge now lay on the floor in front of the passenger seat. The world was suddenly soundless except for the tinkling of the music from one of the books. *Santa Claus is Coming to Town* wafted softly into the still, snow-filled air. There was no one to hear it.

There was nothing left for Lily Rose Smith to cry about; nothing left for her to worry over.

CHAPTER FIVE

There's nothing sadder in this world than to awake
Christmas morning and not be a child.
Erma Bombeck

They sat at the kitchen table spooning cereal and milk from matching bowls.

"This cereal is different," Bitsy said,

"Different?"

"Yeah, there's no crunchy things."

Madison smiled. "No crunchy things. Is that the kind of cereal you like? One with crunchy things?"

"Mmmm," the child murmured, slurping some milk from her spoon. "But this is okay. Different," she repeated. "All gone," she said, pushing the bowl away.

Madison reached across the table and wiped a drop of milk from Bitsy's lips.

"Tell me about you and your mommy, Bitsy."

Bitsy blinked then shrugged. "Mommy's little. She says I'll be bigger than her soon. When I'm ten." She giggled and covered her mouth and Madison grinned. She found this habit endearing.

"Does your mommy work?"

"Yep. But she goes to work mostly at night. I'm asleep but if I wake up Mommy says I have to be quiet as a mouse and wait for her." Bitsy nodded her head vigorously, setting the dark curls bouncing. "She always comes home though." She stopped and frowned. "She didn't say when she was coming back this time though."

Madison saw tears filling Bitsy's eyes. She stood and picked Bitsy up, cuddling her to her chest. "She'll come back whenever she can, honey. For now you're safe with me."

Holding the child close to her for a moment, she remembered helping her sister with her children when they were young. She remembered the scent of warm milk and clean hair. *Now Caitlin and Jason are teenagers. I can't believe those years have flown by so quickly.*

She held Bitsy's hand as they walked down the hallway to the spare room. "This is where we'll sleep tonight," she said, snapping on the light. They faced twin beds with royal blue bedspreads; a matching valance topped silky white curtains. A table between the beds held a small lamp and a clock. She felt Bitsy's fingers stiffen. "I don't want to sleep here," she said, pulling back on Madison's hand.

"Why? It's a lovely room. You'll sleep there," she said pointing to the bed nearest the closets, "And I'll sleep in the bed next to the windows."

"No."

"What do you mean, no?"

"No. I don't want to sleep here."

Madison stooped down and put her arms around the quivering child. "Why, honey? It's a very nice room."

"I don't want to be here—alone," she's sniveled, her eyes pooling with tears. "I want to be with you, Grandma."

"But I told you, I'll sleep in the bed, right there," Madison said, pointing the other twin.

Shaking her head vigorously from side to side, Bitsy lowered her head. "Mommy always slept with me. Whenever we had a bed."

Madison tried to picture the little girl's existence before she'd exploded into her life but she couldn't. *Sleeping in cars? Mother and child in the same bed? Under circumstances I don't even want to contemplate,* she thought. No, she just couldn't imagine.

"Okay, you can sleep on the sofa and I'll sleep in the big chair next to you. But, only for tonight. Tomorrow we'll go to bed like we should."

Madison paused. When had plans for herself and Bitsy escalated into tomorrow?

Bitsy clung to one of Madison's hands as they padded back from the bedroom. "Read to me? Mommy always read to me."

Damn, she thought. *Is there a child's book anywhere in this house? I doubt it. I doubt it very much.* "We'll look for one, Bitsy. I'm not sure we're going to find anything, but we'll try."

"If we didn't have a book, Mommy made up stories to tell me."

"What kind of stories, honey?"

"Oh, about kittens and bunnies. They always had a happy end. Mommy said every story had to have a happy end."

Except hers, it seems, Madison thought. Together they searched the bookshelves. "There are no pictures in these books," Bitsy moaned as she searched the bottom shelve, and just as Madison's hand fell on a small book of poetry, illustrated with pen and ink drawings of children. "Here," she exclaimed as if she'd found a treasure. "*A Child's Garden of Verses*. What a nice book. Do you like poetry?"

Bitsy's eyes widened. "I don't know. What's po'try?"

They settled on the sofa, Bitsy almost burrowing into Madison's side. "Poetry is pretty words that tell a story. The words rhyme and make it almost like a song."

"I had a book that made music," Bitsy said sadly.

For twenty minutes Bitsy sat quietly listening to the cadence of Madison's voice as she read. "Let me see the picture," she'd plead when each poem was finished.

Before long, Madison felt the little body lean heavily against her side. When she looked down and saw the dark smudge of eyelashes on the pale cheeks, she settled Bitsy back against a pillow and covered her with an afghan.

Madison watched the child sleep for several minutes. She looked so peaceful. *Now all I've got to do is find Christmas somewhere in this house.*

But she remained in the chair. Her eyes traveled around the room—so familiar and yet somehow there was feeling that nothing was the same. *And it isn't the same anymore. This will be the last time.*

She closed her eyes remembering the last time they were here— months ago—in the fall. She recalled tipping her head back and looking into the colorful canopy overhead. She remembered saying, "I love the fall. It's like God is taking one more time to amaze you with His artistry."

She opened her eyes and leaned forward, her elbows on her knees, her head cradled in her hands. "Stop it," she whispered. "It's over. Put those memories away."

Bitsy made a soft sound and squirmed beneath the afghan. Madison rose and patted her back softly. "Stay asleep, honey. I have to find Christmas," she whispered.

She began her search in the bedrooms in the wing behind the dining room. In all the times she'd visited this cottage she couldn't remember being in this wing but she knew it was here and knew she probably had seen it once or twice.

In the bathroom that separated the two bedrooms she found a small china box with the face of a tiny angel painted on the lid. "Probably for powder or cotton balls or something." She tucked it into her sweater pocket and continued her search. In a drawer in another bedroom she found a small paisley silk scarf in pink and purple and wondered who had left it behind. *It isn't stealing,* she thought. *Just the giver doesn't know he's doing the giving.* When her search didn't produce anything else, she returned to check on Bitsy, who was sleeping soundly, her body curled into a small soft lump.

Madison's purse lay on one of the end tables. "I don't think I have anything in there that will do. Damn, I've never been so challenged about Christmas gifts in my life," she whispered. Still, she dug through the accumulation that had collected in the bottom of her purse, odd change, a pack of matches from a hotel in the Bahamas, bits and pieces of paper, some with writing and others just crumpled junk that hadn't made it into the waste basket. There was an opened package of lifesavers, hardly in gift condition. Her fingers felt something else—wadded up in a tangle of chain was a small necklace with a silver cross, embellished with turquoise. "I got this in Arizona the last time we were there," she gasped quietly. "It was supposed to be a gift for Caitlin and I thought I'd lost it."

The chain was snarled and knotted. Taking it to the kitchen where the light was better, she sat at the table. Her fingers picked at the links, finally loosening them so that the chain lay flat. "Talk about a miracle—a gift from heaven!" she murmured. "But, I can't miraculously improvise a Christmas tree. Maybe Bitsy isn't accustomed to a Christmas tree. Who knows?" she whispered to herself and went back to the living room.

Puzzling as to where to put these gifts, she stood with her hands on her hips and stared at the fireplace. *The stockings were hung by the chimney with care...* "In a stocking, of course," she whispered, and hurried to her suitcase. Rolled into a small ball in the bottom of the bag was a pair of warm argyle socks she'd thrown in. Madison hated cold feet. She took one sock, found some *Scotch Tape* in a kitchen drawer and hurried back to the fireplace. It took more than a few pieces of tape to secure the sock to the mantelpiece but she did succeed. She hid the necklace in the china box, carefully draping it over some cotton puffs from her cosmetic bag, then folded the scarf into a small square. With a huge feeling of accomplishment, she stood back and marveled at her ingenuity. The Christmas sock looked ludicrously small against the backdrop of the large room and fireplace. Madison tried to see it through a child's eyes. *Let's hope it will look like Christmas to Bitsy*, she thought. Madison sat in the recliner next to the sofa. She faced the fireplace. *Maybe tomorrow I'll make a fire. Grandpa always had a fire on Christmas,* she thought.

As she pulled the blanket over herself, she took one last look around the room before turning the lamp out. Sadly, the darkness didn't prevent her from remembering the past. *When was the last time you were here?* She closed her eyes. She knew when. *October. The mountainsides were aflame with color. We'd driven up to Indian Hills Saddle Club. Meandered along the bridle trails until we reached the river. Later dinner at the Inn on the Lake, then back here. Back here...* "Don't do this to yourself" she whispered but it was a useless statement and the past stampeded back into her mind. *Three nights ago...*

~ ~ ~

"I'm leaving you." The lighting was dim in the century old Inn they were dining in. It was one of their favorite hideaways usually reserved for special, intimate occasions. A velvet box lay on the table between them.

"You've said that before." His grin lifted the corners of his eyes and his fingers pushed the box a little closer to her.

She hated the certainty in his voice, the self-assurance he always displayed. Wasn't everything always *his* way? She slid the box back next to his wine glass. "This time I mean it. I may go away for a little while."

"You'll be back and it will be the same again."

"Not this time, Jim. Not this time."

"You'll be back," he said, the grin still in place.

~ ~ ~

She put the footrest on the recliner up and adjusted the blanket around her. Her eyes rested on the sleeping child. *Why are you here, little angel? Did God send you to me for a purpose? Whatever the reason, right now I'm glad you're here; I'm glad I'm not alone.*

At first her sleep was restless, shifting her body from one side to the other in the chair but then exhaustion took over and she slept, her mind a dreamless, bottomless pit of nothing.

CHAPTER SIX

You must do the things you think you cannot do.
Eleanor Roosevelt

She woke with a jolt—the kind of shock you get when you awaken from a bad dream—the kind of sudden awareness that engulfs you when you think you've overslept.

Madison looked at the sleeping child on the sofa. She was coiled into a small bundle, the fingers of one hand curled around the edge of the afghan; dark curls twisted over the beige pillow beneath her head.

The room was dim and she glanced at her watch on the table next to her. 6:23. Rising quietly, she tiptoed to the front window. Uncurtained and divided into twelve-inch squares, the window was one of a pair on either side of the tiled foyer. They overlooked the circular drive in front of the cottage. Even in the early morning light the landscape reflected the bright newness of a deep coating of snow. Her car wore a muffin crown of white and the tire marks from their arrival last night were smudged into ripples. *Must be at least fifteen inches of snow,* she thought and scanned the wooded area behind the car. Drifts of snow undulated between the trees, giving an appearance of ocean waves frozen in time. The sky was light gray and there were no signs of a rising sun—not yet anyhow.

She shivered and hugged her robe closer to her body. Last night, even though the heat was on, she chose to sleep in the pale yellow robe she'd hurriedly packed—the one that was shabby with comfortable use. The new burgundy red robe, purchased with the hopes of a romantic Christmas Eve, was still in the box at home.

She turned down the hallway and went into the bathroom off the master bedroom. The woman who stared back at her from the huge mirrored wall was familiar yet strange. Why the little smile at the corners of her lips? She shook her head, caught water in her hands and splashed her face. Patting it dry with a thick hand towel she faced away from the mirror. How many times had she been in this elegant bath? Her eyes took in the sunken tub with the jets that turned it into a personal spa. *Large enough for two.* A wide marble deck surrounded the tub. *Perfect for candles,* she remembered, and quickly turned away.

In the kitchen, she measured coffee into the filter, filled the pot with water and plugged it into the outlet over the counter. The instant gurgle it made added a small measure of coziness to the silent house.

From the window over the sink she noted the early morning light filtering through the trees, dappling the unbroken cover of snow. She sighed. "It's Christmas," she said, quietly and remembered the sleeping child in the living room. Bowing her head she leaned against the sink. What was she doing—here—with Bitsy? But she knew she was also asking herself what was she going to do and no answers came to her.

In the living room she picked up her cell phone. Pressing the talk button, she again read the 'no service available' message. She would give anything to be able to call Jo…or her sister but that wasn't possible and the room seemed to shrink around her. Madison glanced at the lone sock hanging from the mantle, then at the sleeping child. "Christmas," she murmured and felt her eyes fill with tears.

Wiping them away angrily, she tiptoed down the hallway to the spare bedroom. From her open suitcase she chose a long-sleeved turtleneck shirt, the cords she'd worn yesterday and clean underwear. Avoiding the opulence of the master suite, she slipped into the guest room bath, leaving the door ajar in case Bitsy came looking for her. Her shower was quick and perfunctory. She wanted to be in the living room when Bitsy awoke but as she was dressing Madison felt eyes watching. Looking up she saw the small, troubled face of the child peering at her through the narrow opening. "Oh, you startled me, Bitsy," she said, hurrying to the little girl and scooping her up in her arms.

"I didn't know where you were," Bitsy said, burying her face in the warm damp skin on Madison's neck. "I was scared you left me."

"I won't leave you alone, Bitsy. I was just in the shower, honey. You were sleeping so soundly." Madison pushed the child away and studied her face. "You had a nice long sleep. How are you this morning?"

"Okay. Where's my mommy?" Bitsy's face was one second away from crumpling, her cheeks pushing her eyes into slits, her chin quivering.

"Oh, don't you remember? She left you for me. At the diner. We're going to be together. For a while," she added and was surprised at the sadness she heard in her voice. "It's Christmas. Merry Christmas, Bitsy," she said with all the enthusiasm she could muster.

Bitsy struggled to get down. Her face a quick change from confusion to expectation. "Did Santa come? Did he find us?"

Taking the small hand in hers, Madison urged Bitsy from the room and down the hallway. "He did. I'm not sure how he did and it must have been very, very late at night but just look," she exclaimed as they turned into the living room. "Look, Bitsy. He left you a stocking. Do you remember the poem about the Night Before Christmas? '*...The stockings were hung by the chimney with care...'*," she quoted, gently pushing the little girl toward the fireplace.

"For me?" she whispered looking at the improbable sock dangling from the mantle high above her.

"You. Here, let me lift you up. Careful. Just pull with both hands so you won't drop it." Madison listened as the many pieces of tape peeled away from the wood.

She put the little girl down on the hearthrug and watched as one small hand began to explore the contents of the sock. Bitsy looked up, her moist eyes glistening with excitement. "I never had a stocking before. Santa used to put my stuff on the kitchen table."

Madison turned away quickly; afraid her face reflected her feelings. *What kind of Christmas had this poor child experienced in the past?*

She squatted down beside Bitsy who held the little china box she'd pulled from inside the stocking in the palm of her hand. "Have you looked inside? Maybe there's something else hidden in there."

Bitsy looked from the box to Madison's face. "It's so pretty. I didn't know it opened." Her voice was muffled with awe.

"Just pull on the top, honey. I think it opens that way."

Several minutes later, with the silk scarf tied around her head like a Polish babushka and the necklace securely fastened around her neck, Bitsy sat on Madison's lap. She cuddled into the warm body that held her. "It's the best Christmas ever," she whispered, then pulled away and looked up into Madison's face. "But, I wish Mommy was here."

"I'm sure she wishes it too, honey. Tell me about the day when your mommy left you at the diner."

Bitsy slid from Madison's lap but remained close to her side. "We drove and drove for a long, long time. First we had bre'fast at McDonalds. I love McDonalds," she added and folded her hands in her lap. "Then we ate at Burger King for lunch. We don't go there very often. Mommy says she makes better stuff for me at home. But it was great. We ate out two times in one day!" Bitsy squirmed around so that she now faced Madison. "Mommy gave me my Christmas present after we finished eating. I had chicken nuggets. They're my favorite. Then she gave me two books!" her voice reflected her excitement and her eyes sparkled. "One book made music. I never had a book that made music before. But," she paused, her face again quick-changing into a picture of distress. "But, Mommy forgot to give them to me in the diner. She left them in the car." The little girl's chin trembled and Madison took one of her hands.

"It's okay, honey. You'll get more books. Your mommy must have been in a hurry. Was she?"

Bitsy shrugged. "I guess so. She told me she had to go someplace and I was supposed to wait for you. She said, 'Your grandma will come and get you.' I told her I didn't have a grandma but she was right. You came and got me." Now it was Bitsy who sought out one of Madison's hands.

Madison rose and paced across the floor. "What's your last name, Bitsy?"

"Smith," she answered with a smile. "S.M.I.T.H. I can spell it." She paused, a slight frown pushing her eyebrows down over her eyes for a moment. "I can spell Bitsy, too. B.I.T.S.Y. but I get stuck on Barbara Ann sometimes. Mommy says I have to know it before I go to real school."

Madison returned to the sofa and sat on the other side of the little girl. "Can you tell me anything about where you lived or what your mommy did, Bitsy. Anything at all?"

Bitsy twisted her mouth and stared at the ceiling, her eyes blinking rapidly. "Well, we lived upstairs and at first Mommy used to run up the stairs. We used to see who got there first but she always held my hand so we got there together. That was silly. Then Mommy got too tired to run so we just climbed." Her shoulders rose and fell with resignation.

"Did you have friends; other children you played with?"

"No," Bitsy replied and slumped against the cushions. "Except for daycare sometimes. Mommy said it was better if I just stayed with her. She said it was too dangerous unless she was with me."

"Well, she was probably right if you lived right down in the city. Did you?"

"There were lots of houses and lots of cars. The sidewalk in front of our house was all tipped up and there were big cracks I could jump over. Mommy said it wasn't good to run down there and she was right. Once I tripped and cut my knee." She leaned forward and pulled up one leg of her pink pajamas. "See? There's the mark."

Madison dutifully examined the small scar on Bitsy's right leg. She sighed. "Well, when you went to daycare, where did you go?"

"It was a nice school at the back of a church. We had books and a playground. The teachers were old but nice. But," she sighed. "Mommy didn't want me to go often. She said it cost lots of money and she wanted me with her."

"Did you go to that church? I mean to services? On Sunday?"

Bitsy nodded. "Sometimes. We sat in the back. It was nice and I liked the music. Mommy always sang real quiet like she didn't want anyone to hear her. When she sang she cried sometimes. I asked her why but she always said, 'It's just the music. It reminds me of when I was a little girl.'" Bitsy looked into Madison's face. "I think Mommy was lonely, too."

Madison slid one arm around the child, noting the *too*. "Maybe she was, Bitsy. Were you lonely?"

"I don't think so. And we both had Missy."

Madison's heart skipped a beat. Another name, maybe a clue to Bitsy's past. "Who's Missy, honey?"

"She lives down the hall. She's so tall her head almost hit the top of the doorway. Skinny too. She's nice, though," Bitsy added, philosophically. "She was black. Mommy said that black skin didn't mean anything. Just another way God made people different. Sometimes Missy wore a blonde wig. It was long and her hair was all over her shoulders which was kind of messy but good because she didn't wear stuff with sleeves—even if it was cold."

Madison smiled and looked across the room for a moment, trying desperately to picture the surroundings Bitsy was revealing. "When is your birthday, honey?"

"Oh," Bitsy said, sitting Indian style on the cushions. "It's St. Patty's Day. Mommy says I'm not Irish but I am a…a…a lep-ri-corn."

The sound of their laughter dispelled some of the chill that permeated the huge room and Madison pulled Bitsy onto her lap again. "Well, let's get you dressed and then we'll have breakfast." She said. "Don't you think it's time we ate? I'm hungry, aren't you?

"It's Christmas so I'll make a nice big breakfast and, since it's almost lunchtime now, we can wait until later to have our Christmas dinner. Come along, honey. You can help me."

While Madison scrambled some eggs and made toast, she let Bitsy put the placemats on the table and, with a little coaching, line up the silverware on the napkins. "These are pretty," Bitsy said, carefully straightening the forks on the cloth napkins. "We always had paper napkins. Sometimes Mommy took some from a restaurant and we used them. She took straws, too."

"Did you have anything special for breakfast? I mean for special occasions like Christmas or birthdays?" She took two plates from the cupboard.

"I don't think so. I can't remember anything special. Mostly cereal. Cereal with crunchy things," she said pointedly.

Madison smiled and scooped some scrambled eggs onto both plates and added the toast. "Here, honey. You sit here. Later we'll look out the front door and see just how deep the snow is. Of course, we can't go out because you don't have boots. I wish your mother had thought to pack boots," she said, sitting across from the little girl who looked longingly at the food on her plate.

"This is special. Sometimes Mommy and me ate at Mister Mo's but that was usually a sandwich for lunch. We shared one," she added, picking up her fork in a tightfisted grip. "If we went to McDonalds I got French toast sticks. I dipped them into syrup. Yummy," she said, forking some eggs toward her mouth.

Madison watched the little girl savor the breakfast and remembered her own Christmas breakfasts when she was a little girl. Her family always spent several days at her grandparent's house for the holidays. Grandma and Grandpa Millhouse couldn't seem to fill the house with enough people.

Christmas Eve was church and lots of food when they returned. Christmas morning, after exchanging gifts and after seeing what Santa had surprised the children with, breakfast was a huge buffet, eaten over several hours so that the kids, Madison and her sister, Lawson, as well as Betty, Marybeth and Henry, her cousins, could marvel at their gifts. There were so many people, so many gifts, and such a lot of food. She glanced around the quiet kitchen, looked at the scarf still around Bitsy's head and the little necklace with the cross at her neck, and she fought back tears.

"You know, Grandma? This is the best Christmas," Bitsy repeated. "Except I wish Mommy was here."

Madison looked at the mixture of emotions displayed on the face of the child across the table from her; the child who thought she was her granddaughter. She forced a grin, gripping her lips together in a grim line that lifted slightly at each corner. "I'm glad you're happy, Bitsy. And you know what? Next year will be even better." She slumped in her chair, her fork in midair. *Next year?* What was she saying? How could she be thinking of next year?

She watched the care the little girl took when balancing the eggs on her fork. She remembered her sister's children and recalled the envy she'd hidden all these years. She could have had a child, a baby girl all her own. She didn't and she searched franticly to find someone to blame. But the blame settled firmly on her shoulders and she felt a tear slip from the corner of each eye. Was Bitsy her Christmas gift? The long, silently sought-after dream that had finally surfaced, finally come true?

She shuddered, pushed her plate of food away and watched with deep awe as the child across from her looked up and smiled.

"Mommy will like you when she comes back," Bitsy said, a forced smile on her face.

CHAPTER SEVEN

Not to be absolutely certain is, I think, one of the essential things in rationality.
Bertrand Russell

Madison didn't find analyzing life difficult. Actually, it was what she was good at. Hadn't she analyzed and created one life after the other in her books? Character after character in the twelve to-date Detective Bloodworth novels by M.J. Millhouse that had evolved from her keyboard. But then, they were all fiction. She was the power behind them, able to make them into what she needed. She created the characters, dreamed up the plots and had everything her way from cover to cover. No, it was her own life that stumped her. Try as she might, she couldn't analyze her life. She had no answers for the turns and twists it had taken. Those events couldn't be cut and pasted to a satisfactory conclusion as in a manuscript.

She lay back in the twin bed, a small night-light emitting a brief circle of illumination next to the door to the bathroom. It had taken her an hour or more to settle Bitsy into the other bed and then she'd had to lie next to the little girl until she was sound asleep.

Her mind ran through the day. Christmas. And what a strange Christmas it was. She'd found colored pencils and blank paper in a desk drawer and the two of them sat at the dining room table drawing pictures. Bitsy had asked Madison to read from the book of poetry they'd discovered the night before.

Sometimes it was just two strangers, picking and poking at each other with questions. She smiled in the dark remembering some of Bitsy's inquiries. "Why don't you have any children?" "Who do you live with?" "Isn't your mommy going to worry if she doesn't know where you are?"

And her own questions—how much had they really enlightened her. She knew Bitsy's last name. *Smith, that's a big help. There must be thousands of Smiths in Philadelphia.* The tidbits of personal information she'd gleaned from Bitsy didn't really draw much of a picture. Madison got the feeling that Bitsy's mother hadn't wanted anyone to know much about them.

She turned on her side, away from the light, away from Bitsy. Still her unrest continued. Maybe if she read it would help but she stayed, entwine in sheets that were grasping at her as if they were restraints instead of sheets. *What if Bitsy woke and I wasn't here? She'd panic.* Besides, she'd promised Bitsy that she wouldn't go anywhere; that she'd be right next to her in the morning when she woke up. Of course, when she'd said 'right next to you' she meant the bed next to her but that was okay. It had soothed the unsettled child.

Madison twisted in the bed again, unable to get comfortable and she knew why. Her mind raced from today to yesterday and the trip and the diner and Bitsy, but if she were honest with herself she knew one of the main reasons for her unrest began earlier. It began the night she'd had dinner with Jim. That last dinner…

~ ~ ~

"You know you're always on my mind. Morning, noon and night. After the first of the year things will be different. I promise… you don't want to do this now, Maddy," he'd said, using a nickname he knew she hated. "It's almost Christmas." He smiled and pushed a long, thin, velvet box across the small table.

"No, Jim, and that silly quote from a Willie Nelson song isn't going to cut it this time. I need to be more than just 'always on your mind'", she said, hating the slight catch in her throat. She shook her head and slid the box back. Her hand disappeared beneath the table, out of sight and reach, twisting the linen napkin that lay across her lap into a tight ropelike lump.

They were sitting at their favorite table in the century old inn on the outskirts of the city. A familiar site where they'd shared many romantic evenings. The candlelight gleamed on his handsome face and she closed her eyes for a moment. "Another bauble isn't going to change things," she whispered. "I've waited thirteen years…"

"And, we can wait another month or so, can't we?" He reached across the table, his hand open, waiting for her fingers. She kept her hands in her lap.

"No. It's always another month or so, another year or so, when your son is out of college; when he's on his own, when… " She swallowed with difficulty, her mouth flooded with the tinny taste of resentment. "When your wife is strong enough to go through a divorce. There's nothing ahead for us, Jim. It isn't *we* who waits. It's *me*. I wait. You go on as usual. I mean it, Jim. I can't go on any longer. I won't."

Madison's voice was brittle with contempt but not as hardened as the lump in her chest where her heart used to be. "All those excuses; they went on and on and I was fool enough to believe them. What a fool I was!"

"You are never a fool, darling. You knew about Joan."

"Yes, I knew and I trusted you. I believed you."

"You stayed."

She lowered her head unable to look at the confident smirk on his face. "That's because I was a fool. All the glamour—the trips—the …"

"The gifts," he said, his measure of self-confidence so evident.

Madison lifted her head and her eyes met his. "Yes, you're right. The gifts, the trips, the sense of being important and included. And the constant promises you never kept and never will. That's what I'm ashamed of. I admit it. A lot of this, maybe all of it, was my fault, but I'm out. Now, not later."

She remembered getting up and walking to the front of the restaurant, gathering her coat from the cloakroom and waiting for him to throw money on the table, have a hurried conversation with the Maitrè d, then join her. The ride to her apartment was quiet. Several times he tried to start a conversation but she sat tight-lipped. She knew if she opened her mouth she'd cry and she wasn't going to do that.

When he held the car door open for her, he tried to pull her into his arms but she stiffened and raised her arms, pressing them against his chest. She glared into his face. He shrugged. "You'll change your mind. You always do."

"Not this time."

"I'll call you when I get back. I'll be back January second."

She said nothing. She knew he and his family were spending Christmas in London—a Dickens Christmas. Why was she surprised? If she ever did see him on holidays it was a quick trip to her apartment for a drink; there was always a gift before he left and then he went back to his family.

He cleared his throat. "You know I have to go, it's an obligation not something I'd chose to do. I'd rather be with you. They expect it. We'll go to London next year, or Paris, maybe Paris. Just the two of us." He grinned.

"There is no next year," she said, choking back emotions that threatened to soften her reserve. She shut the door in his face, turned the dead bolt and leaned against the smooth panel of wood for a few moments. She heard the soft sound of the elevator door when it arrived and then left. She crossed the dark room and stood at the window her icy fingers holding the sheer curtain aside, watching the headlights on his car until it moved out of sight.

~ ~ ~

Madison turned her pillow over, savoring the cool material against her fevered cheek. Besides it was damp from her tears and she was angry with herself for crying. She pummeled her pillow trying to arrange the feathers into a more receptive position. She drew the covers up over her shoulder; willed her eyes to stay closed and forced herself to think about something else. Anything except Jim. Anything except what her life should be, and what plans she must make to fix everything. She was tired. Tired of being confused, tired of being insecure. Instead she thought about Bitsy and how nice it was to be able to bathe her and dress her. How much she enjoyed sharing her day with this child who had miraculously fallen into her life. She loved reading to her and watching her expressions. They had enjoyed a wonderful Christmas day—quiet—different—but nice. Nice for both of them.

CHAPTER EIGHT

A trouble shared is a trouble halved.
Old English adage

Madison lay quietly. A few minutes earlier she'd glanced at her watch and saw that it was after eight o'clock and still Bitsy lay curled under the covers, her head almost buried in the soft feather pillow. Once, during the night, Madison had crept over to the side of her bed and, with the help of the night-light, watched her little charge. Pursed lips and dark eyelashes making half-circle smudges on pale cheeks, she was the picture of innocence and Madison felt her heart stir at the image. *How could a mother just abandon such a precious gift?*

Now, as the morning light brightened the room, she waited for the child to stir. *She needs the sleep*, she thought, *after the excitement of being abandoned and finding herself in a strange place with a strange woman.* Madison turned on her side so that she could detect Bitsy's first movements. *But, she doesn't think she was abandoned; she's expecting her mother to show up some day. And, she doesn't think you're a strange woman—just a new grandma.*

She stretched her hand out and took her cell phone from the night table. Pressing the talk button, she saw the screen glow greenly. A blank green screen blinked at her. *The phone is back on.* She lay back and contemplated what she should do first. *Call Jo? I have to call my sister, she'll be worried because she didn't hear from me on Christmas.* A picture of Lolly jumped into her head. As children they were such look-alikes they were often taken for twins, but two years and an ocean of differences separated them.

Lolly, the older sister with a nickname. The sister who had the perfect life, husband, two children and a career that allowed her to be the stay-at-home mother and wife. As a child and through her teen years, Madison remembered begging for a nickname. If her sister, Lawson, could be Lolly, why couldn't she be... but there never was a nickname. Not a real nickname she could tell the other children to use. Only Sisty, the silly name her sister had lisped. And then only Lolly used it...and now sometimes Jo used it to kid her.

Madison and Lawson, the only children, daughters of James and Martha Millhouse, were labeled with the maiden names of grandmothers from long ago and Madison was Madison no matter what. *I guess that's why I write under M.J. Millhouse*, she mused.

Lolly was the one Madison always turned to. Wasn't that what her therapist told her. "You envy your sister because she has what you want. You want to be like her. You see her life as perfect while yours is flawed."

Flawed because of my decisions, Madison had thought and discontinued the therapy. But it was Jo she called when she needed answers, encouragement or just a shoulder to cry on. Not that Lolly wasn't always sympathetic but she was in California and Jo was just blocks away and right there when she needed her.

Madison grinned to herself. "You reap what you sow, Madison," her sister had often said. And Lolly had no sympathy for her situation with Jim. Over and over again she'd warned Madison, "No good can come of such a dysfunctional relationship. He's using you like a comfortable old pair of shoes. Fit for when it suits him!" Madison remembered her resentment at being classified as "a comfortable old pair of shoes," and, while she agreed with her sister's logic from time to time, something she couldn't put her finger on kept her waiting for a miracle that deep down in her heart she knew would never happen.

She watched as Bitsy stretched and then popped up as only a child can do. "Grandma?" she called anxiously, and then caught sight of Madison in the bed next to hers. "You said you would be right by my side," she accused, her lips pouting, her brow furrowed.

"I am, honey. Right next to you."

"But…"

"No buts," Madison said, slipping from her bed and, sitting on Bitsy's, she opened her arms in welcome.

The child pushed the entangling covers away and climbed onto Madison's lap. "I was scared," she whispered burying her face in Madison's neck.

Madison stroked the dark curls and with her fingers, tilted the little face up. "You needn't be scared, Bitsy. I won't leave you…at least not until we…" *Oh, damn*, she thought. *Until what? Until pigs fly? Until some miraculous event occurs? Where the hell is this child's mother!*

"But Mommy did," she whimpered. "She left me. I want Mommy. Where is she?"

Madison saw tears flood the little girl's eyes and trickle down over her cheeks.

"I don't know where your Mommy is, honey. But she must have had a really good reason to leave you."

"She said you would come and get me. That I had to wait for you," Bitsy said, still sobbing quietly.

Once again, Madison felt her heart tighten. Patting Bitsy's back she whispered, "Now stop that crying. Didn't we have a wonderful Christmas day yesterday? And the telephone is on now, so I can call and …"*And what? Find her mommy?* The confusion was chilling and she hugged Bitsy to her tightly. "Never mind. We'll have breakfast and then you can color more pictures while I think about what we're going to do. How does that sound?"

After a bath and then breakfast, Madison put the paper and colored pencils on the dining room table and watched as Bitsy carefully arranged the pencils by color, the lightest to the darkest.

"I'm going to be in the living room on the telephone. You be a good girl and stay put, okay?"

Bitsy nodded, setting her curls in a slow-motion dance around her face. "You can draw pictures later," she murmured, not looking up. Madison had washed the little girl's hair in the tub this morning and the overhead light made the dark hair shine as if she were sitting in sunshine.

"You have very pretty hair, Bitsy."

"I know. Mommy said I got her sister's curls. Mommy's hair is the same color as mine and real long but she didn't have any curls."

A sister, Bitsy's aunt, Madison gasped. *Maybe another clue to her background*, she thought *but when I asked Bitsy if she had an aunt she said no.* She bent down to kiss her forehead, breathing in the scent of soap and shampoo, the scent of youth and innocence; a scent that prodded strange feelings to flood over her.

She sat in the chair facing away from the dining room and stared out the window for several moments. The sun had not yet broken through the gray sky but the light, reflecting off the white snow, caused a glare.

She scrolled through her saved numbers and paused when she reached the code for her sister. In California it would be just after eight o'clock there but she knew Lolly rose early, ran two miles and would be out of the pool by now. Her routines were orderly and predictable and she could almost see her sister on the lanai, toweling her hair, the newspaper spread around her lounge chair, a cup of hot black coffee and dry toast next to her.

But before she could press the code, the telephone rang.

"Hello," she said, furtively glancing back at Bitsy.

"Where the hell are you?" It was Jo's voice and Madison heard her anxiety.

"Hi. We're snowed in. The phones haven't worked since we got here."

"Well at least you got there safe. You did, didn't you?"

"Of, course; it was a bit iffy at times but we made it."

"You had to go to the top of some God-forsaken mountain where the towers go down on with the first damned snowflake. Are you okay?"

"We're fine. I don't think the roads are cleared yet but the heat and electricity are on. The only things that don't work are the telephone and the television and I can do without them for a few days. I stopped and bought groceries. Even have a bottle of wine, not that I opened it."

"My God, I was worried sick. That storm came in so fast. We have about eight inches here in the city but I had visions of you upside down in a snow bank somewhere. I was thinking of calling the State Police."

"Oh, gosh, don't do that. It should clear up in a couple of days. We're snug as bugs here."

"You keep saying 'we'. You have a mouse in your pocket?"

Madison chuckled softly at the often-used local colloquial. "No, but you won't believe this story. I have a little girl with me!"

There was a weighty pause before Jo said, "A little girl? Whose? What the hell have you been doing that I don't know about?"

"Nothing. It's a really strange story. You see…"

As Madison described the circumstances of her acquisition of the abandoned child, Jo's usually low and well-modulated voice grew higher and higher as she interrupted with comments like 'mother of God'; 'you've got to be kidding'; and finally "are you crazy?" she shrieked.

"What could I do, Jo? I couldn't leave her alone. The guy in the diner was adamant he wasn't going to take her. It was getting dark, snowing like mad. I couldn't use my cell phone to contact anyone. So, we just spent Christmas together. It was kind of fun," she ended lamely.

"Fun. For God's sake do you realize what kind of trouble you might be in? Where the hell is her mother…or some family at least? You can't just adopt a stray kid like you can a stray puppy."

"I know. But right now, with everything…" Madison didn't need to continue that sentence; she knew Jo realized what a turmoil her feelings were in after that last dinner with Jim. Jo knew the reason behind her escape from the city, the need to be alone to think things through.

"I know. I know," Jo whispered. "But you can't just jump from the frying pan into the fire. I thought this little trip was for you to get your thoughts together. See? I told you you'd be better off with us for Christmas. Oh, why the hell didn't you listen to me? Now look what a mess you're in."

Madison sighed heavily and turned to look at Bitsy who was kneeling on a dining room chair coloring her pictures. "Maybe it isn't such a mess. She's a sweet child and is well behaved. I can't understand what her mother did either," she whispered into the phone. "But, somehow I feel a special calm about having her with me. There are times when I just can't wait to find out who she belongs to and return her but that sounds like I found someone's lost library book. She's a child, Jo. She belongs to someone. I've asked her a lot about her life and it sounds like… well I told you. She's from Philadelphia so maybe when we get back I can do some real searching there.

"You're right, she is someone's child but that someone just walked off and left her in a strange place waiting for a fictitious grandmother."

After another pause of several moments, Jo said, "So you're really going to bring her back with you?"

"What else can I do? Surely no one up around this area knows who she is."

"You could call the police."

"I know and I've thought about that. At first I thought that was the only choice I had but now…after being with her and after listening to what she tells me about her life, I'm not so sure. If I call the police they'd just put her in foster care or a juvenile home or something and what if no one claimed her?"

"Then she'd be someone's foster kid. Not yours. I can't understand what you're thinking. Wake up…you've never even had kids, now you're suddenly going to be a grandmother? Are you crazy?" she said for the umpteenth time.

"No. I'm not crazy but sometimes when you've made a major decision in your life you come to a point where major changes just seem right."

"Now you're a therapist?"

"Of course not. But I remember when I was in therapy the therapist said that you have to take chances to make changes."

"Chances to make changes," Jo repeated, her tone was definitely huffy. "Well, since you're so…confused…mentally adrift…maybe you shouldn't make rash changes. Just think this through, okay. When are you coming back?"

"As soon as I can get out."

"Good. Let me know and I'll be waiting for you. You definitely need someone to help you through this and I can't think of anyone better than me. I know you better than anyone. Haven't I been telling you to dump the chump for years? And," she boasted, "I was right."

Madison felt relieved when she pressed the end call button. She flexed her shoulders, feeling the tension lump she'd been carrying around slip away. Moving to the dining room she leaned over Bitsy and looked at the picture she was completing. There were several strewn across the tabletop. "You make very nice pictures, Bitsy. Tell me about them." She remembered her sister using that phrase when her children were young. "You don't ask them what it is," she'd cautioned. "That makes them think you can't figure it out. If you ask them to tell you about them then they have a chance to explain and still feel your interest."

"They're just pictures," Bitsy said, adding a yellow daisy to the lawn three figures were standing on.

The blue sky met the green grass in a severe line across the middle of the paper.

"And who are these people?"

"That one is Mommy," she pointed, "see she has a short skirt. And that one is me, and that one is Missy, she always wears dresses down to the floor. She's black but I used a brown crayon."

"Well, they are all very nice. Maybe we can use some Scotch Tape to put one up on the refrigerator. I remember my sister, Lolly, doing that for some of her children's projects."

"How come you don't have any children?"

"Well, I guess that's just how things ended up, honey. Some of us aren't that lucky." She felt a strange tightening in her lower stomach and straightened and stretched. "How about a cup of tea and a cookie?"

"Oh, boy. Real tea? Sometimes Mommy made me milk…not cold milk but not hot like her tea… with sugar in it and she called that tea but I knew it wasn't because her tea was dark and mine was white." She jumped down from the chair and tugged on Madison's hand. "Come on, Grandma. I can help."

After hearing about the kind of tea Bitsy was used to, she briefly ran a tea bag through some warm milk to give it a bit of color. Adding sugar, she pushed the half-filled mug toward the child. "It's still quite warm, honey, so sip it carefully."

"Thank you," Bitsy said, eyeing Madison's cup filled with darker liquid. "Yours looks like Mommy's did but mine looks really good, too." It was almost, not quite, a complaint.

Later Madison dialed her sister's number.

Lolly didn't wait for her caller to identify herself, she knew it was Madison. "Good morning and Merry Christmas to you. Where the hell have you been? I've been trying to get you for two days!"

"Merry Christmas to you, too. What a nice greeting."

"Well, where are you? I've called a dozen times. You told me you'd be *alone* for Christmas, surprise, surprise."

The sarcasm was not wasted and Madison grimaced. "I'm up in the mountains. We had a huge snowstorm and we're kind of marooned right now. The roads will be opened in a day or two. How was your Christmas? I couldn't call you because the cell phone was down and the landline here is turned off for the winter. Guess the storm closed down the towers up here in never, never land." Her words were hurried and she wondered if she sounded as nervous as she felt.

"We? Don't tell me you and Jim…"

"No. Not Jim. I've got some news… In fact I've got a lot of news."

The line crackled with emptiness for several moments, then Lolly said, "What news?" Her voice had dropped to a croaky whisper.

Madison twisted in the chair. Bitsy had returned to her artwork. "Well, first— Jim and I broke up. I broke us up would be more like the truth."

"No! Get out! Tell me. Oh, little sister, I'm so happy. You couldn't have given me better news. Tell me," she repeated, then added, "When?"

Madison told Lolly about the dinner three nights earlier, her revelations punctuated by her sister's questions, some of which she had no answer to.

"So he's in London with his family. You really mean this, don't you?" Lolly said." This time you mean it?"

"I do."

"So. How come you're up there in his cottage? Why there? Why now when you knew a storm was coming?"

"I wanted to get away, keep out of touch for a little while—to think. I hadn't counted on the storm being this bad. The weather predictions when I left Philadelphia were only of a fast moving storm that would drop a few inches of snow. Somehow it got stalled over western Pennsylvania and by the time it reached us it had gotten a lot worse. We're fine here. The power is on; the phone is always disconnected in the winter. No television, but we're managing nicely."

"You keep saying 'we'," Lolly said, her voice encompassing a huge question mark.

This, thought Madison, *is a repeat of my earlier conversation with Jo. Well, there's nothing to do but tell it.* "That's the other news I have. You see..." *How do I tell this*, she wondered swallowing with difficulty.

"On my way up, I stopped at a diner and... well there was a little girl there. Apparently she'd been abandoned and she, somehow, thought I was her grandmother."

"What?" Lolly screeched. "Now wait. You didn't take her..."

"Of course I didn't *take* her. But she was convinced I was her grandmother and the man in the diner...well, he had to leave and get home to his family. It was Christmas Eve, for God's sake. Could I just abandon her, too?"

"You could have called the police, the children's whatever. You're..."

"Don't you think I tried? The phones were down by then. The storm was getting worse. The only thing I could do was take her along with me. We spent Christmas together yesterday."

"Well, where the hell is her mother? Jeeze, Madison. You can't seem to live a day or two without some kind of soap opera drama taking over."

"This isn't *soap opera drama* and I resent that remark. Actually, it's been kind of fun. She's a wonderful little girl. Her name is Bitsy and she has dark curls and blue eyes. We had a great Christmas together yesterday. She's..."

"Stop! Do you know what you're saying? She isn't a new doll you've found. She's a child. Someone's child! Have you called the police yet this morning?"

"No, I..."

"No? Are you crazy? You could be charged with kidnapping. How do you know she was abandoned?

Maybe her mother just had an errand to run and got caught in the storm."

"I don't think so. Bitsy told me her mother said she had to go away and she was to wait for her grandmother. Listen, it had to be planned, the mother left a backpack stuffed with everything Bitsy would need for weeks. She wasn't coming back for her. I'm convinced of that." Madison kept her voice just above a whisper but Bitsy seemed to be paying attention only to her coloring.

"When I entered the diner everyone had gone but the owner. Bitsy yelled, "Grandma," and came running to me. It was getting late. It was Christmas Eve. She called me 'Grandma', Lolly," Madison swallowed with difficulty trying to erase the emotion in her words but she went on. "The roads were getting really bad and I had several miles to go before we got to the cottage. It just seemed like the right thing to do. I had to take her with me."

"Listen, Madison. You get off the phone right now and call the police. You report an abandoned child and that you took her along with you only because of the conditions, the situation. For God's sake you sound like you've been given a gift."

"You sound just like Jo. She called me earlier."

"Well thank God someone over there has some sense. What did she suggest?"

"That I call…someone…try to find Bitsy's mother."

"You can't just…just…oh, dammit. Do something. Something smart." She didn't add 'for a change' but it was almost implied.

Madison grimaced as she listened to her sister. She knew she was right but… "I'll see what happens, Lolly. She's so vulnerable. I've questioned her about her mother and her life and it's not a pretty picture but I don't know enough to make a decision…"

"A decision? You're crazy. Get on the phone to the police or the Children's Welfare people or someone.

Maybe the mother has turned up and is looking for her baby. How old is the child anyhow?"

"She's four, almost five, she said," Madison whispered.

"Why are you whispering?"

"Because she'd in the next room. Coloring. I found colored pencils. She's…"

"Ohhhh," Lolly screamed. "Hang up. Hang up and call the police. Then call me back later today and let me know what you're doing. Honestly, Madison, you're too much. Out of the frying pan into the goddamned fire!" she screeched, echoing Jo's words.

Madison ended the call but sat quietly looking at the scene outside. Behind her she heard Bitsy humming. She looked back at the child. The Christmas scarf was tied around her neck and she knelt on a chair, her fingers fumbling through the pencils. Bitsy glanced over at Madison.

"You know, Grandma. I think blue is my favorite color now. It used to be purple, but now it's blue." She smiled, her face crinkling with contentment.

Madison sighed. She knew if she called the police, whether they found her mother or not, Bitsy would be lost to her forever. She stood and went to the front door. Pulling it open she felt a blast of icy wind. The temperature was still very low. No snow would melt today. She closed the door and walked back to the dining room. Scooping Bitsy into her arms she nestled her face in the dark curls. Not today. Maybe tomorrow she'd call the authorities but not today. *What will one more day hurt?*

She pressed the child against her chest. *Not today,* she thought. *Not today.*

CHAPTER NINE

Each friend represents a world in us, a world possibly not born until they arrive, and it is only by this meeting that a new world is born.
Anais Nin

Later that same day the afternoon sun, which wasn't ever really visible, was sinking into the woods behind the house. Madison stood in the kitchen looking out the window over the sink. The shadows were creeping longer and longer across the unbroken snow. *Peaceful*, she thought. *Lonely, but peaceful.* Several times during the day, Madison had reminded herself of the problems she faced but the importance of that turmoil was fleeting and she pushed unpleasant thoughts away with an amazing adroitness. Once she thought, *I feel as if I'm Scarlet O'Hara, putting things off until another day.*

During the afternoon she and Bitsy had played dress-up with tee shirts and a sweater she'd packed in Philadelphia. That was only two days ago but it seemed as if it was such a long time ago that she'd thrown these things into her suitcase initiating her escape. When they tired of that play, Bitsy asked for more poems from the precious book and while Madison was reading, the little girl had nodded off. Madison watched the sleeping child for several moments before she tiptoed away.

She turned away from the window and leaned against the sink. The food she'd brought seemed to have dwindled more rapidly than she thought it would but then there were two of them, albeit the little one ate very little. Madison was troubled about that. Children's diets had never been her area of concern before. She opened the pantry and snapped the light on. Surveying the shelves, she found several cans of soup and sighed in relief. *Soup*, she thought, taking two cans from the shelf. *I have cheese and crackers or jelly if Bitsy doesn't like the cheese. It is kind of sharp.*

She put the cans on the counter next to the stove and searched for a small saucepan, finding one in the drawer at the bottom of the stove. She smiled to herself remembering soup and jelly sandwiches as one of her favorite lunches when she was a young girl. The thoughts brought back memories. She and Lolly had a wonderful childhood. Loving parents, good schools, lots of activities. *Gosh, there were times when my parents were taxiing us to dance lessons, soccer practice and swim classes so often it took a good schedule to fit everything in.*

Madison closed her eyes. *Bitsy should have that kind of life, too. She deserves to have security, opportunities...and love. I'm not sure she has had much of that so far. Maybe...* This time the insecurity she felt concerning Bitsy rushed to the forefront and she sat at the table and cradled her head on folded arms. *What do I want? What would be best for both of us? If I only knew...* She stood suddenly, a surge of anger flooding over her. "Damn, her," she whispered in the empty room. "Damn that selfish woman for leaving Bitsy alone. For telling her a non-existent grandma would come to her like a miraculous Christmas gift." *But*, she thought, sinking back onto the wooden chair, *if she hadn't, I wouldn't have Bitsy now. And, do I have Bitsy?* She remembered Lolly's words, 'She isn't a new doll you've found. She's a child. Someone's child!' *But whose child is she?* "Not mine," she murmured and closed her eyes to hold back tears—tears she had no explanation for.

Her mood was suddenly interrupted when she heard the sound of a motor outside. She hurried through the dining room and peeked out the front window. Outside, sitting astride a snowmobile, was a man. He had turned the motor off and she noticed he was dressed in skiing apparel with a helmet and goggles. As she watched, he pushed the goggles up onto the helmet and swung one leg over the snowmobile. She noted he was tall as he strode purposefully toward the front door. Madison turned to see if Bitsy was still asleep. She was.

She hurried to the door and pulled it open just as the visitor was about to knock. "Oh," they said simultaneously.

She slipped outside, pulling the door almost closed behind her. "May I help you?" she said, folding her arms across her chest as some small protection against the bitter chill.

He grinned and she saw that his reddened cheeks bunched up when he smiled, deepening pleasant little lines at the corner of his eyes. "I thought maybe I could help you. I saw a car here and didn't know if Mr. Eldridge had come up unexpectedly."

"No. No," she stuttered. "It's just me. Do you know Mr. Eldridge?"

"Only as a distant neighbor. I'm not usually here in the winter but I took the Ski-doo out for a spin through the woods and when I saw a car I was surprised and thought I'd just stop by and see if everything is okay over here."

"Oh, thanks. We're fine. It was an impromptu visit for me and I guess the timing wasn't too smart. Didn't think I'd get snowed in." She laughed nervously.

He shifted from one foot to the other and she wondered if he was hoping she'd invite him in. Just as she was thinking of something else to say she felt the door behind her open.

"Who's here, Grandma?" Bitsy said, her face poking out from behind the door.

"A neighbor, honey. Stay inside it's much too cold out here for you. He's just checking to see if we're okay." She felt her face flush as she turned back to her visitor. "We're fine and it was very nice of you to stop by."

"Well, that's fine then," he said, backing down one step.

"I appreciate it. Oh," she said," are the roads open yet?"

"Some of them are being plowed. Unfortunately the main road at the end of this lane isn't high on the County's priority list. Not many people stay year 'round up here. In the town, things are opening up. I took the Ski-doo down there for some supplies. Say," he said, the smile returning to his wind-buffed face, "If you need any supplies I'd be happy to get them for you."

She felt like an idiot, chattering to this do-gooder on the doorstep. She re-folded her arms. The cold was seeping into her bones and she shivered. "Why don't you come in for a moment? I'm sorry I've been so…" She was at a loss for words and didn't bother to think of anything else to say. She swung the door open and Bitsy backed up.

"Well, just into the foyer." He thrust his ungloved hand forward and Madison gripped it weakly. "Philip" he said. "Philip Hendershot. I don't want to track icy water into the house," he said, advancing.

Madison shut the door behind him and she and Bitsy stared at the newcomer. She sighed, realizing that she hadn't introduced herself, "Well, thanks for stopping by. As you can see, we're fine. I brought along some supplies and we have heat and water…"

"And you always have the fireplace, too," he said, his eyes roaming around the room.

"Have you visited Mr. Eldridge here before?"

"No. We're neighbors but he's seldom here, mostly in the summer and I live in Florida year 'round. I'm only up here to help with my aunt's estate. She died in November and it's a bit more complicated than we thought. Frankly," he smiled his engaging smile again, "I'd rather be in Florida where it's sunny and warm. I never come north in the winter unless it's absolutely necessary."

She mumbled her sadness at the death of his aunt and forced a smile. Now what? She'd let a perfect stranger into the house thinking perhaps he was a friend of Jim's only to realize he's a stranger. She reached down and took Bitsy's hand. During their brief conversation, Bitsy had slipped behind Madison and peered out at the stranger, her eyes growing with wonder every minute.

"Well," Madison said, inching away and wondering if anyone else found this strange dance they were doing a bit odd.

"Well," he said, holding his ground.

"We're fine," she repeated.

"I see. Well, that's good. I don't know how important it is for you to leave but perhaps I could find someone to plow out your lane when the road is cleared. Why don't I come by tomorrow to let you know what's going on? If the road gets plowed, then we can have someone open up your driveway."

Madison noted the 'we' in his sentence and smiled offering her hand to him this time. "Well, that's very helpful and I appreciate your thoughtfulness. I really do want to get back home as early as possible." She wondered at the truth of that statement. So many things were uncertain. She sighed again.

"Home?"

"Philadelphia."

"Great city as cities go. Well," he said, bending down to look into Bitsy's half-hidden face. "Hope you had a nice Christmas." He straightened up and looked at Madison. "I'll come over tomorrow to check on you. If you need any supplies you can call me. I'm in the book because I still own the little place I have." She noted his glance took in her cell phone that was laying on the end table.

"Thanks so much," Madison said and moved forward hoping this invasion into his space would urge him to leave.

"Merry Christmas," he said and reached for the doorknob.

"Merry Christmas and thanks again," she said, closing the door behind him. Jointly, they moved to the window and watched Philip Hendershot straddle the snowmobile and roar it to life. They watched him circle the drive in front of the house and then disappear into the woods, following the tracks he made when he arrived.

"He was a nice man," Bitsy said, still holding Madison's hand.

"Yes. Thoughtful of him to offer help." *And hopefully, harmless*, she thought turning the deadbolt on the front door.

"Are we going to Philadelphia?"

"I guess so, honey. I have to make some plans, get things taken care of. It's all up in the air right now," she said, and smiled as Bitsy looked upward as if she might see what was up in the air.

"Come on. We're having soup and a jelly sandwich for dinner. Let's put the radio on and see if we can get some dinner music."

Bitsy skipped along behind Madison, through the now familiar living room, dining room and kitchen and Madison smiled. Even though she sometimes felt as if she and the little girl were intruders in the house, right now it felt like home and she couldn't find justification for that thought. "So what," she murmured under her breath but Bitsy heard her and asked, "So what, Grandma?"

"Little pitchers have big ears," she replied and then wished she hadn't said that because she knew it would open up a flood of questions. But the thought wasn't one of annoyance and she already began to plan explanations. She reached for the can opener and a can of *Campbell's Vegetarian Vegetable Soup.*

That evening, after putting Bitsy to bed with a little less of a hassle than the previous night, she tiptoed out of the bedroom and sat in one of the chairs flanking the fireplace. She thought about making a fire and then cancelled that thought. "I'd have to clean the fireplace. Anyhow, we may be leaving in a day or two." The thought of leaving was a mixture of good and evil. She really had to make some definite plans and she'd put it off all day. What should she do about Bitsy ranked first on the list and that surprised her. On her drive up to the cottage her only challenge had been what to do about her own immediate life. Stay in Philadelphia and run the risk of having Jim harass her? Go somewhere? And where would she go? She rose and went to the desk in the corner of the room. Taking a tablet of paper and a pencil she made two columns. She remembered Lolly doing that when she had decisions to make in high school and again in college. Back then, Madison had always found her irritatingly over-organized.

Captioning each column she wrote Pros and Cons. Then she stared at the blank page for several moments and began to list in numerical order, the decisions she had to make. She left room for notes under each item listed. It took a lot of starting and restarting, crumpling the papers as she discarded them. Finally, two hours later she leaned back and tried to ease the knot at the nape of her neck. She had listed:

(1) Bitsy. And under that she had noted: (a) keep her, (b) call authorities; (c) search for her mother; and (d) other. Nothing appeared in the 'other' section of that dilemma.
(2) The second item was Location. (a) stay in Philadelphia, (b) leave Philadelphia, (c) Where?
(3) The third item was simply captioned Bitsy's Mother?
(4) The last item was Books and the only notation there was, (a) you can write anywhere, talk to your agent.

The scribbled notations under (1) (a) and (b) were almost illegible but she knew what she'd written. She poured over her notations then closed her eyes. *That's enough for tonight. I still have time.*

She rose and turned the lights off. As she walked down the hallway to their bedroom she reminded herself that no matter what decision she made, Bitsy's welfare had to come first. Madison also knew that was the most difficult promise to keep. *But,* she thought, *nothing has to be cut in stone, not at first.* She prayed she had the strength to do the right thing.

As she pulled the covers back on her bed, she smiled remembering she had just thought of this room as *their bedroom.* Before sliding between the sheets she brushed Bitsy's cheek with a soft kiss. Still leaning over the sleeping child, she marveled at the perfection of her profile, the tilt of her nose, the curls that spread over the pillow and the tiny fingers that gripped the blanket. Again, Madison wondered bitterly about the child's mother. Who was she? Where was she? How could she?

Before slipping to sleep she folded her hands in prayer. Surely this accident of finding each other couldn't be merely coincidence. She closed her eyes and thanked God for her blessings, listing Bitsy as one of them. Maybe she was being presumptuous but somehow she felt strangely relieved as a peaceful feeling enfolded her body like a soft blanket.

CHAPTER TEN

Often the test of courage is not to die but to live.
Count Vitorio Alfieri

Willie Schmidt, an officer with the Hatter County police, was still called 'the kid' even though he was thirty-five and had been on the county police force for almost twelve years. It was an unwritten rule; the last guy to join the force was called the kid, no matter what. Others had joined after him but hadn't stayed; so the title reverted to Willie.

"Damn miracle the State cleared this road so quick bein' it's right after Christmas," Willie said, leaning forward and peering through the windshield. He and his partner were doing a sweep of the open roads and checking on those that needed to be plowed. In some places the drifts were three or four feet deep. Now, on State Road 742, they traveled slowly, the road open but still icy in places.

"Hey," he said and felt the patrol car slow down as his partner reacted and applied the brake carefully. "Don't that look like tire tracks?"

"It's where that semi went over the side a couple of weeks ago," his partner replied, pulling over to the side.

"Yeah," Willie said as the car came to a stop. "But those tracks are new; dug into the snow where the guardrail should be.

"See that break in the guardrail? Bet the voucher for the repairs is still sitting on a desk in Harrisburg."

"Looks like someone went over in the storm. I'll check it out," Willie called, stepping out of the vehicle.

He knew he would be the one to do the slipping and sliding down the mountainside anyhow. "Looks like the deeper snow piled up on the other side of the road. Drifts over there, hardly nothin' on the this side of the road."

Route 742 ran along the highest ridge in Hatter County, the terrain sloping steeply from each side of the road. In the spring and summer the view from this section of the road was spectacular, a verdant valley of neat farmland that stretched for miles in either direction. He stepped through the break in the guardrail and Willie began his slippery descent.

A hundred yards down the mountainside; Willie paused. Several yards in front of him was a snow-covered car. "Hey," he shouted. "Vehicle in a gully. Upside down. Must have rolled over a bunch of times. Tree damage all the way down." He couldn't see his partner but he knew he was waiting for his report.

Willie crept through an over-the-knees snowdrift and when his feet found the edge of the gully the vehicle rested in, he almost slid under the overturned car. The damage was significant and he cupped his hands around his eyes, peering through a window. He heart turned as cold as his hands. "Looks like one victim inside. No movement," he yelled, then turned and labored his way up the mountainside, trying to follow the trail he'd made.

At the top of the road, facing his partner, he stamped feeling back into his feet and clapped his hands together. "I called it in," his partner said.

"Must have gone over the side early in the storm. Car is covered with about a foot of snow. Someone's inside though."

It wasn't an easy job winching the accident vehicle back up to the roadway but after about four hours, the blue car was hauled onto the road. It also wasn't easy prying the doors open but when they finally did, the body of a deceased young woman was found thrown over the steering wheel, her head against the windshield.

"Looks like she broke her neck. I'll be able to tell more when the autopsy is done," the Medical Examiner said.

Willie crawled across the front seat and picked up a child's book, resting on the floor. When he moved the book it tinkled a few notes of a song, and Willie grimaced and looked into the back seat to see if he had missed anything. "Must have had a kid in the car," he said.

"Well, thank God the kid didn't go with her for her last ride," another policeman said, putting the book into an evidence folder.

A week later the two policemen who had discovered the wreck read the preliminary report. "Somethin's fishy," the older cop said. "Registration is void. The VIN number indicates that car was sent to a salvage yard over a year ago. Should'a been crushed and made into auto parts or somethin' long ago."

"Well, it was a wreck, even before it was in a wreck," Willie said, shaking his head from side to side as he studied the photos of the vehicle.

"Last owner was a Jacob Aaron Johnson, the unfortunate victim of a shootout in Philadelphia six years ago. Gang war." The officer looked at the morgue pictures of the victim. He studied the face of the young woman. "She wasn't bad looking but even dead she looks worried, don't she? Wonder what happened to the kid?" he said, closing the folder.

Willie wondered, too. He remembered the Christmas book and the sound of music when he picked it up. "Must'a happened right before Christmas," he sighed and slid the report back into the box.

When the final report was in from the Medical Examiner's autopsy, the fingerprints were sent to the FBI and Pennsylvania State Police; they reported that the victim was Lily Rose Smith, a known prostitute in Philadelphia. The autopsy report also stated the woman had died from a broken neck as a result of the accident but that the victim was in the final stages of Mesothelioma, a fatal disease. She was a Caucasian woman, between the ages of twenty-one and twenty-five years old and had borne at least one child.

Even though they now had a name for the victim, they found no record of any family. The Sheriff's department ran a photo of the victim requesting any local information, hoping that someone in the area might claim the body. There were no responses to their plea.

Since there was no further information forthcoming, the case was marked open. The case box contained her clothes, shoes, a purse that contained nine dollars and seventy-three cents and a comb, the Christmas book, a small teddy bear found in the trunk and copies of the official reports.

In Philadelphia the police made note of the fact that a former prostitute, Lily Rose Smith, had died in an automobile accident in Hatter County, Pennsylvania on December twenty-fourth. No one checked on the existence or whereabouts of her daughter.

Eventually, Lily Rose Smith was laid to rest, at the expense of Hatter County, in a small local cemetery. The headstone read:

Lily Rose Smith, d. December 24, 2005. RIP

~ ~ ~

Madison smiled as she waved to the retreating snowmobile. This was the third day Philip Hendershot had visited the cottage. Yesterday he'd stopped by to announce the township roads were being cleared and he'd called a friend with a snowplow on the front of his pick-up truck to clear the driveway leading into the cottage. This morning, at seven-thirty she'd been awakened by the sound of the truck plowing the snow from the turn-around in front of the house. Philip, arms swinging in a huge rhythmic arc, was shoveling the remaining snow from around the car wheels.

Yesterday's visit with Philip had expelled all her fears as to any ulterior motives he might have had and reinforced her theory that there were some good people left in the world.

She recalled the relaxed and friendly time they had spent together in the kitchen; Madison and Philip had sipped hot coffee while a glass of untouched milk and her latest colored pencil project were near Bitsy at the other end of the table.

"Do you miss television, Bitsy?" Philip asked.

"Nope. We didn't have television except at daycare and then Miss Natalie didn't let us watch very long." She concentrated on yet another blue sky over a brilliant green landscape, but this time there were no figures, just acres of flowers dotted across the lawn.

"Is that a park, Bitsy?" Madison asked, hoping to get another clue as to where this child grew up.

"No. It looks like a picture in one of the books at the daycare center."

Philip looked at Madison, his brow furrowed. "Didn't have television?" he whispered.

"Her family was kind of…uh…save the earth kind of folks." Madison whispered back, hoping her silly answer would be accepted. Apparently it was, because Philip twisted in his chair to face her directly. "Well, soon you'll be on your way. Back to Philadelphia. I'm sorry you had to have such a barren Christmas, what with the storm and everything."

"Oh, we had a wonderful day. Just the two of us. We get along well."

"I can see that," he said. "Back to the grind I guess? You work?"

Madison smiled. "I guess if you can call it that. I'm an author so I can work anywhere and anytime. It's nice to be able to dictate just what you do on any given day. Of course, there are deadlines," she said, remembering the April 30 one she faced.

"An author? Wow. I love to read. Maybe I've read your book or is it books?"

"Actually there are twelve of them. I write detective stories; it's kind of a series, don't know if you've heard of them— Detective Bloodworth novels.

I'm working on number thirteen now. Unlucky number," she laughed softly. "Maybe it will be the last, at least in the series." Madison stared into space for a few moments. Did the thirteenth novel hold some kind of ominous connotation, she wondered? She shook her head. *What nonsense, this latest mix-up is caused by a strange combination of circumstances—my decision to break away from Jim, a snowstorm and Bitsy's coming into my life all of which has absolutely nothing to do with anything else.*

"I'll definitely look them up. You write under Madison Millhouse?" he said, interrupting her reverie.

"No. I write under M. J. Millhouse. Pen name. Sometimes it comes in handy if I'm trying to avoid critical book reviewers. And, people seem to believe detective stories more if they think a man wrote them.

"My given name is an old family name, belonged to a grandmother. I've never had a nickname so when I started to write I decided to use initials. My sister's name is Lawson, another family name. She's always been called Lolly, though."

"Madison is a nice name. Kind of sophisticated. Anyhow, I'll have to look for your books—M. J.," he said smiling. He rose and put his mug into the sink.

Madison watched him cross the floor and pause to look out the window. His plaid shirt stretched across broad shoulders and she thought *he must work out.*

"What keeps you busy?" she asked.

"I'm a free-lance photographer, so I know what you mean about making your own schedule."

"You do portraits?"

"No. Wildlife, scenery, that kind of stuff. I'm a photo-journalist," he paused, then laughed, "fancy title for a picture taker. No studio portraits. I've been lucky—had some shots get into National Geographic. Took them in New Zealand, Africa, even the Antarctic. Interesting places." He moved toward the archway between the kitchen and the dining room. "See you tomorrow. Need anything today? From the market?"

"No, thanks." She stood, idly running her fingers through Bitsy's curls, patted her shoulder and followed Philip out of the kitchen. "We're just fine and tomorrow we'll get started as soon as the drive is opened." She stretched her hand out to him. "Can't thank you enough for keeping an eye on us, though. It was thoughtful. Will you be here long—in Pennsylvania, I mean?"

"Only as long as it takes to clear up Aunt Maggie's estate. I never thought it would take more than a week or so. But," he sighed, "it's been almost three weeks and the lawyer said it might take months. He said I could go back to Florida, which I'd love to do, but if I have to come back again I might as well stay here and wrap things up once and for all. I'm thinking of putting my place here in Pennsylvania on the market. It's not much more than a cabin but there's quite a bit of land.

"I really love Florida and stay there all year now—when I'm not off on a shoot. If I'd known I'd be up here so long I could have rented the condo. Oh, well," he said. "Bye, Bitsy. Have a nice trip home. Guess you're excited to get back to school and everything."

Bitsy looked up at him, her expression puzzled, but before she could speak, Madison took Philip's arm and moved him into the dining room. "Oh, she'll get back to familiar things soon enough. I've really enjoyed having her all to myself for this short time."

Philip waved his hand at the two women in the kitchen and called over his shoulder, "Bye. Have a safe trip home." He stopped and turned back to her. "Leave any garbage you might have in the can outside. Make sure the lid is on tight so the bears don't get at it. I'll take it over to my place later."

"Bears?" Madison hurried after him. "Well, thanks. I sure didn't think of that."

Just as he reached the front door he turned to face her again. "Will you be back?" he asked.

"Here?"

"Yes."

She smiled. "No. I don't think I'll ever be back here again. I've…" She hesitated. There wasn't any use in trying to explain. “This was a last minute, hasty decision. I wanted to be alone…in a quiet atmosphere…and then…”

“And then you decided to bring your granddaughter along and there went the quiet,” he said, his smile stretching across his face, bunching up his cheeks and narrowing his eyes. “She’s a delight. At least for the few times I’ve been with her. A bright child. You must be very proud of her.”

Madison smiled. “Yes,” she said softly. “I’m proud of her.” She extended her hand again and felt his warm grip. “Thanks again for everything.”

“My pleasure,” he said, his hand lingering on hers.

~ ~ ~

After gathering up their belongings, and mentally noting there really wasn’t much to pack, Madison took one last look around the house. She’d changed the sheets on the beds and cleaned up the kitchen.

Hesitating at the front door, she scanned the room with the fireplace and vaulted ceiling, then picked Bitsy up and went outside. “Stand here on the steps, Bitsy, while I lock the door.” When she heard the solid click as the lock was secured, she sighed. There was something very final about that sound and she was surprised at the feeling that swept over her. It was as if she’d turned a corner, sealed up a package or come to the end of a book. She didn’t feel sad—just resolved.

Madison stared at the key in the palm of her hand for a moment, then pushed it into a side pocket on her purse. Settling Bitsy on her hip, she crossed the shoveled area to the car. Buckling Bitsy into the rear seat she kissed her rosy cheek. “The first thing we do when we get back is get you some boots,” she said, “you’re too big to be carried around.”

“I know. I’m big now,” the little girl said, her head nodding in agreement. “Can we get some books, too, please?” Bitsy begged. They had taken the book of poetry with them and it rested on the seat next to the child. Madison had felt a small twinge of guilt at the theft but when she saw Bitsy tuck the book under her arm as they left, she relented. *I'll explain it to Jim when and if I ever speak with him again.*

Madison smiled. "Okay," she said, then added under her breath "…you little beggar."

She was surprised at the mixed emotions she felt as they traveled down the newly cleared roads. *I feel excited about going home...but anxious about what lies ahead.* "Well, so far things seem to be falling into place," she murmured.

"What things are falling, Grandma?"

She smiled into the rearview mirror, noting the serious expression on Bitsy's face. "Nothing is falling, honey. Just mumbling about what I've got to do once we get home." *I'm going to have to keep my mumblings to myself from now on. God, she takes everything literally and has the ears of a gazelle.*

When they reached the outskirts of the city, she unexpectedly pulled into the parking lot at a Wal-Mart. Was it to take care of an unacknowledged need to postpone her arrival home or to shop for boots? She smiled at the checkout girl as several books and a coloring book and crayons slid along the conveyor belt. They had left the colored pencils in the desk drawer when they left the cottage.

When she pulled into her parking garage she sighed and leaned back.

"Where are we, Grandma?"

"Back in the city, honey. This is my parking place. We have to walk about a block and a half to my apartment." She unbuckled her seat belt and popped the trunk open. Lifting the little girl from the back seat, she held her hand and bent down to speak to her. "Now you stay close to me. I've got to carry our things and I don't want you dashing ahead of me."

When they left the building they walked along cleared sidewalks next to piles of dirty snow along the street. "The snow isn't as pretty here as it was in the house in the woods is it, Grandma?" Bitsy said, skipping next to Madison, her new boots making a scuffing rubber-on-wet-concrete noise.

"No, sweetheart. The traffic makes the snow dirty here. It isn't pretty for long."

As they rode up in the elevator, Madison looked down at Bitsy. She clutched the book of poems in both hands and, with her head tipped up and eyes wide with delight, she watched the floor numbers flash by as they rose to the fifth floor.

"I liked the house in the woods."

"I did, too. But," Madison said, fumbling with her key, "we won't be going there again."

"Why?"

"Just because. That house belongs to someone else and we won't be going back anymore."

"Oh," the little girl said as she stepped into her grandmother's apartment. "Oh, this is pretty, too." Madison watched the little girl slowly swing her body around in a circle in the living room; her arms spread like wings, her eyes wide, open-mouthed with delight. "You sure have pretty places to live in, Grandma."

~ ~ ~

The next few hours were hectic. The first thing Madison did was call Jo. Her fingers trembled as she pressed the keys on her cell phone. She listened to the phone ring across town and when she heard Jo's voice, she felt tears fill her eyes.

"We're home," she whispered.

"I'll come as soon as I can."

"Okay."

"Where's the kid?"

"Watching television."

"You okay?"

"I will be when you get here."

"Are you crying?" Jo demanded.

"Almost." Madison choked back sobs and dabbed at her eyes with a crumpled tissue. She was sitting on the side of her bed, the door to her room ajar.

"Well do something beside cry. I'll be there as soon as I can. I'm finishing up a column. It has to be in by four o'clock."

Madison hung up, blew her nose and crept down the hallway to peek at Bitsy who was sitting on the floor in front of the television set. Cartoon characters danced across the screen, accompanied by irritatingly tinny music but Madison smiled for the first time since she'd opened the front door.

She went into the kitchen and stared at the phone on the counter. The red light blinked rhythmically indicating messages. She pressed the button. "You have seventeen messages," the mechanical voice announced. Sighing, she listened to them in order. There were seven progressively intense calls from her sister, which she erased. She'd already spoken to Lolly and would call later when she…when she knew what her plans were. She grimaced at that thought and continued down through the messages. Three from her agent; the first a comical Christmas greeting, the second one bemoaned the fact that she hadn't even answered the first and asked where the hell was she; the third just demanded she get in touch ASAP. One caller didn't leave a message and Madison assumed it was one of the other callers giving up. Jo called leaving a cryptic threatening message to 'Call me right now you ninny from wherever you are, snow bank, local bar, police… You're more of a worry than my mother is and that's saying something." The click following the message had a resounding hint of the telephone being slammed onto the cradle. There was one furtively whispered, transatlantic message from Jim asking her how her Christmas was. She immediately erased that one also.

Madison made a telephone call to her agent and while waiting for him to answer, drummed her fingers on the counter. From where she stood she could watch Bitsy and she was fascinated by the intensity of the child's attention to the television program.

"Alan Marks Agency," the woman answered and Madison pictured the rotund, gray-haired, very pleasant receptionist Alan and Ian retained.

"Makes the place look so reliable, don't you think?" Alan had remarked when Madison first went with the agency. "A pretty little flighty sweetheart is not our image at all, my dear," he'd grinned.

Jerking herself back to the present, Madison asked, "May I speak with Alan, Mrs. Bronsky? I'm returning his call."

"Oh, Miss Millhouse, he's waiting to hear from you. He was quite anxious this morning."

Madison heard the click as the call was transferred to Alan's office.

"Madison, dear. How the hell are you and *where* the hell are you? You've been a naughty girl, not letting us know where you were."

"I'm home. I've been away for the holidays."

There was a pregnant pause and Madison pictured her agent, ascot carefully arranged under his almost non-existent chin. "You worried me, dear. Needlessly, I hope."

"Of course. But, I have to talk to you. There are some changes…"

"Changes? Now don't tell me you aren't working on your book, darling. We have a deadline you know. You promised."

"Don't worry. The book is not involved in the changes. I can write anywhere."

After another brief pause, he said, "Anywhere? You aren't thinking of abandoning me are you?"

Madison laughed. "Don't worry, I'm not dropping you. Far from it. I just have to make some personal changes and you, my friend, are the only one in on these secrets. For now, at least."

"I'm flattered and agog with curiosity," he crooned. "Tell Alan."

"Not now. I need to come in. What time tomorrow is convenient?"

"Convenient? I can come over there now if it would speed up the news. Why wait until tomorrow?"

Madison looked at Bitsy, her coloring book and crayons lay untouched on the coffee table. *No*, Madison thought, *I can't have Alan over here. Not yet anyhow.* "Tomorrow in your office is better, Alan. I have things to do here. How about ten o'clock tomorrow?"

"Done. I supposed I'll just have to speculate and you know how good I am at that."

"Don't dream up any trouble. I'm okay. Just... well, we'll talk tomorrow."

After she hung up she went into the living room and sat on the sofa facing the television. *Where do I begin,* she thought?

"Come here, Bitsy. Sit with me." She patted the cushion next to her and watched as Bitsy rose and climbed onto the sofa, moving without actually breaking eye contact with the television screen. Madison put one arm around the child and pulled her onto her lap.

"You like the program?"

"Oh, yes. I love TV. I never saw this show. I only saw what Miss Natalie turned on."

"At daycare?"

Bitsy nodded.

"We're going to have company soon."

"Who?" Bitsy turned to look up into Madison's face.

"Jo. She's my friend...my best friend."

"Trinny was my best friend, only I wasn't her best friend."

"Why was that?"

"'Cause she and Judy went to daycare everyday so she and Judy were best friends."

Madison grimaced at the sadness those few words evoked. "Well, you'll have other best friends." Her arms tightened around the child on her lap. *Don't make promises you can't keep. Now you're going to guarantee a new 'best friend'?* Her mind raced, jumping from scenario to scenario, none of which made any sense; she recalled the past few days and looked forward into a blank future. *Oh, where was Jo?* She looked at the hands on her watch, which barely seemed to move.

At ten minutes before five her doorbell rang and she dumped Bitsy on the sofa and rushed to the door.

"Jo!" she cried, and fell into waiting open arms, unable to stem the tears that cascaded down her cheeks.

CHAPTER ELEVEN

No trumpets sound when the important decisions of our life are made. Destiny is made known silently.
Agnes de Mille

"Won't we wake her?" Jo asked, eyeing the sleeping child curled up in a corner on the sofa. Madison had draped a soft mauve shawl over her once she finally drifted off to sleep while the women talked softly. The shawl was one her grandmother had made for her when she was a little girl and as she settled it around the child, old memories burgeoned through her mind and she sighed audibly pulling herself back.

"Once she's asleep you could invite a brass band in and she wouldn't hear it. It's getting her to sleep that's the difficult job."

"I noticed. She doesn't like her bed, I gather."

"She loves it. I guess it's having a stranger here that made her so stubborn. She's still getting used to the changes in her life."

"Not surprising. I can't believe most of this and I'm supposed to be a grown up."

"The first night we were together," Madison continued, "she wasn't going to go to sleep unless I lay on the bed with her. She told me her mother and she shared a bed. That was after she indicated that sometimes they didn't have a room of their own. God only knows where this child has been." She paused and looked at the sleeping child feeling the same surge of emotion coursed through her body that had puzzled her for days. It was as if an old ache had returned only she couldn't identify the old ache…or could she?

"Then we progressed to me sleeping in the twin bed two feet away. When we got here I had to promise to leave both bedroom doors open and a night light on. Yesterday she went to bed without a whimper."

"Sorry. I put a monkey wrench into your domestic act," Jo said, twirling the wine in her glass. "Now what the hell is going on? Talk to me."

Madison shrugged. "I…we…" She looked at her friend. Tall, dark and…not handsome, not even pretty, but exotic, that's the description that fit Jo best. Dark hair, usually pulled back severely so that her classic features captured whoever was looking at her. Almond shaped eyes, ringed with dark, thick lashes. Her mouth was full and wide, quick to laugh and just as quick to cut you down with a lashing you most probably deserved. A brilliant columnist who wrote for the Philadelphia Inquirer, her opinion columns were often the topic of letters to the editors, other columnists and even television talk shows. She had a small row home two doors from her mother's house; the only other house she'd ever lived in. She'd grown up on Reed Street in South Philly. "That's where I'll die, I guess," she'd once said to Madison when they were talking about dubious futures.

"Let's talk sense, okay? Do you know what you're taking on? Are you really serious about running away to Florida with this abandoned kid?" She stared meaningfully at Madison. "You don't know a whole lot about kids. What makes you think you can and why go to Florida? You haven't any contact there."

"I might. Remember that guy I met up at the cottage? The one who helped us get the driveway plowed? He lives in Florida. He has a condo there. When we were talking he said he would have considered renting if he knew he was going to be in Pennsylvania for such a long time. He thought he'd only be there a couple of weeks.."

"And you think he might just out of the blue rent it to you? He doesn't even know you. What's with this guy? Is he a hunk?"

"Oh, really, Jo. Do I look like I'm interested in a hunk right now? Haven't I had enough…men? Give me a break. That's as about as far from my mind as…as going to the moon is."

"Well," Jo countered, "You have to admit I'm right when I say you don't know a whole lot about kids."

"I know but I love them. You know how much I enjoy your nieces and nephews. I love my sister's kids."

"You haven't been around your sister's kids for six years."

"I see them every year."

"Yeah for a week, maybe two, in the summer. Then you come home and rave about how much they have grown and how they are impossible to understand."

"They're teenagers now."

Jo rose and filled her wine glass from the bottle on the kitchen counter. "Want a refill?"

"No, thanks."

Madison watched Jo return to the living room, stare out the window for a few moments and then return to the wing chair she'd left. They were sitting facing the couch where the sleeping child remained, silent and curled into a soft mound. "I don't know, Sisty," she said, using the nickname Madison's sister used. She was the only other living soul who had permission to delve into that secret place. No one, not her brother-in-law or even her parents when they were alive had called Madison, Sisty.

"What don't you know?" Madison curled her feet up into the well-padded button-backed chair she occupied.

Jo sighed. "I don't know what to tell you. You're taking off, leaving me, leaving everything familiar, your agent, your home," she flung one arm out encompassing the cheerful room that had been part of Madison's life for over ten years. "It's so unlike you."

"I know, but it's something I think I have to do."

"I can understand you wanting to get away for a while. I even endorse putting some miles between you and that…bastard. But why take the kid along? Surely you would be better off on your own. You don't know a thing about her background except the little bits you've learned from her and how much of that isn't just speculation? What if her mother shows up, starts looking for her kid and you're off in Florida somewhere?"

"I don't think that will happen."

"Still, someone someday might begin a search. What if they found the mother? People know she had a kid. Wouldn't she, or someone want her back?"

"I don't think so."

Jo propelled herself from the chair and skirted the coffee table, pacing across the carpet to the hardwood floor of the dining area. "You don't think so? What the hell does that mean. You have no idea where she is or what her motive was for dumping that kid on you, or anyone who came along and looked slightly like a grandmother. You, by the way don't even fit the bill."

"Oh come on. I could be a grandmother."

"It's kind of difficult to do without your own kids first," Jo said, her hands clutched behind her as she paced. "That's the scheme of things. You learn about grandchildren by raising children."

"You know where this is coming from, don't you? You know, better than anyone how much I've always longed for a child, for a husband and a normal family life. Well, maybe I'll never have the husband but I might just have that child I've always dreamed of. Is that so bad?" Madison watched as her friend lowered herself into the chair again.

"You wanted a child with that bastard. Yeah, I know."

"For years I wanted a child. I was even stupid enough to accept that I'd be virtually raising the child by myself. Today…," she paused and dragged in a deep breath. "Today single women raise children…women whose biological clocked has ticked its last tock. Gay women. Lonely women. I knew he wasn't going to burden himself with another child but I wanted one. I remember…" she drank the last of her wine and pushed the glass onto the coffee table next to Jo's. "I remember begging." She didn't try to hide her tears now.

The room was so silent, sounds of the night traffic on the street five floors below sifted through the windows. "I was such a fool," Madison whimpered, covering her face with both hands.

Jo rushed to kneel at her side. "You weren't the only fool. He was so selfish and controlling and you just couldn't see it. I saw it but said nothing. I thought it wasn't any of my business."

"And it wasn't," Madison said softly, wiping her eyes. "It wasn't anyone's business but mine and I did a royal screw up, didn't I?"

"Well, you've come to your senses now. You know how happy you made me when you said you'd finally called it quits...and sounded like you meant it."

"I do." Madison pushed a big breath of air from her lungs, lungs that felt as if they were encased in concrete. "I was stupid for too long but...but," she said rising, "but I'm so thankful I did it. Now all I have to do is leave before he comes back and tries to contact me...not that it would make a bit of difference."

"Well," Jo said, "you better not get wishy-washy now."

"Oh, no chance of that. Now I have Bitsy. That's a wonderful motivation to make a new start. A brand new life for both of us," she said, rising and spreading her arms as she were going to take flight. "Come on into the kitchen. I feel like a cup of coffee...or tea. How about you?"

"Coffee," Jo said, putting her arm across Madison's shoulders.

Jo took her usual seat at the kitchen table. She looked around the small and efficient room. "You have a great place here. What are you going to do with it if you leave?"

"Not 'if', Jo. 'When'." She counted scoops of coffee into the filter-lined basket. "I'm not going to do anything with it yet. Who knows I might not like Florida. I might end up somewhere else...or back here.

I'm counting on you looking after things for me Just looking in once in a while. Alan will help too, if I need him."

"You know I will."

Madison watched the last few drops of coffee fall into the carafe and the pot make its final gurgle. "I'll establish a change of address once I get to Florida. In the meantime, will you pick up my mail and then forward it as soon as I get in touch with you?"

"You know I will. I'll miss you. I can't believe you're really thinking of leaving. It…"

"I'll miss you, too." She shrugged and poured two mugs of coffee and put sweetener and creamer on the table.

Jo shook her head. "Listen," she said, vigorously shaking two packs of *Splenda* and them dumping them into her mug. "We need to talk some more but right now I feel kind of overwhelmed by all this. I'll call you tomorrow."

Madison nodded.

"What are you going to do tomorrow?"

"I'm going to try and find Bitsy's mother or at least more about her if possible. I know…that's kind of a turn-around but if I make some effort to find out anything it might help."

"Help who? You? Bitsy? And that's another thing. If you're going to run off with the kid maybe you shouldn't be using her mother's pet name for her."

"You're right. I'll take care of that tomorrow."

Jo stood and placed her coffee mug, which remained half-full, in the sink. "I have to leave. I've got an interview early tomorrow; some kid who went to Temple and has made quite a name for himself through the debating club. Might be something political and then again…you know." She moved behind Madison's chair putting her hands on her friend's shoulders. "Stay put, I'll see myself out."

Madison jumped up. "No such thing. I need a hug and you need one in thanks. What would I do without you?"

"You're going to have to find out if you move twelve-hundred miles away," Jo said, trying to put some humor into her voice and failing.

They walked arm in arm to the front door, stopping to look at the sleeping child. "She's beautiful," Jo whispered.

"I know. Oh, Jo, do you think this might be an answered prayer? Won't this be better for Bitsy... and me?"

"You're looking for sanctions and I'm not ready to give that yet, honey. You know I'll always be in your corner but if it's going to hurt you in the long run..."

Madison sighed and threw her arms around her friend. "I know. See you tomorrow?"

"I'll call you during the day. You going to be here?"

"I have that early morning appointment with Alan. If I do go out after that I won't be long. Leave a message and I'll get back to you."

"Listen. About that searching for Bitsy's mother; it might be dangerous. Why not wait until you've given it more thought. Maybe even hire a private detective or something."

Madison smiled and nodded. "How about dinner tomorrow night. The three of us?"

Jo scanned her friend's face, searching for anything that made her believe her friend. Shrugging, she said, "Let's have something better than Chinese take out we had tonight, okay?"

Madison smiled and gave her friend a hug as she left. Just having Jo nearby, handy to talk to, made a difference. She watched Jo walk down the hallway to the elevator.

After Jo pushed the button she turned to look at Madison in the open doorway. "Don't do anything stupid for the next twenty-four hours, okay?" she called softy.

"Cross my heart," Madison said and slowly shut the door as Jo entered the waiting elevator.

CHAPTER TWELVE

Let us not look back in anger or forward in fear, but around in awareness.
James Thurber

At six o'clock the next morning, Madison and Bitsy sat at the kitchen table as Bitsy spooned cereal into her mouth. Madison, still not accustomed to rising with the sun, sipped a cup of coffee and paged through the Philadelphia telephone book. There were pages and pages of 'Smiths' "Bitsy, honey," did your mother have a telephone?"

"Nope," Bitsy answered, a dribble of milk on her chin. "Mommy said we didn't need one. She got messages sometimes at Mister Mo's."

Madison remembered Bitsy mentioning a restaurant. Maybe she would be able to find out something about Bitsy's mother there. She paused, her hands resting on the closed telephone directory. *Do you really want to find anything*? she asked herself feeling the unwelcome chill of uncertainty flow through her veins.

Stop that. Didn't you decide last night to try and find the missing mother she thought? She pushed the heavy book away and went and looked out the front window. The scene below was depressing. Piles of dirt-smothered snow, wet pavements and street; people bundled up against a cold wind that blew mercilessly between the tall buildings. Her mind flitted back to her conversation with Philip. *No wonder he misses Florida,* she thought, *but at least, the snow up there in the mountains is white and pretty.*

Madison hurried back to the table. " Good girl. Want anything else?"

"No, thank you Grandma. Can I watch television?"

"Why don't you practice your letters and numbers as I showed you? Remember, I have to go out later this morning and you're going to stay with Mrs.Thorson."

Bitsy stopped suddenly. "I don't want to stay with Mrs. Thorson," she whined. "I don't know her."

"She's a nice lady. She has grandchildren. You'll like her, honey and I'll be back for you as soon as I can. Okay?" Madison said, ruffling the dark curls. "Here are your papers. Remember, it's like going to school and you'll be going there in the fall. I'm going to be in my bedroom, honey. Have some work to do on the computer. You'll be okay here won't you?"

Bitsy nodded. She seemed anxious to learn and Madison felt pleased that she had thought of this minor home schooling project. At least for now. What lay ahead? Well, that was another thing…another worry…for another time.

In her bedroom Madison opened her laptop and Googled Philip Hendershot, hoping she was spelling his last name correctly. She was amazed at the number of listings for this surname that appeared and noted that some spelled Hendershot with a second 't' but found only one Philip. She scrolled down the site and learned that Philip Hendershot, born in Clearfield, Pennsylvania, was a graduate of Penn State, had several honors and awards in photography and was listed on several other sites for acclaimed photo-journalists. She read some of the accolades and was impressed. Pulling up a selection of his photographs she instantly recognized his artistic abilities. Many of the pictures were of exotic wildlife and beautiful scenery in Florida.

"Hmmmm. Seems he is quite famous in his field." She noticed there was no reference to a Mrs. Hendershot, then switched sites to check on an address and found one for him at RD #3, Laurel Ridge Road,

Skippington, Pennsylvania and another for Oceola Beach, Florida. She wrote the information in the notebook she always carried in her purse. "Might come in handy," she murmured and pulled the screen down and closed the laptop.

Again, seated at the kitchen table, Madison glanced at her watch and then paged through the telephone directory once more looking for Mr. Mo's restaurant/diner. She gasped when she found a listing for Mister Mo's, then grimaced at the address, recognizing it as being in a section of the City she had always avoided. Quietly she closed the book and pushed it away*...after I leave Alan's I'll try and find Mr. Mo's,* her thoughts determined and without a hint of indecision.

Madison stood and looked out the small window over the sink. The view was uninspiring. The window overlooked a space between two buildings on the side street and exposed a small part of a little park. In summer it was a refreshing reminder of green grass and trees. Now it revealed piles of snow and trees tossing their bare branches in the brisk wind.

Turning she walked through the living room and down the hallway to her bedroom, her steps determined, her mind made up. She had to do something. "Bitsy," she called over her shoulder, "I'm getting ready for my meeting. Put your coloring book and crayons in that plastic bag on the coffee table for me will you?"

CHAPTER THIRTEEN

The greatest mistake you can make in life is to be continually fearing you will make one.
Elbert Hubbard

She drove cautiously along unfamiliar narrow streets; the neighborhood, a collage of old, brick row houses, abandoned factories and small businesses, was completely alien to Madison. *It's like a street scene in a television drama...like Cold Cases or Law and Order,* she thought. Never before had she ventured into this part of Philadelphia. Circling the block again, she moved slowly down the street. For the third time, she glanced to the right and looked at Mr. Mo's Diner. The one-story, brick-fronted building had two large plate glass windows flanking an inverted entranceway. The windows and the glass in the door were covered with metal grillwork. The diner was sandwiched between a dry cleaner and a pawnshop. The pawnshop's windows were protected by similar grillwork. Apparently the dry cleaner wasn't afraid of intruders because those windows didn't have any protection, just huge paper signs that were obviously hand-lettered with the current bargains. The businesses were in a line of stores, some of which had large sheets of plywood covering the windows. Each time she'd passed there were people going in or coming out of Mr. Mo's.

She glanced at her watch. 11:40. It seemed as if she'd been on the go for hours, dropping Bitsy at Mrs. Thorson's apartment on the first floor at 9:45, she'd had to bite her bottom lip when she saw the panic on the child's face before they left the apartment.

"I'll be back as soon as I can, Bitsy."

Bitsy's eyes filled with tears and her lower lip trembled. The knuckles on her hands stood out like white marbles as she clutched her coloring book. The box of crayons lay on the table next to her. "You promise?" she whispered, her voice filled with apprehension.

"I have to take care of some business, honey."

"I can come with you. I'll be good. Mommy sometimes let me come with her."

Madison stooped down next to the terror-filled child. "But you said you also went to daycare and sometimes stayed with… Was it Missy?"

Bitsy nodded but her expression didn't change. Madison read fear and pulled the child into her arms. "Mrs. Thorson is really nice, honey. You'll like her. She's a grandmother, too. She tells me all about her grandchildren whenever I see her in the hallway or at the mailboxes," Madison whispered into Bitsy's ear. She felt the child shudder.

"I'm afraid."

"Of what?" She watched Bitsy bite her lower lip.

"You won't come back for me," the little girl stuttered.

"Of course I will. I wouldn't leave you for a minute if it could be helped, honey. But, I have to take care of some business first." Madison crushed the little girl to her chest. "I promise, honey. I'll be back to get you. You'll be a good girl for Mrs. Thorson?"

Bitsy nodded, her curls bouncing around her tortured face.

In the apartment on the first floor, Madison looked at Mrs. Thorson. "She's a little jumpy at being left. Here's my cell phone number if you need me, please call right away." She leaned down and kissed the soft cheek and whispered, "I promise, sweetheart. I'll be back as soon as possible."

Her visit to Alan's office was briefer than she thought it would be. Alan was shocked at her announcement at 'grandmother-hood' as he put it. Once she'd assured him that her writing schedule would be resumed as soon as she had relocated. That, apparently, was his biggest problem. "Dolly, I won't get to *see* you," he said, elongating the word 'see' by adding another four or five 'ees'.

"Come off it, Alan. I'll be a keypad away anytime you need to convey messages and there is the good old telephone so we can speak word to word," she joked.

Once the details, sketchy as they were at the moment, were explained he felt better. "Not that I don't disapprove heartily, dear, but I do understand. Sometimes personal trauma takes hold and there you are," he said, arms outspread. "I'm glad you dumped that popinjay, though," he added with a sneer.

"Remember, not a word to anyone about my plans until I'm established. And, for God's sake don't let even a hint at what I'm doing get to Jim. He might call you when he realizes I'm not around. I'm counting on your promise."

Alan solemnly crossed his heart and mouthed the words, 'hope to God'.

When she left his office she felt as if giant steps had been taken. Now Jo, Lolly and Alan knew of her plans. *Well,* she corrected, *maybe not everything but at least they are out in the open as far as they are concerned.*

She pulled her attention back to her mission. The morning traffic wasn't heavy, at least not on these streets.

Park and get out, she told herself. *You're never going to find out anything this way.*

Madison pulled into a parking space almost a block away from Mr. Mo's. Locking the doors, she pulled the collar of her parka up to her ears and pushed her hands into the pockets. It was still bitterly cold and a cruel wind rushed between the buildings. As she walked she noticed an empty lot next to the drycleaners. Remnants of a chain link fence poked out of the snow that bore the imprints of some children she saw building a fort in the relatively pristine snow. Their voices rang with excitement as they pelted each other with snowballs.

She'd dressed carefully this morning; old jeans, a turtleneck and a parka she'd had for years and rarely used any longer. Only her feet were clad in stylish leather boots; she didn't have any shabby footwear. After she'd left Alan's office she'd pulled on a knitted cap she wore skiing years ago and tucked her hair up into it. She'd thought about wearing sunglasses but decided that perhaps that was just a bit too Hollywood. She didn't want attention—just some answers.

At the time of her meeting earlier this morning with Alan, she'd wondered if he was curious about her attire because she usually was smartly dressed whenever she visited him. He hadn't commented and some of their conversation began to replay through her head. *Stop that. Concentrate on what you're doing now. That's all taken care of.* She pushed all thoughts of this morning's visit with Alan away. She was on a self-assigned mission and she had to concentrate on that and nothing else. For now Bitsy was safe and that was all that mattered.

She'd changed her purse for an older, smaller shoulder bag and she felt it bounce against her hip as she strode along the cracked sidewalk.

At the door to Mr. Mo's she hesitated for a moment, then pulled it open and stepped into the warm room inhaling the smells of food and damp clothes. A small bell announced her arrival. Several men seated on stools along a short counter turned to see who had entered. They immediately returned to their food and conversation.

She felt conspicuous and uncomfortable; nevertheless she slid into a booth and took a plastic menu from behind the napkin dispenser, ketchup and mustard bottles and salt and peppershakers. An older woman wearing a ridiculously big red holiday bow on the top of her gray hair sidled up to the booth. "Coffee?" she asked. Her uniform was pristinely white and clean and Madison felt a small sense of relief.

"Decaf, if you have it, please." Madison said feeling so out-of-place she blushed.

"Eatin' breakfast or lunch?" the woman said, flipping open an order pad. "Lunch special is chicken soup or beef stew. Hamburgers are good here." She licked her pencil point.

"I think I'll just have toast and coffee," Madison murmured, sliding the menu back into place. As she watched the woman retreat, Madison noted the floor was relatively clean given the wet sidewalks outside. The table and seats looked as if they had been wiped carefully. She sighed.

Trying not to call attention to herself, Madison looked around the small diner. Several booths were occupied, one with a woman and three children who were arguing about what soft drink was the best. "Pepsi," one shouted and received a punch from his brother who sneered, "No way—Coke beats Pepsi every time."

Two elderly women sat in another booth directly across from Madison. Coffee mugs and plates with what looked like the remains of breakfast were on the table but the women seemed more intent on talking. Each had an oversized cloth shopping bag folded on the bench beside them.

Several younger women were in a large booth in one corner of the restaurant. They were vigorously discussing plans for the evening and what they should wear.

The only other occupant was one very large, black man who lounged in the last booth against the wall. He faced Madison and was speaking into a small cell phone, which was further diminished in size by the enormity of his shaven head. Their eyes met as she scanned the room and her face warmed as she quickly looked away. *I must stand out like a sore thumb,* she thought, again taking the menu from its hiding place to read the offerings. She was amazed at the selections under the heading of *Dinners*. *Baked fish, ham steak, roast chicken*...Under *Lunches* she noted *Daily Special*, *soup and half a sandwich* and remembered Bitsy saying she and her mother shared a sandwich. She sighed heavily just as the woman put a coffee mug and plate of toast on the table in front of her. "There's butter and jelly," she said, sliding a dish containing various plastic containers onto the table. "You want anything else?"

"No. No, thanks. This looks fine," Madison said, smiling up into the aged face of the waitress.

As she sipped her coffee, which was exceptionally good, she looked around, carefully avoiding the man in the last booth whose cell phone rang almost constantly. The diner was a small hive of activity and obviously most of them were regulars, calling to each other and sharing gossip.

Behind the counter was a short, very muscular man dressed in white with a multi-stained apron tied around his waist. He appeared to be the cook and cashier and Madison wondered if he was Mr. Mo. A small white paper hat with a crown of mesh rode precariously on top of his bushy hair caught back in a thick ponytail. He appeared to be either badly in need of a shave or was growing a beard.

She watched two of the men at the counter rise, calling friendly goodbyes to the remaining men. They move to the cash register at the end of the counter nearest her and she noticed their trousers were tucked into heavy boots. The man at the cash register looked up, caught her eye and smiled. "Everything okay?" he called.

"Oh, yes. Thank you," she stuttered, taking another sip of her coffee.

"Free refills," he called to her, pulling bills from the cash drawer and handing them to one of the men. Madison noticed the men were younger than she had thought at first and she watched them walk to a large truck parked along the curb.

The black man extricated himself from the booth with effort and Madison was amazed at his size. *Must weigh 300 pounds if he weighs an ounce,* she thought, carefully keeping her eyes lowered. She noticed that he didn't visit the cash register, merely nodded to the man behind the counter, tucked his newspaper under one arm and left the diner, the bell announcing his departure. But, before he closed the door behind him, Madison thought he looked directly at her as if memorizing her face. An icy tremor ran up her spine. Through the window she watched him walk away. He disappeared from her view and she thought, *At least he walked away from my car. That probably stands out too.* She shivered again. There was something ominous about the man and she quietly chided herself for being judgmental about someone she didn't know and never would.

The waitress appeared at the side of Madison's table with the coffee pot. "More decaf?" she asked and without waiting for a response poured coffee into the half-filled mug.

"Thanks." Gathering all the courage she could muster, Madison reached out and touched the back of the woman's hand. "Wait, please." She kept her voice low and the woman leaned closer. Madison caught the scent of Clorox.

"Do you remember a young woman who came in here with a little girl. The little girl...about four years old...had dark curls, blue eyes..."

The waitress straightened up. "Get lots of folks in here. Can't remember all of them. We're busy most of the time. This is quiet," she said, backing away from Madison. "We're usually packed for lunch. Must be the weather."

She turned and hurried away, disappearing behind the counter. Madison noted the man must have gone into the kitchen as she saw the top of his head through the serving window.

Well, she shrugged. *What did you expect? You're looking for a needle in a haystack and you don't even know if this is the right haystack.* She pushed her crumb-filled plate away and sipped her coffee. *At least the coffee is good.*

Draining her mug she picked up the check the waitress had left. She twisted the long purse strap over her shoulder and went to the cash register. The waitress came through a doorway from the kitchen and took the check and five-dollar bill Madison offered. "Keep the change," Madison said, turning away. "Thank you."

"Come again," the waitress said, pushing the bill into the cash drawer and stuffing some money in her apron pocket without making eye contact with Madison.

Outside, Madison didn't hesitate. She hurried along the sidewalk to her car. Just as she was about to click the door opener she felt someone rush up behind her. Clutching her purse to her side she whirled around only to come face to face with the man behind the counter. "Oh, you scared me," she murmured, her face white, her hands gripped into tight fists. He wasn't wearing the white cap and was bundled into a thick plaid wool jacket. She saw the bottom of his apron beneath his coat.

"What the hell are you doing? Askin' about a woman and a kid." He took her elbow gently and pushed her nearer the car. "I ain't gonna hurt you but you must be nuts." He looked furtively over his shoulder and said, "Walk with me."

Madison felt him tug on her arm and moved forward with him. "Where are we going?" she asked but there was no reply.

They passed several tall houses, each with a flight of stone steps to the front door. The windows were all curtained or covered with plywood and she was frozen with fear. Her feet automatically kept pace with his. When they reached the corner, they turned in unison, his hand still on her arm. This street was even more dismal than the other and Madison hunched her shoulders, not only against the wind, which was stronger here, but also for protection against the unknown that seemed to surround her.

He paused and turned to face Madison. "What you lookin' for this woman and kid for?" he whispered.

"I'm...," Madison didn't know what to say—or how much to say. "I know of a child... I think she came from this neighborhood."

He took her arm again and she wondered if anyone noticed the unlikely pair as they walked along the sidewalk in front of an endless row of tall brick row houses.

"Who are you?" he said, keeping his eyes forward.

"I'm...a friend."

"Whose friend?"

"The little girl's."

He slowed his pace and she did too. "You know her mother?"

Madison sighed, the puff of breath turning into a frosty white cloud as it escaped her lips. She pushed her hands further into her pockets. "No."

"I know a little girl. Like you said, dark curls. Mother's a hooker."

"Oh," Madison gasped and stopped.

He tugged on her arm again. "Keep movin'."

"But if you know Bit..." She hesitated. *It might not be a good idea to give her name away.* "You think you might know such a little girl?"

"I might. Disappeared. She and her mamma. Right before Christmas. Been some talk."

"What kind of talk?" Madison asked, trying to keep her excitement low.

"Rumors. Street talk. Who wants to know?" the man said, glancing briefly at Madison's profile. "Don't get many rich folks in this neighborhood. Don't get many strangers and if we do they don't go asking questions."

"But you came outside. Found me. You're the one who's talking to *me*." She felt defensive but her anxiety forced her to continue. "I don't mean any harm to her or her mother. I just want to find her...the mother...if I can."

"You know where the kid is?"

Madison stopped and again the man tugged on her arm but she resisted. "I might. I only have her best interests in mind." She glanced around. Not a soul in sight. No sound coming from any of the houses, most of which looked boarded up. *Are you crazy? Standing here with this man you don't know in a section of the city like this? You're asking for trouble. Jo would be appalled.*

"You with the city? The state? The government?"

"No! Tell me if you know where her mother is."

He shrugged, pulling the collar of his plaid jacket up to his ears. His ears were red; his face was burnished by the cold and he squinted into the breeze. "If it's who I think it might be…the kid…is she with her mamma?"

"No, that's why I'm looking for her mother."

He squinted up at her, she was several inches taller than he, but for several moments they were face to face. They might have been on another planet they were so isolated. Madison felt as if she should inch back but she stood her ground.

"A woman disappeared. Right before Christmas," he repeated. "Had a little girl. Used to come in the diner. Ate there. I took messages for her sometimes. Not the kind of messages you'd wanna know about."

"And you don't know what happened or why she disappeared?"

"No, but even if I did I wouldn't tell you."

"Why? I only want to help…the child…and the woman, too, of course."

"There ain't much you could do to help that poor bitch. The kid…who knows?"

He turned away and stared intently down the empty sidewalk in front of them. "Listen, lady. If you know where the kid is, take care of her. She ain't got no family or anyone else that'd give a rat's ass about her. Her mother was a skank, for God's sake. What's the kid gonna be? She kept her away from as much as possible, but with what she did for a livin'… ain't no life for a little girl like that. No future. Go away and quit askin' questions, okay? It ain't safe here. For you or for the kid, if she's still around. Questions only stir up trouble," he philosophized.

A gust of wind caught several plastic bags from an overfilled garbage can and they tumbled toward the two standing on the sidewalk. They watched them in silence. "You better get outta here if you know what's good for you. I'll walk you back to your car," he said.

He turned abruptly and began walking away. Madison remained frozen to the sidewalk.

"C'mon," he said, looking over his shoulder. "You're in way over your head, lady. Get back to where you belong before you get into real trouble. So far the police ain't involved but they might be some day and you don't wanna be anywhere around. It might not be pretty."

"But…" she said, hurrying to catch up to him. "But…"

He stopped short and she almost ran into his back. "But nothin'. Look lady. I prob'ly shouldn't even talked to you. I felt sorry for the mother and the kid. Sometimes they seemed a cut above the garbage we have around here," he said, gesturing to the derelict neighborhood. "But the old lady wasn't no good really. I knew that. They're gone and maybe it's better no one cares; no one's lookin' for them. At least not very hard. It's bein' kept quiet for now.

"If you know where the kid is, and I don't wanna know, and if her mother ain't with her, then it'd be bad news, for you and for the kid, if you get involved. Don't come back. Take my word for it. It'll be best for everyone if you don't make any waves. Let it be," he said, then turned away and disappeared down a narrow alley near the diner. Madison hadn't noticed it before.

She ran to her car and pulled away, driving for several blocks before she allowed herself to draw in a deep breath. There was only one thing she wanted right now and that was to scoop Bitsy into her arms.

CHAPTER FOURTEEN

Tears may be dried up, but the heart – never.
Marguerite de Valois

Madison cried. She crushed Bitsy to her chest, feeling the child's body quiver with fear. "It's okay, honey. It's okay," she whispered

A few minutes earlier, when she'd arrived at Mrs. Thorson's apartment, she'd found Bitsy sitting in a chair in the living room facing the front door. Wide-eyed and stiff with tension, the little girl had leapt from the chair and rushed to Madison. "Grandma," she cried, wrapping her arms around Madison's legs. *Just like she did when I found her in the diner,* Madison thought, pulling the little girl into her arms and buried her face in the dark curls. Both of them were crying unashamedly.

"She wouldn't do anything but sit in that chair waiting for you," Mrs. Thorson lamented. "Just stared at the door. I tried, television, cookies, nothing…"

"It wasn't anything you did, Mrs. Thorson. She's very timid. Things have been a bit difficult for her lately." Madison wiped tears from her cheeks. "Thanks so much for watching her. I call you later," she pressed a twenty-dollar bill into the puzzled woman's hand.

Madison rushed into the hallway and waited impatiently for the elevator. During the short trip to the fifth floor, she kept Bitsy in her arms. Once safely in her living room, Madison sank to the sofa, still cradling the child against her body. She felt Bitsy's incredibly soft wet cheek pressed into her neck, felt her body quiver with each sob. Emotions flooded her heart…feelings she probably couldn't identify even if she tried and she didn't. She just savored the moment, eyes closed, heart beating with an unusual fervor.

"Don't cry, honey," she whispered.

"I thought you weren't coming back," Bitsy sobbed, her breath coming in stuttered gasps.

"I told you I would." She leaned back and pushed the child away slightly, looking into the tear-stained, fear-ravaged face. "I know," she whispered. "That's what your mommy said, too, wasn't it. But this is different, sweetheart, and you have to trust me. Your mommy must have a very good reason to leave you and she told you I was coming to get you, didn't she?"

Bitsy nodded vigorously.

"And I did, didn't I"

Again the curls bobbed. "But Mommy didn't. She didn't come back…yet."

"Okay," Madison said, swinging Bitsy across her lap. "but we're together. I just have to work things out, honey, but we're going to be together even if I have to come up with some miracles. Somehow I'll make it happen. Is that okay with you?"

"Yes," the child whispered, her lips folded into a tight line, her eyes still filled with remnants of insecurity.

"I'll never lie to you, okay? And you have to promise never to lie to me." She waited for a response. "You know what a lie is, don't you?"

"Yes," Bitsy replied a slight sparkle returning to her blue eyes. "That's when you don't tell the truth. And," she added, "that's a bad thing to do. It makes everyone sad. Even God."

Madison laughed softly. "Oh, Bitsy, how did I get so lucky."

"I don't know." Bitsy pressed her head on Madison's shoulder, her hair tickling Madison's neck. " I love you, Grandma," she said, brushing her lips across Madison's chin. She paused, her brow crumpling into a frown and looked up into Madison's face. "But, I miss Mommy. Where is she? Is she coming back?" She began to cry again, softly this time. Madison felt her tiny fingers digging into the back of her neck.

"Of course you love her, honey. And you will always miss her. I don't know where she is or even if..." but she paused, unable to put the into words the thought that Bitsy's mother had abandoned her child forever; that she was never coming back.

She hugged Bitsy tightly, feeling the little girl snuggle even closer into her body. After this morning's events, she truly doubted the mother would ever return. Who knew where she was or even if she was alive? The thought of those consequences sent a glob of fear roiling from deep within her body to the back of her throat. Remembering the fatalistic expression on Mr. Mo's face just before he turned and disappeared, she feared the worst. But, was it the worst? Wouldn't Bitsy be better off with her? Wouldn't she be better off with Bitsy, away from Philadelphia, making a new life for both of them?

"Your mommy said she'd try to come back, honey, but sometimes things happen. If she can't, well you have me and I have you and that's a good thing."

She squeezed the child to her chest again and for several moments they rocked back and forth, together. *This has to be a good thing. For Bitsy,* she thought, *and for me.*

~ ~ ~

That evening Madison, Jo and Bitsy went to a neighborhood restaurant for dinner. It was a restaurant familiar to both women, one they had met in many times, especially when there was need to commiserate over a problem, real or imagined; a need to share or to celebrate something. They knew the waiters and managed to get a nice table near the front window so Bitsy could look out at the passing traffic. Jo noticed their waiter's eyebrows rise when he heard the little girl refer to Madison as Grandma.

"Lots of cars, Grandma," Bitsy said, kneeling on the chair. "Lots of people too."

"I know, honey, but you have to eat your dinner." Madison put the fork in Bitsy's hand. "Just eat two more bites of chicken, okay?"

Jo laughed. "You are something else, lady. You act like you know what you're doing."

"You don't think I do?"

"I'm impressed, that's what I mean."

"You have time to come back to my apartment?"

"Sure. I've got all night."

Once Bitsy was settled for the night, this time in her bed with the night light lit and the door open, Madison and Jo sat at the kitchen table again. "Coffee" she asked.

"No, thanks. Had enough at the restaurant.

"You'll never guess where I went today."

"Your agent's? What did he say about this hare-brained scheme of yours?"

"Oh, not much. He's confused but supportive as long as I stay with him. You know Alan, the bottom line with him is always fees. No, I mean what else I did today."

"Well, what did you do, and please don't tell me it was something stupid. You promised me last night..."

"I went looking for Bitsy's mother. It was..."

"What?" Jo shrieked and Madison put her finger to her lips. "Quiet. You'll have Bitsy in here with that yelling?"

"I thought you said she'd sleep through a brass band."

"A brass band doesn't sound like a scream."

"Sorry. What...Oh, damn, just tell me."

Jo fixed her eyes on Madison's face and didn't move or say a word until Madison finished her story. "You mean to say you were in this Mr. Mo's? Alone? Then you were strolling along the sidewalk with this guy you don't know and who warned you to leave the whole story alone? You are crazy you know. You really are. Do you even have a clue as to what might have happened? How dangerous that whole scenario was?"

"Well it turned out okay and it made me make up my mind in a hurry. There is no way I'm going to abandon Bitsy. No way. She'll be safer and better off with me. I can't worry about the legal aspects right now. All I know is that I have to get her away from Philadelphia. She's coming with me."

Joe studied her friend's face. "You really mean that."

"Tell me you agree," Madison whispered.

Jo stood and paced across the tiny kitchen floor. "If what you say and what you gather from this…character you met…this Mr. Mo…then maybe, just *maybe* the kid would be better off with someone who is totally divorced from that kind of life, that part of town. But," she paused and came back to the table, "but there is so much more to consider. How are you going to settle anywhere and get the kid into school? What about a birth certificate? What about looking for other family members?"

"I've thought of some of those things and you will probably be able to help me with more. I know my mind is going sixty miles an hour right now and there are things that might come up and I won't know what to do."

"You need a lawyer."

"No. Not right now. Maybe when we get settled somewhere."

"That's another thing. Do you really feel good about going to Florida? You could go to California and be near your sister. Not that I'd like that but it might make for a shorter duration, being close to your sister who apparently got the brains in the family."

"Oh, shut up. I don't want to be that far away from home."

"Well, that's one point we agree on. But have you even considered getting help. Professional help"

"What kind of professional help? You mean counseling?"

"I mean a private detective. I could put you in touch with someone…"

Madison stood and rinsed her mug at the sink. "I know you could and I know you want to help but right now, the way things seem to be coming into place, I think I'm going to wing it and at least get away. Maybe things will look different from a new location. You're right; I will miss things. Mostly you, but Philadelphia has been my home for a very long time. Or at least this part of Pennsylvania." She returned to her seat across from Jo. "The thought of Bitsy going into foster care frightens me. You hear things…"

"I know. Crazy as this sounds I've begun some research on that subject. I think I'm going to do some writing on that. Things like how many children stay in one foster home and how many others get shifted and how often. The ratio of educational abilities between the kids who get moved a lot and those who don't, and even to the kids who have normal homes with parents whether it be one or two parents. Then there are stories of abuse… It's a huge subject and I wish I could have more facts and figures for you."

"See?" Madison smiled at her friend. "It is something to think about and right now all I can see if Bitsy were to be taken away from me, are the negatives. I know there are good people out there who take in foster children. But…I want Bitsy to get the best and I think I can do that for her."

"You are…"

"Crazy? You've called me that quite a few times. It's a good thing I really know you and forgive easily," Madison laughed softly.

"I was going to say… 'a good person'. I just hate the thought of you getting hurt. You make yourself vulnerable you know. At least you have in the past. Maybe this is a new Madison sitting across from me." She, too, laughed, her face draining of the stress she'd been carrying for several days. "Okay. I'll help you 'get away', as if you are escaping. I'll keep an eye on your place. But you have to promise that you'll call every day and let me know what's going on. If I hear anything here, I'll let you know."

They both stood, eyes coated with tears, and leaned over the table, giving awkward hugs

"What's your next step?" Jo asked, stepping away from the table.

"Tomorrow I'm going to contact Philip and see if he'll consider renting me the condo. If he decides not to, that's okay, too. I'll find something else down there. Naples Florida is about 1300 miles away. I could fly back to Philly in a day if I have to for anything connected to the books.

"California is much farther away. It would make dealing with Alan difficult. No, somehow the sound of Florida feels right. The weather would be a whole lot better," she smiled. "I know you are worried about me. I appreciate it, Jo. We've been so close for so long this separation is going to be tough…on both of us. Who knows? Maybe I'll be able to work something out. After all, I may be able to get Philip's condo for three months. After that I'd have to make other plans anyhow. Let's leave it like that for now, okay?"

They moved into the living room. She opened her arms. "I'll pray for you, Sisty."

"And Bitsy?" Madison added, giving her friend another hug.

"And the brat too. But, I really think you must consider calling her another name. That one is just too settled in the past." They turned and walked toward the front door

"I know. I've thought of a way. I'll talk to Bitsy tomorrow, promise."

"What about a birth certificate. You know her last name. You think she was born here. You'd be able to get her mother's name that way too."

"I know but I think it might be better to do that from a distance. When I have the information then I can make more decisions."

Jo sighed loudly. "I still think you need an attorney or a private eye."

"I'll get an attorney in Florida, or wherever we end up."

"I'll call you tomorrow," Jo said, picking her purse up from the end of the couch.

"Okay. We'll be here. I'm going to call Lolly after you leave. She was pretty upset with me after I spoke to her earlier, telling her all about Mr. Mo and that stuff. Somehow I don't think the idea of me acting the private detective in that section of town gave her a warm and fuzzy feeling."

"I didn't get a warm and fuzzy feeling either. Call your sister."

"She's as worried about me as you are."

"And well she should be."

"Go home. Thanks for everything."

"Like what?"

"Like dinner tonight, a shoulder to cry on, a sounding board. You're a special friend, you know that don't you?"

"I know. You're a special friend, too. I just wish you weren't such a worry."

"Get out of here. Go home. I'll call you tomorrow."

Jo brushed a soft kiss on Madison's cheek. "I said last night not to do anything stupid and you didn't listen."

"I'll listen tonight, okay?" She watched Jo walk down the hallway toward the elevator. "Good night and thanks," she called as the doors closed. Somehow Madison felt calmer than last night. A mysterious peace settled on her shoulders. She couldn't identify the cause of this peaceful sensation but she welcomed it. For the past week there hadn't been a whole lot of mental peace.

"Tomorrow's another day," she murmured to herself as she closed and bolted her door and picked up the telephone.

"I've made up my mind, Lolly." Madison leaned back in her chair next to the window.

"But how are you going to pull this off? Just whisking a child away is crazy. How are you going to do it?" her sister bemoaned.

"I'm not sure of all the details yet but it will work out. I just know in my heart that this is the right thing to do."

There was a lengthy pause and, on both sides of the country, the sisters contemplated the conversation they were having for the second time today. Earlier, once Madison had made up her mind following her visit to Mr. Mo's, she'd called her sister in California. At first Lolly was aghast. The decision to take charge of this child, to move her away from Philadelphia, to begin whatever she had to do to make this decision feasible, had frightened Lolly and now she pleaded once more. "Don't do this, Madison. You may get yourself into terrible trouble. God only knows who's looking for Bitsy—unsavory characters… You said so yourself. You're dealing with people who have no…scruples, no sense of right and wrong."

"I know, that's just what Jo said earlier this evening. And that's why I have to do what I feel is right. She'll be safer with me. We're leaving. I told you earlier," Madison referred to her hushed conversation with Lolly earlier. "You know the situation with her mother. I did try to find her," she rationalized.

"You didn't go to the police," Lolly answered, her voice filled with uneasiness.

"If I do that then Bitsy will be put into foster care. You know I can care for her better than…than some stranger. She thinks I'm her grandmother."

Lolly didn't respond immediately, then said, "But *you* know you aren't. This flight from Philadelphia—this new life you're seeking— it's because you've broken up with Jim, isn't it?"

"Partially, that was my decision after I…after I told him it was over."

"Does he believe it's *over?"*

"Frankly, Lolly, I don't care what he thinks. As far as I'm concerned it's over and that's that. But, now that's not the whole story. I can handle Jim. It's Bitsy's welfare I'm most concerned with."

"Oh, Sisty," she said, "I have bad feelings about this. Not about you leaving that sanctimonious, lying pig… I've prayed for that for years. We're both so glad you finally did that. It's the situation with the little girl that worries me."

"You don't think she'll be better off with me?"

"Of course, she'll be better off; but, under what circumstances? You don't have a clue as to what you're going to have to face. You realize that you'll have to be able to support your claim as that child's grandmother in the future. What about registering her for school? What about her birth certificate? There are things…"

"I know there are things that will come up. But, I just feel this was meant to be. Think about it. What are the chances of a little girl being abandoned and thinking her grandmother will be picking her up if she waits long enough? What are the chances that *I'm* the one who comes along at the right moment in the right place? It has to be more than fate, Lolly."

"What about your career? You've worked so hard and you're successful, Madison. You can't just turn your back on that. For God's sake, you're going to have to support this child if you insist on doing this hare-brained scheme."

"It's not hare-brained." *That's the same phrase Jo used. Am I really unhinged about all this? No.*

"I've thought things out pretty carefully. I told you, Lolly. I spoke to Alan today. He's going to make sure no one knows where I am, not that I'm actually thinking anyone will be looking for me. That will give me some time to…well, anyway, he's also promised never to tell Jim anything about any of this. In fact, he thinks this will all evolve into a best seller. He's rubbing his hands already in anticipation of a new book he says I'm going to produce…you should hear the prospective titles; *Bizarre Grandmother—Christmas Angel—Abandoned?* He's having a field day with that," she chuckled softly as she recalled the offbeat reaction her agent had when he heard about her decisions to keep the mystery child and continue the fantasy about being a grandmother.

For a moment she drifted back to her meeting with Alan and remembered him saying," You don't even have children, love. How are you going to explain a grandchild?"

She'd responded, "I'll work it out, Alan. Just be sure to keep everything I've told you confidential. I'm counting on you."

Lolly broke her reverie. "Well, where *are* you going?"

"I told you," Madison said, remembering another earlier telephone conversation today with Philip Hendershot. But, Madison hadn't had a reply yet and knew her probable destination hung by a thread. She frowned. *I'll hear,* she promised herself optimistically and told Lolly she'd call when she had more information for her.

~ ~ ~

At just after three o'clock that afternoon, Madison's fingers trembled as she carefully dialed the telephone number and listened to the phone ring, counting the number of rings. "Maybe he's out," she mumbled as she got to six.

"Hello." His voice was breathless.

"Oh, I've made you run from someplace to catch the call, haven't I?" she asked.

There was a brief pause and then he said, "Madison?"

"Yes, Philip. I hope I haven't called at a bad time."

"Of course not. I was out in the shed working on my snowmobile. Ran over some hidden logs this morning. How are you? Is everything okay?"

"Oh, yes. Bitsy and I are doing fine. The weather here is very cold but no more snow. Of course, the snow in the city is now dirty and ugly. I keep thinking about how wonderful and white the world is up there. How's the weather?" She felt ridiculous. It was such inane conversation she was embarrassed.

"It's cold here too but no additional snow. In fact, I don't think we've lost an inch because the temperature hasn't gone above 20°. The roads are cleared though, so things are back to normal."

She heard the confusion in his voice. *I know he's wondering why I called and thinking it wasn't to ask about the weather,* she thought, gripping the receiver so hard her fingers were cramping.

She stood and with the toe of one foot, pushed the door to her bedroom almost closed. "Philip, I have a very strange request to put to you. I remembered you saying you thought you should have rented your condo in Florida. Are you still considering it?"

She heard him take in a deep breath. "Well, actually I wasn't but not because it isn't a good idea. If I'd have thought of it before I left, I would have been able to screen the renters before signing a lease. It would have to be for three months, my condo complex requires that. You see, I have some valuable things there and if I'd thought of renting the condo sooner, and taken care of it before I left, I'd have put them safely away." He paused. "Why do you ask?"

She inhaled deeply and wondered if he could hear it. "Something has come up and I need to get away. I was wondering if you would consider me as a tenant for your condo. It would be for about three months, until I can find out where I want to live. Then I'd get a place of my own. I know this is really stretching things. You really don't know me. I'll have my granddaughter with me, of course, but she's very well behaved and I'd see that your condo was very carefully taken care of. I could provide references," she added, realizing she was talking much too fast. She also wondered just who, on such short notice, she could get to recommend her character and financial stability. *Alan? Maybe someone from the bank or her publisher? Certainly not Jim,* she thought, although if things were different he would, but then again would he ever sanction her doing something completely on her own like this? Her thoughts seemed so scattered and she gripped the telephone tighter and waited for his response.

"I think something might be arranged, Madison. I know you wouldn't ask if it wasn't important. Frankly, this has come out of the blue, so to speak. Let me call a friend I have in Florida and see what he says. He's looking after my place while I'm gone. I spoke to him yesterday, as a matter of fact, to tell him I'll be up here for at least two more months."

Madison's heart swelled in her chest. Could something as urgent as this really be taken care of with a couple of phone calls? Of course, she'd insisted to herself earlier, if this didn't work out she would contact a realtor in Florida. Something would turn up. Her feeling of euphoria, after making the decisions she had made, was continuing on an unprecedented high. Somehow the thought of Florida seemed very right. Enough distance, better climate, that was for sure, and she could write anywhere as she had repeatedly assured Alan. She smiled.

"That sounds wonderful, Philip. Will you call me with your decision soon? I have to make plans and don't have a lot of time. If this can't work out, I'll contact a realtor or rental agency in Florida. Perhaps you could help with that. I'd like to be able to leave by the end of next week."

When she hung up she remained sitting on the side of the bed. Sounds from the television in the living room drifted down the short hall. Television had been such a treat to Bitsy that Madison wasn't limiting it as much as she had the first couple of days they were in the city. And, it was a good way to occupy the child while she implemented her plans.

"But," she'd cautioned Bitsy. "I have to know what you're watching, so don't use the remote to change the channel. If you want it changed just ask me, okay?

The child nodded in agreement, her face turned to the screen, her eyes filled with wonder.

~ ~ ~

Following her late night telephone call with Lolly, Madison peeked out the window. The street below her was dark and quiet but the glow from the city brightened the sky leaving a familiar silhouette etched against the sky. The wind had died down and now the bare branches of the trees lining the street cast eerie shadows.

"Lolly will come around. She'll see I'm right," she whispered, then tiptoed down the hallway to look in on Bitsy. She remembered the difficult time it had taken to convince Bitsy to sleep in the small guest bedroom across the hall from Madison's. Now the little girl was curled up in a soft lump under the sheets and quilt. Madison had promised that the door to this bedroom and her own would always be open just in case Bitsy needed her. So far, after sleeping in her own room through the night, Madison believed Bitsy knew she'd keep her promise.

She remained in the doorway listening to the child's soft breathing. *My grandmother made that quilt,* she mused. *I never realized how much something like that meant to me. All those memories. All those stitches. I thought I'd never be a grandmother and now...*She entered the room and brushed a soft kiss across Bitsy's cheek, her body filled with such intense emotions she felt her knees quake.

CHAPTER FIFTEEN

The cure for boredom is curiosity. There is no cure for curiosity.

Ellen Parr

"Do you know what New Year's Eve is, Bitsy?"

Madison and Bitsy were at the grocery store. Bitsy stood on the lower rack of the grocery cart and held onto the side as Madison shopped.

"It's when one year ends and a new one starts," Bitsy said, face set in her serious mode. Madison had become good at reading Bitsy's inner feelings by the set of her face. She was a bright child and sometimes amazed Madison with her studied statements.

"That when Mommy *always* had to work but she brought me a surprise. I had to be very quiet no matter what I heard outside. Mommy said, I couldn't open the door or look out the window, no matter what," she added, nodding her head in agreement with her words.

"You mean you stayed in your apartment all by yourself?" Madison stopped in the middle of the aisle, annoying the woman behind her who pushed her cart around the stalled one, shaking her head and casting an angry glare at Madison.

"Why didn't you stay with Missy?" Madison smiled inwardly at her incongruous first name basis with Missy, the character Bitsy described as her sometime babysitter.

"Missy had to work, too."

"Oh." A picture of the little girl alone in the rooming house, chilled Madison and she pushed the cart ahead. These small peeks into Bitsy's earlier life always left Madison with an empty feeling that sometimes stretched into anger. “What kind of cereal do you want?” she asked, trying to erase the unpleasantness.

The long, well-stocked cereal aisle loomed ahead and Madison knew it would take a while for Bitsy to make her selection but she didn’t hurry her. Watching her move along the aisle, touching one box and rejecting it for another was reward enough for Madison. Finally a box of Fruit Loops was tossed into the rapidly filling cart.

“Well,” Madison said as they reached the snacks aisle. “We’re going to have a New Year’s Eve party of our own tonight. You can stay up an extra hour, how does that sound?”

“Oh, goodie,” Bitsy clapped her hands silently beneath her chin.

“Soda, treats, all kinds of good stuff. You can choose one soda and one treat, okay?”

Bitsy’s eyes widened and she jumped from the moving cart. “Careful,” Madison cautioned. “You might fall leaping from the cart that way.”

“I know what I want,” the little girl said, skipping down the row of bagged chips and other goodies. She paused in front of a huge bag of Doritos on the top shelf. “These,” she said pointing.

“That’s a strange choice,” Madison said, pulling a smaller bag from another shelf.

“Mommy liked them, do you Grandma?”

“No, but you may choose whatever you want.”

She added a can of salted mixed nuts and some crackers, putting them in the cart next to the cheese and dip mix. A bag of fresh vegetables and six cookies from the bakery counter completed the party fare. Madison had even picked up a bag of fancy napkins and foil-coated party hats for the festivities.

“Let’s get the soda and then we have to get home. I don’t like the evening traffic on this holiday.”

While waiting at the checkout counter as her purchases traveled along the conveyor belt, thoughts of previous New Year’s Eve celebrations rushed through her mind. It was the one holiday Jim didn't feel obligated to spend with his family and it was usually a special event for them as a couple. She remembered how handsome he looked in his tuxedo. She knew that the many gowns she'd chosen for these special occasions still hung in her closet. "Now they're just so many sequined empty reminders," she muttered, wondering if the Salvation Army would take them.

The cashier looked up. "Did you say somethin' Ma'am?"

"Just talking to myself," she apologized.

"Grandma does that a lot. And, sometimes she doesn't tell me what she said," Bitsy announced to the clerk and everyone else within earshot. The clerk smiled and the packer just kept stuffing things into the plastic bags.

At nine o'clock that night they held their celebration. Madison used her grandmother's wine glasses for the soda and wine. *I remember grandma setting the table for holidays and birthdays with these glasses. Snippets of the past,* she mused, sipping her wine. The chips, cheese and crackers were arranged on pieces of her best china.

Madison wore a cone-shaped blue plastic hat with a small bill. It was covered with silver stars. Bitsy had a gold crown with little white feathers waving with every motion of her head. "I'm a princess tonight, Grandma." She paused, then added. "You look like a circus man, Grandma. You need a big red nose."

Madison laughed so hard tears streamed down her cheeks. "Of all my past New Year's Eve celebrations, Bitsy, this is the best," she giggled, pouring more root beer into Bitsy's stemmed glass. "Happy New Year, honey."

Later following the bath ritual, which amazed Madison by the importance it had taken on, and after reading a story from one of Bitsy's new books, she tucked the covers around the sleepy child. The scent of soap and talcum powder filled her nostrils. "Sleep well, honey. I'll be across the hall. See you in the morning." She kissed the soft cheek again.

"Good night, Grandma. We have lots to do tomorrow, don't we?"

"We do. It's going to take both of us to get ready to travel to Florida."

"I want to see the palm trees and coconuts you showed me in that book," Bitsy whispered, settling her head in her pillow. "And beaches," she added, sleepily. "Do you like beaches, Grandma?"

"I love them, honey. And you will, too."

She tiptoed out of the room and glanced back at the child who was almost asleep. *What a difference from the first couple of days here,* Madison thought; remembering when she'd picked Bitsy up from Mrs. Thorson's apartment. *Different for both of us. It all came together after my visit to Mr. Mo's.*

She poured a glass of wine and took the book she was reading to the couch. She smiled as she put her feet up on the coffee table. *Have I ever known such contentment? Maybe when I was a child. Children should have a contented childhood. I did and so will Bitsy.*

But as she opened the book, she had to acknowledge there might be areas of life ahead of her that might contradict this blissful feeling. She opened her book and sighed. *The day after tomorrow is January second and Jim will be back*. She felt a small twinge of angst run through her. "Well," she murmured. "He won't change my plans or interfere in anything I do from now on." Still, silently she wished she and Bitsy had been able to leave Philadelphia this week instead of next. She closed her eyes and mentally ran through what had to be accomplished before they could leave. In the dim room it seemed like an uncomfortably long list of things to do and she pushed her book aside, rose and went to bed. *Grandma always said things looked better in the light of day.* Madison smiled as she pulled the spread back on her bed. As she snuggled down between the cool sheets, she realized that over the past few days she'd referred to her grandmother several times. *Well, I couldn't have a better example to follow*, she thought, pushing the pillow into a more comfortable position. "But she had Grandpa to help her," she whispered into the dark.

CHAPTER SIXTEEN

The grand essentials of happiness are: something to do, something to love and something to hope for.
Allan K. Chalmers

New Year's Day was cold, windy and sunny. Madison and Bitsy took a walk around the neighborhood. "Come on, sweetheart Let's see what's stirring outside."

Madison was aglow. *This is the first New Year's Day I've gotten up this early and didn't have a headache. Who says all that hoopla is fun.*

She wore jeans, a thick sweater and her leather coat and Bitsy was clad in her two-piece snowsuit. *The one she wore when I found her in the diner,* Madison thought and took her hand as they crossed a street. They both had scarves wrapped around their necks and chins. Bitsy sported new mittens and Madison wore gloves.

There weren't many other souls braving the cold and they walked several blocks before turning the corner to go home. "We'll have cocoa and cookies when we get back, okay?"

"Two cookies?" Bitsy said, swinging the hand that was firmly gripped in Madison's gloved hand.

"Two. And then we'll play a game."

Bitsy stopped. "What game?"

"Do you know how to play cards?" Madison said, tugging Bitsy in motion again.

"No. But Mommy sometimes played…I think it was sole tear…"

"Solitaire. That's a game you only need one to play. We're going to play Go Fish. I'll teach you."

"Oh, goodie," Bitsy said and began skipping along the wet sidewalk.

They cut through the small park around the corner from their apartment building. Here the snow was whiter than that along the streets and Bitsy tramped across some open areas. "Look, Grandma, you can see where I walked. This is all white and shiny like the snow at the house in the mountains."

When they reached the edge of the playground area Bitsy stopped. "Oh," she gasped, then frowned. "Where are the swings?" She stared forlornly at the empty metal framework.

"It's winter, honey. They take them in for winter and put them out when the weather is nice and warm and you can play outside."

"At day care, when I was there, Miss Natalie and Miss Jane pushed us on the swings. If we were good, they let us stay outside for a long, long time. They caught us at the bottom of the slide, too." Madison heard a hint of longing, a recall of old pleasant memories in Bitsy's voice.

Bitsy stood staring at the barren swing set then turned to look at the sliding board She dropped Madison's hand and rushed over to it. "It's all icy," she called.

"Come on, honey. We can't play here yet." She stooped down and cuddled the child to her. "Just think. When we're in Florida it will be warm all the time and the playgrounds never close. We'll have such fun there, won't we?"

Bitsy continued to stare at the icy sliding board. "Okay," she said, turning away. "When are we going to Florida?"

"By the end of the week, honey, if I can get everything taken care of"

"I can't wait to go to Florida."

Madison frowned. "Why, Bitsy? You don't even know what Florida will be like."

"I do too. You showed me pictures on your computer. Beaches and different trees…" She turned to face Madison. "And you'll be happy in Florida."

Madison held her breath. "Why would you say that, honey? I'm happy here… with you."

"Sometimes you look sad."

Madison took Bitsy's hand. "I'm always happy with you, sweetheart. If I look sad it's because I have so many things to think about so that we can go away…together…so we'll be…" She was going to say safe. *That might sound too scary,* she thought. "So we can be warmer and happier. Okay?"

Even to Madison it sounded kind of lame but Bitsy smiled and leaned forward to kiss her cheek. "I love you, Grandma."

Madison stood and took her hand. "I love you too, honey. I may have to go to my agent one day and if that's the case, you may have to stay with Mrs. Thorson."

Bitsy stopped short, her hand tugging on Madison's. "No. Please don't make me stay with Mrs. Thorson." Her face was twisted with concern.

"Why, Bitsy? She's a nice lady. She has two little grandchildren."

"I know but she…"

Madison squatted next to Bitsy. "What did she do, honey?" Madison asked, her chest tightening around her heart.

"She kept asking me questions about my mommy. You told me not to say anything about Mommy." Bitsy's eyes filled with tears and she wiped at them with the backs of her wooly mittens. "I don't know where Mommy is," she wailed softly.

"I know, honey. But you have me. Remember your mommy wanted you to be with me." She bit her lower lip to keep it from trembling. She straightened up, took Bitsy's hand in her's and walked along the sidewalk. "We'll find someone else to watch you if I have to go anywhere, okay?"

Bitsy marched along next to Madison, her boots scuffing along the wet sidewalk, one hand firmly clutched in Madison's gloved hand. "Okay, Grandma."

Back in the apartment, Bitsy put her boots into the coat closet near the front door. "I can take my snowsuit off by myself," she said, running down the hallway to her bedroom.

"Okay, but lay it over the side of the bathtub. The bottoms of your pants are wet from where you tramped in the deep snow in the park."

In the kitchen, Madison put the kettle on and got out the cocoa. She stared at the pantry shelves. "Do I leave all this stuff or take it with me?" she wondered aloud. There were so many little decisions to make she felt overwhelmed for a moment. Then, shrugging her shoulders she placed four cookies on a small plate, took two mugs from the cabinet and a bottle of milk from the refrigerator. "Rome wasn't built in a day either," she murmured.

"Come on, honey. Cocoa's ready" she called.

"Yum," Bitsy said thundering into the kitchen and climbing onto one of the two kitchen chairs at a small table in an alcove between the kitchen and dining areas. "Oh, goodie, two cookies," she said reaching for one.

"Wait for your cocoa, sweetheart. You don't want to eat your cookies before you get your cocoa, do you?" Madison stirred cold milk into Bitsy's cup of cocoa.

For several minutes they sipped their cocoa, ate the cookies and talked about their walk. "Mommy didn't take walks much. She said the sidewalks weren't safe." Bitsy looked up into Madison's eyes. "Our sidewalks weren't nice and straight like yours are," she said nodding at her own wisdom. "They were all cracked and tippy."

Madison was about to reply when the telephone rang. She jumped up, saying. "Finish your cocoa at the table, honey and then you can color if you'd like." She hurried to answer the phone in the living room.

"Can I watch television?" Bitsy begged.

"Okay, but I'll do it for you. Stay there until you've finished your cocoa and wipe your hands and mouth on a napkin before you come into the living room." She reached for the telephone. When she recognized her sister's voice she smiled. "Happy New Year to you too, Lolly. How's the weather in sunny California?"

"Sunny. Just wondered how you were doing. Bitsy okay?"

"Wonderful. We had our own celebration last night. Soda and cookies. We even had party hats."

Lolly hesitated then said, "Sounds like fun. Steve and I stayed home this year, too. Guess the noisy crowd doesn't have the same lure it used to. Watched the ball come down in Times Square and then went to bed. The kids were out at a friend's house and we don't expect them to come home until later today. But they called just after midnight. I still haven't come to grips with teenagers."

Madison heard her sister sigh. "They're growing up. Much too fast, but that kind of happens, doesn't it?"

Again Lolly hesitated before speaking. "Madison, have you made any more decisions?"

"You mean other than what we talked about last time? I'm going to take Bitsy and go away for a while. I've cleared a lot of things with Alan. He's being just wonderful and very understanding." She heard herself vocally underline *understanding.*

"I'm trying to understand, Madison. I really am. We're just worried that you may be biting off more than you can chew. Remember when Dad cautioned us about that."

"I do and I'm trying to be as reasonable and sensible as I can under the circumstances. I'm waiting to hear from Philip about the condo in Florida. But," she said, "even if I don't hear from him, we're leaving by the end of the week. We'll find somewhere down there. I'm sure."

"It's the height of the season there. You might not find many places for rent. And," she said, "You won't want anything with a long term lease."

"I know. I just have this feeling that things are going to work out, Lolly. I know you are concerned but please..." she paused, taking in a deep breath. "All I need right now is for you to understand and be supportive. Please?"

"I'm trying to be supportive but we're still worried."

"I know. Wait a minute, Bitsy needs the television on." She put the phone on the coffee table, checked Bitsy's face and hands for chocolate and switched the television set on. Flipping through the channels she found the Rose Bowl Parade. "Here, honey. Watch the parade. It's full of bands, horses, flowers and all kinds of good things."

She picked up the telephone again. "Where was I?"

"Making plans to leave by the end of the week."

"Okay. I'll let you know when we are leaving and where we're going, if we know. I have an idea of where I want to be even if we don't get Philip's condo. I'll try the same area because it sounds really nice. He spoke so highly of it. Let's hope it works out. I've checked it out on the Internet. Please don't worry, we'll be okay. I'll call you when I know anything for sure."

"Wait," Lolly said. "Don't hang up yet. Have you heard from Jim?"

Madison bit her bottom lip before responding. "No. He won't be back in town until tomorrow and I'm hoping that I won't hear from him at all until after I'm gone. And then," she laughed softly, "after I'm gone I surely won't hear from him."

Madison heard Lolly sigh again. "Take care, Sisty and keep us informed. We're praying for you but it's hard to know just what to pray for."

"Pray for us to be safe and happy. That's all we really want. That and to be together," she said, looking at the back of Bitsy's head. The little girl was sitting cross-legged in front of the television and Madison's heart swelled with emotion. "She's a wonderful little girl, Lolly," she said lowering her voice. "I love her." She paused, then added, "I love her more than anything or anyone I've ever known."

"That's scary. You may be opening yourself to a lot of hurt, little sister."

"I know but down deep I think I can handle it. I'll call you, Lolly." She slid the telephone back onto the stand and stood silently watching Bitsy. *Maybe true love does hurt a little,* she thought, feeling her chest contract and her heart swell with emotions she was unfamiliar with. But, the feeling of doing the right thing, the feeling of being on the right track far outweighed any concern and she stepped forward and ran her fingers through Bitsy's hair.

"What?" the little girl asked.

"Nothing, honey. I'm just so happy you're here with me. Sometimes I have to touch you to believe my heart."

CHAPTER SEVENTEEN

Nothing in life is to be feared. It is only to be understood.
Marie Currie

When the telephone rang at eight o'clock in the morning Madison stopped what she was doing. Her body froze. *It's January second. Is that Jim? Should I answer?*

She crept across the living room carpet, as if any noise she made would alert the caller to her presence. When the answering machine came on and repeated her recorded message in a voice she barely recognized, she stood helplessly next to the end table, her hands in tight fists at her side. Following the beep she heard Philip's voice. "Madison, it's Philip. Sorry if I've called too early. I just..."

Madison's hand shot out and snatched the receiver from the stand. "Philip," she gasped.

"Oh, hi. Sorry. I must have called at an inconvenient time. You sound all out of breath. Did I wake you?"

"No. I mean, no it's not inconvenient. I was...I was in another room," she lied.

"Well, I spoke to David Logan. He's the fellow who watches my condo whenever I'm away. A retired lawyer. Great friend. Lives on the same floor as I do."

Madison forced herself to sit on the couch, her knees quaking with anxiety. "I'm so glad to hear from you Philip. Have you made any decision? About the condo, I mean?" As she listened to herself, her voice sounded higher pitched than normal and she hoped she didn't sound over-anxious but then how could she keep her voice calm when it was being driven by her racing heart.

"Yes, I have, Madison. David agrees with me. If you would sign a three-month lease…he has the papers, you can have the condo. Of course, when I return I'll need it back but by then you will probably have found other arrangements. We'll work it out if that sounds okay to you."

Madison took in the first real breath in several minutes. "Oh, Philip, that sounds just wonderful. You don't know how relieved that makes me feel. I'm sure staying at your place will be very temporary. It's just until I get settled. Things…" Her mind churned at a pace close to that of her heart and she paused, dragging in another huge breath of air. "How will I get the keys? Where exactly is it?"

She heard his soft chuckle. "David has the keys and I'll email you directions. How are you traveling to Florida?"

"By car. I'm driving."

"Have you been to the west coast before?"

"No," she said softly. "I've been to Miami and the Keys but that's all." As she said those words brief flashes of the past crowded her mind. Trips with Jim to exotic hotels and beaches, filled with yacht trips and luxurious accommodations. Things from the past that she wanted to erase.

"No trouble. I'll email you directions from Philadelphia to Osceola Beach. It's near Naples. It's not hard to find and I'll alert David to watch for you. Do you know when you'll arrive?"

" I don't. I still have things to do here but it will be as soon as possible, that's for sure. I'm aiming for the end of this week. Can I call you when we're ready to leave and then you can call your friend?"

"Sounds good. And, Madison," he paused. "I hope everything works out for you and your granddaughter."

Madison felt herself go limp and her eyes filled with tears. She struggled to keep the rampant emotions she felt at this moment hidden from her voice. "Thank you Philip. You'll never know what this means to us. We're so grateful for your kindness..."

"No thanks necessary. The condo's empty for at least the next two months. I might have a photo shoot scheduled before I can return to Florida so whatever happens, you'll be okay once you get there."

Madison thanked him and they hung up promising to connect before she and Bitsy left Philadelphia. As she sat there recalling what she could remember about their conversation she wondered if there was more hidden in Philip's last words. *Well, I can't worry about that. Once we're settled...*

"We have lots of work to do today, sweetheart. I'm going to need your help packing. That was Mr. Hendershot. Remember the neighbor when we were in the mountains at the cottage? We have a place to go in Florida. In a few days we'll be off. Isn't that exciting?"

"Uh huh," Bitsy said, her eyes glued to the television program. Madison went into her bedroom and pulled the entire set of luggage from her closet. Her hands trembled with excitement not fear as she began to empty bureau drawers into the cases on her bed. "Bitsy," she called. "I need you." She laughed quietly at the intensity and true meaning of the words.

The feeling of euphoria was suddenly interrupted as the telephone rang again. *Philip again? Or was it Jim this time?* She reached for the telephone on her nightstand.

~ ~ ~

The clock on the dashboard showed 11:14 as she signaled a right turn and began looking for a parking space. She watched Bitsy in her rear view mirror. The child was as stiff as a statue and hadn't spoken since they began this hurried trip. "You have to trust me, honey," she said. "Remember? We promised…never to lie. I'll come back for you."

One block past her destination she pulled into a tight spot in front of a tall building which, she knew, housed hundreds of lawyers. After all, they were only three blocks from the Court House. She turned the engine off and looked at her passenger, buckled into the back seat. *I've got to get a car seat for Bitsy before I get a ticket. That would certainly not be good right now.*

"Listen, honey. You know I promised never to leave you but that doesn't mean I don't have to go somewhere I can't take you once in a while. I'll only be a couple of hours."

Bitsy, who had been wide-eyed and exceptionally quiet ever since they left the parking garage, looked at Madison's image in the mirror. "Okay," she said in a small voice.

Madison got out, put money in the parking meter and helped Bitsy from the car. She reached across the back seat and retrieved the plastic bag that held Bitsy's favorite storybook, her coloring book, crayons and a package of cookies.

Taking the child by the hand they hurried down the block to the office building where Alan's agency was. They rode the elevator to the ninth floor.

Mrs. Bronsky looked up, startled, as Madison burst through the door and hurried to her desk. She was dragging a little girl by the hand.

Madison hurriedly looked around the waiting room and noted two young men, magazines open, their eyes looking intently at the newcomer.

"Mrs. Bronsky," she whispered, "do you have grandchildren?"

"Yes."

"Oh, good. I have a *huge* favor to ask you." Bitsy crowded into the back of Madison's knees. "I have an appointment in about twenty minutes and it's a good forty minutes away and I need a babysitter. Can my granddaughter stay with you for an hour or so?" She knew Alan, who had promised to tell no one about her granddaughter, had probably already told his faithful receptionist.

Mrs. Bronsky slowly rose from her chair and looked over her desktop. A little girl with dark curls peeked from behind Madison. "And who is this little charmer?"

"This is Bitsy. Bitsy, say hello to Mrs. Bronsky."

Bitsy folder her lips into a tight line and blinked rapidly.

"She's a bit shy but she's a very good girl, aren't you, honey," Madison said, tugging the child from behind her. "I'll be back to get you as soon as I can, okay?" She looked at the puzzled receptionist. "I'll explain it to Alan."

"You go along. It will be okay with Alan, I'm sure. You're late already. Bitsy and I will be just fine, won't we dear?" Mrs. Bronsky came around her desk and bent low to speak into Bitsy's face. "I have some orange soda in the kitchen and we have some wonderful toys in a box in the closet. Let's see what's there, okay?" She held out her hand.

"Toys?" Madison said.

"For clients who can't leave their children somewhere. It's not unusual."

Madison watched as Bitsy looked from one to the other then slowly put her hand into the extended fingers. She stared up into Madison's face and bit her upper lip.

Madison stooped and gave Bitsy a hug, brushing her lips across one cheek. "You'll be okay, honey, and I'll be back as soon as I can. I promise."

To Mrs. Bronsky, she said, "You have my cell phone number. Call me if anything…anything at all comes up. And…thanks Mrs. Bronsky. You don't know how much I appreciate this."

With a wave to Bitsy, Madison whirled and rushed to the door. She turned and took one last look. Bitsy was holding Mrs. Bronsky's hand and clutching her plastic bag. Madison blew her a kiss and closed the door.

In the car, pulling away from the curb she tried to swallow the lump in her throat. *This will get easier. It has to,* she thought and then concentrated on the traffic. She had fifteen minutes to get to the restaurant and she knew it was at least thirty minutes away.

~ ~ ~

"You're late." His broad grin deepened the creases at the sides of his eyes.

"I know. Couldn't help it." Madison slid into the booth across from him. "I told you on the phone this morning, I'm very busy and I don't know what we have to meet for anyhow. It's over, Jim. It's over, I thought I'd made that very clear," she repeated. She put her jacket and purse on the bench next to her and folded her hands quietly in her lap, marveling at her calm.

"I'm not so sure, Maddy."

"Please stop calling me that ridiculous name. You know I hate it."

"Okay, Madison. We need to talk. Let's order lunch." He pushed a large menu across the table.

They were sitting in a restaurant they hadn't visited before…not as a couple anyhow. Madison had chosen it as neutral ground. Earlier, on the telephone, Jim had suggested a restaurant they'd frequently visited in the past, one that held tastes of the past, memories that could easily be revived. But Madison objected; that was not the setting she envisioned, not that she had envisioned any setting. In a perfect world, she had hoped she could get away from Philadelphia without any confrontation, without seeing him again.

But, Jim had suggested…no insisted…they needed to talk, and asked if he could come to her apartment. Madison recalled the terror those words evoked.

"No," she'd said. "No, that isn't convenient at all and anyhow, I've said all I'm going to say. As far as I'm concerned, we have nothing more to say."

But, as he always did, he pressured to see her 'one more time' as he put it. "Why?" she'd asked.

"To settle some things." She couldn't pin him down and rather than risk an unexpected visit from him where he'd see Bitsy, she'd settled on a meeting for lunch as the lesser of two evils. She didn't want to see him. "But this is the last time," she insisted. "I'm going away for a while."

In the restaurant she opened the menu. She wasn't hungry. All she wanted was to get this over and get back to Bitsy and get on with her life.

"What will you have?" he asked.

"A cup of soup and a buttered roll."

"That's all?" he said, looking at her. "You look lovely, by the way. New suit?"

"No. You've seen it dozens of times." She'd chosen her attire carefully. She wanted to look business-like, independent and sure of herself. The cream suit with matching embroidered blouse, smart brown boots and her brown suede jacket seemed to fit the bill.

"Well, it's very becoming. Sure you won't have something more than soup?

"I'm sure. Listen, I don't know what you want but I can't see any purpose in this meeting. I've made up my mind. I'm not changing it. I think I made everything quite clear the last time we…" she paused, "…we were together." She scolded herself mentally for the hesitation.

He looked down to study the menu. "Think I'll have the broiled fish." He closed the menu and pushed it aside. "I don't believe you, Madison. Not after all these years…after all we've done together. We had a great time…a good relationship…hell, we didn't even fight…often." He grinned, the smile reaching his eyes, his innate charm in tact.

She sighed. "You just don't get it do you. We did have some great times…but it wasn't what I wanted and you knew that years ago…and you promised me," she swallowed carefully, "Our relationship only lasted as long as it did because I was weak…stupid. You promised me we'd be married and I believed you…for far too long. I think I was more than patient. But, during the last few months, I finally realized it would never happen. Do I have to go over all that again? You are not going to leave your wife," she said looking directly into his eyes. "And that's okay. For you…but not for me."

"What prompted this? You've always understood before. We've had these discussions…

She looked across the big room and saw the waiter nearing their table. "Please order me the chicken rice soup and a buttered roll," she said quickly, closing her menu.

After the waiter left, Jim reached across the table. "Give me your hand, sweetheart. You've got to forgive and forget. It's always best. We've only been apart a week. I've missed you."

She glared at him. "Missed me? Was that while you were in London with your family…your wife? Excuse me? Haven't you been listening to me at all? I'm not giving you my hand…or anything else. What don't you understand about '*It's Over*'!" she hissed, her voice rising with her annoyance.

Driving here she'd thought the meeting might be confrontational but once she sat across from Jim she didn't feel anxious or nervous at all and her confidence soared. It was truly over. The only thing she was worried about was that Bitsy was all right with Mrs. Bronsky. She opened her purse and took her cell phone out, turning the ringer off and the vibrator on. She placed the phone on the bench next to her, close to her thigh.

"Expecting a call?" he asked.

"Maybe. I've a lot to do in a short time."

"You said you might be going away? Where? For how long? Is this just a fun trip, a get-away? Maybe Hawaii? I'd be happy to make the arrangements."

"I'm going alone," she said with a pinch of guilt because she was not going anywhere alone. From now on wherever she went, Bitsy went too, at least that was her plan. And, it certainly wouldn't be to Hawaii. "No thank you. Besides, I'm never again going anywhere you pay for. Is that clear?"

He settled against the back of the bench and shrugged his shoulders slightly. "You'll change your mind. You always have."

"Stop it," she said, leaning forward. "For once stop being so smug and sure of yourself. Get this straight. I'm not going to come back; there is no relationship... You can't lure me with gifts and promises. I am not going to change my mind. Is that clear? "

The waiter put their food on the table. "Will there be anything else, sir?" he asked.

"Another beer," Jim said pointing to his empty glass.

"And the lady?" the waiter said, smiling at Madison.

"I'll have coffee, thank you."

They sat staring at their lunches for several moments. "You can't mean that, Madison. You've been my whole life for twelve years." Jim's voice was solemn.

"Thirteen," she corrected. "And I was never your 'whole life', you know that. If that were true we wouldn't be sitting here." She picked up her spoon and tasted the soup. It was hot and she replaced the spoon on the saucer. "I'm moving on."

"Another man?"

"Of course not."

"Why 'of course not'. You're a beautiful, vibrant woman."

"I knew that's what you might think. Your thoughts are always driven by your... needs," she finished lamely. "I have other interests. My writing, for one thing."

"You've always written. That's never interfered with us. I never did anything to stop you doing that." He made himself sound so magnanimous. "Why go away now? Everything you need is right here."

She laughed softly. “Everything I need? You mean you?”

“I’ve been in your life for a long time.”

“In it but not really a part of it. Look, Jim. I know I’m to blame for this, too. If I hadn’t been so weak, so trusting, so gullible…”

“So well cared for… Remember the Bahamas? The cruises? San Francisco? The ski trips. Europe? I could go on…”

She looked at him and noticed, for the first time, a small worry line between his eyes. “You were always generous. We did have fun; I’m not discounting any of that. But, in the end I needed more and I told you almost from the very beginning… I wanted a husband, a family, a normal life. I didn’t realize how much I wanted that until recently and I also realized that I was the one sacrificing, not you. You had the best of both worlds. Family…and me…”

“What epiphany made you change?”

“Don’t be smug.”

“Well, something must have happened. Up until just before Christmas I thought everything was okay. And, I was willing to do anything to keep it that way.”

“Anything? I don’t think so and you know it.”

“Well, what happened?”

She leaned back and studied him. Handsome, wealthy, the kind of man most women would have loved to have as a companion. “I think it was when my dad died in September. I thought about him…and my mother…they were married over fifty years. I began to remember… remember their life together. They didn’t have a lot of money but they were comfortable and their lives were beautiful, fulfilling, normal…” She felt her eyes begin to burn as tears threatened. She took a long drink of her water.

“I thought you ordered coffee,” he said, looking for the waiter.

“Forget it. I don’t want it now.”

“It won’t be any trouble…”

"Forget it!" She sighed. "I don't want the coffee. I don't want lunch with you. I don't want to see you again. How can I make that any clearer?"

He took a forkful of fish and moved to toward his mouth but stopped midway. "You mean that don't you."

"Yes," she said, trying another spoonful of soup, which had gotten considerably cooler. She pushed the dish away. She didn't want to eat. The roll she'd ordered lay untouched on the plate, a fluted paper cup held whipped butter.

"Well," he said, forking some salad into his mouth. "There are some things we need to settle."

"Like what?"

"Like money."

Her eyes widened. "You mean you think I owe you something? Money?"

He shrugged and took more food from his plate, chewing carefully. "Not exactly. No, you don't owe me money. There's the ring though." She saw him glance at her left hand. There was no ring on her ring finger.

"The five diamond wedding ring," he said. She noticed a change in his eyes, a steeliness that wasn't there when she first arrive glinted back at her. The harsh 'this is going my way or else' look she'd seen before when he was transacting business.

"A wedding ring without a wedding. It was just so much window dressing when we went out as Mr. and Mrs. Eldridge wasn't it. It was to protect you…not me. Don't worry…you'll get that back," she whispered.

"I'll buy it from you. What's it worth? Ten thousand new. Now, five thousand maybe? After all, it's used."

"You bastard," she whispered, her voice a harsh noise she almost didn't recognize. "If I had it with me, you'd get it back right now. It's home, I haven't been wearing it. I'll have it delivered by messenger this afternoon. To your office, of course."

"Come on, sweets. I'm willing to pay you for it. Don't tell me you can't use a few extra bucks?"

She felt a shudder run down her spine and looked at him. He ate calmly, carefully, his attention on the food on the plate in front of him. "That's what it's always been, hasn't it, Jim. Money. The bottom line for everything. You can afford to be who you are and you think everyone should accept you for that. Money is your power, it gives you control over everything. You once told me 'money can buy anything…anything worth having'. You are pitiful," she said and saw him look up sharply.

"Pitiful?"

"Guess that's not an adjective often used to describe the great Jim Eldridge. Well pitiful doesn't mean poor, Jim. It means pathetic and deplorable. It means you are lacking in something."

"And what am I lacking?" he said, sipping his beer.

"Not money, not success, not even luxuries, that's for sure. No, what you're lacking is understanding, being able to love without strings or control. There's a lot more but I'm not going to give you a lesson in grammar, or social behavior." Her voice held steady and she felt a wave of satisfaction flow over her.

"I'm leaving. I'll see you get the ring today." She rose and shrugged into her jacket. She looked at the man she'd loved for too long. "I feel sorry for you, Jim. You just don't get it. Please don't call me again."

At the door she wanted to turn and look at him once more. She wanted to see some emotion, hurt, bewilderment; anything, but she steeled herself and pushed the heavy door open. What she didn't want was to see him casually eating, not even looking at her as she left. She walked quickly to her car and pulled out of the parking lot without another glance at the restaurant.

A few blocks away she pulled into a small parking lot in front of a series of small businesses. She turned the motor off, and pressed her shoulders against the back of the seat. She blew a large puff of breath from her pursed lips and looked into the mirror, smiling at her image. "And that's that," she murmured. Reaching into her purse for her cell phone she dialed Alan's office. "Mrs. Bronsky, it's Madison. Tell Bitsy I'm on my way back."

CHAPTER EIGHTEEN

Confusion and despair make for poor traveling companions.
Author unknown

At nine o'clock on Friday morning, Madison closed the door softly, turned the key gently and picked up two canvas carryall bags at her feet. She paused a moment looking at the door with the familiar brass 5-A; somehow the occasion seemed to merit a moment of speculation and remembrance.

Shrugging her shoulders as if to adjust the load she carried, she began to walk toward the elevators, her purse swinging from one shoulder. Bitsy followed her down the hallway. She carried a small tote bag with her coloring book, a favorite storybook and her crayons. Madison had slipped a covered plastic cup filled with dry cereal and raisins into the bag just before they left the apartment.

"Where is Aunt Jo?" Bitsy asked. "She said she'd be here when we left."

"She's probably at the parking garage, supervising the packing of the car," Madison laughed. "Come on, honey," she said, urging Bitsy into the elevator while she held the door open with her shoulder. "Mr. Weslowski is way ahead of us with the rest of our bags.

The air outside was warmer than it had been all week and a timid sun tried to push it's way through the gray sky overhead. "Look, Grandma. The snow is almost all gone."

"Let's hope that's the last snow we see for quite a while," Madison said as they hurried to the garage. She had to remind herself to adjust her pace to Bitsy's and slowed down a little. "We don't want to run into any snow on our way south, do we?"

"No," Bitsy said, skipping next to Madison. "Soon we'll see beaches."

"Well, not real soon but that's the way we're headed," Madison said, pushing the elevator button in the dreary lobby area of the parking garage. They stood silently while the elevator creaked to the third floor.

Madison was right about Jo. When they got off the elevator she heard Jo's voice supervising the stooped handyman as he placed a small suitcase into the trunk. "Put that small box on the back seat, it won't fit in the trunk. Where did you put her laptop?"

"Hi, Jo," Madison called hurrying across the concrete floor, Bitsy jogging behind her.

"Hi. Are you sure you've got everything?"

"I'm sure and if we forgot anything we will either have to live without it or replace it. That's not the biggest question for me right now." Madison handed the two carryall bags to Mr. Weslowski who was standing next to the open trunk. "Have room for these in there?" she asked and watched as he carefully stowed them next to the suitcases and a fairly large cardboard box.

She dug into her pocket. "Here, Mr. Weslowski." She pushed two twenty-dollar bills into his hand. "Thanks so much for helping me with the heavy stuff. If you need to get in touch with me, Miss Jo here will take a message and get in touch with me. We'll be traveling."

He put his hand to the brim of his cap, a lopsided grim twisting his face. "You are a good tenant, Ms. Millhouse. Have a nice vacation." He backed away a few feet and then turned and walked to the elevators, pushing the hand truck he'd used to take the luggage and boxes from the apartment house to the garage. From the elevator he gave a final salute to the three women standing next to the car.

"Vacation? Is that what you told him?" Jo said as the elevator doors closed.

"Sure. I wasn't going to tell him we're leaving indefinitely. I have a feeling Jim might just try to check up on me, especially when he tries to phone and finds out the service has been discontinued. I asked at the phone company what kind a message they put on the telephone when the service isn't terminated but just discontinued for a while. They said it would be something like 'service is temporarily discontinued', or maybe she said 'interrupted, at the customer's request'."

"That's good. Of course, if he calls me, which I don't think he will because he knows all too well what I think of him, I'll tell him you are presently on a different planet and to bug off.

Madison and Jo giggled and Bitsy looked from one to the other and then joined in as if she understood the reason for their laughter.

"Listen," Jo said. "Are you sure you've tied up all the loose ends? Mail? Television cable? Telephone? Garbage? Is the refrigerator empty? Do you want me to take a look around after you go?"

Madison smiled and tossed Bitsy's bag on the seat next to her car seat. "I think I've done everything. What was left in the refrigerator this morning went into the garbage. You don't have to go in today. Just once a week would be great and I really appreciate this help.

"You're in charge of the mail until I give you another address. You have the key. I've discontinued the telephone and cable temporarily until I notify them. The garbage was sent down the chute right before we left. You're going to take my plants to your place or you can leave them there and just come in and water them once a week."

Madison ticked off these items on her fingers. "Of course, I'll also be in touch with Alan regularly. As soon as I get where we're going I have to get back to that book. I'm weeks behind as it is. If you think of anything else you can call me on my cell."

"Oh, don't worry about that. I'll probably be calling you three times a day."

"Don't," Madison said, opening her arms to embrace her friend. "We'll be okay and if we aren't, for any reason, I'd call you. I don't want to have to worry about you worrying about me."

They laughed again.

"I'll keep in touch as we travel south anyhow. I'm not making this a marathon race. We'll get there when we get there. I told Philip we were leaving today but were not sure when we'd arrive in Florida. He said that was fine, that his friend, Dave, will be looking for us anytime after three days."

"You're sure of your route?"

"I have the instructions Philip emailed and I also got triple-A to give me a trip-tick. We're going to be fine," she said squeezing Jo's shoulders.

"I know. I'm just worried. It's not like you're going off for a week or so on some fun-filled vacation. This is the real thing and I still don't like it. I'm going to miss you," she said, her voice catching in her throat.

"I'll miss you, too," Madison said, turning to lift Bitsy into the car seat. "Say goodbye to Aunt Jo, Bitsy."

"Goodbye Aunt Jo," Bitsy repeated softly.

"Bye little one. You be good for…for your grandma," Jo said, glaring at Madison. "I thought you were going to do something about that name," she croaked.

Madison closed the rear door and tugged on Jo's arm. "Listen, I've thought and thought and I'm not sure that's a good idea. It's kind of like taking her identity away. She's had enough changes for now. I'm going to leave it Bitsy, at least for a while. We aren't likely to run into anyone who would know who Bitsy Smith was anyhow."

Jo shrugged. "Maybe you're right. I just thought it might be a constant reminder of her…mother…or at least her past."

"When she goes to school she'll probably be Barbara or Barbara Ann and who knows, maybe she'll grow into another nickname, kids do that."

"I was just trying to help."

"I know and I love you for all the help you've been. This change is…" She wiped her eyes. "It's for the best."

"I'll pray that it is. You take care. Call me as often as possible, okay?"

Madison nodded and hugged her dear friend one more time, then went around the car and slipped behind the wheel. Jo moved to the front of the car, her face a study in control. As Madison back out of her allotted space, she fought back tears and Jo waved a half-hearted, non-joyous wave. Madison made the turn toward the down ramp. She glanced at the clock on the dashboard—11:04—she didn't look back—it was too painful.

~ ~ ~

Neither passenger made any attempt at conversation for several minutes. Madison drove automatically along familiar streets, pausing at stoplights, watching crowds of people hurry to offices or lunches or shops. It was just like many other days when she'd driven through the city. And yet today everything seemed to be so anonymous, as if she were passing through a space in time that had little or no relationship to her. Every once in a while she looked into the rear view mirror to catch sight of Bitsy. The child sat calmly, eyes focused on the window next to her as they passed through the city.

Madison watched the street signs carefully as she drove south on Broad Street. She had to be sure and make the turn on I-95 toward Philadelphia International Airport. She'd been there many times, but never when she was driving. Never when she alone was responsible for getting through the mad traffic, the streaming rivers of fast-paced cars and trucks all determined to get there first.

The traffic became denser and traveled at a greater rate of speed. She gripped the wheel then relaxed slightly as she saw the next sign she was looking for—exit 11 to get to I-495 toward Wilmington. Once up onto the interstate highway she settled into the middle lane.

She'd stop at the first rest plaza and check her maps, directions and AAA trip-tick. Maybe she had too much information. She sighed. It was all pretty confusing and she didn't realize how little she'd paid attention when Jim was doing the driving between Philadelphia and Washington D.C. They'd gone there every year for conventions and meetings and she'd been an idle passenger, clueless as to where they were driving, only happy to arrive safely at their destination.

She felt the muscles in her shoulders tighten and tried to shrug off the tension. Now all the route numbers jumbled through her mind, I-95, I-495, I-695, I-295. Names that appeared on the directions like Richmond, Virginia and Rocky Mount, North Carolina were familiar in sound but she had no idea what lay ahead. *Maybe this wasn't a good idea,* she thought. *Maybe we should have flown. How could we have done that? Too late now,* she mentally whined, her mind leap-frogging from worry to worry like an out-of-control video game.

She checked on Bitsy again who appeared to be asleep, her head bobbing with the motion of the car. "God, how wonderful it must be to feel so relaxed and at ease," she muttered enviously. "Well, this was your idea." She stiffened her spine and pulled into the right-hand lane. She was getting off at the first rest area she saw along this misplaced theme park ride. She needed a breather and another look at the maps.

They sat on a concrete bench in the sunshine. Protected by the building that held the vending machines, Madison felt her tension melt. With one arm protectively around Bitsy they watched the constant changing of vehicles and people at the rest stop.

"Are we near Florida yet, Grandma?" Bitsy said, squinting into the sun.

"I'm afraid not, honey. I only stopped here to get another look at the maps. For a while I was kind of confused as to whether I was on the right road."

"Are we on the right road?"

"We are. And, I feel better. There's a lot of traffic and we will probably have to go a long way before we stop again so are you okay? Need to go to the bathroom?"

"No, I just went," Bitsy said, carefully folding the paper around the package of cookies she'd chosen from the vending machine. "This place is neat, Grandma. You can even get ice cream from a machine back there."

"I know. But, we're not getting ice cream now. Maybe for dinner. Let's go, honey. I'm ready to get back on the highway."

Madison had awakened Bitsy when they first arrived, then found a table and benches in a fairly deserted picnic area. She'd spread the maps and papers out and studied them carefully. "I thought I did this last night but what a rude awakening I got this morning when I barreled my way onto the interstate," she said.

"What's a 'rude awakening', Grandma?"

"It's when you realize that you don't know as much as you should."

"Oh." Bitsy kicked her heels against the bench and ate her Cheerios and raisins, while Madison rechecked her directions.

"I think my problem is that I have too many maps." She folded the auto club map and put it into a folder. "These directions from Philip will be good once we get to Florida and this map," she tapped the one in her atlas, "is the one I need for right now. At least until we're past Washington." She stood. "I need a cup of coffee. How about some milk?"

"And cookies?"

"You have cookies," Madison smiled and took the little girls hand. "You are a regular Cookie Monster aren't you?"

"I love cookies. You always have cookies for me."

~ ~ ~

Jim leaned forward, his elbow on the desktop, the slim phone to his ear. "If you hear from her, know where she is, will you give me a call?"

He waited for a response from Madison's agent, then said, "Well, I appreciate your honesty." He hung up and looked across the desk at his attorney, long-time friend and college buddy, Spalding Henderson. "That fairy prince won't give up her whereabouts. Frankly, right now I don't think he knows where she is, but he will. She has to keep in touch with him."

Spalding, known to Jim and only the closest of friends, as Inky, a nickname resulting from a college prank and relating to an ink bottle once used as a missile, folded his hands across his increasing paunch and shook his head sadly. "I told you. How many times have I told you? You should have used protection right from the get-go."

Jim smiled. "I did use protection."

Inky jerked himself forward in the plush client's chair his hands hanging loosely between his knees. "Yeah, you used a rubber."

"Better than that. I had a vasectomy she didn't know about."

The attorney stood and paced away from the desk. "You know damn well what I mean. A pre-nup. I could have fixed all this for you a long time ago."

Jim rose and joined his friend, staring out the large window with the view of downtown Philadelphia. "A pre-nup means an anticipated 'nup' and that was never in the cards. You know that."

"I could have worded it so that it covered…you know it's all in the wording, Jim. How many times have I saved you money…thousands…with the right wording? Now you've left yourself open to all kinds of suits."

Jim turned back to his desk and sank slowly into the Spanish leather covering on his high-backed desk chair. "You're thinking like a lawyer."

"That's what I am. And, I've saved your ass more than a few times, and not only about money."

"I don't think she'll cause trouble."

"You don't know that," Inky said, walking closer to the desk but avoiding the chair. "Then there's that Goddamned ring…"

"She sent it back," Jim said, opening his desk drawer and pulling out a small jewelry box. "Sent it back special messenger, insured."

"Yeah, and you sent a stupid check for five thousand dollars. I told you…"

"Which she returned."

"She could have made a copy. She didn't have to cash the check to acknowledge receipt of it and the money leads right to a commitment on your part." He ran his fingers through thinning hair.

"She didn't open the envelope. It was returned just as I sent it."

Inky sank down on the edge of the seat. "You don't know that. She could have steamed it open, made a copy of the check and if so, your ass is in the drink, my friend."

"I really don't see any trouble on the horizon."

"Ha! You didn't see this coming."

Jim leaned back and laced his fingers behind his neck. "Yeah, I did. She's been different for the past few months. I saw it coming but I didn't think she'd stick to it. She's pulled this before but I was always able to coax her out of it. This is the first time she disappeared."

"You always got her back with money, trips, gifts… I warned you."

Jim stood and stretched his hand across the desk. "You're a good friend, Inky and a damned good attorney but this time I think you're wrong. She's got something else. I don't know what and I really don't think it's another man. If I get any hint of trouble I'll let you know right away. Now, go have a good stiff drink on me. You've probably worked up a pretty good fee in the half hour we've been talking.

" I'd go with you but I have a client coming in in fifteen minutes." He glanced at his watch and gripped his friend's hand. "How about dinner tomorrow night? I'm at loose ends," he said with a mischievous grin.

~ ~ ~

Madison couldn't identify exactly when the change took place but something definitely happened just south of Washington. The road was still choked with impatient drivers who changed lanes erratically—but something was different—she wasn't part of the hectic pace anymore. It was okay if they traveled in the outside lane, slower than the others. The need to keep pace had disappeared. The dynamic rhythm she had felt earlier on the roadway after they left the rest stop, the traffic entering and leaving the highway as they bypassed Baltimore and then Washington, was pulsing to a slower beat or maybe she was slowing down. Maybe she had returned to a more sensible pace, or maybe it was the fact that with every turn of the wheels, the distance from Philadelphia increased. She felt her shoulders relax a little; her fingers no longer clutched the wheel with the same intensity.

She glanced in the mirror and saw Bitsy looking out the window. She was about to say something when Bitsy asked, "Grandma, where are we?"

"In Virginia, honey. See, even though it's still winter and the trees are bare, there's very little snow. It will get warmer as we drive south."

She watched as Bitsy's brow furrowed and her mouth purse, pushing her lips into a soft, moist rosebud. She recognized the look. Bitsy was pondering something.

"Grandma," she said again. "Florida is a long way away, isn't it?

"It's a lot of miles, that's for sure. But we won't hurry. We'll get there in a few days."

"But, if we go to Florida how will Mommy find us?"

Madison sighed. "I'm not sure, honey. Sometimes we have to have faith. We have to believe that things are going to work out." She watched Bitsy return her stare in the mirror. “We’ll talk about it later when we stop for the night, okay?”

“Okay. But, Mommy said she was coming back. She said I should wait for you and be good and stay with you. But…where will she look for us?”

“She must have a plan, honey or else she…let’s just wait and see what happens, okay? We’ll talk later.”

“Okay. When are we going to get to Florida?”

“In about two or three days. It’s a long trip but we’ll stop often so we don’t get too tired.”

That evening, after checking into a motel, Madison took the small suitcase from the trunk and held Bitsy’s hand as they walked down the carpeted corridor to the elevators. The hallway and carpet smelled musty and the inside of the elevator held the scent of a recent passenger…a combination of vanilla and roses. At the door to their room, she fiddled with the card that opened the door, then pushed it with her foot, put the suitcase on a small rack just inside the door and flicked a light on.

Bitsy remained in the doorway, her storybook clutched in both hands. She gazed around the room, her eyes wide and her mouth agape. “Wow, Grandma. You sure do get pretty places to live.” She tiptoed into the main room and looked first at one queen-size bed, then the other. Then she pointed to the television set propped on the end of a large, mirrored bureau. “Is that for us?”

“Yep, this is our room until tomorrow morning when we check out and get back on the road. But first, young lady, you’re going to have a nice hot bath then watch television while I take a shower and then we’re going out to dinner.”

Bitsy balanced on her tiptoes, a sign that she was excited. Madison smiled as she recognized these signals.

“Oh goodie. I like to eat out. Where do I sleep?” the little girl giggled turning a small circle at the foot of one bed.

“Right there, in that great big bed. Do you think you’ll fit?”

“Yeah,” Bitsy laughed, putting her fingers over her mouth. “It’s so big we could both fit.”

"I know, but what did I tell you?"

"That I have to sleep in my own bed." Bitsy nodded approvingly and carefully placed her book on her bed.

Madison smiled at the reverence Bitsy always reserved for books. "Your mommy must have really like to read. Is that why you love books?"

"Yeah. She really liked books. She always had a book. She told me that being taught to read was the best thing that ever happened to her."

"Do you know who taught her to read?"

"She said some lady that took care of her when she was alone. Mommy was going to teach me to read but she didn't."

Madison put the bathroom light on and began to run water into the tub. "Well, I can help you and soon you'll be going to school. You'll like that won't you?

"Look, honey, they've left us some bubble bath. Won't this be fun?"

Later in the restaurant, Madison ordered a cup of soup and half a sandwich for Bitsy, then when it was served pulled out all the unwanted things in the sandwich, things like onion and tomato slices and a bit of lettuce. "You're going to have to learn to eat salads young lady," she admonished, wiping her fingers on a napkin.

Madison enjoyed her small steak and relished the glass of wine that came with it. She felt comfortable and relaxed and after the day's trip those emotions surprised her. She watched Bitsy chewing carefully, her back straight, a white linen napkin tucked carefully into the neck of her sweatshirt with the angel on it. *Her most recent favorite shirt.*

When Madison stopped at the counter to pay their bill the hostess presented Bitsy a lollipop, saying, "You're such a good little girl." She looked up at Madison and continued, "You don't see many children so well-mannered these days. You must be very proud of your daughter."

"Granddaughter," Madison corrected with a smile, "and, yes, I'm very proud of her." She turned to Bitsy. "Save the lollipop for tomorrow, okay?"

They walked around the small lobby and peeked into the windows of a small gift shop near the front door. "Can we go inside, Grandma?"

"Sorry, honey. It's closed for the night and we'll be on the road early tomorrow morning. We'll go shopping in Florida. You'll probably need summer clothes there."

Bitsy skipped across the lobby to the elevators and stretched to reach the button. "Let me press number three, okay Grandma?" she said as the shiny doors opened. She had to have help reaching the button for the third floor but nevertheless she grinned proudly at her accomplishment.

Inside the room, Madison set the chain lock and the deadbolt. "One story and then bed, Bitsy. It's been a long day," she said

Bitsy stood close to Madison, something Madison noticed she did whenever they were in strange surroundings. "But you said we were going to talk."

"I did. I'd forgotten but you didn't, did you?"

Bitsy shook her head, setting the dark curls in motion. "No. I didn't forget."

Madison smiled and stooped to hug the little girl. "Get your pjs on and into bed and then we'll talk."

When Bitsy was tucked into bed, leaning back against two pillows, her legs pulled up Indian style, Madison sat next to her. "Okay. What were we going to talk about?"

"About how Mommy is going to find us in Florida."

The threat of this conversation hadn't left Madison's mind during the evening, but she had hoped that perhaps Bitsy might not remember. She sighed. *Bitsy remembers everything,* she thought and then reversed herself. *No, I wish she remembered more.*

CHAPTER NINETEEN

Somewhere, something incredible is waiting to be known.
Carl Sagan

Madison sat next to Bitsy and put one arm around her shoulders while her other hand reached for Bitsy's. "Sometimes we just don't have the answers to all our questions, honey. I think this is one of them. We know your mommy wanted you to wait for me and I came and got you. What we don't know is why she had to leave you right then. We also don't know where she went or how soon she'll come back."

Madison paused. She'd promised herself that she would not refer to Bitsy's mother negatively or in the past tense, even though in her mind she was convinced there was little hope of the mother ever again coming into Bitsy's life. She wasn't sure why this conviction was so strong, but after her visit to Mr. Mo's and the talk she'd had with him, the weight of the speculation seemed to focus on the fact that something terrible had happened to the child's mother.

She shivered. "So? What do we do when we don't have answers to questions? Do you know?"

Bitsy, her wide eyes glued to Madison's face, shook her head slowly from side to side. Her intensity was almost palpable.

"We trust in God, honey. Remember when we talked about always telling the truth? You said telling lies made God unhappy didn't you?"

Bitsy nodded.

"Well, one way to get answers from God is to pray for them. Have you ever prayed?"

Bitsy straightened up and some of her fear retreated. "Mommy said prayers sometimes. Sometimes she kneeled at the side of the bed and folded her hands," Bitsy demonstrated. "She closed her eyes and she whispered."

"Did you pray too?"

"No. I didn't know the words but she always made me sit very still, on the bed not on the floor, and be very quiet."

Madison closed her eyes and tried to envision the picture Bitsy's word drew. She saw a dismal room, a distraught mother and an innocent child but the details were shadowy. How could she truly picture such an event? As a child she'd been taken to Sunday school regularly. Her grandmother had taught her simple prayers to be said before falling asleep. At home she and her sister and parents had said grace before meals but only on special holidays. At her grandparents' home it was a ritual for every meal. She remembered not having any trouble switching traditions as she moved from place to place. As a teenager she'd thought these rituals tiresome at times but the messages had never left her. A small tug of regret pulled at her heart as she remembered almost abandoning prayer for the more sophisticated life. *What a fool*, she thought and tugged on Bitsy's hand. "Let's pray."

She slid off the bed and extended her arms to the confused child who willingly moved into the embrace. "Do you know the words?" Bitsy whispered.

Madison knelt next to the bed, Bitsy at her side. "You don't have to have special words, honey. Just words from your heart. Close your eyes." Madison's heart hammered in her chest and she wondered if the precious words would come to her. She watched Bitsy fold her hands and close her eyes. Years and years slipped back and she felt an amazing peace surround her. She pictured the room that she and Lolly shared when they stayed at their grandparents' farm. She smelled the clean scent of laundry soap and fresh air that always permeated the sheets on their bed.

"Heavenly Father," Madison began. "We love you and ask for your help…there are questions that we don't know the answers to. We need to know what you want us to do, to prepare us for what lies ahead. Please show us the way and help us to do the right thing. We ask for your guidance and forgiveness for the times we have failed…thank you for all the blessings you have already provided to us. Keep us safe and carefully covered by your love. In Jesus' precious name, we pray."

Madison paused, then continued, slowly repeating the Lord's prayer. "Our Father…" When she whispered 'amen' she heard Bitsy repeat the word. Tears flooded her eyes and she turned to pull the child into her arms. The rush of emotion that engulfed her shut out everything but the two bodies pressed close together. She felt Bitsy's fingers lace at the back of her neck, the soft curls brush against her cheek and a small shudder ran through her body.

When she rose, she lifted the little girl with her. Still holding Bitsy close to her, Madison whispered in her ear, "I'll teach you the Lord's Prayer. Then we can say it together, okay?"

"Okay," she whispered and let Madison place her back in bed, pushing one pillow to the side and folding the sheet and light blanket up under her chin. "I don't think I want a story tonight. Is that okay, Grandma?"

As Madison smiled and kissed the child's soft cheek, Bitsy turned her head and brushed her lips across Madison's chin. "Do you think God heard you?"

"I'm sure He did. But, you have to remember lots of people are praying for lots of things. Sometimes answers don't come right away. We can be patient, can't we?" Her fingers touched the soft curls over the child's forehead and Bitsy nodded.

"You're tired, sweetheart. So am I. Go to sleep and tomorrow we'll have another adventure. Just you and me, honey. Just you and me."

"I love you Grandma."

"I love you too Bitsy." She snapped off the light next to Bitsy's bed. "I love you very much."

Later that night Madison sat in the dim room, the only light coming from the bathroom where the door was left ajar. Sitting in one of the two chairs at a small table next to a heavily draped window, she listened to the soft rhythm of Bitsy's breathing. The small lump the child made in the huge bed seemed to her to be an indication of how small the little girl was and of how large her responsibility was.

"I'll take care of you...protect you...provide for you...and love you my little granddaughter. No matter what," she whispered. *That's another prayer,* she thought and climbed into her bed. But, as tired as she was, and as much as she knew tomorrow would be another long day, she didn't fall asleep quickly. It wasn't as though there were worries grinding at her. No, she felt a strange need to relive bits and pieces from the past two weeks and the memories scanned across the backs of her closed eyelids bringing to life the time she'd had Bitsy with her. The Christmas stocking...the first time she bathed the little girl...the joy she saw and heard when they shared the simplest of things... the sound of Bitsy's laughter...so many precious memories that built into... *What,* she thought, *what have they become?* She blinked rapidly in the dark, as if the fluttering of her eyelids would clear a path to the answer. But she knew the answer, or at least prayed for it. It was the beginning of a life together, she and Bitsy, whether she was truly her granddaughter or not. She was happy about her choices, at peace with herself and she drifted into a tranquil sleep.

~ ~ ~

"They left this morning as far as I know," Philip said, propping his feet on the coffee table, the one made out of half a barrel and a polished piece of maple from a tree on this very property. His great-grandfather had made it almost a century earlier. Philip's eyes wandered around the rustic room, part of the summer home his family had enjoyed for generations. Every corner held a memory. It was going to be tough to abandon the place but who was left to enjoy it? Not him.

"How warm is it there?" he asked, closing his eyes and picturing the scene from his condo balcony.

"Must be 70°, bright, sunny, you're a damn fool for staying there." David Logan twisted the cap off a bottle of beer and stretched his bronzed legs on the poolside lounge he occupied.

"I know, but I dread that damned 1300 mile trip and I swear I've made it for the last time. Once I get everything settled here the only time I'll head to frozen wasteland is on a shoot and that chance might be few and far between if I have any say so. I'll take the Congo anytime."

"Can't be all that cold up there."

"We still have half a foot of snow along the roadways and more in the forests."

"Well, when do you think your lady friend will arrive? I've cleared out all the things you told me to and a bunch more—knick knacks and things like that. Stored them in your studio, locked it up and kept the key."

"Thanks. I don't know when they'll get there."

"Well, it only takes two good days of driving. You've made it in less."

"I know, but she's traveling with a child. I imagine they will take longer."

"A child," Dave scoffed. "Are you sure you want a kid romping around in your place? Sticky fingers, dirt, destruction."

"Madison's granddaughter is well-behaved. I was with her a couple of times. She was very quiet. A nice little girl. I can't see any reason to be concerned." Philip smiled to himself as he remembered sitting at the table with Madison and her granddaughter.

"Your decision. Frankly, I wouldn't have a kid within one hundred yards of me at any time if I could manage that. Maybe you're falling for the dame." He paused. "Are you?"

"No. She seemed to need help and I could help. You're an old curmudgeon."

"I'm not old," Dave said, tipping the last of the beer into his throat. "You're missing some good stuff here, old man. That gal in 210 is across the pool from me and in an itsy-bitsy bikini. She's sunning her back now and the top is underneath her, no strings tied. Think I'll go over and startle her. Think she'll jump up?"

"You're not only a curmudgeon you're a dirty old man."

"Enough of the 'old man' stuff. How long do you think the terrible twosome will be in your place?"

"Madison's signing a three month lease. You have the paperwork so just take care of that for me and back off. Actually, I think she'll be looking for a place of her own right away. Something's going on there but I haven't a clue. Apparently this trip was unplanned, even the visit to Eldridge's cottage seemed strange. Must be family trouble, maybe something to do with the child's mother or something. Who knows? Anyhow, she's a nice woman, an author and her granddaughter looks like a good kid. They won't be there long. Don't you go stirring up things. By the time I come back she'll be off on her own."

"Let's hope so. We've been petitioning to have the condo association prohibit children for ten years now. We don't need another kid, even a temporary one. I thought we were getting somewhere when the Lansky's moved out with their three hellions. Only have two teenage girls now and outside of parading around half dressed, the don't cause any trouble."

"Well, be nice. I'm just offering a helping hand to someone who needs one, no commitment of any kind. I'll see you sometime in the spring. Call me if you need to or if you want to vent some of that sarcasm you're so famous for."

Philip chuckled to himself and hung up the telephone. He walked to the window and rocked back on his heels, his hands clenched behind him. The scene was like a Christmas card, pure white snow, most of it undisturbed except for where he'd taken his Ski-doo. The trees cast long shadows and the sunlight made the tops of the drifts in the open areas sparkle.

He closed his eyes and pictured Madison the day he'd gone over to check on the strange car in his neighbor's driveway. It wasn't often that anyone was there whatever the season. He remembered her face, pale and drawn, her arms crossed tightly across her chest. Her body language was fear and insecurity. He read defensiveness in her voice. She was attractive and as an artist, he took in her warm complexion, her soft brown eyes and hair the color of polished walnut. What had made her take refuge there? Why the day before Christmas…in the worst snowstorm of the season? And with a child? He'd tried to make sense of it but found nothing that made it any clearer.

Then when she'd called him with her strange request to rent his condo, his mind had churned through possibilities. It was pretty obvious she was running away, and taking the child with her. A kidnapper? *Don't be silly,* he'd warned himself. *The child called her Grandma.*

In the cabin in the woods, Philip shrugged his shoulders. *Why do I have this sense of…* he struggled for the right word*…responsibility for Madison…and the little girl?* He sighed and went into the kitchen where the ever-present pot of hot coffee awaited him. He poured the dark liquid into a large mug and returned to the living room. Again looking through the window, his thoughts continued to confound him. *Something is wrong there, something is wrong for both of them.* He shrugged and sipped his coffee. *Maybe I'll find out someday but for now all I can do is hope that she's safe. I'll call her in a few days, just to welcome her to Florida. Just to see if they need anything.* He could almost hear the comments Dave would make if he could read his mind.

~ ~ ~

Madison knocked on the door to unit 330 and waited. This was the unit where Philip's friend David lived and who Philip had instructed her to visit so that she could get the keys and the lease agreement. When the door opened, Madison and Bitsy both looked up into the face of a very tall, thin man who sported an untidy beard. Bare-chested and in wrinkled and slightly soiled khaki shorts, she noticed he was also barefoot. He glowered at them for a moment, then turned and took two keys on a small chain from a table just inside the door. He handed them to her. "You're Philip's friend. I'll be down in thirty minutes with the lease." He closed the door.

Slightly intimidated by the brusque greeting, Madison and Bitsy walked to the door with 310 in brass numbers. Once they entered, they both stood very still for several moments. The condo was luxurious—They'd walked into a large open living room, dining and kitchen area. Since the unit was a corner one, the windows faced both west and south and gave them not only a view of the pool area but a glimpse of the Gulf seen across the tops of a thicket of palm trees. The patio, which really was a balcony, held two matching lounge chairs, a table with an umbrella and two small chairs, all surrounded by a black wrought iron railing.

There were three bedrooms and two baths. The third bedroom, or that's what she assumed was behind the locked door, must have been where Philip did his photographic work. *A dark room possibly?* There were a few very obvious blank spaces on the walls in the spacious living room. *Probably some of his framed work,* she mused, *in the locked room.*

At first Madison thought she'd made a mistake…or Philip had made one. *How could he rent this place to a stranger…with a child,* she thought?

When David knocked on the door exactly thirty minutes later, she felt the hostility he didn't do much to hide. *He's not pleased we're here*, she thought as he presented her with the papers for the lease agreement. She did notice, however, that he had put a shirt and sandals on and changed his shorts to something more presentable. He briefly went over the terms, handed her a pen and then stood next to the dinette table. "If you have any questions, I'm just down the hall. My phone number is there," he pointed to a manila folder. There was no hint of an invitation in his words and he added, "The condo rules are in that folder, and," he added with some emphasis, "they are strictly enforced." He stared at Bitsy who was sitting on the couch, her hands folded on her lap, her eyes moving from one adult to the other. He took the lease, leaving a copy on the table, then offered his hand to Madison for a handshake and left.

That evening Madison and Bitsy were introduced to one of Florida's spectacular sunsets as they sat on the patio after a dinner of soup and jelly sandwiches. The evening breeze was cool and they both had pulled sweaters from their suitcase to take care of the slight chill.

The next morning, over a breakfast of cereal and milk Madison had purchased at a convenience store before finding the condo complex, she smiled at Bitsy. "Remember, we have to be very, very careful not to disturb anything. This all belongs to that nice man who helped us get away from the cottage and back home."

"I know," Bitsy said. "His name was Philip. Can we go out on the patio?" She pronounced the word 'patio' carefully because it was a new word she had learned and she loved to use new words.

"Not today, honey. I don't want you ever to go out there without me, okay? And, I know I promised you a trip to the beach today, but I have some work to do. We have to get some groceries, although I don't think we'll be here long. That's another thing we have to do…look for another place to live." Madison heard a quiver in her voice that identified her uneasiness.

"Why? Don't you like this one?" Bitsy asked, her eyes still rounded in wonder at this magnificent new home.

"I love it, honey. But we only have it for a short time and the sooner we make other arrangements, the better. Here. Take your new books and look at them while I clear up." She looked at the disappointment on Bitsy's face, smiled and then said, "Well, maybe we have time to go down to the beach and look around before I get started on all those other things.

"Why don't you sit next to the windows and look at your books? I have to call Aunt Jo and Aunt Lolly to let them know we arrived safely." *Or they'll be calling me in a panic*, she thought, taking her cell phone from the counter top.

The two calls were almost identical. "We're fine... No, I didn't have any trouble finding it; Philip's directions were perfect... It's a beautiful condo unit, much too fancy for our tastes but we'll be looking for another place soon...The weather is wonderful. It must be 70°, bright and sunny...No, we haven't been to the beach yet but we're going right after I hang up...You don't have to worry about us. I have everything in hand...Yes, I'll be working on the book soon...I know...She's fine. She was a wonderful passenger on the trip and she's such a big help; no trouble at all..." Madison paused and smiled at Bitsy who she knew was listening to every word. "I'll call again soon...please don't worry...You can call me anytime on my cell...I love you, too... Honestly, we're fine." *How many times have I said that*, she thought, carefully disconnecting the phone after the second call.

"Aunt Jo and Aunt Lolly send you love, Bitsy." The little girl looked at her expectantly but Madison remained on the couch, staring out the sliding glass doors to the patio. She saw the expectation. *She wants to go to the beach,* Madison thought. *She looks to me...for everything...Oh, Lord, what have I done?*

She stood and pulled the door open and walked out onto the patio. She stood next to the railing and gazed across the tops of the palm trees between the condo and the Gulf. A gentle breeze set the fronds in a mesmerizing motion that reminded her of a seductive dance. Everything looked so peaceful but an unexpected storm raged inside her. *Is it because I just spoke to Jo and Lolly? You have to be strong. You have to be in control.*

She bowed her head. *I've made myself responsible in an irresponsible situation. How am I going to continue this masquerade? I can't even think ahead a few days and I've committed myself to a lifetime...a lifetime made out of whole cloth. Is any of this fair? To either of us?*

She felt the presence of Bitsy next to her and looked down. The child gripped the iron bars and looked through them. A few women were in the pool bobbing to some taped exercises. They all wore hats that looked much too fashionable for the pool. *More fitting for a patio tea party*, Madison thought.

She struggled to bring her thoughts back to reality. Some of the things that Jo and Lolly had said echoed in her ears. "How are you going to get her into school? You'll need a birth certificate…What are you doing to find the child's mother?"

She sighed. "One step at a time," she murmured.

Bitsy looked up at her. "One step where, Grandma?"

Madison stooped down beside the little girl. She looked through the railing and realized that Bitsy had such a limited view. *Her view is limited to what you decide it will be.* She picked her up. "Look, Bitsy. From here we can see the Gulf of Mexico."

"What's a Gull of Mexico? Is it a bird?"

"No, honey," she said, laughing softly. "The Gulf of Mexico is that big blue area of water. It is like a huge lake only the bottom part," she pointed south, "is open and it becomes a bigger sea. Isn't it pretty? Later I'll get the map out and you can see where we are in Florida."

"Wow, and that's where we're going to the beach?"

Madison put the child back on the patio and, taking her hand in hers, led her to the lounge chairs. "Yes, honey," she said placing Bitsy in one and settling herself in the other. "But, we have to keep in mind that this isn't a vacation. It's where we're going to live...for a while at least. There are things we need to do...that I need to do...and you're going to have to help me. Will you help me?"

Bitsy nodded enthusiastically. As Madison looked at the child who had commandeered her heart in such a short time, she wondered if anyone was really looking for her. *Who?* she thought, *would look for her except her mother and wasn't she the one who had literally given her away? Oh, if I only knew?* She leaned back, closed her eyes and felt the warmth of the morning sun on her face. By this afternoon, facing west as it did, it might be hot with the evening sun on the patio. "If we have dinner out here we'll have to put the umbrella up," she said, thinking out loud. She stood and once more looked across to the water.

The scene was serene, like a postcard you'd send to friends in the chilled north. The sky was an unreal blue and the clouds were so light they looked like skimpy feathers being blown by a light breeze. The sun licked the tops of small waves leaving streaks of gold that disappeared as the next wave gobbled them up.

"My grandmother always said looking at water, whether it was a stream, a river or a lake, washed away your troubles," she said taking Bitsy's hand and opening the doors to the living room. "Oh, if that were only so."

Inside she paused for a moment. "First things first, honey. Get your sandals on; we're going to look at that beach. Then we have to get you some shorts and summer clothes. We need a few groceries, too. Maybe there's a Wal-Mart near here. We'll look later today," she said, mentally recounting all the things she'd already scheduled for the coming hours.

While she was locking the front door she glanced down the passageway toward Unit 330 but there was no sign of anyone. The whole complex was very quiet and she wondered if most of the occupants worked during the day. *Probably a mixture of working folks and retirees. We'll probably find out soon.* She recalled that David had not offered much information about the area.

She held Bitsy's hand as they took the open stairs down to the pool area and the parking lot. As they walked past the fence between the parking lot and the pool area she heard the soothing voice of the taped instructor. "Kicking forward, then to the side, right and then left. Shoulders up, ears up, nice rhythmic breathing."

"What are they doing, Grandma?" Bitsy asked, trying to see through the thick hedge of Oleanders.

"They are exercising in the pool. Sounds like fun, doesn't it. Maybe, if we have time this evening, we'll go down to the pool but we can't do everything the first day, can we?" Madison said with a sigh.

"Nope," Bitsy said, skipping toward their car. "Mommy says everything takes time."

CHAPTER TWENTY

God answers sharp and sudden on some prayers, and thrusts the thing we have prayed for in our face, a gauntlet with a gift in it.
Elizabeth Barrett Browning

The nagging uncertainty, the physical insecurity that plagued Madison in the morning stayed with her all day. As she watched Bitsy scampering excitedly along the water's edge, jeans rolled to her knees and bare feet eluding the gentle waves that rolled up onto the sand, Madison wondered if this was truly where they should be. A paradise filled with tribulation?

Later as they strolled from store to store in a Mall they had discovered several miles inland, she wondered if they really needed these new, more tropically-appropriate clothing; shorts, sleeveless tops and two bathing suits each with coordinated cover ups? She purchased a newspaper and searched the want ads for real estate while they ate lunch at the food court, but nothing seemed suitable. How long were they going to be here? Oh, if there were answers where were they?

As they were leaving the Mall, Bitsy suddenly stopped short in front of Madison. "Oh, look," she gasped, "a kitten."

Madison looked where Bitsy was pointing. The store window was filled with stuffed animals—an elephant, a dolphin, arched as if gliding through a deep blue sea somewhere. There were puppies, kittens, monkeys, small and large and Bitsy now had her nose pressed against the glass gazing longingly at the tiny gray kitten posed on a pink pillow.

"Oh, she's so pretty," she murmured.

Madison remembered hearing Bitsy's wish for a kitten, a real live kitten that her mother has told her wasn't practical under their circumstances. Not a lover of cats herself, she would have joyfully agreed with the missing mother but seeing the longing in Bitsy's face urged her to pull the door open. "Come on, Bitsy. Let's look inside."

She shifted their plastic bags to one arm and took the child's hand. Bitsy was tiptoeing along the aisle, looking from side to side, each display a wonderment of reality made of fake fur and button eyes.

"Would you like a kitten?" Madison asked, tripping over Bitsy as she stopped in front of her feet.

"Oh, could I?"

Madison grinned. "Of course. Pick one out."

"I want the one in the window," she said with determination.

"Well," Madison said, looking around for help and seeing a very tall young man behind a small counter, arranging a miniature African scene with tiny zebras and giraffes.

Looking up he asked, "May I help you?"

"Would it be possible to purchase the small gray kitten that's in the window?"

"Of course, let me see if we have one on the shelf first. If so, it would be in a box."

"Does the pink pillow come with it?" Bitsy asked, surprising Madison with her boldness.

The young man smiled down on the child. "No, I'm sorry. The pillow is just window-dressing."

He left them at the counter and disappeared into a back room separated from the store by string after string of bright beads.

"What a funny door," Bitsy said.

"I guess it's supposed to look African or Indian."

When the young man returned empty-handed Madison's heart sunk for a moment but then she saw his wide grin.

"Nope, we'll have to get you the one from the window."

When he returned to the counter he held the gray striped kitten and the pink pillow. "Seems like we can sell you the pillow for an extra three dollars," he said, putting them on the countertop. "I asked the Manager while I was in the back."

"Thank you. Thank him for us," Madison said, extracting some bills from her wallet.

"Please don't put her in a bag," Bitsy said, just as the young man was tucking the pillow into another plastic bag. "Can I hold her?"

The young man laughed. "Sure you can. I think Tabby would much rather be carried that poked into a bag." He rang the sale up, handed Madison the receipt and the bag containing the pink pillow and bending over the counter to speak to Bitsy, said, "I'm happy that Tabby found a good home. Take good care of her."

When they left the store, Madison was carrying several bags and Bitsy was hugging the little cat to her breast. "Oh, thank you, Grandma. Now I really have a kitty."

Madison sighed and walked toward some benches in the middle of the walkway. "Bitsy, let's sit down for a few minutes, okay?"

For several minutes she watched the shoppers, families with several children, many of them stopping at the window filled with the replica animals. As she watched them and then turned to look at Bitsy, caressing her make-believe pet she realized that she had overlooked something very important. Bitsy was four-years old and yet all she had played with since she came into Madison's life was books and crayons. "Bitsy," she said softly, "if you could have anything you wanted what would it be?"

"A baby doll or a teddy bear," she answered quickly. "I asked Santa for a baby doll or a teddy bear and he said I might get them if I was very good." She paused, staring across the walkway at the store she'd just left. "But, I didn't get them," she said her face turning from glum to glee. “But now I’ve got a kitty and that’s the best anyhow.”

Madison stood and reached for Bitsy’s hand. “Come on, honey. We haven’t finished shopping yet. But before we go on I’m going to see if I can get a big bag to put all these bothersome little ones in.”

They re-entered the store and again the young man looked up. “Can I help you?” he said, hurrying around the counter.

“Do you have a large bag I can put all these others in? We have more shopping to do and they are so cumbersome like this.”

“I can do even better. I’ll put them in a big bag and then hold them in the back for you. You can pick them up on your way out.”

“Oh, that would be wonderful. Thank you so much.”

With springier steps, Madison and Bitsy retraced their way into the heart of the mall. For a few moments Madison checked the board listing the stores in the two-tiered mall. She found what she was looking for and urged Bitsy over to the escalator going up to the second floor. When she found the store she was looking for she glanced down at Bitsy’s face. The child stood, open-mouthed in front of Singer’s Toy World. Still clutching her kitten, Bitsy looked up into Madison’s face, her face reflecting puzzlement tried to cover the anticipation she attempted to suppress. “Are we going in there?” she whispered.

“We are. And, we are going to find you a baby doll and a teddy bear.”

Madison was surprised at the feelings that rushed through her. She hadn’t been in a toy store for years and recalled the fun she’d had choosing dolls and trucks for her niece and nephew when they were children. Some of the joy of Christmas shopping had disappeared as they grew older and now she just sent a generous check each year asking that she get a report of what they spent the money on. Now it was DVDs and electronic gadgets she didn’t even recognize.

They walked along an entire store-length row, shelf after shelf of dolls. There were elegant Victorian beauties on the higher shelves and so many Barbies, Madison had to smile remembering the first one she'd purchased for Caitlin. There were display boxes containing tiny newborns together with all the accoutrements that a real baby would need. At the end of the aisle, there were bins of soft dolls, looking like old-fashioned hand-made dolls. Still Bitsy hadn't stopped in front of any doll offered.

"See anything you like, honey?"

"Oh, Grandma. There are so many and they must be so 'spensive."

Madison stooped down, her arm encircling Bitsy's shoulders. "You just pick out one you'd love to have, okay. Let me worry about the cost. After all, you were in a strange place this Christmas. Santa didn't really know how to find you. But he did. Now he's giving me a chance to help him out, just this once," she added.

Bitsy studied her grandmother's face for a moment and then scooted around her and ran to the center of the aisle they'd just viewed. "This one," she exclaimed, pointing to a box on a shelf that was at Bitsy's eye level. The box held a baby doll complete with outfit, diaper, baby bottle, receiving blanket and rattle. Madison smiled as she read the box. 'Life-like skin, eyes that open and close. Feed Melissa water only,' the box warned. Tucking the box under one arm, she reached for Bitsy's hand. "Now for a teddy bear."

They found bins and bins of all kinds of stuffed toys but Bitsy's hand fell on a small teddy bear with a red satin bow under his chin. "This one," she said.

Watching Bitsy wait for the clerk to ring the sales up and put the toys into a large bag, Madison felt a wave of intense emotion surge over her. *How thoughtless and foolish I've been,* she thought. *Imagine a little girl not having a doll and a teddy. I've watched her with books and crayons and it never dawned on me she needed more?*

Memories of her childhood toys flooded her mind, Lorelei, her last doll, dressed in a plaid satin dress and shiny patent leather shoes. The almost hairless teddy bear she'd given childhood haircuts to until he was almost bare. The stuffed lamb she received for Easter one year, the one that was left out in the rain one summer and disappeared because it became mildewed and her grandmother spirited it away.

As they left the mall her mind again reverted to the worries that had been her companion all day, all day except for the past hour when she'd realized that the only true blessing in her life right now was Bitsy. Her heart fluttered as she buckled the child into her seat. She kissed Bitsy's cheek and ran a hand over the kitten's furry head. "What are you going to name your kitten, honey?"

"She going to be Rosie because she has a little pink tongue, see?" she said, pushing the cat's face up so that Madison could see. "There was a girl in school who was called Rosie. She didn't have a pink tongue but she did have pink cheeks." Bitsy giggled, her fingers covering her mouth.

"Rosie is a lovely name."

Bitsy shook her head. "Yes, much better than Tabby like the man called her."

"Well, he didn't know she was so special and needed a very special name."

Madison went around the car and slid behind the wheel. For a moment she watched the little girl in the back seat, head down, murmuring something to the new pet she had acquired.

Later, in the grocery store Madison's uncertainty returned and she picked and chose food as if she were shopping for a brief stay because… well, that was another unknown, wasn't it?

That night, before tucking a tired and happy little girl into bed, she was advised that the new baby would be sleeping in the bed with Bitsy and the kitten would be appropriately arranged on the pink pillow next to the bed. "I love you, Grandma," Bitsy said, sleepily, one arm around her new baby. She hadn't decided on a name for the new acquisition yet. "I'll think of a good name for my new baby doll soon," she said, stifling a yawn.

"Good night, sweetheart," Madison whispered, backing away from the bed. In the hallway she walked slowly, as if reluctant to leave the room with the already sleeping child and her new possessions. "God help me, I love her so much," she said softly and went into the kitchen. Standing at the sink and staring into the darkness outside she bowed her head. Her quiet prayer was easy to compose. "Lord, help me as I take care of this precious gift. If it is your will that we make a life together, show me the way."

She poured the last of the coffee into a mug, zapped it in the microwave and grabbed a light blanket from the foot of *her* bed, but it wasn't really *her* bed, just one she was using right now.

She took her coffee and blanket out onto the patio and stretched out on one of the lounge chairs.

The sky was a dark velvet canopy dotted with tiny bright asterisks. The soft breeze coming off the water ruffled the palms and even unseen, she knew their feathery fronds were swaying; she could barely hear the soft rattling sound they made, like the rustling of a long silk gown. It was a delicious tropical evening. She was safe, at least for now, so why was she lying there as if she were on an operating table. Pulling herself upright, she wrapped her arms around her knees and stared off into the darkness.

"This is stupid. You're where you planned to be. You've made your decisions. Coming down you were all happy and upbeat about the trip. Now what's your problem?" But she knew what her problem was…her many problems…and that was her problem…the inability to focus on one thing at a time. The uncertainty of their future, because it wasn't just her she was planning for. It was Bitsy, too. She remembered her last look at the child, already drifting off to sleep, her profile etched against the pillow, curls spread like a dark stain against the white case, and her heart swelled in her chest. Wasn't this child the blessing she'd waited for all these years? This had to be right. She felt her eyes fill with tears but didn't wipe them away. She looked at the sky with blurred vision then said a silent prayer, a petition for help, a plea for answers.

She was reaching for her mug when she heard her cell phone ring; she'd left it on the coffee table. Bolting from the chair she ran to answer it.

"Hello," she gasped, returning to the patio and closing the door quietly behind her although she knew her fears of waking Bitsy were unfounded. The child was exhausted.

"You sound out-of-breath. Where were you?"

Madison slipped into one of the chairs next to the table. The umbrella was furled in a tight column above her head. "On the patio. Oh, Jo," she murmured and felt the stemmed tears slip down her cheeks.

"You okay?"

"Yes, it's just been a tiring day. I tried to put too much into one day, I guess. What's up?"

"You sure you're okay? You sound terrible."

"Well, thanks. You sound crummy too."

"I do not and you know it."

"Well…"

"Listen. Where's the kid?"

"In bed, why? We had a very busy day and I think the sun and fresh air wore her out early. She's usually still begging to stay up a bit longer at this time of night." Madison felt her spine stiffen and her courage surge, and she knew she was speaking too fast. *Jo. It's just hearing Jo's voice that's what it is,* she thought, relaxing her grip on the phone at her ear.

"Okay. Listen, I've been doing some real heavy-duty thinking about your situation."

"Situation? Come on, Jo. I've got things pretty much in hand." She grimaced in the dark at the lie, remembering the anxiety she'd been struggling with just minutes earlier.

"I know you think you do but just listen to me, okay; without interruption for a few minutes. Promise?"

"Promise."

"You know when you broke up with that rich pig I was so happy. I thought now's the time for you to relax, have some fun, do what Madison wants for Madison's sake and then…then you jumped into the grandmother business without any thought or direction. Wait, I know you're straining at the bit to defend yourself, but you promised.

"You think of Bitsy as the child you always wanted, the one you thought you'd never have. That's not all bad. But, the way she came to you is definitely strange, unorthodox to say the least. I've done nothing but concentrate on how to make things easier for you ever since you left. I've heard the tension in your voice mounting. You can't fool me, you know."

"I know, but…"

"Whoa. Give me a chance. As I said, I've been thinking and I've come up with a solution…" she paused. "Maybe that's not the right word but at least some suggestions that might make what you're trying to do easier. Not that I totally approve of what you are trying to do, but you know me. I'll always be in your corner, no matter how weird a corner it is."

"I know," Madison whispered, her words drifting away on the night breezes.

"Where are you right now?"

"I told you, on the patio. It's a beautiful night. Peaceful, tropical…almost romantic." She heard the hitch in her voice.

"Well, let's get practical before we get romantic, okay? I think the very basis of your problems is that you don't know anything about Bitsy's mother. You need to know why she did what she did. Why she left her child at that diner with that cock-and-bull story about a grandmother coming to get her. And," she paused again, "I've come up with an idea."

Jo paused and Madison listened intently to the silence.

"I'm going to do an in-depth investigation."

"What?" Madison gasped.

"Wait. You know my investigative methods, how I research everything for my columns and articles. I'm good at it."

"You are, but how are you going to do anything like that about Bitsy's mother? And is that the first answer I need?"

"I think it is. And, you have more information, probably than you realize because you're too close to the problem. You can't stand back because you're involved in the day to day survival and you have been ever since you picked up that little package of charm."

"Bitsy's…"

"Oh, don't go getting all defensive on me. You know I love the little brat, almost as much as I love you. This is aimed at making it easier for both of you."

Madison stood and walked to the railing. The lights around the pool punched an oval of brightness in a very dark night. "I know you mean well, Jo. But…what can you do?"

"Well, first of all give me every singe bit of information you've learned from Bitsy about her mother, her life…absolutely everything you know; starting with Bitsy's birth. Where was she born? When? I'm going to try and find her birth record. Then we'd have the mother's name. I know you said her mother was called 'flowers' and if that isn't ridiculous, what is? We might even find a father's name. Who knows?"

Madison leaned her back against the railing, looking into the dimly lit elegant living room. Her laptop was on the coffee table. Earlier she'd promised herself she'd get back to her book but that promise died quickly. She was too tired. Her mind was too scattered. She changed the phone to her right ear. "Bitsy said she was born in Philadelphia on St. Patrick's Day. She's going to be five this coming March."

"Great," Jo said, scribbling the information on a sheet of paper. "I can check that easily. Then when we know the mother's name we can begin a search. Check death records, accident records, and things like that. Maybe even find out where the mother came from. There might be other family somewhere."

"Wait, Jo. Digging into her mother's life might be very dangerous. You know what I told you I learned, or at least it was hinted at, when I spoke to that Mr. Mo. I have a strong feeling that Bitsy's mother is dead." She paused after putting that up-to-now unspoken thought into words. "There might have been…foul play." She felt almost foolish using those words, they sounded so theatrical. "It might be too dangerous for you to get involved any further. Why don't you…?"

"Don't worry. I have help. Do you remember me speaking of Walter Kalik? He's a freelancer. Writes articles about follow-ups to crimes and criminals for the paper. He was a Philadelphia cop for twenty-some years, a homicide detective before he retired. Before that he studied law but ran out of money and dropped out of college. A real nice guy. I know him well and would trust him with my life."

"I don't remember you speaking of him."

"Well, I've already asked him if he could help me find out what happened."

"Jo," Madison squawked. "This is supposed to be quiet. I asked you not to tell anyone…"

"Hold on, I haven't mentioned specifics yet. Just gave him a hypothetical situation. Don't worry, if anyone can help and keep it quiet, he can." She paused. "Well, what do you think?"

"I think you're some super kind of friend, Jo." Tears poured down her cheeks. "I've been so…so distracted trying to think about what has to be done first and if I've done the right things so far…"

"I know you have. I've heard it in your voice even when you were trying to convince me that you're happy and carefree. Poop! I know you kid."

The two friends spoke for another ten minutes, exchanging information and ideas. When Jo hung up, her last words were, "Help is on the way, kid. Say a prayer and don't give up. Try and relax. Pretend you're on vacation with that little bundle of joy. You need a break way more than you realize. Love ya'."

Madison lay back on the lounge chair and pulled the blanket up to her chin. Was it her imagination or did the sky look even more intriguing? Darker yet brighter? She closed her eyes. A vacation? Hardly, but somehow she felt as if a huge bolder had been lifted from her shoulders. She closed her eyes and drifted to sleep in a very short time, waking hours later and creeping to bed after glancing in at Bitsy. Was this scheme of Jo's going to work? She'd counted on Jo in the past for helping her through tough emotional times but this was different, not hurt feelings, not disappointments in her life with Jim. *Maybe it's because it's not just me she's helping now. It's Bitsy too,*" she thought as she punched a comfortable dent in the pillow, then folded her hands and prayed silently.

CHAPTER TWENTY-ONE

The truth must dazzle gradually or ever more be blind.

Emily Dickinson

Madison watched Bitsy playing at the water's edge. It was a beautiful morning again and she wondered if people living in Florida ever got complacent about the pleasant weather. Was it only three weeks ago that they were stranded in the Pennsylvania mountains? Was it only a week since they had made their first visit to the beach? Already Bitsy was becoming a soft shade of brown.

They had begun to go to the pool in the late afternoon, too, when it wasn't so crowded. Madison and Bitsy had made a quasi-friend of another resident—Mrs. Quinlan, a grandmother who knitted beneath an umbrella every afternoon. She was making lap robes for elderly patients at a local nursing home. "They always seem to be cold, no matter what the temperature. Of course, they keep the place like an icebox.

"It's the least I can do and I feel it's kind of a payback for my good health. You should visit sometime, my dear. They love to see children, too. Your little granddaughter would be most welcome." She checked her stitches and then continued, "You are very fortunate having your granddaughter with you. All my children and grandchildren are scattered about the country. One son in North Caroline, another in Michigan and Sally, my only daughter, in California." She sighed audibly, putting sound to her discontent.

She was a pleasant lady and easy to talk to. One thing that Madison admired about her was that she didn't ask questions. Her only comment when they met was, "Oh, my, you are a young grandma."

Now, Madison squinted in the bright sunshine. "Come here, honey," she called, reaching for the suntan lotion. "Can't have you getting burned. You've already been here long enough."

"I'm getting tanned," the little girl in the purple bikini said, admiring her shiny arms and legs as they were covered with another coat of suntan spray.

"Fifteen minutes more and then we have to leave. We'll have a nice lunch and then I'm going work all afternoon."

"At your computer?"

"Yes, Uncle Alan is getting nervous and wants three chapters by next week. We'll go to the grocery store and get a few things before we go home, okay?"

"Okay," she called over her shoulder, already heading back to jump in the small wavelets that quickly erased her footprints.

Later, driving along the street to the nearest shopping center. Madison asked, "Are your feet sandy?"

"A little," Bitsy said.

"Well, brush them off. No, wait. I'll brush them off when we get out of the car." She entered the parking lot and cruised along the rows of spaces until she found one. "Boy, they are crowded today—they must be giving the stuff away."

"No they're not, Grandma. You're being funny." Madison saw Bitsy cover her giggle with her fingers.

"We just need a few things. I think I'll make chicken tonight. Sound good?" Madison smiled. She was adapting quickly to these mundane domestic chores. Dinner at six o'clock or thereabouts, regular breakfasts and lunches. A far cry from the haphazard mealtimes she'd enjoyed for years when she was on her own. And yet, it was so normal, so natural, and so comfortable.

"Mmmm. You make good chicken. Can I have a wing?"

"There's no meat on a wing. How about a leg?"

"Okay. We don't need cookies; we still have those little teddy bears. I like them."

After their brief shopping trip, Madison headed back to the condo but as she approached the light at the corner, she turned left instead of right.

"Where are we going?" Bitsy called from her backseat perch.

"I thought I'd take another way home and we could get familiar with other places nearby." At the back of her mind was keeping an eye out for a place of their own even though with the urging of both Lolly and Jo, she didn't feel as pushed as she had before Jo's call. After all, she had another two months at Philip's place. Still, when she thought of the next move her pulse raced a bit.

As she drove along the unfamiliar road she found that it wound it's way away from the coast, the landscape becoming more open and jungle-like in areas. Houses, all nicely landscaped were scattered on both sides of the road but they were further apart, leaving areas of untamed countryside. Madison began to think she'd made a mistake coming this way as there seemed to be few crossroads and when she came to them it looked as if they went nowhere but into more wilderness.

She slowed when she came to a larger building, built low to the ground. There was one main building facing the road with a wing at each end. A sign in the front read, "Collier Country-Day Academy; ages 4 to 15; hours 8:00 to 3:00 daily; registration open."

"Why are we stopping?" Bitsy asked.

"We're not stopping. I'm going to turn around. This road seems to go nowhere." She pulled into the parking lot of the school, again reading the sign on the front lawn. It was a neat building and there were several cars in the side parking lot. The landscaping was attractive and when she turned the car around she could see playground equipment and what looked like a large fenced field behind the school.

"Are we going in here?"

"No, honey. I was just looking. Maybe…"

"Maybe what?"

"Maybe we'd better get home and get those groceries in the house. We'll take a ride another day," Madison said, pulling back onto the road and retracing their route to the familiar intersection.

She's bright, Madison mused as they entered the elevator. *She could get a head start on school even if I can't afford to have her there for a long time. Hmm, maybe my little exploration trip wasn't so dumb after all. I'll have to think about this.*

" I can read some of my new book by myself now," Bitsy boasted as she clutched a small plastic bag of lighter groceries. "I can read to my baby doll, too." She hesitated. "Do you think I could call my baby Jo after Aunt Jo?"

"Well," Madison paused before pushing the button for the third floor. *Not that Jo wouldn't be flattered,* she thought, but *it just doesn't sound like a name for a newborn baby.* "How about Joanie? That's a nice name and it's very like Aunt Jo's name. Then you wouldn't get your baby mixed up with Aunt Jo."

Bitsy laughed. "You're being silly again, Grandma. I won't get my baby doll mixed up with Aunt Jo. But," she said, a slight frown pushing her eyebrows together, "but maybe Joanie would be better." She hummed softly to herself, watching the numbers on the panel next to the door. "Won't Mommy be surprised when she sees my new baby doll and teddy and my kitty? And," she boasted, "that I can read some of the words in my books now."

When the elevator doors opened they came face to face with David, again unshaven and disheveled, his left hand gripping a can of beer partially concealed with a foam holder. Since he remained standing in the center of the doorway, Madison shifted slightly to the right and said, "Excuse us."

He remained solidly in place. She repeated, "Excuse us," this time adding a little emphasis on the word 'excuse'. He remained immobile and continued to stare at her, eye to eye, then blinked artificially and grinned an undisguised leer.

Although his eyes moved to the grocery bags she held, he said, "Been out looking for new digs, have you?"

"We've been shopping. Would you please move out of the way! What is your problem?"

"Me, Madam? I don't have a problem. It's you who has the problem."

"I have no problem but you at the moment," she sniped.

He leaned against the open elevator door. "Oh, but you do. I recognized it as soon as I saw you. In fact, I knew it as soon as I knew of your coming."

"Really," she said and moved to the right attempting to move past him, but he straightened up and extended his elbow, further blocking the narrow doorway. "Get out of my way," she demanded."

"Gladly," he said, moving aside so slightly that if she did attempt to pass him she would have had to brush by his body.

"What business is it of your if I've started looking for our own place," she demanded, shifting one of the grocery bags and freeing up her right hand, which she extended to Bitsy who was cowering behind her.

"I know your kind," he said, jutting his face toward her so that she caught the sweet-sour scent of beer on his breath.

"And what kind is that?"

"Oh, you're a user. A user of men, friends, whatever you can for your own good."

Stunned, Madison began to feel threatened. At first she thought he was just trying to be annoying, which he had succeeded in, but now she felt fearful. "Get out of my way or I'll scream for help." She felt Bitsy's fingers dig into her palm.

"You're a user, Madam, that's what you are. Oh, Philip you are such a fool." He swayed slightly, his eyes boring into hers.

"I'm not a user, *Sir*," she said mimicking his formality, "but *you* are a drunk. Now get out of our way or you'll be sorry."

"Sorry? I don't think so," he said, weaving in front of her. "I'll admit I'm a drunk. But, Madam," he said eloquently, "I can sober up, you, on the other hand, will always be a user."

Madison stepped forward, elbowing him with her left arm, her heavy bag of groceries swinging into his groin and, dragging Bitsy with her, squeezed past him. "If you don't leave us alone, I'll have to take steps," she called over her shoulder as they hurried to the door of Unit 310.

Inside she double locked the front door, put the plastic bags on the kitchen counter and leaned with her back against the sink, exhaling a huge sigh. She gripped her hands together to stop them from trembling.

Bitsy stood in the kitchen still holding the plastic bag assigned to her, her eyes wide, her face ashen. "He's a mean man," she whispered.

Taking the bag from her, Madison stooped and hugged the terrified child's shoulders. "He's a jerk. Don't you worry, sweetheart. I'll take care of him." But her bravado was on the surface only. Inside her stomach was churning. *What was his problem? Why did he hate me and Bitsy? And what was that intimation that I should be looking for another place to live? Has Philip called him with a change of mind about us occupying his condo?* Her hands still shook as she put the food into the refrigerator and cupboards. She put several cookies on a small plate and poured a glass of milk.

"Here, honey. Have this snack while I make a couple of telephone calls. I'll make lunch in a few minutes."

Bitsy climbed up onto the kitchen chair. "He's not a nice man, Grandma. Why is he so mean?"

"Don't you worry about him. I'll be back in a minute."

Hurrying into her bedroom, she pulled her cell phone from her purse. *Thank goodness I put Philip's number into my phone,* she thought. "Oh, be there," she prayed silently.

When Philip answered the telephone, Madison hesitated. Was this what she really wanted to do? Was it wise to be tattling on a stupid man to someone who had helped her?

"Hello?" Philip repeated.

"Philip," Madison stuttered. "I shouldn't have called you."

"You mean you misdialed? Oh, that's okay I do that sometimes. Especially if the number is in the memory and I think I know it or just hit the wrong number. How are you?"

"Oh, Philip, we're fine and I didn't misdial," she hesitated, "I have to confess I dialed your number but had second thoughts after I had done it."

"Why?"

"Oh, just a slight little problem…"

"With the condo?"

"No. No, not with the condo…" again she hesitated. "It's just…well, I had a slight run-in with your friend David a little while ago and now I'm ashamed that I called you. But he did say something that made me wonder…"

"Wait. David did something…"

"He'd been drinking. He had a can of beer in his hand. It's nothing, Philip. I'm ashamed of my reaction and shouldn't have bothered you."

"Damn him. I should have warned you. I thought he'd…well, he does have a drinking problem and he can be…surly sometimes. I'll talk to him. Are you all right?"

"Yes, we're fine. It was something that he said that made me want to check with you."

"What?"

"Well, now I feel even more foolish." She took in a deep breath. "He sounded like he thought we should be out looking for another place to live and I thought maybe...maybe you were having second thoughts about us being here."

"No, not at all. I was going to call you today or tomorrow. Things are wrapping up here quicker than the attorney thought..."

"Then you're coming back soon?"

"No. That's the second half of the story. I just got a telephone call not two hours ago and I was offered an assignment in South America. It's for a nature magazine and I'll be somewhere along the Amazon. It sounds interesting so I'll be leaving the States sometime in late January or early February. The job should take about a month so you have nothing to worry about."

"You're sure you won't want this place sooner?"

"Hell, no. It would have been empty for at least another two months if you weren't there. You take your time in finding another place and I'll keep in touch. I'll also call Dave and straighten him out."

"You don't have to do that. What worried me most was that I thought perhaps you had changed your mind...or regretted having us here."

"Never. Listen, I'll speak with him. Dave's a strange duck. He doesn't like women. And, unfortunately he is anti-child. He's been worrying the Condo Board for years to get them to change the complex to adults only."

"I got the feeling from the very first minute I met him that he didn't approve of me or Bitsy," Madison said, feeling her anxiety calm. "We'll try to stay clear of him. I don't want you to get involved. I can handle this. It was just his obviously being inebriated and his blocking the elevator doorway so we couldn't get out..."

"He did that? The idiot. No, you can be sure I'll talk to him. I'm so sorry you had to experience his dark side. He can be fun when he's sober. We've been friends for years but he can get nasty. When it's just the two of us he usually minds his manners because he knows I shut him up if he gets too annoying. Damn him. I'm sorry. Maybe I should have warned you but I thought he was on the wagon. At least he sounded like it whenever I spoke to him on the telephone since I've been up here."

Madison heard his soft chuckle. "Let's forget it. Thanks, Philip. I still feel foolish for calling you. And, I'll get started finding us another place as soon as I can. We..."

"You don't have to rush into anything, okay? I'll keep in touch until I leave for South America."

"Thanks. You've been so kind. I don't know how we'll ever really thank you but we'll try."

No one spoke for several moments and then Madison said, "Well, thanks for everything, Philip..." and Philip interrupted..."Wait. I might need some things from my studio. I might pop in before I leave the country. I'm trying to think what I'll need on the shoot. What cameras and things like that I'll want to take along. Let me make my travel arrangements and then I'll let you know when I'll be coming by. I won't be staying long so don't plan to disappear. I'm looking forward to seeing you...both. How's your granddaughter?"

"We're fine and getting used to this wonderful weather."

"That's something I miss." He chuckled and she could picture his bronzed cheeks, his eyes ringed with laugh lines.

Madison laughed. "If you want us to disappear while you're here we can. It's your condo."

"Not necessary at all and...it's yours while you're there," he said softly. "I'll bunk in with Dave for a night before I leave."

Madison felt her cheeks flush.

After a slight pause, he said, "I'll call you when I know my plans, and in the meantime just try and ignore that stupid friend of mine. I'll straighten him out."

When Madison snapped the phone shut she stared at her image in the mirror. She was sitting on the side of the bed and hadn't realized how tense she was until she allowed her shoulders to settle back in place.

She smiled at her reflection. *So, Philip is coming back, briefly, but back here before he goes away again.*

Rising, her cell phone still in her hand, she was about to leave the bedroom when the phone rang. Flipping it open she thought, *Philip? Did he forget something?*

"Hello?"

"Hi."

Madison recognized Jo's voice and backed toward the bed again, settling down on the foot. "Hi, I was just about to make lunch for us. What's up?"

"Hold on to your hat. I've got news…and some answers."

Madison drew in a short anxious breath, "Already?"

"Uh huh. Told you Walt was good. He's found Bitsy's birth records and knows her mother's name."

"What?" Madison gasped.

"Yep. Little Miss Bitsy was right. She was born on March 17, 2001 so she'll be five in March. She was born in Hahnemann University Hospital to Lily Rose Smith; father listed as unknown. Actually that's about all the information he got but he says he can scan records for Lily Rose Smith now and see what comes up. It's not much but it's a start and you can get a copy of the birth certificate."

"Oh, my gosh. I'm overwhelmed. I didn't think you'd find anything, at least not this quickly. How do I go about getting a birth certificate, I wonder."

"I'll check it out and let you know."

"Thanks, Jo. Gosh, I'm…overwhelmed," she repeated. "Maybe today is a turning point. I just spoke to Philip and he's coming back to Florida a the end of this month and when I heard that I was panicking about where we would go and then he said he wasn't staying he was just coming by to pick up some stuff he needs for a job in South America which will last at least a month. Then this morning I was driving along a road I've never been on and saw a school that might be perfect for Bitsy and…" She paused. "I'm running on and on, aren't I?"

Jo laughed. "Yes, but it's okay. You sound happier than I've heard in a long, long time. You're right…maybe things are going to take a turn for the better."

"With your help and a few answered prayers, it looks like that, doesn't it? I'm almost afraid to believe it," Madison said, running her fingers through her hair. "Thanks, Jo. Thanks for everything."

"What? I didn't do anything. Just contacted Walt. Told you he's good."

Madison paused a moment. "I'm going to pay him, of course."

"Don't worry about that now. I think he's enjoying it. He was practically rubbing his hands together when I saw him. He's probably already scaring up sites on the Internet. He said he still has friendly police contacts that he can trust…call up favors…so don't worry. I'll keep you posted."

After Madison ended the call she stood in the hallway a few moments before going into the kitchen to begin their lunch. *I don't think I'll say anything to Bitsy yet. Just in case nothing really changes,* she thought. *But, two good pieces of news in one day must mean something...something good.*

That afternoon her fingers flew across the keyboard on her laptop for the first time in almost a month. When she looked at her watch and saw it was almost five o'clock, she'd completed the chapter she was working on in book number thirteen in the Detective Bloodworth Mystery series. Flexing her fingers she watched Bitsy out on the patio. The little girl had wrapped her doll in the receiving blanket and was talking to the kitten on her pink pillow. After careful consideration, Madison had realized that not allowing Bitsy to play outside the open sliding glass windows was a bit over-protective. *After all,* she thought. *She's almost five years old and the most sensible four-year old I've ever seen. Why would I think she'd climb over the railing?* She laughed softly and stood, stretching her arms above her head. *Maybe some wine for dinner*? she mused.

She stepped outside. The afternoon sun was brilliant and she shaded her eyes and looked toward the blue waters of the Gulf. "It's nice out here," she said, sinking onto one of the lounges.

"I know. Better than inside."

"What are you and baby and kitten doing," Madison asked, sleepily.

"We were pretending to be on a bus going to the Mall. Do you want to play Go Fish or Old Maid?"

"No, not now. Let's do that after dinner. I'm going to close my eyes and rest for just a few minutes. In fact, how about we go out for dinner instead of having chicken here. We'll have a girl's party, just you and me."

"Can Joanie and Rosie come too?"

"Just Joanie. I'm sure Rosie will want to stay on her pillow. She looks so happy there."

Bitsy nodded her head, and brushed a soft kiss over Madison's cheek. "I love you Grandma."

"And I love you too, sweetheart."

Twenty minutes later, Madison stood. "Okay, Bitsy, let's get ready for dinner."

Bitsy grabbed Joanie and Rosie and skipped ahead of Madison, crossing the living room and heading down the hall. "I'll brush my hair and wash my hands and face," she called happily. "I'll wash Joanie, too, so she's pretty for dinner."

Madison felt her eyes fill with tears. *All this joy*, she thought. *Can it be real?*

CHAPTER TWENTY-TWO

In times like these, it is helpful to remember that there have always been times like these.
Paul Harvey

Jo Petrillo's office was the direct opposite of her home and life in general. At home things were arranged in such precise order that she had a difficult time finding someone to work for her. Housekeepers had thrown their hands up in despair when she complained that the dishes in the kitchen cabinets were in the wrong order after they had emptied the dishwasher. Her clothes were hung in the closet by type and color, hangers exactly two inches apart and everything facing the same direction. Her bureau drawers so orderly they looked like display cases in department stores. She valued her time and that of others when it came to her schedule. She was never late for appointments

When Walter stepped into her cubicle at the newspaper, he hesitated a minute. Jo sat behind her desk, which, except for the space her laptop took up, was completely covered with papers, books, two coffee mugs and stacks of manila files. Piles of papers were leaning against the wall and both chairs were full of boxes and papers.

"Oh, just move that pile of stuff," Jo said, pointing to a stack of folders, papers and magazines on one of the two chairs facing her cluttered desk. "But don't get anything out of order. That's research."

"Research? How do you find anything in this rabbit hole?" he said, shifting the pile neatly to the floor.

"It's my rabbit hole and it's too small. I've been complaining for eight years now that I deserve a bigger hutch." Jo smiled at her friend as he settled his huge bulk into the uncomfortable chair that was obviously designed for a smaller body. "What's up? More news?"

Walt unzipped his jacket and removed a small notebook from an inside pocket. He flipped it open. "I ran a check on Lily Rose Smith. She has a sheet. Three counts of solicitation…she was a hooker."

"We thought we knew what she did."

He shrugged. "You didn't say."

"You told me to give you the bare basics so you could run whatever searches you thought you'd need."

"I checked out the address they had listed for her but she moved right after the last bust."

"I guess that's not surprising," Jo said, idly tracing her fingers over a shiny magazine cover.

He nodded. "Well, they were minor collars, a group of them were rounded up at the same time. She spent a night in jail and then was released. Apparently she had a pimp who paid the fines but he's more into drugs than sex. Three hundred pounds of useless flesh, a nasty s.o.b. He's got a long record and is now in jail awaiting trial on drug charges and aggravated assault on a police officer. I asked my buddy to look him up at the Philadelphia House of Corrections. He asked the dirt bag if he knew where Lily was and his response was, 'If I knew where the bitch was you'd never find her. Damned slut cost me money, man. She's gonna pay, if I find her first.'

"We did notice there was a black hooker by the name of Missy Harris who was booked on all three of the busts our gal was so I'm going to see what she knows, if I can find her. They move around a lot." He waited, staring past Jo's head at the scene outside the fifteenth floor window behind her.

"You're in charge, Walt. As I said before, Madison is willing to pay whatever you charge to find out what happened to the kid's mother. That's her only goal…that and keeping the child safe."

"This Madison handy?"

"No. I told you, she took the kid and ran after she tried to find the mother on her own. They're in Florida. I called her and told her about the birth information and that we had the mother's name now. She was very grateful. Maybe she can get a copy of the birth certificate. She'll need it to get the kid into school."

"If you're okay with it, I'd like her phone number so I can talk to her."

"Sure." Jo scribbled Madison's phone number on a scrap of paper. "This is her cell phone, she doesn't have a permanent address yet."

Walt stood and slipped the paper into the notebook, then put it back into his pocket. "I have a guy who's running the woman's name through the State records but so far nothing else has come up. I'm trying to find out if she had a car or anything that would be registered in the public records. Hooker's don't pay taxes; they move around a lot and don't leave much of a trail."

"I understand."

"She apparently was on welfare right after the kid was born… just WIC…but that lasted for about six months. The address they had for her then is no good now. After that ended I guess she was back in business," he said with a smile.

Jo stood behind her desk. "Find this Missy. If anyone knows more about her it has to be a close friend, don't you think? Apparently Lily Rose Smith was a real loner except for her work and in that kind of business they don't exactly keep records, do they?"

She walked around the desk and slid her arm around his back. "Keep track of your time, Walt. Madison can afford to pay for this info, okay?"

Walt leaned down and brushed a kiss across Jo's cheek, his five o'clock whiskers scratchy against her soft skin. "Have time for a drink?"

"Not today. Deadlines," Jo said, waving her arm over the stacks of papers on the desk. "Another time…really, though, give me a call sometime. It's been a long time."

“Too damn long, Jo,” he squeezed her shoulder and reached for the doorknob. The door was set in the floor to ceiling windows separating the side offices from the main area, which was seething with activity. “Looks like a madhouse out there, doesn’t it?”

“It is a madhouse. I just thank God these hutches are soundproof so I don’t have to contend with the noise.”

He opened the door and a cacophony of voices, phones and office equipment invaded the quiet space. “I see why,” he said with a grin. “I’ll check out this Missy and get back to you.”

“Thanks,” Jo said, closing the door behind him. Through the glass wall she watched the large man weave his way through the maze of desks to the elevator bank. She turned back to her desk, surveyed the mess, sighed and picked up her telephone. Still standing and looking through the window at the quickly darkening sky, she waited—listening to the phone ring in Florida.

~ ~ ~

Following Jo’s phone call, Madison felt her fears intensify. It wasn’t anything Jo said that was upsetting…*I guess just talking about it stirs the fire,* she thought. *A fire that isn’t going out until this is settled…and when, or will it ever, be settled.*

She stood next to Bitsy’s bed, the night-light shedding just enough light for her to watch the sleeping child. Her fingers touched the dark curls then trailed along the satin binding on the light blanket tucked under Bitsy’s chin. On the pillow next to her the lifelike face of the doll rested, eyes closed, fake eyelashes making dark smudges on rouged cheeks. She smiled remembering their prayer time; a time that had become a bedtime ritual for them, a pleasant and peaceful ending to whatever had filled their day. *Bitsy is very quick to learn*, she thought, remembering the child’s soft voice repeating the words to the Lord’s Prayer with her.

Madison sighed, reluctant to back away. *Will I ever get over the miracle of having this wonderful child in my life?* she wondered.

Her decision, whether to leave the bedroom or not, was made for her when she heard her phone ring. She'd purposely left it in the kitchen so if it rang it wouldn't wake Bitsy. *As if anything short of a runaway freight train would wake her,* she thought, hurrying to the kitchen.

When she flipped it open, she didn't recognize the calling number and hesitated a moment before answering..

"Hello?" she said, her voice a tentative whisper.

"Madison? This is Walter."

Madison sighed. "Yes, I was expecting to hear from you."

"Hope I haven't called too late?"

"No. I was…" she was going to say, 'I was expecting you to call' but she'd already said that.

"I talked to Jo this afternoon. I guess she called you. I have a couple of things I'd like to ask you, if that's okay." His voice was deep, a comforting rumble that eased the tension at the nape of Madison's neck.

She slid onto one of the kitchen chairs. The light over the ceramic-topped stove was the only illumination in the room. But, instead of being forbidding, the dim room looked comfortable… *safe*, Madison thought, and felt her anxiety melt a little.

"Anytime, Mr. uh…. I'm anxious to learn whatever you can find out for us."

"It's Walt, and I'm finding a little here and a little there. Did you know about a woman called 'Missy'?"

Madison's heart jumped in her chest. "Yes. Did you find her? Bit…my granddaughter spoke of her as being a friend of her mother's." Suddenly Madison's mind was jumbled. Did she dare tell Walt Bitsy's name? Should she openly refer to the child as her granddaughter? *Oh, damn all this secrecy. I'm not used to this furtive stuff unless it's in one of my books and I'm doing the plotting.* She smiled. Wasn't that a kick? She really did think of Bitsy as her granddaughter.

"I've uncovered police records that show the woman we're looking for, Lily Rose Smith, was charged with prostitution a few times and that a woman by the name of Missy Harris was also arrested during those same arrests. I'm going to try and find her and question her," Walt said, cautioning, "but don't get your hopes up too high. Hookers aren't very reliable."

"I understand, but anything you can learn will be a help." Madison heard a familiar puff and pop sound after Walt spoke. She smiled. Walt was smoking a pipe and she remembered the sound from her grandfather; she could almost smell the cherry scented tobacco she'd watched him carefully pack into his pipes.

"Can you think of anything else you can tell me that might help? Anything about Lily Rose's habits, her activities." He paused, then added, "Except her...her livelihood."

Madison folder her lips in a tight line. "Well, I don't know exactly where she lived in Philadelphia but I did find out she often got phone messages at a small diner apparently nearby. It's called Mr. Mo's and I went there and..."

"You went there," he interrupted.

"Yes, I guess it was stupid but I thought I might find out what happened to Bitsy's mother." She stopped, realizing that she'd just given Walt her granddaughter's nickname. "Anyhow," she went on, "I spoke to someone I thought was Mr. Mo and he made me feel that something terrible had happened to her mother. He warned me to leave and stay away, and I did."

"Good advice. Jesus, lady, you were crazy to do that."

"I know now. Jo and my sister had a fit."

"What did he tell you?"

Madison related everything she could remember about that terrible day. Just telling the story brought back memories of the cold wind, the desolation she had found herself in, the look in Mr. Mo's eyes as he warned her to leave and never come back.

They spoke for a few more moments, then Walt asked, "You did get the information on the birth certificate? Did you follow that up yet?"

"No. I'm not sure how to go about that exactly."

"All you do is go online, Google birth certificates and check Pennsylvania; that will lead you to it. You can download the application form right there. I was just looking at it. It's easy enough. You'll have to have a current driver's license that matches your current address so the birth certificate goes to the right person. It costs ten dollars. Just list yourself as the grandmother."

Madison paused. "That might be a problem, Walt. My official address is in Philadelphia. That's also what's on my driver's license. Can I get it sent to another address…down here?"

She listened to the silence for what seemed like several moments, then heard Walt say, "I don't think that's possible; from what I remember about the form, your current address and the address they send the certificate to has to be identical. You could get a Florida license and that would solve that problem."

"But I don't want anyone to know where I am right now. If I get a Florida driver's license that could be checked, couldn't it? I mean it would be in the public records, wouldn't it? Or am I being paranoid? Besides," she added, her voice an echo of her confusion, "where we're living right now is only temporary." *And do I want to make a permanent commitment to…living in Florida?* she wondered for a moment but decided not to put that thought into words…not yet.

Again there was silence as Walt thought through this problem. "How are you getting your mail? Did you put a change of address through the post office?"

"No. I'm having Jo pick up my mail and then forward it here. Again, I didn't want a record someone could check leading to me, not yet anyhow. I plan to get a post office box as soon as possible. In fact, I should have already done that."

"Good girl," Walt said, as if congratulating a child on an achievement. "That's the way to do it. Well, in that case, use your Philadelphia address, have the birth certificate sent there and have Jo forward it to you in Florida."

"Oh, gosh, thanks, Walt. You're such a comfort."

Walt chuckled. "Haven't been called that in a long time…if ever," he said. "I'll keep in touch as soon as I have any other news. How's the weather there?"

Now it was Madison's turn to chuckle. "It's like a little piece of paradise right now. Balmy breezes, warm temperatures; all the stuff you read about and envy during Pennsylvania winters."

"Sounds good. Maybe someday I'll get smart enough to escape the cold. This winter hasn't been any piece of cake. Well, take care. I'll be in touch."

"Thanks again," Madison said, ending the phone call.

She sat quietly in the dim room for several moments, going over the brief phone call from Walt. She tried to picture him. *Older? Just because he smokes a pipe?* She also briefly wondered about the connection between Jo and Walt. *An old flame*? Surely she would have heard of him before if that were possible. Shrugging, she stood, poured half a glass of red wine into one of her stemmed glasses and walked through the living room to the patio. At first she leaned against the railing, a soft breeze brushing her hair back from her face. She thought about the call from Jo, Walt's call, the addition of Joanie and Rosie to her growing family, the news about the birth certificate, the possibility of finding Missy and the suggestions Walt had made.

She also remembered seeing the school she might consider for Bitsy. *I'd definitely need the birth certificate if I decide on that,* she thought. Madison laughed softly. "What are you getting yourself into?" she murmured. Sitting on one of the lounge chairs she held her wine glass in both hands. Whatever it was she was facing, it seemed much brighter than it did a few hours earlier.

Progress, she thought. *That's what it is.* She had almost drifted to sleep when she remembered she was holding the wine glass and sat up to put it on the table next to her. Was it the sudden upright movement that erased part of the complacency she'd just felt? Abruptly she was brought to the present and the thought of hookers, pimps, jails and all those hints of dire activities that Mr. Mo had planted in her mind came rushing forward. "It isn't over yet. It may never be; but Bitsy and I are safe here and for now that's all I have to lean on." Her words sounded empty and cold in the soft, balmy night and she stood, closed the doors behind her and pulled the drapes across the windows, shutting out paradise and moving into reality. She and Bitsy were in temporary surroundings. She needed to find another place to live, get a post office box and make arrangements for Bitsy's school, whether it was that one or public school in the fall. Suddenly all those demands seemed to be a heavy load and her shoulders drooped. Today was today. Yesterday was gone and tomorrow awaited. But what really awaited them?

She poured the wine down the kitchen drain, put the glass in the dishwasher and went to her bedroom; the one that wasn't really hers. *Well, at least*, she thought, as she settled between the sheets, *at least Philip will be down here in a couple of weeks. Hang on to what you have and don't worry about what you don't have. That was what Grandma often said.* But as she closed her eyes she realized that perhaps she didn't even have what she thought she had and with that miserable thought she began to pray, hoping that the peace she was looking for now began right after the amen.

CHAPTER TWENTY-THREE

Research is the process of going up alleys to see if they are blind.

Marston Bates

Walt climbed the stairs quietly. Years of experience had taught him it was better to arrive unexpected than to broadcast your arrival when you were on a furtive mission. He purposely didn't slide his hand along the wooden railing; God only knew what residue the occupants left there. The smell of the stairwell and hallways assaulted his senses—an elusive aroma like the combination of a badly kept litter box and rotten food, mixed with years of unmoved dirt and dust.

He hesitated at the third floor landing and peered ahead. Even though it was four o'clock in the afternoon, the interior hallway was unlit and he squinted as he counted three closed doors on each side. Walking to the door farthest from the front on the left side he knocked firmly on the scarred door with tarnished numerals 316 tacked to the wooden panel.

There was no answer and he leaned forward and pressed his ear against the panel. Sure enough, someone was moving around inside. He knocked again and waited, then repeated his knock, firmer this time. Someone inside murmured, "Who's there?"

"Delivery."

"Ain't 'speckin' no delivery. Go 'way."

"Got a package," Walt insisted.

"You're fulla shit," was the response

"Come on lady. I climbed these damned steps to get this to you. Open the door."

"No way, mister. Don't want no package. I ain't openin' no door."

Walt hesitated, tapped softly again and, lowering his voice to just above a whisper, said, "It's about Lily…" He waited, then heard soft movement and finally the sound of the dead bolt being turned, the chain being moved and he watched the doorknob slowly twist. He pushed the door open, coming face to face with a tall, thin black woman. Her head was shaven clean and it glistened even in the dim interior of the room. Her makeup was almost theatrical with brilliant blue eye shadow from her eyelids to highly arched, painted-on eyebrows.

"What you know 'bout Lily?" she said, backing slowly away from him. "You a cop?"

"No. A friend." He moved further into the cluttered room, pushing the door closed behind him.

"I don't know nothin' 'bout Lily," the woman said, increasing the space between them.

"Sure you do. You were her friend," Walt said softly.

"No. She just lived down the hall. I don't know nothin' 'bout her."

"You knew her. You knew her little girl," he said, watching her eyebrows climb up her forehead. "Sure you knew her. You're worried about her aren't you? You're worried because she's disappeared. I'm just trying to help them."

He reached into his pocket and pulled out a fifty-dollar bill, pressing it into her hand. "Just between us, okay? This is for you. No one needs to know."

Missy slumped into the corner of the couch, drawing three velvet pillows next to her. "She been gone. I don't know where. Honest."

Walt moved closer. "That's what I'm trying to do—find her."

Missy straightened her back and put one long arm casually across the back of the couch, her attempt at feigning ease lost in her expression of wariness. "What you want her for?"

"To help her."

"Maybe she don't need your help."

"Maybe she does. Maybe the little girl does." He watched her expression flash from suspicion to confusion. She turned to look away, "I don't know nothin'."

Walt moved so that he forced her to look at him. "You like Lily. You like the little girl," he said softly. *Damn what was the kid's name,* he thought, regretting he hadn't made sure he remembered it.

"I did," Missy said, forcing her eyes from his.

"You still do, don't you? Wouldn't you like to help them? They were your friends."

"Look," Missy said, springing to her feet. She was at least two inches taller than her visitor. With forced courage she stared him in the eyes, this time her eyes held the power. "You get outta here. I don't know nothin'." She lowered her eyes and then moved toward a door at the back of the room.

Walt reached out and grabbed her arm with enough finger strength to prevent her from moving. "I don't want to hurt you…or hurt Lily or the kid. All I want is some information. Something to make it easier to find her. I swear I mean them no harm…just want to help them."

Missy looked at the intruder. "You're a cop," she whispered.

"I was…a long time ago. Now I'm just someone trying to help someone who needs help. That's all," he said, removing his fingers from her arm.

"What you want to know? I don't know nothin'," she whined.

"Tell me about Lily."

Missy grinned, her parted lips an ugly gash across her face revealing gold-capped teeth. "You think I trust someone who was a cop even if he ain't now?"

"I need your help," he answered, spreading his arms wide.

The static in the room was plain, the uncertainty on her part, the need on his.

She moved to a small chair next to a table covered with plastic saints and statues. A candle flickered behind them giving the space the appearance of an altar. "She was better than what she did," Missy whispered.

Walt moved closer. "I know."

"She lived for the kid. Hardly let her outta her sight, 'cept with me."

"I know," he repeated.

"You know so much how come you don't know where they are?" Missy's voice was bolder.

"They got into some trouble. The little girl is separated from her mother. I'm trying to find Lily so they can be together again." He hesitated, wondering if he'd given too much away but watched at Missy leaned forward, elbows on knees, her head in her hand.

She began to moan and sway and Walt watched for several moments, then reached forward and touched Missy's shoulder. "Lily's in trouble, isn't she?"

"I don't know," Missy moaned into her hands, shaking her head from side to side. "I don't know. She been gone. They's lookin' for her. She ain't nowhere to be found. She was sick." She looked up at Walt. "You think she's dead?"

He shrugged. "Do you?"

"I don't know," Missy said, tears streaming down her glossy cheeks, beads of perspiration on her head glittering in the candlelight. "She was bad sick," she said, her head bowed, arms crossed across her chest, her fingers gripping her upper arms.

"Tell me what was wrong with Lily. You said she was sick. Maybe she's somewhere needing help. We could get that for her. You and me," Walt said, standing directly in front of Missy.

"She was sick. Went to a clinic, then the hospital for tests. I took care of Bitsy," Missy said, and Walt immediately catalogued the child's name.

"What was wrong with Lily?"

"Some disease. I can't 'member the name. Big word. Bad, it was. She wanted to find someone to take care of her baby. Not me," she said, wiping her eyes with the backs of her hands.

"Who? Who did she want to take care of Bitsy?"

Missy shrugged. "I don't know. Some kind of stupid plan to find a grandmamma for her baby. She just drove off. That's all I know," she said, standing. They were close, too close and Walt moved back a step.

"She drove off? She had a car?" he said, his heart leaping in his chest.

"Weren't much. Some old junker a dude gave her."

"What kind of a car?"

"Who knows cars…not me. It was blue, beat up, all dents and funny paint. I tole her it was a damn fool mistake to even take it. I tole her it would get her into trouble. No papers. Cars costs money." Missy strode across the small room, her hands clutched in front of her, her brilliant caftan swaying as she swung around to face him again.

"Where's Bitsy?"

"She's with a good lady."

"Where?" Missy demanded, her brows now knit in a deep frown.

"Can't tell you, but she's safe."

Missy's face relaxed. "Well, if that's true, that's good."

Walt studied the pathetic woman before him. Every once in a while, even when he was a cop, Walt was amazed at how compassion could be found in the most unexpected places and people. He saw Missy's compassion for her friend and the child and marveled that she hadn't forgotten how to care during the years she'd been on the streets. He shrugged his shoulders. *I've probably got all I'm going to get,* he thought, then remembered one thing Missy had said. "You said 'they were looking for her'. Who's looking for her?"

Missy immediately reverted to her defensive attitude. "No one."

"You said *they* were looking for Lily when I first got here. Who, Missy?"

"Poison."

"Someone called 'Poison'?"

She nodded.

"He the pimp?" Walt remembered his friend report that the man in the detention center on drug charges and assaulting an officer was also known as Paul Oyson giving rise to the nickname 'Poison'.

Again she nodded. "But Jeremy's takin' over. Skinny, mean as a snake. He's bad news. Poison…he was mean but not like Jeremy," she said, shaking her head from side to side. "Poison done got into trouble, big trouble. He gonna be in jail a long time."

"Why are they looking for Lily?" he asked, already knowing the answer.

"Just 'cause she's gone." Missy turned away. "Money," she said softly. "They don't like it when you don't get the money for 'em."

"What other contacts did Lily have, Missy? Contacts here in the neighborhood?"

"No one. She don't contact with no one, just…" she looked up, her huge eyes glassy with suspicion. "…Just business," she murmured.

"Where did she go around here? Was there one spot you could always find her? Anyone she spoke to? What about the child? Did she have any friends?"

"No. Lily don't talk to no one…and her baby…she ain't got no friends. Lily kept her real close. Daycare sometimes, but not often."

"What daycare?"

"How the hell do I know? It ain't my business to watch them," she said, her eyes flashing her annoyance.

"You go out together…anywhere…except 'business'?" he asked.

"Just Mr. Mo's to eat once in a while. I don't eat out much," she said, her eyes traveling to the curtained doorway at the back of the room.

"What's back there?" Walt asked.

"Nothin'. Just a kitchen I don't use much. Can't get fat. Men don't like fat women. Not white men, anyhow. You tirin' me, Mister. Get outta here. I don't know nothin' more about Lily."

Walt realized his interview was over. He smiled. "Listen, Missy. You don't need to tell anyone about me, okay? About my coming here and asking about Lily. This is just between us. I promise if I find Lily, I'll let you know.

"Wait," Missy said, taking a tentative step toward him. "Mister, if you find Lily and she's okay, tell her I miss her." She hesitated, then continued, her voice husky with emotion, "but, don't come back…and don't tell me where she is."

He looked at her fear-riddled face.

"You can't tell what you don't know," she said, the true meaning behind her words a bold statement of what might lay ahead of her if she knew where her friend was.

When he closed the door, Missy was still standing in the middle of the cluttered room, the money clutched in one hand, the other across her breast. As he slipped down the battered stairs and opened the door to the street, some of the old feelings he'd had as a police officer flooded back. The poverty, the dirt, the smell of fear and hopelessness were the same. It would never change.

CHAPTER TWENTY-FOUR

A strong positive mental attitude will create more miracles than any wonder drug.
Patricia Neal

Madison and Bitsy left the air-cooled interior of the post office and stepped out into brilliant sunshine. She felt relieved that she had already accomplished two of the things on her 'to do' list. She'd mailed the parcel with her latest chapters to Alan and rented a post office box. "I've got to get us some sunglasses," she said, squinting both ways before crossing the street to her car.

"We could go to Wal-Mart," Bitsy chirped.

"You're getting to know your way around here, aren't you," Madison laughed. "We'll go later. Right now we've got an appointment with a real estate lady.

"The one you called this morning?" Bitsy said as Madison snapped the safety belt across the car seat.

"Yep. We're going to find us a new house...or apartment...or condo."

"I like the one we have."

"Well," Madison said, sliding behind the wheel and looking at Bitsy in the rearview mirror, "that doesn't belong to us, you know that. Besides, it's way to expensive for us. We'll find something nice but a bit more economical."

"What's ec-o-momical?"

"Eco*nom*ical, honey. It means more than we can afford."

"Oh. Mommy said we couldn't go to movies because they were too 'spensive and besides, she had to work."

Madison grimaced. *Work,* she thought, *Oh, Lord, honey if you only knew* and then she silently thanked God that the innocent child didn't know and prayed she never would.

"Let me know if you decide you'd like to look at any of those listings," Janet Molina said as she held the door for Madison and Bitsy to leave.

"Thanks for your time," Madison said, grasping Bitsy's hand. "I'll look these over this afternoon and give you a call. You know my price range, so if these are in that bracket, or can be negotiated to fit, we may be able to do business. After we've seen them, of course."

Madison hurried Bitsy to the car. "Why don't we look at those houses today, Grandma?"

"Because I want to think about them before we look at them. Sometimes when you see something like a new house and it's all fixed up you make a quick decision. That's not always a good idea."

She pulled out of the parking lot at the real estate office. Madison had been impressed with Mrs. Molina's demeanor, no hard sell and yet a businesslike eagerness *to find the perfect fit*, as she'd said.

Back at the condo after lunch and with Bitsy feeding her baby doll make-believe food on some of the small kitchen plates and pouring water into an empty oleo container for the kitten on the patio, Madison spread the listings on the kitchen table. Three were of small homes, one not far from the school she had seen. She had mentioned that location to Mrs. Molina and had been assured that all the listings were within reasonable travel distance. "Good locations, all of them," she'd said. "Near schools, medical facilities and shopping. Just what you'd want with your little granddaughter with you." Madison wondered if she automatically read some doubt about her role as grandmother into other people's random comments, then dismissed that thought as being overly paranoid.

One of the listings was for a condo in a small complex closer to the beach but Mrs. Molina had indicated that perhaps the renters there would be more temporary, students at the local college, or visitors from the north who wouldn't stay the full year. Madison pushed that listing to the bottom of the pile along with a couple of others that she rejected for one reason or another.

After an hour of making notes, weighing one against the other she had narrowed her choices down to four. Three houses and one apartment. She picked up her phone and called Janet, arranging to see these listings tomorrow morning.

~ ~ ~

The following afternoon Madison lay on one of the lounge chairs on the patio while Bitsy sat at the table under the opened umbrella. She concentrated on a circus picture in her coloring book, her back to Madison, the breeze ruffling her dark curls. "I love this page, Grandma. I can use almost all my crayons."

Madison held a glass of Arizona iced tea in one hand, the other lay across her forehead. She had a headache. The patio was still partially shaded and a soft breeze blew in off the Gulf. She sighed, recalling their travels this morning to the four listings she had chosen as possible new homes. She'd had such high hopes. *Jerk*, she thought.

Now I know what cute and cozy means. It means impossibly tiny and outdated. Compact but needs a little tender, loving care means it's not only small but in need of more help than I could ever give it. And, spacious means built like a barn and partially furnished. The latter identification applied to the apartment, which was built over a three-car garage so far from town it was almost in the Everglades.

Janet had assured Madison she would have more listings to show her later in the week. "They might be a bit higher than your limit but it's worth taking a look. We can always negotiate."

When Madison had relayed her morning adventures to Jo when they returned to the condo, Jo had said, "They always show you the crummy stuff first so that the next bunch will look like real bargains at any price. Take your time and don't be hustled into anything."

Madison had assured her friend she had no intention of being hustled into anything but the nagging need for another home stayed with her. Especially since, upon their return, they had run into their surly neighbor at the top of the stairs leading to the third floor.

This time, however, he stopped, then moved to the right. He wore swim trunks, a brightly patterned shirt and carried a towel over one shoulder; he looked neat and clean and she could smell the soft scent of his aftershave lotion. Madison looked at his hands to see if he also carried a supply of beer but his hands were empty.

"I believe I owe you an apology," he said, smiling and bowing his head slightly. "I was truly out of line the other day. A bad day." He sighed, waiting for her response.

Madison hesitated a moment. "We all have bad days. Apology accepted." She moved toward the door to their unit but he remained standing at the top of the stairs. As she put the key in the lock she glanced toward him. "Have a nice day," she said, pushing the door open. Bitsy darted inside as if a demon was behind her.

Still he stood looking at her. "I am sorry. I didn't mean anything…guess I scared the little girl."

"Let's let it go," Madison said, her hand still on the open door.

He nodded, turned and began his descent to the pool area.

Now on the patio she realized that it wasn't only David that added urgency to her finding another home, it was more than that. Philip would be coming back at the end of the month. *Not to stay*, she thought, *but it was a harbinger that he might want to return home sooner than he'd first expected. Then there was school for Bitsy.*

Do I want to put her into pre-school right away? Well, it would make things easier for me in a way. I could spend more time concentrating on writing. And, it would be good for her. She'd have friends, a schedule and she's so quick I think she needs it.

"Bitsy, honey, do you think you'd like to go to pre-school?"

"What's that?"

"Like that school we saw the other day. You would go there and make friends and learn all kinds of things. Things that you'd need before you go to real school." She remembered Bitsy's comments about *real school* and the eagerness she'd expressed about going to school.

Bitsy jumped off the chair she was sitting on at the table. Her face was alive with excitement. "Would it be like real school?"

Madison sat up, putting her glass on the table next to her. "A lot like it, I think. I would take you in the morning and come and get you in the afternoon."

Bitsy frowned. "I'd go all day? Like daycare?"

"Oh, probably half a day. It would be much more interesting than daycare I think. You'd have classes. Things like reading and numbers and the alphabet."

"I already know the alphabet," Bitsy countered, her face cautious now.

"I know you do and you'd do well but they could teach you what to do with the letters. You could write, too."

Madison saw the child rise up on her toes, an indication of her excitement. "Well, maybe, but wouldn't you be lonesome?"

Madison opened up her arms. "Of course, I would. I will miss you but I'll also be happy that you can go to school and make friends. All you have right now is me."

"I like being with you."

"Yes, but you have to practice for real school. At least, we could try it. There would be all kinds of interesting things for you to learn. You know how you love to learn. New words. New places. Remember the fun we had looking at our maps on the way down here and how you love to be able to look at the map of Osceola Beach and pick out the Gulf and the rivers?"

Bitsy moved into Madison's waiting arms. "I might not like the school. What if I wanted to come home? I like being with you," she repeated.

"Why don't we go there soon, just for a visit and you can look around? We don't have to make any decisions right away, especially since we don't know where we're going to be living. It would just be to see what it's like."

Bitsy buried her head into Madison's shoulder. "Okay," she murmured, then leaned back and looked into her grandmother's eyes. "We'll just check it out, like we looked at the houses today."

"That's all," Madison said, hugging the child to her. *Maybe I'm rushing things*, she thought and wished she hadn't broached the subject of school yet. *Maybe she's smarter than I am. Oh, why am I so impetuous sometimes?*

Later that afternoon Madison called Lolly. "What's new," her sister asked.

"Not much I guess."

"Heard anything from that investigator?"

"Only the birth information and how to get a birth certificate. I think he might have found some more but he didn't elaborate. I guess he doesn't like to feed information in dribs and drabs. At least that's the feeling I got when I spoke to him."

"You spoke to him?"

"Yes, he called. Jo gave him my cell number."

"Well what else is new? Enjoying the weather?"

Madison laughed. "You know that's the first question anyone who calls me asks. It's just beautiful. I can't believe how warm it is for January and Bitsy is already getting a nice tan. We go to the beach a couple of mornings a week. Today we went house-hunting instead."

"Oh, that's good. What did you find?"

"Nothing. Absolutely nothing. I've set a price limit and the realtor showed us things either just under that or in that range but they were awful. Jo says realtors show the crummy stuff first and then they get to the more expensive so that we can make a comparison."

Lolly hesitated. "You know, Sisty you sound good. Better than I've heard you in years. It must be the weather…or Bitsy."

"I think it's both, but mostly Bitsy. Honestly, I'm really enjoying having her with me. You'd be surprised at how domesticated I've become. Meals on time, a regular bedtime and prayers before bed. She's so quick to learn I've even thought of putting her in a private school we discovered on one of our trips."

"I'm still worried about you but I do feel a bit better now that there's some distance between you and…"

"And Philadelphia? Me too and I didn't think I'd ever say that. If I can just put a period at the end of the matter of Bitsy's mother I think I can move on."

"Have you heard anything from Jim?"

"No. I don't think he's even trying to find me."

"Well, you don't want him to, do you?"

"Of course not. You know," she paused, "I guess if it hadn't been for Bitsy I might have done a turn around just like I did all those other times when I tried to break it off. It was a comfortable rut."

"That's just what it was, a rut, only not so comfortable. I heard the disappointment and frustration in your voice. I didn't think you'd do it or stick to it and maybe you're right…maybe Bitsy did make the difference."

"I think she's made differences that neither of us recognize yet." Madison listened to the silence that stretched three thousand miles between them. "I miss you. Maybe you could come over for a visit once we get settled. I spoke to Philip yesterday and he's coming down to Florida at the end of the month. He's got a photo shoot in South America and he's picking up some equipment he'll need."

"Oh, is he coming back to his condo? Does that mean you have to move right away? Is that why you're doing house-hunting?"

"Not exactly. I intended to look for a house or apartment anyhow. This just spurred me into to doing something sooner than I had anticipated. No. I'm ready to get settled. This is a beautiful condo but it's not ours and we need to make a move."

"You're going to rent rather than buy aren't you? Buying is such a commitment and you're really not sure where you want to be, are you? You still could come to California, you know."

"I know that's what you'd like, Lolly, but I don't think that will work. At least if I'm on the east coast I'm closer to my agent, the publishers and my contacts in New York."

"Oh, nuts. With computers you're just a click away from anywhere in the world."

"Still, there's the importance of putting in a personal appearance once in a while, especially right after the book is released."

"When is the release date for the latest one? And, by the way, how is that going?"

"I finally got back to writing. I was only away three weeks and Alan was having a fit but he's pleased now. I spoke to him yesterday, too."

"I have another call coming in," Lolly said. "Call you in the next day or two. Don't do anything rash or impetuous."

Madison laughed, "I'm not usually impetuous."

"Not until recently," Lolly snickered. "Bye for now."

~ ~ ~

Spalding (Inky) Henderson raised two fingers to the bartender, signaling they were ready for another round. He watched him put two glasses of scotch and water on a tray and hand it to the waitress at the end of the counter. The girl was pretty and barely old enough to serve. She had that full-of-wonder image so many have when they're just starting out in the adult world. "College kid," Inky whispered to his companion, Jim, who was slumped against the over-padded, high back of the booth across the table from him.

"I can't understand it," Jim muttered, his right hand circling the fresh, cold glass the pretty waitress had just placed before him. Inky noticed that Jim didn't even follow her with his eyes as she swished her way back to the bar. He grimaced.

"She's been gone weeks. I've gone by her apartment. Even ran into that Polack maintenance man. He said, 'She's on vacation. Her and the little girl' What little girl?"

"Who knows? Who cares? Just be glad there's been no fallout."

"But what little girl? And where the hell did she go?"

"Look, Jim. She's gone and so far there's been no trouble. Count your blessings. Who knows, when she comes back there might be trouble."

"Something you're always looking for," Jim mumbled, twisting the icy glass on the paper napkin under it.

"That's my job. Besides, who's looking for trouble? You are if you're going to continue to look for her. She might have one of the kids from the Italian girlfriend's family with her. God knows they always seem to have a couple dozen kids around."

"How do you know? You don't even know that family."

"Neither do you but that kind of family always have a bunch of kids."

"Why would Madison take one of them with her?"

"Who the hell knows? Drop it for God's sake. Just pray she stays away…from you at least. It's time for you to move on."

"She always came back before," Jim murmured, then recognizing the whine in his voice, said, "You're right. Good riddance." He took a deep swallow of his drink, grimaced as the cold liquid slid down his throat, and pushed the glass away. "I've got to go. See you next week. You're going to that City Council meeting, aren't you?"

Inky stood, threw some bills on the table. "You know I am. I'm representing you."

The two men walked from the dim interior of the tavern into the weak late day sunshine. Jim looked up at the sky. "At least it looks like we're going to get a break in the weather." He turned to walk toward the garage where he parked his car. "See you," he called over his shoulder.

Inky stood for a few minutes watching his friend. He smiled as he saw the familiar swagger return to Jim's steps. *He'll be okay in a week or two, back on the prowl. I'm surprised he hasn't already replaced Madison. Damn stupid Bitch. But I'm sure glad she bailed out when she did. That was getting tricky and smart as he is, Jim Eldridge was getting in too deep for comfort,* he thought, turning to go to his car. Daylight was fading fast and he wanted to be on his way out of town before dark.

As Jim turned toward the parking garage elevator bank, he spied someone he knew. Waving his hand in the air, "Jennifer," he called. "Over here. How the hell are you?"

The woman who walked toward him could have been a model but she wasn't. Jennifer Alban was once of the best criminal lawyers in Philadelphia, and by far the best-looking woman in court no matter who was present. Her hair, the color of highly polished silver, was cut so that it fell chin length and curved under provocatively, capturing every male eye in sight, and some female eyes, too.

"Haven't seen you in a long time, Jim," she extended her hand and he took it and pressed it to his lips while circling her shoulders with the other arm.

"Busy, busy," he responded. "There's always so many holidays parties, you know how it is. I'm surprised our paths didn't cross. Then I spent Christmas in London this year."

"I'd love to hear about that. It's something I've dreamed of but never got around to. One of those 'some day wishes'," she laughed.

"How about a drink? You have time?"

She glanced at her watch as if her schedule was crowded. If the truth were known she was on her way home to a frozen dinner and Friday television.

"I could. Just one, though."

They did an about-face and walked back to the sidewalk. The streetlights were on now and they cast golden circles of light on the pavement. The air was crisp but not bitter and she welcomed his arm around her. "Martino's is just around the block," he said, leaning into her so that her soft hair brushed his cheek. Inky was right. *Time to move on,* he thought, picturing that soft gray hair spread across a pillow. *At least I got the ring back and the rest...? Well, my dear Madison, I'll just write that off as collateral damages*. He grinned, his steps quickened and he hurried toward an evening he was picturing as even better than he'd first contemplated.

"Martino's sounds fine," Jennifer said, picturing the upscale restaurant with the secluded bar; a drink, or maybe more, followed by dinner; a much better prospect for the evening than a few minutes earlier.

Across town, Walt Kalish studied the notes he'd just entered in his notebook. He leaned back and closed his eyes. Missy Harris had given him more information than she realized. He knew Lily Rose protected her child as much as possible, kept her isolated. The news of Lily's illness was a surprise. AIDs? He wondered and then dismissed that. They had medicines for that. These days people could live a long time with AIDs.

He also knew Lily had a car. He could check the registration records. Maybe he'd get lucky and be able to do a search on the car, find out what happened. An accident maybe? A blue car, with lots of dents? That wasn't much to go on but he remembered slim chances that led to solutions in other cases.

He made a note to check out Mr. Mo's too, but that might not be anything of value and he didn't want to stir up any interest in Lily. He was beginning to feel he knew his quarry a little now, enough to be on a first name basis, anyhow. He smiled then returned to business. He reviewed his notes from his telephone call to Madison, especially the ones on her visit to Mr. Mo's. Shaking his head he muttered, "What a chance that gal took."

His eyes scaled down the other information he'd noted from his conversation with Madison. "Imagine a woman dumping her daughter in a remote diner and telling her a grandmother was coming to pick her up? And on Christmas Eve, for Christ's sake," he muttered. *Well,* he thought, *in desperate times people do desperate, dumb things.*

He flipped through the thin file he'd begun to collect on his quarry. He pulled her sheet and looked at the mug shot. "Where are you Lily?" He studied the pained face but he didn't see the usual look of defiance that women in her trade often had. No, Lily looked sad and perhaps sorry. He whistled softly as he studied the grainy image of Lily Rose Smith. There was something there that he hadn't seen in other hookers, something different, not that it made much difference. She was what she was.

Shrugging his shoulders in dismissal, he closed the notebook and slid it into his desk drawer, next to his back-up service revolver and the 'second badge'. He smiled as he remembered getting the badge to replace the one he'd 'lost' because he knew when he retired he'd have to turn in his badge. "Have to keep some souvenirs," he said, sliding back into his recliner and turning the television set on. He loved a mystery, the feeling of excitement in arranging clues, the challenge of finding answers no one seemed to have. No one but he knew how much he missed being on the job.

CHAPTER TWENTY-FIVE

If a child is to keep alive his inborn sense of wonder, he needs companionship of at least one adult who can share it, rediscovering with him the joy, excitement and mystery of the world we live in. Rachael Carson

Madison remembered her sister's warning but right now she didn't feel at all impetuous. She couldn't believe her eyes either. It was love at first sight, literally. The minute she stepped into the house on Thunder Creek Road she knew she'd found the home she was looking for.

After the initial shock of finding such a perfect little home, and after they had gone through the rooms, one by one, she asked the realtor if she'd mind letting them look around alone. Now standing in the master bedroom she felt a sense of belonging she'd never felt before. How could that be? Wasn't her apartment on the fifth floor of that brick building in Philadelphia the culmination of her dream...the perfect home? How many years had she been completely content there? But she couldn't really bring a true picture of the place to mind because she was overwhelmed by the sense of belonging right here, right now, and while it was comforting and so strong it seemed to smother any doubts, she was also confused. Bitsy stood next to her and every time Madison turned she followed.

"This is nice, Grandma," the little girl whispered, as if the same aura that had captured Madison had overtaken her too.

"It's perfect, honey."

Madison opened the double French doors in the big bedroom. The doors led to an enclosed porch. The room was the only room completely unfurnished. The rest of the house was partially furnished and it looked as if the former owners had been in the process of filling in the empty spaces. The essentials were there. Some of the necessary extras she could move from her Philadelphia apartment. She looked around this extra room, envisioning her bookcases, her desk and computer. This was a perfect studio—a quiet and comfortable place for her to write.

"Are we going to live here?"

"I hope so, sweetheart. Let's go talk to Mrs. Molina" She took Bitsy by the hand and they walked slowly down the hall, past the bedroom she pictured Bitsy in; past the second bath and into the living room with the cathedral ceiling. A small dining area led to the sunny kitchen that had a separate breakfast room and doors leading to a screened Florida room. Huge pin oaks shaded the house and lot and she heard the sound of birds in the tall trees and watched a slight breeze stir the Spanish moss that adorned the branches.

Outside, Janet Molina was sitting in her car, the door ajar, the air-conditioner running. "Everything okay?" she asked, standing.

"Well, I really like this one the best so far," Madison said, trying to muffle her excitement.

"Let's go talk to the owners," Janet said, turning the engine off and closing the car door. They began to walk across a wide lawn to a sturdy ranch house. "These folks are renting the house which is on their property. They had to get a zoning change in order to build it and it was built for their only son when he got married. They planned on having their son, his wife and only grandchild live right next door," Janet said, skirting a small hedge of flowing shrubs. "Unfortunately, their son was killed recently in Iraq."

"Oh, how awful," Madison said, stopping her progress. "Perhaps…"

"Don't worry. They really want to rent it. Their daughter-in-law and grandchild, I think he's three, have moved back to Indiana where they lived originally. She's going back to college and her parents are going to care for the child. Of course, the McWalters miss the little boy very much. I think they want to have people in the house to help ease their pain. She told me the empty house reminds her of their loss even more."

Madison looked across the lawn at the house they had just visited. It stood alone, probably a hundred yards away from the house they were heading for. She sighed, took Bitsy's hand and continued up the path to the front door. "Maybe we should wait outside."

"No. Let's go in and speak with them." Janet lifted the shiny doorknocker and the threesome listened to the metallic clunk it made.

When the door opened they faced a pretty woman in bright coral colored shorts and golf shirt. She smiled at Madison and then glanced down at Bitsy. Madison saw her expression go from polite welcome to surprise. "Come in," she said, opening the door wider.

The living room they stepped into was bright and tastefully decorated in tropical prints and light wood furniture. Two ceiling fans slowly circulated above them. The wall to the right was entirely sliding glass doors and a huge pool and patio lay beyond the windows. The entire outdoor room was enclosed in a screened cage. Madison saw Bitsy's eyes widen.

A tall thin man dressed in tan shorts and shirt rose from one of the chairs. "Welcome," he said, stretching his hand toward the three women. Madison and Janet felt the firm grip. "And welcome to you, too, little lady," he said, stooping so that he could take one of Bitsy's hands.

"Thanks for allowing me to show your house this morning," Janet began. "My client is interested in talking to you about it."

"Why don't we go outside on the patio? There's a breeze and we can sit in the shade of the overhang," Mrs. McWalters said, leading the way.

Half an hour later, an agreement had been reached. Madison agreed to sign a one-year lease. She'd been hoping for something month to month because of all the uncertainty that surrounded their stay in Florida but the thought of missing out on the perfect home persuaded her to take the step. Somehow she had a feeling deep within her heart that any decision she made concerning this matter would surely be for the best.

"After the first year, if you want to go month to month we might consider it," Mr. McWalters said as they stood outside the front door. "We don't however, plan to sell it…not now."

"That suits me fine. Right now I'm not sure what my long-range plans are."

"We'll be happy to see you and your granddaughter in the house," Mrs. McWalters said, her eyes brightening with tears.

"I'm so sorry for your loss," Madison said, her hand touching the older woman's arm. She watched as Mr. McWalters' arm quickly circled his wife's shoulders.

"It's been a terrible loss for us, but we know we must go on. It was hard to see Marcy and little Ian leave but it is for the best. And," she said, with a weak smile, "Who knows maybe when she finishes school they'll return."

"And then…" Madison stopped. *Would Bitsy and I have to leave if the daughter-in-law and grandson decided to return to Florida? What...* but before she could contemplate future trouble, Mr. McWalters smiled and said, "We'll cross those bridges when we come to them. Marcy has at least two more years of school." He extended his hand to Madison. "We'll see you in February but if you need to come back to look at room sizes or anything, just give us a call."

As Madison, together with Janet and Bitsy, walked back to the smaller house, she felt an elation she couldn't contain. Her mind reeled with things she would have to do in the next ten days. *Call Jo first*, she thought, *make a list of the things we'll need from the apartment.*

I'll have to get a breakfast set for one thing but I'll have to purchase that locally. Then...there's my books, all my clothes, china, silver, the precious things I saved from my parents' home... The list seemed endless.

Riding back in the car with the realtor, Bitsy sat quietly belted into the back seat. Madison was quiet also, her mind racing as fast as her heart was. But every time she even hinted to herself that she might have been hasty, she buried those feelings under the joy she felt. "It has to be right," she muttered.

"I think you'll be very happy there. You'll have to keep your car in the carport as there isn't a garage and I don't see that as a big drawback. There is that nice roomy shed at the back but you probably won't use that for anything much but storage. You heard Mr. McWalters say that he intended to do all the yard work. That's his hobby you know and I think he's pretty fussy about how the grounds are kept."

"That's good. I'm certainly not a gardener. I thought perhaps they were the ones doing it because both places are so nicely landscaped and taken care of. You can see the tender loving care the lawn and plants get."

"The property is nicely located to shopping, schools, medical centers and not that far from the beach that you can't make that trip as often as you'd like, too."

"You don't have to sell me," Madison laughed. "I was sold the moment I stepped into the house."

"I knew you'd like it."

"Why did you save it for last then?"

"Because then you had all those others to compare it with. And, besides, I just had a feeling that you would be the right tenants for those landlords."

~ ~ ~

Madison's hands shook, but it was from excitement rather than the fears that had dogged her for the past weeks. She dialed Jo's office number.

"Jo Petrillo," she answered, reaching for the phone from across her desk where she'd been sorting through some files.

"It's me."

After a very brief pause, Jo said, "What's up? I hear excitement in those two little words."

"I just signed a lease on a house."

"What!" Jo slumped back into her chair and swiveled it around so that she was looking at the skyline. "You didn't!"

"I did. Oh, Jo, it's just perfect. Two bedrooms, two baths, a studio for me to work in, a great living room, small dining area, the sunniest kitchen you ever saw with a breakfast room and doors leading onto a screened patio. It's in a really nice, quiet residential neighborhood. It's a manufactured home."

"Wow, sounds great. What about the cost? And, what the heck is a *manufactured home*?"

"The cost is in my range, and a manufactured home is one that's built in pieces in a factory somewhere and then shipped to the lot and assembled. It's kind of an interesting concept and seems to be a real good solution to a quick home."

"How did you find it?"

"My realtor. Doesn't that sound uppity? My realtor took us there this morning. You won't believe the story behind it."

Madison related the sad story of the son's death in Iraq and the daughter-in-law and grandson leaving.

"One man's sorrow is another man's joy," Jo quoted. "But I know your joy is only in finding the place. You signed a year's lease? What if you have to leave before that?"

"I thought of that and I'm going on instinct. The couple who own the property seem so nice, in fact they remind me of my mom and dad. I think if something really came up that we had to leave they'd understand. At least that's what I'm hoping. Actually, what I'm hoping is that we don't have to leave. Not for the next year anyhow."

"You know that kind of hurts, kiddo. That means you'll be 1300 miles away from me for a year…or more. I miss you already."

"I miss you too, Jo. You'll have to come down and visit. What a great place for a vacation. You won't believe it."

"I'll believe it. And, you just might have to come north when your book's released."

"Yes," Madison said, feeling calmer. Jo's voice had a way of doing that, of bringing her back to ground. Madison sighed. "But there are things…"

"What kind of things?"

"Well, for one, I'm going to have to fly back to get some things in my apartment shipped down here. I'll have to bring Bitsy too and that might not be…" she hesitated, hunting for the right words. "…might not be safe I guess is what I'm thinking."

"Wait a minute. Why should you and the kid fly up here? Just tell me what you want packed and I'll get it done for you."

"Oh, I couldn't ask you to do that."

"You didn't. I just volunteered. How hard can that be? Tell me what you want."

"But it's a lot of work."

"I'd hire a moving company, silly. I'm not sitting there wrapping Grandma's china in newspaper. These moving companies do a great job. My brother, Al, just had his stuff moved from Philadelphia to Atlanta, much to my mother's chagrin. Another bird has escaped the nest. Anyhow, he just contracted for them to move him and they came packed up the stuff and trucked it to Atlanta."

Madison held the telephone in a vice-lick grip. Could this be possible? "But it would take a lot of your time just getting the stuff together."

"No. He and his wife did a walk through with the moving company representative and basically told him what was being moved. Of course, they took almost all their possessions but there were things they left for

Sam to pick up. He's the youngest brother and he needed things in his dorm room at college. It worked out great."

"But that takes a lot of time. You'd…"

"How much stuff are you going to move?"

"Well," she hesitated. What did she want? "My clothes, books, bookcases, china and all the kitchen stuff," she began. "Maybe that swivel rocker in the living room…"

"Make a list and fax it to me tomorrow. I'll call a couple of movers and get an estimate and get back to you tomorrow evening."

"Oh, Jo. What would I do without you?" she whispered, her throat choked with emotion.

"Well, one thing you did without me was move to Florida. Do I hear tears?"

Madison unconsciously sniffed. "Yes," she whimpered.

"Get a grip, girl. You don't have time to be a wimp now."

After they hung up, with promises to speak tomorrow evening, Madison stood and paced around the condo.

She glanced out the window to the patio and watched Bitsy at the table with her books, baby doll and Rosie. She seemed so content. *Somehow that kid knows when I'm tense and just calms down all by herself. She's never a problem. What a gem*, Madison thought.

Madison took a notepad and pen from her briefcase and went out on the patio with Bitsy.

"Do you want something to drink, honey?" she asked.

"I had a bottle of water before," she said, pointing to an empty water bottle. "I shared it with Joanie and Rosie."

"You're such a good little girl. When did you get the water?"

"While you were on the phone with Aunt Jo. Did you tell her about our house?"

"I did and she's so excited for us."

"Me, too," Bitsy said with a confirming shake of her head.

"I have to make a list of things I want to get from home so Aunt Jo can send them to us."

"How's she going to do that?"

"You know, honey, Aunt Jo is a wonderful friend. Wonderful friends do lots of nice things for other friends."

"When I go to school will I have friends?"

"Yes, honey. You'll have wonderful friends, too."

"Can I sit with you?" Bitsy asked, Joanie tucked under one arm.

"Of course," Madison said, sliding over to make room for the little girl. "Are you feeling okay?" she asked.

"Uh huh. I just want to sit with you. It's time for Joanie's nap."

Madison put her paper and pen on the small table next to her lounge chair and felt Bitsy snuggle into her side. She ran her fingers through the soft dark curls. There was plenty of time to make up the list for Jo. The shade of the overhang covered the occupants of the chair, the breeze drifted rather than blew, the rattling palm fronds were soothing and the noise of nearby traffic was a muted swishing of tires on the road next to the beach. *Not like the streets of Philadelphia*, Madison thought as she closed her eyes.

~ ~ ~

The next morning Madison finished up a brief note to accompany the list of furnishings she hoped Jo would send to her. She scanned the list. Was it too much? Then rationalized that if the truck was going to bring some things, how much really didn't matter. She also wondered if the list was complete and, most importantly, if this was too much to ask her friend. "She said she volunteered but did I manipulate that volunteerism?" Madison wondered. She re-read her note.

Hi, Jo. I can't imagine how I'm going to repay you for all this help. If you have any questions about anything on the list, call me. I'll talk to you tonight. I'm still riding on cloud nine, everything seems to be falling into place and I'm listening for the other shoe to drop.

You're the best friend in the world and I love you, *Madison*

She put the list and the note together and reached for her purse. "Come on, Bitsy. We've got to find a place to fax this to Aunt Jo," she called.

Bitsy was sitting Indian-style in front of the television set. "Just one more minute, Grandma? The lady is going to show the Word of the Day."

Madison perched on the arm of the sofa and watched the program Bitsy was watching. Kid Class, a morning program led by Miss Audrey, one of Bitsy's favorite shows and one Madison heartily approved of.

"The Word of the Day this morning is…" the television teacher paused dramatically pointing to a blank blackboard behind her. "Information", she chirped and the word magically appeared. "That means 'facts learned; news or knowledge'."

She turned to the camera. "Let's use the word in some sentences, shall we?" Taking a pointer she tapped on the magic screen behind her and read, "'I learned some interesting information today'; 'I need more information to make a decision'; 'Please send me information on the weather'" all of which suddenly appeared in sequence. "Now let's see if you can make up a sentence of your own."

Bitsy hit the power button and the television screen went black. "Don't you want to watch the rest of the show?" Madison asked. "It's only another five minutes."

"No, that's okay. The rest is mostly commercials and I just wanted to see what the Word for the Day was."

Madison stood and picked up her purse and the papers to be faxed. "Do you have a sentence using the word 'information'?" she asked, locking the door behind them.

"Let's see. Well, 'when Aunt Jo gets your *information*, she'll know what to send you." Bitsy laughed, covering her mouth with her fingers.

"That's very good, honey. I'm proud of you. But, Aunt Jo won't get this *information* unless we get going."

They were both laughing as they started down the stairs.

"What's the joke of the day," Dave said, meeting them at the second landing.

That sent them both into a fit of giggles and Madison struggled to contain her laughter. "There is no joke. It was just…" she giggled again.

"Just what?" Dave stood to one side.

"Well, we were discussing the 'word of the day' when you said 'joke of the day' and that made us laugh. I apologize if we seemed rude," she said, still grinning. "It just struck us funny."

Dave laughed softly. "And it was." He hesitated. "Well," he said. "Have a nice day."

"You too," Madison called starting down the next flight, noticing that Bitsy actually smiled at her nemesis. "We're going to hunt down a fax machine," she added, waiving her papers in the air.

"You can do that at the condo office. They charge a small fee but it's convenient," Dave called after them.

"Thanks," she called from the bottom level.

Madison went to the condo office and introduced herself to the older woman who sat behind a huge, unencumbered desk.

"I understand that I can get a fax sent."

"Sure," the woman said, standing. "You live here?"

"We're staying temporarily in Mr. Hendershot's unit. For three months," she added, remembering

Philip's statement that he had to rent to a tenant for a minimum of three months.

"Thought I didn't recognize you. Well, welcome to Gulf Shores." She put the pages into the fax machine and watched as they rolled through, one hand on her ample hip.

"Here you are. That's three dollars. A dollar a page."

Madison took the money from her wallet and handed it to the woman. "Can I also receive fax messages?" she asked.

"Sure but only during office hours. 10:00 a.m. to 4:00 p.m. There's a dollar a page charge for that too," she paused. "We have a twenty page limit per month," she added and handed Madison a business card. "Not many people in here use a fax though. Here's the information," she said and Madison suppressed a giggle. She looked quickly at Bitsy who had her fingers over her mouth.

Their next stop was Wal-Mart. As she pushed the cart along the aisles she tried to remember what the color of the two bathrooms in their new home were and was annoyed at herself for not making a note of that information. She smiled. *That word is going to haunt me all day*, she thought.

Her towels in the apartment in Philadelphia were a deep garnet for her bathroom and a very light yellow for the guest bathroom. "I think the towels Jo will be sending will be okay for the new house, honey," she said to Bitsy who was walking next to her. "Let's just get some small accessories."

She chose one yellow set and one dark pink set made up of a glass, a toothbrush holder and a pretty soap dish.

When she checked out, the cart contained those items plus new pillows for the beds, sunglasses for both of them, a new book for Bitsy, a pair of sandals for each of them and several items from the grocery department.

“Wow,” she said, putting the packages into the trunk of her car. “No matter what I come for when we go to Wal-Mart, we always seem to fill up the cart.”

“I love Wal-Mart,” Bitsy said.

“No wonder. You get something new every time we come. That, young lady, is going to have to stop. We might have to watch our pennies for a little while.”

“I don’t have any pennies.”

“Neither do I. It’s just a saying. It means we might have to be careful what we spend until we get settled in our new house.”

“Oh,” Bitsy said, and, looking into the rear view mirror, Madison saw a serious frown develop on the little girls forehead.

“Don’t worry. We’ll be fine. I just want to be a little cautious for a while.”

“I know,” she said knowingly.

CHAPTER TWENTY-SIX

I never see what has been done; I only see what remains to be done.

Marie Currie

Jo could be bossy and downright demanding when she wanted to and now was a time she wanted to. She cupped the phone to her ear and drummed a pencil on her desktop. "Don't tell me you can't do it. How many people do you move in January? Not many, I'll bet. I want the apartment packed and shipped by January thirtieth."

She listened to the person on the other line, giving him time to complain and then said, "It isn't impossible. Walking on the moon isn't impossible so why would packing a few items in boxes and shipping them off to Florida be impossible?"

She waited. "Well, January thirty-first will be okay. I'll meet your representative in the apartment this afternoon after four." She listened, still drumming the pencil. "No I can't make it any earlier. I, too, have to work."

At three thirty Jo entered Madison's apartment. She took a quick tour through the rooms, identifying the things on her list. "I can't see a problem, kitchen things, bath things, closets and drawers, I'll watch what they take," she muttered, opening and closing drawers and doors. In the kitchen she surveyed the cupboards and pantry. "I don't think she wants all that stuff in the pantry," she said, closing the door firmly.

In the dining room she surveyed the china in the hutch, knowing it was Madison's grandmother's. "Extra careful with that stuff," she said, making a check mark on the list.

At four o'clock she ushered the moving company representative in. When she saw it was a woman, she smiled to herself. *She'll understand,* she thought and smiled a welcome.

An appointment was made for Jo to be present on January twenty-eighth to supervise the move. After she watched the woman leave, Jo sat in the swivel rocker that would be shipped to Florida. "Damn that woman. I'm going to miss her…I already do." She blinked away threatening tears and took out her cell phone and dialed.

Thirteen hundred miles away Madison answered her phone.

"I'm sitting here in your apartment. Your things will be moved on January twenty-eighth and I'm getting sadder and sadder," she said.

"Oh, my God, Jo. You are a miracle worker. How did you do it?"

"With my usual dynamic presence, how else," she answered.

"You are something. How is it going to be accomplished?"

"I called three companies and chose the one with the most reliable record and the best price considering the short notice. They all acted like it wasn't possible to arrange this move without six weeks notice. I straightened them out. It wasn't really a problem and on January twenty-eighth I'll be here supervising."

"There's going to be a special place in heaven for you, Jo. How am I ever going to thank you?"

"Oh, they're pretty easy words. As a writer you should be able to come up with something."

They chatted, as always finding things to talk and laugh about. Jo did get a kick out of the information of the day/joke of the day meeting with the *dreaded neighbor*, a name she had singled out for him.

When she left Madison's apartment she paused in the doorway, then shook her head slowly and closed and locked the door.

~ ~ ~

Madison sat on a blanket and watched the waves etching a watery line along the beach. Bitsy, a few feet away, was digging in the sand and arranging portions of the castle she was building. Madison remembered the day she showed Bitsy how to build a castle. Her eyes misted for a brief moment. *These memories are so precious*, she thought.

There were fewer people on the beach this almost brisk morning and most of them jogged along the sandy stretch.

The breeze was cooler than usual and she and Bitsy wore light jackets over their bathing suits. Neither of them had ventured into the water…it was too cool today to get wet. She smiled as she thought about what the temperature must be back home and then bit her lip. Was she already thinking of Philadelphia as *back home*, a remote place distanced by more than just miles?

"Bitsy, do you know what today is?"

Not looking up, the child vigorously packed sand into her bucket with the back of her shovel. "Nope. What is today?"

"It's our one month anniversary. I ran into you…or you ran into me… I don't know which. Anyhow, it was December twenty-fourth when we met in the diner in the mountains. Do you remember?"

Bitsy put her shovel down carefully, dumped the packed sand next to a previously formed turret and turned around slowly. "I remember," she said, brushing her hair from her eyes. "Mommy told me to wait for you." She stood and walked to the edge of the blanket.

Madison held her breath for a moment. She never discouraged Bitsy to talk about or mention her mother but on the other hand she felt that for now it was best to let the subject be totally controlled by Bitsy. If she wanted to talk about her mother, Madison encouraged her.

"Let's brush some of that sand off first before you sit down," she said, taking a towel and dusting sand from the child's tanned legs.

"One month?" Bitsy said, sitting next to her grandmother.

"Thirty days. That was December twenty-fourth and this is January twenty-fourth It seems longer, doesn't it?" She didn't think it was the time to go into the variations of days in the months now. That would come later. She smiled looking forward to another teaching opportunity and slid her arm around Bitsy's shoulders.

Bitsy scooted closer.

"We've done lots of things in that month haven't we?"

"We lived in lots of places," Bitsy said. "The mountains, your 'partment in Philadelphia, motel houses when we drove to Florida and Mr. Philip's condo," she said, counting the places on sandy fingers. "Now we're going to have a new house," she looked up into Madison's face. "Are we going to stay there a long time?"

Recognizing the uncertainty that tainted Bitsy's voice, Madison realized that this hectic change of residences must have had an impact on the little girl she hadn't acknowledge or even considered. As long as they were together that was what had selfishly been important to Madison.

"Of course we are, honey. For at least a year anyhow because I signed a lease for that long. Who knows? Maybe we'll be here for years and years."

The ease with which Madison committed to years and years surprised her. Surprised her but didn't dismay her.

"Soon we'll move into the house on Thunder Creek Road. Aunt Jo is sending us furniture, blankets, towels and all kinds of things we'll need in our new home." She squeezed the little girl's shoulders and felt her rest her head against her side.

Pushing herself away and rising to her knees, Bitsy looked intently at Madison. “Am I going to that school?”

“Let’s see, honey. Why don’t we visit it first before we make any decisions? Maybe we need more information,” she said with a smile, remembering the word of the day. Of course, there had been more words of the day since then but somehow that first shared memory was the one Madison remembered most.

“Okay. Can I finish my castle?”

“Oh, sure. Let’s go to Wendy’s for lunch today. A baked potato will be good on our cool, winter day,” she said, laughing. Her heart swelled as she heard Bitsy’s giggle and watched her squat down on the gritty sand and return to her castle building.

“This is going to be the best castle ever, Grandma. Better than the one the water washed away.”

That evening after bedside prayers and when Bitsy was safely asleep, Madison took her coffee out on the patio. She had her pjs on, her robe tied around her waist. Still the night air was cool and she sipped the hot coffee, warming her hands on the mug.

“What a gorgeous night,” she whispered. The sky overhead was clear and a million stars twinkled. The breeze was coming from the east so the building protected her; still the temperature was the lowest she had experienced since moving down.

She sat at the table, the umbrella furled above her. “Another great day,” she murmured. Her mind recalled the activities; beach in the morning, lunch out celebrating their anniversary, a short trip to the new house to measure windows for curtains even though she wasn’t sure what she wanted yet. “It seems a shame to cover the windows, Bitsy,” she’d said as they left Thunder Creek Road. “I love the sunshine steaming in. Still, we have to have a bit of privacy here and there. We’ll see about curtains after we’ve moved in.”

On the way back to the condo they had stopped at the post office and mailed in the completed application for Bitsy's birth certificate. "Let's hope that works without any complications," she murmured.

"What complications?" Bitsy asked and Madison remembered her vow not to put thoughts into words.

"Oh, nothing really, honey. Let's just hope that everything goes well. And," she said, taking the child's hand, "it will. I have a good feeling." But the good feeling wasn't actually quite up to the level she'd hoped for. *More like a pray-this-works feeling*, she thought.

That was all earlier and now she forced herself to push the conflicts aside and enjoy the winter evening; the winter evening where she could sit outside in her pajamas. She laughed softly to herself and finished her coffee, the mug already cool in her hands.

Sliding the doors open, she pulled the drapes across the windows and settled into a chair. Somehow the cream-colored leather sofa seemed intimidating to her and she rarely sat on it, nor did she allow Bitsy to climb up on the soft, shiny cushions. With her eyes closed she recapped what lied ahead. Before the moving truck arrived she would pack up their belongings here ready to move. But, she thought, *Philip will probably be here before that. Too bad we couldn't have been moved into our new home before he came down. Then he wouldn't have had to 'bunk in with Dave' as he put it.* She didn't notice that her heart thumped an extra beat when she thought of Philip's arrival and, if she had, she would have discounted it as just another consideration to organize in her head that had absolutely nothing to do with her heart.

Yesterday, she and Bitsy had picked out a small breakfast set that fit perfectly next to the windows in the breakfast room. *What fun that had been*, she thought. Finding a perfect set, a small square table with two chairs that were listed as a 'honeymoon' set. The set was light oak and the tabletop was covered with white ceramic tiles. *Honeymoon set,* indeed, she laughed. *It will be delivered tomorrow, making for another opportunity to visit our new house.*

Later in the afternoon, she'd spoken to both Jo and Lolly, separately, of course, and she remembered they had both commented on her improved attitude. "That's because I'm happy," she'd said. "I've found a wonderful house, things are falling into place and I have high hopes of getting information about Bitsy's mother. Whatever Walt finds, I know I can deal with." She paused, "And, I'm in love."

She heard them gasp. "In love with Bitsy," she hastened to add.

Now in the quiet dim room, Madison paused a moment to remember their cautions not to get too complacent. Not that either was predicting problems, but until it was over they advised caution.

"If only," she whispered. If only what? What if Bitsy's mother was never found? Would she live with that worry hanging over her forever? *And if she's found...dead...is that the answer I'm looking for?* A shiver crept over her and she pulled the robe closer together, covering her legs but the chill came from inside. She noted silently that she hadn't addressed the possibility that Lily Rose Smith might be found alive and well…and wanting her daughter returned. Madison rose, checked the lock on the front door and then peeked in at Bitsy.

When she slipped between the sheets in the elegant yet masculine master bedroom, her mind and heart welcomed her prayers. She waited quietly for the peace that conversing with God always brought to her.

"Please, dear Lord, keep us safe. Continue to guide me in the right direction. You know all I want is to make life better for Bitsy, to love and protect her. I pray this is your wish too. She is a miracle…one of your miracles and I thank you for all the many blessings you have provided us." She prayed silently for several minutes, ending as always with the Lord's Prayer even though she had already led Bitsy through that earlier. When she wiggled into her usual position for sleep, her mind and heart were lighter and she pictured a serene and happy life for both of them ahead of her. Today has been good; tomorrow could be even better and the future…? Even though that remained an unanswered question, Madison felt calm and safe as sleep overtook her.

~ ~ ~

For the past two weeks, Walt had explored every avenue looking for Lily Rose Smith, even if they were more like dark alleys than avenues. His covert visit to Mr. Mo's produced nothing. Nothing that he wanted to stir up by asking questions. No, he'd just listened. He'd nursed a sandwich and drank endless cups of coffee listening to the lunchtime gossip. The main topic today had been a drug bust and roundup of prostitutes, all of which seemed to be ho-hum occurrences somewhere in the vicinity. An occasional knifing was almost too bland to deserve comment.

His police buddies hadn't found Lily's name in any other jurisdiction for any crimes. He thought about using Bitsy's DNA to search for her mother but decided that was too risky. First of all, he didn't now if Madison would want to submit the child to a test and then where would he look? Lily hadn't been listed anywhere as a victim of violence although he suspected she'd had her share of violence in one form or the other. If he could get to her medical records where would that lead? He already knew she was very ill and he already knew she was the child's mother. It was very iffy that by knowing her DNA it would lead to her whereabouts.

As he drove home, the file he'd set up for the case rested on the passenger seat. While stopped at a red light, he flipped the file open and gazed at the mug shot again. "Where the hell are you, Lily?"

He sighed, closed the file and moved forward on the green light. He thought of the case and then thought of Jo. Maybe he'd call her. See if she was free for a drink tonight. It would be nice to sit across the table from a smart, attractive woman for an hour or two. Not that he thought it would go beyond conversation and a drink. He'd tried that route several years ago but somehow either Jo was involved or just not interested in any possible involvement. "A pleasant woman's company is enough sometimes," he uttered to himself. After all, he wasn't exactly a Don Juan either. The love of his life had departed this world far too soon and much too tragically and he didn't want to think about that. Other ladies often brought those memories back. He pulled into his parking space, flipped his phone open and dialed Jo's number at the newspaper.

~ ~ ~

Walt sat across from Jo in a booth at Wrangler's Bar and Grill, a place he'd frequented often in the past. It was only three blocks from his old precinct house and he had never entered in the evening and not found at least one old buddy to commiserate with.

"Thought Tony would never leave," he said to Jo with a smile.

"He's an old friend. I didn't mind him joining us for a while."

"Yeah, well I did. I can talk to that old dog anytime. It's a real job getting you to come out for a drink once in a while."

"I'm not trying to be difficult, Walt. You know that. I've been extra busy lately and that's good. It pads the paycheck." She stirred her old fashioned slowly. She enjoyed Walt's company. He was older than she was by a good ten years but ever since they'd met years ago, she was taken by his calm honesty and sincerity. She smiled inwardly betting he'd hate those adjectives to be applied to his name.

"What's new with your friend, Madison?" Walt asked.

Jo was pleased that he'd broached the subject. When she'd accepted his invitation she had cautioned herself not to pry into his investigation unless he opened the door. He'd just opened the door.

"She's doing well. They've found a place to rent. She and Bitsy were staying in a friend's condo temporarily. I know she ordered the birth certificate.

Things are going well for her but I know this business of Bitsy's mother is weighing heavily on her mind."

She smiled and watched Walt lower his head for a moment. "That's a problem, Jo. I wasn't going to talk about the damned case but it's never far from my mind." He shrugged and pushed his nearly empty glass away. "I've run into more blank walls than I've ever had in a case. But, I know there has to be an answer. It's just finding it that's getting to me."

Jo reached across the tables and drew her fingers over his clasped hands. "You can only do your best, Walt, and I'm sure you have. Maybe there aren't any answers to the question, 'Where is Lily Rose Smith?'"

"I've asked myself that damned question a thousand times. Maybe if I go over the whole thing from the beginning I'll discover something I overlooked."

"Do what you have to, Walt, but no one is going to blame you if you can't find her."

"What's the very first thing that happened? You know her better than anyone. What was Madison doing?"

Jo thought a moment and then tipped back her glass and swallowed the last of the drink.

"Want another?" Walt asked, and Jo nodded. He signaled the waitress and ordered another drink for each of them. "How about a sandwich?"

"I don't know…are you hungry?"

"I am. I had lunch but it was pretty awful and I wasn't eating I was listening." He told her about his earlier visit to Mr. Mo's. "Didn't learn a damned thing but then I really didn't think I would." He smiled across the table at her. "Have a sandwich with me?"

They poured over the plastic coated menu on the table and when the waitress delivered the second round of drinks they both ordered Philly cheese steaks.

"Now where were we?" Jo asked, centering her drink on the paper coaster.

"Go back to the very beginning," Walt coached.

Jo squeezed her shoulders up toward her ears, easing a knot that had formed earlier in the day when she was hammering away to make a deadline. "Well, maybe the beginning really doesn't have anything to do with Bitsy." Jo began to relate the story of Madison's romantic break-up. "She was running away and didn't realize the storm would be so bad. She was headed to a friend's cottage way up in the mountains. When the snow got really bad she stopped in a diner to get a cup of coffee and take a little break. Driving was apparently pretty bad.

"The diner was almost empty and the guy who was running the place was pretty mad at her."

"Why?"

"Well, it was Christmas Eve and he was waiting to close. He told her someone had left a little girl there to wait for her grandmother. When Madison stepped into the diner and a strange little girl ran up to her shouting, 'Grandma', he thought Madison was her grandmother. It's Christmas Eve, there's a terrible storm outside and he's stuck there waiting for the little girl's grandmother to come. Naturally when he thought she was the grandmother, he left and she had to take Bitsy with her. By that time the phone towers were down and for the next couple of days they were stuck in the cottage in the mountains."

Walt closed his eyes, trying to recreate the scene Jo had just spoken of. His hands twirled the glass in front of him. "I feel as if I'm missing something. Something that's right there but I can't get to it." He sighed and took a sip of the amber liquid. "Thanks, Jo. You've given me a couple of hints I'll look into. I'll have to see if I can open another door somewhere. There has to be an answer," he said, his fingers gently stroking the back of her hand.

When the sandwiches arrived the couple in the booth looked as if they were celebrating something and perhaps there were and didn't know it. Jo laughed at his jokes and he was interested in her latest project. For two hours they shared a good time and when they separated Jo planted a soft kiss on his cheek, but he pulled her toward him and pressed his lips on hers, a soft, tender kiss. “Nothing funny, sweetheart. Have a great night. I’ll keep in touch and if I find anything…well, we’ll celebrate again.” He patted her back and then walked with her to her car parked a block away.

CHAPTER TWENTY-SEVEN

A pessimist sees difficulty in every opportunity.
An optimist sees opportunity in every difficulty.
Winston Churchill

Madison checked her list and smiled. Everything on the list had been taken care of and it was January twenty-sixth. Philip had called last night letting her know he would be here on the thirtieth. *Four days,* she thought, sipping her iced tea as she sat on the patio. Bitsy had opted to stay inside and watch television. Madison glanced through the windows and saw her sitting with her legs in a yoga position, eyes glued to the television screen.

The furniture was scheduled to arrive on February fifth, even though Jo had threatened bodily harm, that was the earliest they could promise. It didn't matter; it wouldn't change Philip's plans or interfere with them, he'd already made arrangements with Dave, who was surprisingly pleasant every time their paths crossed. Already there were packed boxes in both her bedroom and Bitsy's. The move should be relatively easy. Twice they had visited the house on Thunder Creek Road, measuring and picturing the furniture she planned to add and mentally rearranging what was already there. Mr. and Mrs. McWalters couldn't be more accommodating, already offering whatever help they could to make their move easy.

Madison sighed a sigh of contentment. *Is this really all going to fall into place?* A frown momentarily creased her brow. The only thing unsettled was the matter of finding Bitsy's mother…or what happened to her. Every day she found herself wishing the telephone would ring and Walt would be calling with any information. Again the nagging uncertainty overwhelmed her. *Will it ever end*? she thought. *Will what end?* she asked herself. *The search? Or the doubt? And what doubt do I have? Not that I want and love, Bitsy. No, no matter what, I'll do everything and anything I can to make that dream a reality. I just pray we'll find out what happened to Lily Rose, or where she is,* she added, reluctantly.

Just then she heard the door sliding open and looked up to see Bitsy standing in the open doorway. "Grandma," she said, stepped forward and threw up on the patio floor.

Madison flew from her chair, tipping the glass of iced tea she had put on the floor next to the lounge chair. "Bitsy," she screamed, snatching the child into her arms.

"I'm sorry, Grandma," the little girl sobbed.

"Don't be sorry, sweetheart." Madison stepped over the mess and hurried down the hallway to the bathroom. As she carried the little girl, she felt a hot forehead buried into her neck. "I think you have a fever. Do you feel like you're going to be sick again?"

"I don't know," she whimpered. "I'm sorry."

"Please don't say that, honey. You couldn't help it." She ran cool water on a face cloth and wiped Bitsy's face and neck. Then, carrying her to her bedroom, she laid the child on her bed. "Tell me how you feel, Bitsy?" she cooed, stroking the hot forehead.

"I feel…sick," she said, her voice trembling.

Madison sat next to her. Never had she felt more helpless that at that moment. "Do you want a drink of water?" she asked.

Bitsy shook her head from side to side.

"Are you sleepy?"

The child nodded, closing her eyes.

"Try and rest honey. I'll be right here. If you need me call, okay?"

Bitsy nodded again, eyes still closed. She rolled on her side, curling her legs up and sliding one hand under her pillow.

Madison tiptoed out but paused in the doorway watching the drowsy child a few moments. She appeared to be asleep already.

What can it be? Something she ate? We ate the same things and I feel fine. Madison tried to remember what her mother had done in a situation like this but nothing came to her. *Surely Lolly and I must have had upset stomachs*, she thought, her mind rushing from thought to thought. "Lolly! She'll know what to do," she murmured rushing into the living room for her telephone. But the scene just outside the open door brought her to a halt. "I have to take care of that first," she said grimacing at the thought then hurrying to the kitchen for a bucket and some rags she knew were in the pantry.

Fifteen minutes later she stood in the kitchen her phone to her ear. When she heard the receiver on the other end being picked up, she croaked, "Lolly, I need help."

"What's the matter," Lolly shouted.

"It's Bitsy, she's sick."

"Sick? How sick? What happened?"

"I don't know; she threw up. She's hot. What do I do?" The panic in Madison's voice was palpable.

"Hey, don't panic, that never solved anything. Tell me what happened. Calm down!"

"She threw up on the patio, on the tiled patio. Well, it's not really tiled but it's stone and… I think she has a fever."

"Think? Have you taken it?"

"No. I don't have a thermometer. Not here, it's back in my medicine cabinet in Philadelphia."

"Well, welcome to motherhood. Never go anywhere without a thermometer, baby aspirin and some Pedialyte."

"I'm not a mother," Madison whispered. "I'm a grandmother."

Lolly didn't respond immediately, then said sadly. "That's the problem. Grandmother's have already gone through fevers, chickenpox and upset stomachs. You haven't." She listened for Madison's response but there was none. "Listen, it's probably just something very minor. What did she eat?"

"The same things I did," Madison moaned. "And, I'm not sick."

"Well, that doesn't make any difference. Kid's stomachs react to stuff differently. Just keep an eye on her. Could be a little virus, or maybe too much heat or activity. It's doesn't take much to upset a tiny tummy. What's she doing now?"

"Sleeping, I think," Madison said, walking through the living room and tiptoeing down the hallway to Bitsy's door. "Yes," she whispered, "she's sleeping."

"Good. That just might fix it. Be sure she gets enough liquids. Watch her when she gets up and if she still seems sick go the drugstore and buy a thermometer and something to calm her stomach. Get a thermometer even if she's better. Geeze, I'll bet you don't even have baby aspirin do you? If she looks or feels sicker than when you put her to bed, go to one of those walk-in clinics. You'll have to get a doctor, though. All children need checkups and come up with these things from time to time. It's part of the whole package, Sisty. You bought in and you're going to have to go through it all. Just wait until she's a teenager."

Madison slumped into a chair in the living room. "Thanks for the warning."

"It isn't a warning, just a fact of life, Sisty. Kids do damn fool things and need rescuing; they get sick over nothing; later she'll probably cry over nothing. It's part of the whole picture. You wanted it."

"I still do. Thanks, Lolly. I guess I did panic. She's been such a healthy little girl the whole time, I never thought about her getting sick. God, what if it was something serious. I was scared."

"The whole time is just over a month. That's not a complete picture. Take it as it comes and call me whenever you need to. I didn't mean to sound flippant but I've been there done that and you haven't."

"Chickenpox?" Madison questioned.

"That and measles and mumps. Has she had her shots?"

"I don't know."

"You need a doctor. And, be honest with him. Tell him you have absolutely no records of what health care she's had in the past. You'll have to make something up, I guess."

"I already have. If I need to I'm going to say that her mother was my daughter. That she went wild, had Bitsy and then drifted away and I have custody of her now."

"Can you back up that custody bit?"

"Not really, but I ordered her birth certificate. That might help."

"What did the birth certificate say?"

"That Lily Rose Smith was her mother and the father was unknown."

Madison heard her sister's harrumph. "It happens today," she said.

"I know. Much too often. I worry about Caitlin."

"She's not…"

"Sexually active? God, I hope not. We've given her all the information we can. Life is such an uncertainty with teens."

"What about Jason?"

"He's…he's two years younger than Caity. Dad's had the birds and bees talk and I know they have some pretty good sex education in the schools here. They're pretty liberal in being open about sex, I still haven't decided if that's a good thing or not. There's a program for unwed teenagers at the schools and even daycare so the mothers can finish school."

"Gosh, I never thought about any of that," Madison whispered.

"Well, it's on the horizon, honey, so watch out. You'll have to do some research. I have a couple of pretty good books. I'll send them to you."

"Thanks, Lolly. You're such a good sister."

"I know. What would you do without me? Only do what you damned well please…but that's okay, Sisty. You're a good sister, too, and over the years I've come crying to you. I'm happy that you seem more content than you have in years. These things, puking on a tiled patio…they'll come and go. You'll be okay."

"Thanks for everything," Madison said, trying to remember when Lolly had needed her help. Nothing came to mind.

Ending their conversation with promises to call tomorrow, she tiptoed back down the hall and stood in the open doorway watching her granddaughter. "Whatever happens, sweetheart, you'll always be my granddaughter," she said, turning away and wiping tears unashamedly from her cheeks.

For two days Bitsy wasn't her usual bubbly self, and Madison spent hours every days watching her carefully and calling Lolly frequently. Finally she felt comfortable that this was nothing to worry about. As Lolly said, "kids get sick over nothing, you have to learn the signs. Motherhood is a cope and clean up science."

It's not easy, she thought, brushing Bitsy's hair from her forehead, a covert way to feel if she was feverish. Of course, the same day Bitsy was ill, as soon as she woke up, Madison had rushed out to the nearest drug store and stocked up on things the pharmacist, Alice W. Hawkins, R.PH, recommended she have on hand. She also bought a thermometer but she remembered the pharmacist's caution about not taking a child's temperature too often. "Just keep an eye on her," she said, looking down at the pale little girl clutching her grandmother's purse strap.

Madison wondered about the smile that twitched at the sides of Ms. Hawkins' mouth. *Did she think I was a bit old to be so unprepared for a child's illness,* she thought, going on the defensive; but then perhaps she was being a bit sensitive whenever anyone thought Bitsy was her daughter and she had to explain that she was her granddaughter.

Bitsy improved steadily, although slow at first. The following morning, Bitsy didn't want to eat anything and Madison coaxed some soda and saltines into her, pursuant to Lolly's suggestion. Later Bitsy graduated to toast and weak tea and this morning she asked for cereal. "Feeling better?"

"Uh huh. Can we go to the beach today?"

"Let's wait one more day. I thought we'd go back to our new house and take another look. I also want to find the library and get us library cards. You love books and so do I so I think we should belong to the library. Have you ever been to a library?"

"No, I don't think so. They have books?"

"Oh, honey," Madison said, lifting the little girl high in the air. "You never saw so many books. Come on, let's get cleaned up and be on our way, okay?"

On the drive back from the new house, where Madison had stopped in to see Carol McWalters to get the name of a pediatrician she could refer her to and directions to the nearest library, Madison quizzed Bitsy.

"Tell me, honey, have you had any shots?"

"Shots?"

"You know. Injections at a doctor's office." She looked in the rearview mirror to see Bitsy's face puckered with confusion.

"I don't think I ever went to a doctor's office. Mommy took me to a clinic but that was once when I had a bad cold and the stuff Missy gave me didn't work."

She doesn't remember a doctor. What kind of mother was she? But she answered her own question…*a troubled mother, probably young and inexperienced in the things she should have known, not that you're very bright about childhood illnesses. Still, basic health care...but, I guess she didn't have health insurance.* Another worry popped into her head. How would she get Bitsy on her health insurance?

"You don't remember getting any shots?"

"Nope. I saw a television show once where everyone had to get shots because a bad dog bit them. Yuck. It looked awful."

"Okay. Well, we're going to have to look into that."

"I don't need shots, do I?"

"You may, honey, but they don't really hurt and they are good for you."

"But I'm better. I won't throw up again, I promise."

Madison laughed. "You don't need shots because of that, honey. You will have to have them before you go to school, though."

Again she studied the child in the back seat. Puzzlement skewed her face and Madison smiled. "Shots are just part of life, Bitsy. Over and done with quickly. Everyone gets them at one time or another."

"Do you need shots?"

"No. Not any more, at least not that I know of. But I had to have them when I was a little girl. And, once when I went on a trip to Europe after college, I had to have three."

"Wow," Bitsy said. "Let's not go to U-rope."

Madison pulled into the parking lot at the library branch nearest to Thunder Creek Road. She mentally congratulated herself on checking out the location first and then finding out what she needed to become a patron of the library. She noted that the cross street was one that she would take to go to the Collier Country-Day Academy; if she chose to look into that. *So many things to think about*, she thought, getting Bitsy from the back seat of her car.

Inside, if Bitsy was staring at the Grand Canyon for the first time, her face couldn't have been more awe-struck. They were standing at the registration counter in the library and while Madison was getting their library cards, Bitsy wandered around in a circle, eyes taking in shelf after shelf of books.

She moved to stand in front of a display case filled with brightly colored pieces of clothing and rough tools and bowls made of wood. "That's our current collection of native Florida Indians…the Seminoles," the librarian called to her. "We change our display every month. Next month it will be exotic shells from Sanibel Island. Have you been there?" she asked Madison, handing her two library cards.

"No we haven't but it sounds like we should. We haven't been here in Florida very long. Thanks," she said.

"Well, I'm happy that you had a copy of your yearly rental lease with you. That way there is no charge for the cards. We have other plans for our guests who come to Florida for shorter periods of time and can't establish a residency." She smiled at Madison. "Enjoy your visit to our library."

"Where is the children's library?" Madison asked.

"Just down that hall. The double doors are closed but just push them open and go on in. We keep them closed because sometimes the children get excited when a special program is being given." The librarian was gray-haired and matronly and her smile was warm and friendly and she looked lovingly at Bitsy. "Your daughter might be interested in some of our children's programs. Just ask the children's librarian for a flier on the current programs."

"Bitsy is my granddaughter and thanks for your help. I'm sure she's going to be interested in the programs. She loves books," Madison said, proudly.

Bitsy was enrolled in two events at the library that day. Of course, Madison had to ensure her that she would be in the library waiting for her. She wondered if Bitsy had been difficult for Lily Rose to leave at daycare because she obviously didn't want to be away from Madison. "Did you like to go to daycare, Bitsy?" Madison asked as they were leaving.

"I cried sometimes, but Mommy promised to come and get me…and she did until…"

"Well, that time was different, Bitsy. She knew she had to go somewhere very important and she didn't leave you alone…not for very long, she left you for me. I came and got you, remember?"

"Yes," she said, her voice muffled.

Madison hurried to change the conversation. "Well, I think you'll really enjoy the Wednesday Read to Me class, don't you? And then there's a movie on Friday morning. That's the day Philip is going to arrive but he said not until later in the day."

"I like you to read to me, too," Bitsy said, guardedly.

"And I love to read to you, honey. But this will be extra reading and you'll be with other children. I think you'll like that." She pulled into their parking place, reminding herself that on Friday she would have to park in a guest space and let Philip have his parking space.

They climbed the stairs instead of taking the elevator, which they now used only if they were carrying groceries. "The exercise will do us good," she'd rationalized to Bitsy. *I wonder,* she thought as she plodded up the stairs, *if I'm going to have a problem with Bitsy going to school, whether it's the academy or public school in the fall? She seems afraid to let me out of her sight.* Her anger flared as she opened the door to the condo. *Well, that's because her mother dumped her. If I could speak to that woman I'd give her a piece of my mind.*

As she put the books they had checked out on the coffee table, she looked at Bitsy, already paging through one of the books she had chosen. *No,* she thought, *if I could speak to Lily Rose I'd thank her for producing such a wonderful little girl. I won't ever let her go, but I'd thank her.*

She ruffled Bitsy's curls. Realistic thoughts? She didn't know but she said a silent prayer of thanks and request for guidance as she settled into a chair just to watch the little girl.

CHAPTER TWENTY-EIGHT

For every failure, there's an alternative course of action. You just have to find it. When you come to a roadblock, take a detour.

Mary Kay Ash

Walt shifted his coffee mug to the other side of the desk, next to his cell phone. The top was neat, much neater than any desk he'd had while a cop and he enjoyed the uncluttered area where he could write his columns and keep his investigative files.

This morning his laptop was to the right, unopened, his cell phone was to the left and one lone manila file folder lay centered between those two items. He tilted back in the chair he'd bought at a thrift store, the chair that squeaked at his every move ever since he brought it into the living room where he'd designated this corner as his office. He'd also purchased the small desk from the same thrift store, both several months after retiring from the police force.

He sat in the chair, and with one hand he raised the mug to his lips and with the other he flipped open the file on the desktop. Just yesterday he'd changed the tag from Missing Woman to Lily Rose Smith.

After reviewing his notes for the umpteenth time, he leaned back rewarded by the squeak he anticipated. *Got to oil this damned chair*, he thought, draining the last of the black coffee from his mug. He closed his eyes and mentally went over all the notes he'd just read. The words raced across the backs of his closed eyelids like the ticker tape that ran along the television screen when the news was covering the stock market.

Walt leaned forward with a thump. "Damn there has to be something I'm missing," he grumbled, looking into his empty mug. He rose and paced across the living room in the one bedroom apartment he and his wife, Gloria, had leased right after their whirlwind courtship and marriage. *Thirty-four years ago*. He paused and looked around the room. Nothing much had changed since her sudden, untimely death. Nothing except the addition of his desk, which stood where her small piano had been. Walt grimaced and returned to the desk. "Don't think about that. Twenty years and you still go back." For a moment the old hollow feeling returned as he remembered the day she died. *A bust gone bad*; *she was a good cop, too.*

He picked up the mug shot and stared at the face of Lily Rose Smith. *Why? Why can't I find you?* He thought about Jo and what she had told him about the case, about Madison, a voice on the telephone, he re-heard her anxiety, her need to find this woman.

Suddenly he closed the file and picked up the phone. He dialed eleven numbers and waited as the phone rang.

When Madison answered, he said, "This is Walt. I have a question for you. Where was that diner where you and the little girl came together?"

He heard her gasp thirteen hundred miles away, then she said, "I'm not really sure where it was but I know I'd gone past the road that leads to Kleinsville and it was before you get to the turn off for Little Hollow. It was almost dark and snowing hard. I remember it was on the right going north."

"Okay," he said. "Thanks."

"Wait. Do you have something? A lead or something?"

"No, just going to go back to the place where this all started."

"But the man I saw that day insisted he didn't see Bitsy's mother," she faltered, *was this a break? The break they needed?*

"I know but sometimes if you prod them just right they might remember something. It's a chance. Was there anyone else that you know of that might have been there when Lily dropped the kid off?" In Philadelphia, Walt smiled at the first name comfort he'd assumed during this search. In Florida, Madison grimaced. Bitsy's mother had become a real person with a first name that was easy to use, but still remained a mystery. A complete mystery.

"No one that I know of. There must have been customers, waitresses..."

"Well, thanks for the help. I'll let you know if anything comes of this. Don't hang your hat on it too quick. I've been stumped so far but who knows, something might break when you least expect it. Hang in there. I'll be in touch."

Madison folded her phone and put it next to her laptop. She'd been working at the kitchen table so there were papers and research books, scattered over the table and the countertop. Her eyes scanned the screen to re-read what she had just written but her mind wasn't where her eyes were. *Did Walt have a new clue? Was this going to help find Lily?*

"Bitsy, what are you doing," she called.

"I'm fixing Joanie lunch," she answered from the patio.

"Okay, honey. I'll be finished in a few minutes and then we'll go to the library for your Read to Me class."

For the rest of the day Madison's mind kept coming back to Walt's telephone call. *What could he find in that diner? I was there for such a short time. I don't even know the name of the diner or the man I'd been speaking to. All I can remember is being so angry with him and annoyed at having to take Bitsy along with me.* She tried desperately to relive the time and became angry with herself for not being able to remember much.

"I wouldn't know him if I met him face to face this afternoon," she moaned as she paged through a magazine in the library, waiting for Bitsy. She'd exhausted herself with the struggle to understand what might be happening. She'd tried to rationalize…*after all I was running away from a tense situation. My mind wasn't functioning on anything but getting away, breaking the ties with Jim.*

She looked up. Wasn't that strange? It was the first time she'd thought of Jim in almost a month. Madison lips lifted at the corners of her mouth in a small, discrete smile.

That's because you're happy…in spite of everything you're happier than you've ever been. That's what comes from dreams that come true. She laughed softly and looked up to see the librarian watching her. "Something funny?" she called.

"Something pleasant," Madison answered as the double doors to the children's library swung open and Bitsy ran to her side.

"Was that fun?" Madison said, hugging the little girl.

"Oh, Grandma, it was so good," she said, throwing her arms wide. "We had two stories and then Miss Eileen had pictures and a stuffed green turtle, he wasn't real, just a toy. We learned all about turtles, too." Bitsy held a piece of paper. "And, look. I drew a turtle. He's green," she said, thrusting the paper at Madison.

"It's wonderful," she said, standing. "And look at all the friends you were with in there. I'm so happy you had a good time."

Madison watched other children hurrying down the short hallway to be greeted with mothers and fathers who were waiting. The hubbub was a pleasant combination of excited children's voices and inquiring parents. She felt so at home, it shocked her.

As they walked to the car…she walking and Bitsy bouncing like a bubble caught in a breeze, she sighed. "Just enjoy the day," she counseled herself, "and look forward to tomorrow and all our tomorrows."

Bitsy didn't pay any attention to what she was muttering. She jumped into the back seat and waited to be buckled in, carefully holding her picture.

They drove home, Madison listening and Bitsy chattering about turtles and a boy named Mark and a girl named Betsy. She giggled, "She's Betsy and I'm Bitsy. Miss Eileen laughed," she said, her eyes snapping with delight, her cheeks once again colored with a rosy hue.

~ ~ ~

An atlas, opened to Pennsylvania, lay on the seat next to Walt. He'd carefully gone over the route Madison had described and reckoned he must be ten or fifteen miles from the diner.

The scene around him was typical for north central Pennsylvania, thick woods on either side of the road, broken occasionally by a dirt road that disappeared from sight. Tall, thick green pines and fir trees stood in stark contrast to the gray thatch of bare branches the maples and birches made in this nature collage. In a couple of months green sprouts would soften the hillsides with a harbinger of the lush green vistas he knew would follow. He loved Philadelphia but going up into the Pennsylvania mountains was something he also enjoyed. It was a soul-cleansing experience. How could such a pristine paradise be the setting for turmoil, trouble and...he hesitated...even death? Was that what he expected? He exhaled a deep breath through pursed lips, as if blowing out a candle on a birthday cake.

Walt slowed as he came to a wide curve and whistled softly when he saw a shiny aluminum diner set in a paved parking lot ahead on the right. "Bingo," he said, slowing and putting on his turn signal. When he pulled into the lot he glanced at the clock in the dashboard. Ten fifty two. The roadside sign identified the diner as 'Riegel's Place—Good Country Food.' There were three cars and a pickup truck in the lot.

Sliding out of his car, Walt tucked a copy of the mug shot into his inside jacket pocket. The wind caught his hair, whipping his thick gray mop into an untidy thatch. As he hurried to the door he used his fingers as a temporary comb.

Once inside the scene was typical of many country diners in Pennsylvania. A long Formica counter ran the length of the diner to his right, an army of red leatherette stools marched along a parallel line next to it. Booths, padded seats and backs of the same red material lined up along the front windows. Stainless steel behind the counter gleamed spotlessly.

Walt straddled a stool near the cash register that occupied the end of the countertop. A waitress, bone thin with white hair tucked into a net with a paper tiara over her brow, smiled at him and pushed a plastic sheeted menu along the counter. “Coffee?” she asked, a broad smile splitting her lips and reveling good dentures.

“Yes, black please.”

“Specials are up on the board,” she said, pointing to a chalkboard hung over the stainless steel divider between the grill and the kitchen.

The first two items were breakfast and he chose one of them. “I’ll have the short stack with bacon,” he said, sliding the unread menu to one side. He watched as she scribbled his order on a small ticket and pushed it over a spike next to the grill.

A tall young man dressed in white tee shirt, matching pants and a huge white apron manned the grill. He wore another paper crown, this one with a mesh insert over his hair.

Walt watched as he poured three generous dollops of batter on the grill and separated some bacon from a huge pile near the end of the cooking surface.

Country western music provided a nice background, not too loud so the diners couldn’t talk and loud enough that he could recognize Randy Travis’ voice. When his food was placed in front of him, his mouth watered. The pancakes were perfect, the bacon crisp but not burned and the waitress, whose name was Milly according to the badge she had pinned to her uniform, filled his cup with hot coffee.

When he leaned back, his plate cleaned, Milly hustled up to him. "Anything else?" she asked. "We have homemade apple pie, just out of the oven this morning."

"Couldn't eat another thing," Walt said, rubbing his stomach. "I'll let you top up my coffee though."

He twisted on his stool and looked at the other diners. In a booth near the rear exit he saw three men. They had been there when he came in. They wore thick plaid shirts, camouflage caps and as he caught some of their conversation he noted they were anxiously awaiting the opening of fishing season two months away.

Further along the counter, two elderly men sat nursing coffee, sharing a newspaper and talking about local news.

Two women with woolen hats pulled down over their foreheads left shortly following his arrival and a family of mother, father and three children, one in a high chair positioned at the end of the booth, were loudly enjoying an outing.

The last booth held two younger women, coats and scarves piled on the bench next to them. They were engaged in a quiet conversation and Walt couldn't quite put a label on them. Going shopping later? Just out of the house for a while? They didn't seem to belong here mid-morning.

"Nice crowd for a Thursday," Walt said.

"We have a nice business here. The lunch crowd will be in soon. Starts at eleven thirty and goes until three. We close then. Bill is a good chef. Even went to culinary school," she said with obvious pride.

"Family business?" Walt asked.

"Yep, this is a family business. Been here over twenty years. Bill's dad and mother started the business. She's back in the kitchen. The pies are hers. Bill's my nephew. His dad died not three years ago. Hunting accident." She became solemn with the memory, then brightened. "Bill has three kids. Nice kids, not this wild kind you see sometimes. Especially in summer when the tourists are coming through." Her grimace spoke loudly of her opinion of tourists. "His wife, Shirley, is a teacher," she added, another measure of pride in her voice.

"Were you here on Christmas Eve this past year?" he asked.

He noted a hint of caution as she frowned, then said, "Sure. We was all here. Always have a good crowd the day before Christmas and New Year's. Other holidays too, but not like those two. This is a real meeting place before holidays. Like one big party," she grinned a toothy smile. "Closed early as usual 'cause we leave early. At least Shirley and I left early. Bill had to wait on…something," she ended lamely.

"I wonder if I could get you to look at this picture," he said, pulling the photo of Lily Rose Smith from his pocket. It was grainy because it was taken from her mug shot and he'd made a copy at Office Max before he left the city. He slid the copy across the Formica top and watched as she picked it up. Holding it close to her face she squinted her eyes and spent several moments studying the photo.

Handing it back to him, she said, "Don't know her. Looks kind of sad, don't she?"

"She's missing. I'm trying to find her."

Milly took a step back. "You the police?"

"Used to be. Now I do some private investigations. Just to help folks out. Someone thought she might have been here on Christmas Eve…sometime during the day. With a little girl?" his words urged her to rethink her assessment.

"It was so crowded that day but…" she turned toward the young man who was scraping the grill. "Bill, this fellow wants to know if you remember this lady."

The young man came to where Walt was seated, He wiped his hands down the sides of the apron and extended one to Walt. "Bill Riegel. Owner. How can I help you?"

Walt took the offered hand and felt the firm handshake. "I'm looking for a young woman who we think might have come this way on Christmas Eve. She's missing. I've been asked to do some ground work trying to locate her." He handed Bill the photo.

The young man took a long time studying the photograph before he handed it back to Walt. "You with the police?"

"Used to be. Twenty some years with Philadelphia's finest," he grinned. "Now I'm retired and fill in the empty time trying to help folks."

Bill nodded his approval. "Wish I could help you, but I don't think I've ever seen her before. Most of our customers are local. A few hunters in season and tourists in the summer." He tipped his head back and studied the shiny ceiling above him. "Christmas Eve, you said? Had something funny happy back then."

Walt stood. "What happened?" he said, controlling his interest as he had for years when he wore a uniform and later in plain clothes. Never project your interest, was one of his slogans.

"Well, as I recall," Bill said, propping himself against the wall, one foot resting on the wall behind him. "There was that thing about a little girl. Someone, I guess it was her mother, the kid didn't say much…anyhow someone left the girl here. Told her to wait for her grandmother."

Walt's stomach tightened. He waited for the boy to continue.

"Seems the kid was told to wait for a grandmother to pick her up and I got the feeling she didn't even know the grandmother. Damned fool thing to do on Christmas Eve. I felt sorry for her but I had to get home. That was some dilly of a snowstorm. I had three kids home waiting for Santa Claus," he grinned and the family smile was obvious. His smile echoed his aunt's. "Anyhow I was pissed by the time the woman came and got her. And, the strange thing was she kept saying she wasn't the kid's grandmother." He shook his head and shifted his weight to his other leg.

"But you never saw the little girl's mother leave her."

"We were really crowded that day. We always kind of celebrate with our regular customers that day. New Year's Eve, too."

"So your Aunt Milly told me." Walt took the photo and looked at it intently. *Was there any hope here,* he thought? "You think any of your customers might recognize this woman?"

"Lord, Mister. I don't even know who all was here and they aren't around now anyhow. Work, mostly, or mothers at home. We're a quiet neighborhood. I'm tellin' you though, the story made the rounds. A little girl, abandoned, Christmas Eve. Lots of talk for a while then it died down. No one knew anything about it really. Just gossip."

An elderly couple entered the diner and headed for a booth. Milly took her order pad and followed them. Apparently, by the way she greeted them, they were two of the regulars for an early lunch.

Walt turned back to the young man. "I know you're busy but if you could think back, remember anything at all about the situation. It might help." He smiled his most earnest smile.

The young man was about to speak when the two young women from the first booth walked up to the cash register. "Here you are, Bill. The omelets were great." Each woman had a green order check in her hand, which they handed to Bill with some cash.

Walt watched them as they joked with Bill and each other. He reached for the photo and turned to face them. "Hey, ladies. Either of you remember seeing this woman in here on Christmas Eve?"

He held the photo out for them to take but instead they crowded around looking at the picture still in his hand. "I don't think I know her. Christmas Eve you said? What time? I was here for a while but had to leave early to get the kids from church. Special kid's thing in the church basement that day but I had to pick them up by two o'clock." She turned to the other woman. "You know this lady, Alice?"

"Nope. I was here, too, but I don't remember her. Hey, wasn't that the day someone left that little girl in here? I think that should be a crime," she said, shrugging into her coat.

But the first woman remained, still studying the photo. "Seems like I saw this woman before. Not here. Maybe somewhere else. Maybe in the newspaper? I guess not," she said, backing away.

Walt's pulse raced. "If you can think of anything, anything at all could you let me know?" He handed her his card, a simple business card with his name, land, cell phone and fax numbers. "Call collect if you remember anything."

She tentatively took the card. "What do you want her for?" she asked.

"Nothing really. Just want to find her."

"Her family looking for her?"

"Yes," Walt lied. Well, Bitsy was family and even if she wasn't looking for her, well… "If you think of anything it might help us find her…"

"Hey," Bill said, still standing behind the counter. "What happened to the little girl?"

Walt hesitated just a second. "Well, the woman who took her wasn't actually her grandmother but she was family. The little girl is with her. We just want to find her mother."

"Oh, poor baby," the first woman said, her face crumpling with passion. "You mean to say that poor child hasn't seen her mama since before Christmas?"

"Now that is a crime. If she just left her she don't deserve to be a mother," the other said, carefully buttoning her coat.

"Listen," the first woman said, "if I think of anything I'll call. You just have to find that woman and make her see how bad she's treating that poor child."

They hurried from the diner and Bill moved back to his grill. While they were talking Milly had put an order on the spike and Bill began to grill two hamburgers.

Walt pulled a ten-dollar bill from his pocket and left it with the check. "Keep the change," he called as he headed for the door. He couldn't hang around any longer unless he ate lunch and that thought made his full stomach twinge.

As he walked to his car he saw the two women still sitting in a small van. He opened his car door but before he could slide behind the wheel, he heard, "Hey, Mister. Wait."

The first woman hurried across the parking lot. "I think I remember something."

The wind, which had picked up, whipped her blonde hair around her face and she tried to push it behind her ears as she spoke, "I think I saw that woman's picture in the newspaper but I can't remember when or why." She turned to face into the wind, her eyes drawn into slits, her forehead creased with concern. "Maybe I'm wrong," she began and Walt interrupted. "No matter. You've given me another place to look. What newspaper?"

"The Morning Herald. It's printed in Connerstown about fifty miles up in Hatter County. It's the only paper delivered around here."

Walt grasped the woman's hand. "Thank you. You don't know how much I appreciate this."

"I might not be right."

"Even so. It's another place to look." He grinned widely, brushing hair from his eyes. "Thanks."

She turned to go, then looked over her shoulder. "I hope you find her. I hope the little girl is okay."

"She is," he called to her retreating back. "Thanks again."

CHAPTER TWENTY-NINE

The most important questions in life can never be answered by anyone except oneself.
John Fowles

Saturday morning Madison cleaned the condo as if it were awaiting a military inspection. Bitsy stayed on the patio with her books and toys, avoiding the flailing dust cloth and the vigorous vacuuming that drowned out the television. When the kitchen shone with a gleam only found in model homes, Madison called to Bitsy, "Come on, honey. We're eating lunch out so we don't mess up the kitchen."

As they paraded down the outdoor staircase, Bitsy asked, "Where are we going for lunch, Grandma? Know where I'd like to go?"

"No, where?" Madison said, keeping a close eye on Bitsy's feet as they bounced from step to step. "Be careful, Bitsy. Walk down stairs carefully, remember?"

"Uh huh. I want to go to the Mall and get pizza."

Madison frowned. She knew they must pass a dozen pizza places on the way to the Mall. She was just about to tell Bitsy that when she realized that the Mall would be a good place to spend some time this afternoon. She didn't look forward to sitting in the condo waiting for Philip's appearance. That just sounded too nerve wracking and then she wondered, *what are you all a' twitter for? You know he's coming later today and you've been...*Again she hesitated. Did she want to use the word eager? *Well, it sounds better than excited*, she rationalized.

At the bottom of the steps she grasped Bitsy's hand. "Okay, then. It's the Mall. Maybe we can look around a little."

Bitsy skipped next to her. "Maybe we can go in K-Mart, too?"

"Maybe but we are not buying any more books until we move and I can get a small bookcase for your room. When you have books you have the responsibility of keeping them neatly."

"I know. Miss Eileen told us about how important it is to be careful when you take books out of the library. She said, 'No dog ears'," Bitsy put her fingers over her mouth and giggled. "Dog ears," she repeated.

Strapping Bitsy into her seat, Madison asked, "Do you know what dog ears are?"

"Miss Eileen showed us. You can't fold over a part of a page to mark your place."

"Yes, she's right. I'm so happy that you like your new class and friends."

"I can't wait for Wednesday," Bitsy said.

~ ~ ~

When the door chimes rang at three-thirty, Madison's heart skipped a beat. Hurrying to the door her eyes quickly scanned the elegant living room. Nothing was out of place, everything looked bright and polished, and Bitsy was in her room, playing with her baby doll. She now owned three blankets and several new outfits for Joanie courtesy of their earlier trip to the Mall.

Pulling the door open she looked into a familiar face and instantly wondered how it could be familiar when she'd only seen Philip three or four times. Their eyes locked. Neither spoke for an extended moment and then she stepped back, "Come in," she invited.

Philip stepped forward; they were still face-to-face, inches apart. "Oh," Madison stuttered, as she crept backwards," it seems weird to be inviting you into your own condo."

"Not my place right now. I told you, it's yours until the lease is up." He smiled and extended his hand and she gripped the firm warm and completely dry hand. Her's felt embarrassingly cool and damp.

"Well, it still seems strange and I can't say how much we appreciate your help."

Philip moved across the carpeted floor and looked out the sliding glass windows. "You're going to have to stop all that nonsense about appreciating the condo. You, my friend, are doing me a favor."

"Still…" Her mind lingered on the phrase 'my friend'.

"Oh, boy, have I longed for this view." He sighed contentedly looking through the broad glass doors.

Madison moved next to him. "It is lovely. Morning, noon or night, it's a wonderful view."

He slid the door open and stepped outside, inhaling deeply. "I've missed this," he said, leaning on the railing.

"Would you like something to drink? Beer? Iced tea? I could make coffee…"

"I'd love a beer. Will you have one too?"

"Sure," she said, turning away.

In the kitchen she opened two bottles of beer, took two tall glasses from the cupboard and put them on a tray she'd found on top of the refrigerator. She hesitated a moment, then slipped some crackers from a package in the pantry and placed them on a small plate, adding that to the tray.

She left the kitchen and moved through the living room but before she went back to the patio, she rested the tray on the coffee table and tiptoed down the hallway to peek in on Bitsy. The little girl was on her knees, tending to her doll, propped up on a pillow on her bed. "Time for your nap, Joanie," she heard the child whisper. Once again, Madison marveled at how content Bitsy could be for hours with her small collection of possessions.

On the patio she found Philip sprawled on one of the lounge chairs. “Thanks.” He said, reaching for a bottle and glass. “I used to come out here every night before going to bed. It was a great way to unwind at the end of the day.”

Madison took the other lounge, noting that Philip had chosen the one she always chose. “I do too. Stress seems to just blow away with the breeze out here.”

“I agree. Where’s your granddaughter. Bitsy, isn’t it?” he asked, sipping his drink.

Madison swelled with pride, noting that he’d actually remembered the little girl’s name. “She’s in her bedroom…I mean the spare room.” Madison felt her face flush.

“Don’t do that.”

“What?” She sat forward, a frown pinching the flesh between her eyes.

“Don’t keep making careful use of words indicating that this isn’t your home right now.”

“I didn’t mean…”

“I’m sorry. I didn’t mean to sound cross. It’s just that I want you to be comfortable here. I want you to enjoy your stay. I’m passing through and won’t be back for at least another four or five, maybe even six weeks.”

Madison relaxed against the colorful cushions. “Thank you again. We’ve found a wonderful place. We plan to move as soon as my furniture arrives. I think I told you. Too bad we couldn’t have been out of here now and then you wouldn’t have had to bunk with Dave.”

Philip stood. “You aren’t going to quit, are you? Forget I’m barging in. It’s your home until you leave. Let’s leave it at that, okay?”

She rose and walked to the railing. Leaning on it she gazed out over the Gulf. “My life has been in such a turmoil these past few…weeks,” she said softly. “I’m sorry if I’m overdoing the thanks but this act of kindness is…”

He joined her at the railing. “It’s an act of kindness that has been sufficiently and eloquently acknowledged. Let’s move on,” he said, the breeze brushing his hair from his forehead. “Tell me about your new home.”

Madison faced him. He looked so content, so comfortable. “We found a house for rent on Thunder Creek Road. It’s really lovely. I signed a lease for one year.”

“Thunder Creek Road. That’s a good location. Quiet but not too far from everything.”

Madison began to describe the house, trying not to include too much minutia but the excitement in her voice couldn’t be completely contained. “And,” she finished, “I think it might work out well because there’s a private school not too far away that Bitsy can attend. At least that’s the tentative plan for now.”

“Collier Country-Day Academy. I’m familiar with it…it’s a very good school. I’m happy for you…both.”

Just then Bitsy slid the door open, “Oh,” she said, staring at Philip.

“Come and say hello to Mr. Hendershot,” Madison said, holding out her hand.

“Hello,” Bitsy said, tentatively, her face a study in caution.

Philip squatted in front of the child and held out his hand. “Hello, Bitsy. I’m so glad to see you again. And this time we’re not stuck in a snowstorm.” His smile was engaging and they watched Bitsy relax. “Have you been enjoying our wonderful Florida weather?”

Bitsy’s face brightened. “I love the beach and Grandma sometimes takes me in the morning. She says we can come more often once we move into our new house.”

“We’re still establishing routines,” Madison added, sitting on one of the chairs at the table and pulling Bitsy onto her lap.

For the next hour the time flew. Bitsy brought her doll and several books out to the patio and Philip was duly impressed. Madison watched them carefully. Usually Bitsy was very hesitant when confronted by men but she chatted to Philip with no reservations at all.

"You have a way with children," she commented.

"Don't know why," he answered. "I love kids but they just haven't been in my life much. I guess because I chose a…" he hesitated and Madison saw a far away look briefly pass over his face. "The career I chose doesn't bring me in contact with children much and my personal life is usually spent with a few friends or alone."

No one spoke for a few moments and then Madison said quietly, "I know what you mean. Writing is kind of a one-man job, too."

Philip laughed and reached for the last cracker on the plate. "These are good," he said.

"My favorites. They're really good with wine. Oh, I should have offered you wine instead of beer."

"No, the beer was fine. Hit the spot. Wine is for later." He stared at her, then smiled. "How about letting me take you out for dinner. It would be a real treat for me before I leave tomorrow."

Madison stood and looked down at Bitsy, who was paging through one of her newest books. "Oh, thank you, but I don't think so. I mean it sounds great but there's Bitsy…"

"My invitation includes Bitsy," he said, his eyes crinkling above his smile.

"But…"

Philip stood and again they were eye to eye. "But nothing. I know a little place out on the island. Have you been out on the island?"

"No, but…"

"Quit saying 'but'. It's not fancy, the seafood is great and it has the best view of our Florida sunsets you can find. Say yes…please?"

~ ~ ~

They chose to sit on the covered deck outside the main dining room. A wooden railing ran along three sides of the deck, broken by a stairway down to the beach. Little colored flags on a rope that edged the roof, flapped in the breeze. The tables were covered with a tablecloth that was clamped at each corner so the wind wouldn't blow it off. The chairs were molded white plastic with brightly patterned cushions. Bitsy knelt on her chair, refusing the booster seat that had been offered. She polished off the fish fingers she had ordered. "Yum, Grandma. These were good. Better than the ones we get at the grocery store."

"I should say so," Madison smiled. "I think you should thank Mr. Hendershot for such a nice dinner."

Bitsy studied the man sitting across from her grandmother, folded her lips in for just a moment, then smiled and said, "Thank you Mr. Hendershot."

Philip grinned. "You're quite welcome, Bitsy. I knew this would be fun. You're a very grown up little girl and I'm glad you liked your dinner."

He looked across the table at Madison. "Thanks for making my last meal in the US, for a while at least, so pleasant. Lord only knows what kind of food lies ahead."

"Thank *you* for a wonderful dinner. You were right…the food was excellent and the view is great."

"I must have a thousand photographs of Florida sunsets and yet they are always new. Each night the picture is different. I always miss them when I'm away."

"Where are you going this time?"

"To the Brazilian rain forest. We could be there for about five weeks or even longer. It depends on conditions.."

"That's a long time to take pictures, isn't it?"

"Not really. Some shoots take months. It might sound tedious to someone who doesn't do this but the excitement is there, just waiting. Waiting for flowers to open, the light to be just right…and if you're dealing with animals, well that's another story. Sometimes you lay in a wooden box up in the trees for days just trying to get the right combination of light, action, content and so forth."

Madison leaned back as the waitress removed their plates and asked," Any desserts tonight?"

Philip looked from Madison to Bitsy. "Dessert?" he asked.

"Not for me," Madison answered, "and I think Bitsy has had enough, haven't you sweetheart?"

Bitsy hesitated.

"Why don't you bring the little lady one of those key lime sherbets," Philip said. He leaned forward and whispered to Madison, "They aren't very large and I think she'll like it."

"Thanks, Philip. You're making her feel very special tonight."

"That's the whole idea. How about you? An after dinner drink?"

Madison hesitated. "Just coffee, thank you." Philip ordered coffee for both of them.

The light was fading fast and they were the last diners out on the deck. The sky changed, still blue but with a slatey tinge; some of the clouds looked as if they had been brushed with soot others were rimmed with gold. Bold colors, pale orange, pink and a milky mauve pressed down on the horizon. One golden spot lingered sending a narrowing path of light across the top of the water. "The sunsets are beautiful here, I've never seen such a spectacular array of colors. I guess it's all the water and reflections that make it so different."

"Yes. Have you ever been to Key West?"

Madison hesitated. She had been to Key West several years ago with Jim but they were on a cruise ship and missed the sunset because they were in the casino. She shook her head, "Not really. I was on a ship that docked there but we didn't see the sunset. I understand they are famous."

"They are. It's a quaint little town with many sides...rowdy, romantic, carefree...I guess you can find whatever you want there and won't have to look very far. You should go sometime when you can really delve into it, Truman's little White House, Ernest Hemmingway's home with all those six-toed cats. There's a Civil War fort and it's only 90 miles from Cuba. It's very historical, artsy and..." he paused, then grinned widely, "...I guess robust would be a good word to describe Key West."

"Maybe we will visit it someday," Madison smiled. She was more relaxed than she could remember being in a very long time.

Bitsy's dessert came and she loved it, scraping the little bowl with her spoon so as not to miss a drop. "That was good, Mr. Hendershot. Thank you."

"You know that *'Mr. Hendershot'* is bothering me. I think we should come up with some other name for me. What do you think?"

Bitsy looked from her grandmother to the man sitting across the table. "What?" she murmured.

"I don't think she should call you Philip."

"How about Uncle Phil? I have two sisters and they both decided on careers rather than children," he countered. "Would you object to that?"

Madison paused then looked across the Gulf. The sky had now turned a vibrant magenta and dark clouds near the horizon seemed to be edged in gold. "Philip, I'm not sure..."

"It's just a suggestion to make things easier for Bitsy...and me. Am I out of line?"

Madison sighed. "Not out of line but maybe..."

Philip took some bills from his wallet and placed them in the folder the waitress had left when she brought the coffee and Bitsy's dessert.

He stood and came around behind Bitsy's chair. "You know what, Bitsy? We can go down on the beach for a little while. There's a place for children to play at the end of the deck. The area is full during the day with kids careening up and down on those gizmo's that bounce on big springs." He turned to Madison. "It's lighted and perfectly safe and we could sit on a bench. How about it?"

"Can we go, Grandma? Can we go with Uncle Phil?"

Madison smiled. *Well, that question seems to have been answered already,* she thought lifting Bitsy from her chair. As soon as the child's feet hit the deck she was running toward the stairs down to the beach. "Be careful," she called.

Philip took Madison's elbow and they followed. "She'll love it and it's perfectly safe. I've watched other children on those things."

By the time they had descended the wooden steps, Bitsy was already astride a huge yellow duck. "Look at me, Grandma. I'm riding a duck like a horsey."

Madison laughed softly. "Be careful, honey."

They sat on a nearby bench. The breeze had died down and now the little flags moved cautiously in the dying wind. Madison looked up at them. "They look like the flags that are on some ships."

"They do. I think on ships they might send a message or designate ownership or something. I'm not up on that." Philip leaned back and put his arm along the back of the bench.

Madison leaned forward. *Was that a message? Are we moving toward something I'm not ready for,* she thought, suddenly becoming stiff and quiet. *Or I am being paranoid again?*

"I enjoy being with you and Bitsy, Madison," Philip began. "Maybe once you are settled in your new home and I'm back home, you'd allow us to do this again." His question hung in the silent night air.

"Philip," she whispered. "I'm not sure…"

"Neither am I. I just know that when I met you I knew I liked you. You're interesting and I'd like to know you better. I'm not rushing you into anything. Honest," he said, turning toward her. "Can't a couple of friends share a dinner occasionally?"

"I guess so."

Philip stretched his legs and crossed his ankles. "I don't know what you were running from…and I don't want to. But, I remember when we first met. You were…defensive…frightened…and seemed too alone."

"Too alone?"

"Well, maybe that's not the word I want, but I felt something. A need to be your friend maybe? Does that make sense? Sometimes we all need a friend and I wanted to be yours. That's why when you called about the condo, I was happy to be able to help."

Madison shook her head from side to side in the near dark. "I can't believe I had the nerve to call you. You don't know how many times I've thought about that. Why you? Why then? What a nerve," she said, her voice a hint above a whisper.

"Watch me, Grandma," Bitsy called as she left the duck and climbed on a purple elephant."

"Be careful. That's a big elephant," Madison called.

"He has to be bigger than a duck," Bitsy answered, bouncing and lurching backward and forward.

"She's a nice little girl," Philip said, leaning forward, one elbow on his knees and his hand resting beneath his chin.

"She is. She's a blessing," Madison said.

Philip heard the emotion. "Has she been with you a long time? I shouldn't ask should I. Forget it," he said.

"No. No, it's all right. I've had her with me for several months…this time," she added. She stiffened, anticipating more questions but Philip remained silent.

The sky was dark now, all the brilliant color faded, the sliver of light on the horizon a mere line of gold drawn across the top of the water.

"I can't explain, Philip," she began and he interrupted. "You don't have to. I'm not questioning you, Madison. Not about her or anything."

She sighed. "Thanks. Maybe someday…" She shivered, drawing her sweater around her shoulders. "Bitsy, are you getting cold? Maybe we should button your sweater, honey. It's getting dark. I think we should be going."

Philip stood and walked to where Bitsy was playing. "Come on, little girl. Time we left." He bent and scooped her up into his arms, almost tossing her over his shoulder.

Bitsy screamed with laughter and Madison's heart swelled as she watched the tall man and the tiny girl approach. "You've been captured, Bitsy," she said, reaching for the child.

The threesome climbed the steps, then walked through the almost empty dining room. The man behind the bar called a greeting to Philip and Madison got the feeling he was well known there.

In the car driving back to the condo her mind raced through the evening. The small talk, the lovely meal, the beautiful sunset and then the time on the beach in the dark, little lamps around the bottom of the deck casting just enough light for them to watch Bitsy enjoying her romp in the small beach playground. She remembered those last few minutes. *Philip seems so...sensible I guess is the word I want. Nice and sensible and kind. He's good with children even if he insists he isn't. Bitsy likes him.* She sighed, smiling to herself. It was fun.

They rode up in the elevator, Madison sure that Bitsy was too tired to walk up three flights of stairs. In fact, as soon as they got to the condo it was apparent that Bitsy was almost asleep on her feet. Madison hesitated at the door.

"I'll need to come in and get some equipment from the back room," Philip said, softly.

"Oh, sure. I'll just get Bitsy to bed. You go ahead and do what you have to do. We'll stay out of your way."

Philip took her arm. "You don't have to stay out of my way. I'll only be a short time." He leaned down and took Bitsy's tiny chin in his hand. "Hope you had a good time tonight, little lady," he said.

Bitsy blinked sleepy eyes. "Oh, Uncle Phil, I did. Can we do that again?"

"Bitsy," Madison gasped. "That wasn't polite."

"Sure it was," Philip said. "And, yes, when I come back we'll do that again. Good night little lady," he called as Madison took the child by the hand and went down the hall to the spare bedroom. She was sure her cheeks were aflame.

"He calls me *little lady*," Bitsy said sleepily, as Madison turned back the sheets.

In fifteen minutes, Bitsy was sound asleep, too tired even for evening prayers but she did manage to murmur as Madison pulled the light blanket up under the little girl's chin, "Uncle Phil is nice."

Philip stacked several boxes and long plastic tubes against the wall next to the front door. The last thing he brought from the back bedroom was a canvas duffle bag. *He must have clothes stored back there, also,* Madison thought.

He looked at Madison who sat in one of the padded chairs covered with soft pastel tropical flowers.

"I think that's it. I have some things in my car." He stood near the door.

She rose and walked to him. "Thanks for a lovely evening, Philip. Thanks for both of us." She extended her hand, which he took in both of his. It definitely wasn't a handshake.

"Would you like to see some of the photographs I have stored back there?" She hesitated and he said, "Unless you're too tired."

"Of course, I'd love to see them. I thought you probably had some treasures locked up in that room."

"I always do but David stripped the walls, I noticed. He was convinced that any child you brought would be hell-bent on destroying everything in sight. How wrong he was and I told him so."

"He was just being careful with your things. I don't blame him. He didn't know us."

Philip moved closer, still holding Madison's hand. "I want to show you a couple of things," he said, tugging on her hand and urging her down the hall.

In the room, Madison was amazed at the number of framed photos that leaned against the walls. Two tables were also stacked with folders and she assumed they also held photographs. Along one short wall, metal shelving held boxes, papers and some empty frames. Mirrored doors hid a large closet and there was a six-drawer bureau against the wall next to the closet.

"Wow," she said, still standing just inside the door.

Philip snapped on more lights. "I thought you might like one or two for your new house. Those," he pointed to several leaning against a wall, "are scheduled for a show in Miami in April. But, these," he said, turning some around. "These are extras. I always seem to take dozens more than I need and somehow they become part of me. I don't seem to be able to part with them."

"Oh," she gasped. "You shouldn't give them away. They're too precious."

"Well, I can't paper the walls of the condo with them and it seems a waste to just leave them alone in this room. They should be enjoyed and I do give them to family and friends. What do you think of these two?" he said, turning them around for her to see.

They were of tropical birds caught in natural settings. "They are breath-taking," she whispered. "Where did you do these?"

"In Tahiti," he said. "It was a good shoot. I got hundreds. After that I went down to New Guinea. Those are over there but I think these are better." He leaned against the doorway as she inched closer to the photos.

"They're beautiful," she whispered. "I feel as if they just might fly out of the frame, they are so real."

"Pick two to take to your new home. That is if you think they will fit in with your décor."

"They would fit into any décor, especially in Florida." She turned toward him. "Philip I think these are beautiful but I'm not sure you should just give them away. I'd like to buy them from you."

"They're not for sale…I want to give them to you. When I come home next month maybe I'll have others that are even better." His grin was infectious and she smiled at him.

"Thank you," she said, grasping her hands in front of her. "You are too generous, Philip."

"I don't just give them to anyone, you know. Just someone whom I think should have them. Art is to be shared. It's useless stacked up in a room somewhere."

"I know how you feel. When I create a book it isn't just for me. It has to be shared or it's no good."

"I know. I've read all your books. You're a good writer."

"You have? Thanks."

He picked the framed photographs up and started for the door, Madison following closely. She closed the door and trailed down the dim hallway after him. As she passed Bitsy's door she glanced in. The nightlight gave just enough light for her to see the sleeping child.

In the living room, Philip leaned the pictures against the back of the sofa. He turned to her. "Thanks for a lovely evening, Madison. I'll keep in touch while I'm away, if you don't mind. I know you'll be busy moving and I'll be miles away from a post office most of the time, but a card once in a while, maybe," he said, the infectious grin again capturing her.

"Thank you for the evening, Philip. It was…" she hesitated. "It was special and we both enjoyed it very much." She reached her hand toward him, felt his soft hand enfold hers and they seemed frozen in that moment.

He squeezed her hand, turned and began to pick up the boxes he'd stacked. "I'll come back in a minute for the rest of that stuff," he said, disappearing out the door.

Madison remained where she was. When he returned, he stuck the long tubes under his arm and picked up the duffle. Saluting with the other hand, he said, "See ya'."

When the door closed after him, she took one step forward and then stopped. He was gone and yet the night didn't feel as if it were over. She turned the dead bolt and wandered back into the living room.

Walking to the sliding glass doors she reached for the cord to close the drapes, then hesitated, opened the door and walked out onto the patio. She leaned against the railing, feeling the soft breeze caress her face. It was cool and yet her face still glowed with a warmth she couldn't identify.

He was gone but he would be back. She smiled, went inside, closed the drapes and went to her bedroom. She stood in the doorway trying to imagine Philip there. She tried to picture his clothes in the closet where hers hung, his things on the nightstand where her bible and alarm clock rested. *Where are his things?* she wondered. *Tucked away by Dave so they wouldn't be compromised by mine?*

She smiled. When Philip returned she would be on Thunder Creek Road. Would she see him again? As she washed her face and brushed her teeth she studied the woman in the mirror. Somehow she seemed younger, less stressed and yet she knew the same worries she'd had hours earlier were still there. Still, the evening had erased something. Erased something and left another something in its place. *What?* she asked her reflection.

CHAPTER THIRTY

"The past is not a cold grave but a window to the soul of who you were."
Author unknown

Walt felt as if he were on a roller coaster. Not that the road was exceptionally hilly, it did climb and dip as all mountain roads in central Pennsylvania do; no, this was an emotional roller coaster he was on.

Could this possibly be the opening he needed? But how reliable was his source? A woman who *might* have seen Lily's picture in a newspaper weeks ago? On the other hand, she sounded pretty confident even given her last minute insecurity. Of course, he'd know if he found a picture of Lily in the Morning Herald. Still he wavered from hopeful to natural pessimism as he hurried north. "Won't know until you get there," he muttered and took pressure off the accelerator; there was a big curve ahead. He slowed when he saw a sign indicating a junction with Rte. 742.

The Morning Herald was situated on the main street, a busy thoroughfare in a moderately sized city. After parking his car in a lot half a block away, he walked back to a three story brick building with an impressive front door and a nice, rather old-fashioned reception area. The hallway leading to the left was busy with people coming and going into offices.

He identified himself as a retired police officer from Philadelphia looking for a missing woman and requested permission to review all the issues of the Morning Herald from January first through the current issue.

A young woman with a bright red turtle necked sweater that left little to the imagination as to her attributes, pulled a binder from a rack at the back of the area. Sliding it across the counter, she pointed. "There's a room where you can look through these," she said, her cheeks flushed with color. "First door on the left. Let me know if you need anything else."

Sitting in the small room equipped with chairs and wide, bare wooden tables, Walt felt right at home. How often had he poured over copies of the Philadelphia Enquirer on case after case, looking for information that was right there for anyone to find. He smiled as he paged through the papers beginning on January first, skipping the sport and financial sections. Still his hopes rose and fell with every page he turned; his eyes scanned every photograph. His mind skipped from place to place; rising to *Lily Rose has to be here* and then dipping to *this is probably another dead end.*

He reached the issue for the tenth and his eyes widened. There she was. The photo was an obvious touched up autopsy photo but it was Lily all right. Eagerly he read the news story, noted the name of the reporter and made some notes.

> *Lily Rose Smith was killed in an automobile accident on December 24 on Rte. 742 during the devastating snowstorm of that date. Fingerprints identify her as being from Philadelphia. The Hatter County Sheriff's Department is seeking information on any connection she might have with someone in the area. The officer to contact is William (Willie) Schmidt.*

"Bingo," Walt whispered. "Next stop, Hatter County Sheriff's Department. He took the binder to the front desk, requested a copy of the article and thanked the young woman for her help. Tucking the copy in his inside pocket, Walt's footsteps as he left the building were bordering on jaunty. He'd gotten directions for the

Sheriff's office and he felt a rush of expectancy as he pulled out of the parking lot. He whistled all the way to the squat brick building on the outskirts of town. A sign in front identified it as Hatter County Sheriff's Department.

He pushed the heavy metal door open, noting there were three squad cars parked to the left of the front entrance and several cars and pickup trucks were lined up along the right side. At the front desk he asked the young officer for William Schmidt.

"Willie?" the officer smiled. "He's out on patrol now. Due back in…" he paused and looked at the board behind the counter. "He's due back in at three."

Walt looked at his watch. It was two-thirty. "I'm Lieutenant Walter Kalik, retired, Philadelphia police," he said, showing his identity card and reaching across the counter to offer his hand to the young officer on duty. "Looking for a woman who disappeared around Christmas. Mind if I wait for Officer Schmidt? I think he might know something about the case."

"Yes, sir. You can wait right there," the young man said. He pointed to a wooden bench along the wall opposite the front desk. "I'll tell them in the back that you're waiting for him in case he comes in that way."

Walt smiled. It never hurt to mention rank. His eyes scanned the area and memories flooded back. On a smaller scale and obviously newer, it was much like the city precinct house he'd spent so many years in, only the detective's desks were upstairs back in Philadelphia. Here it appeared everything was on one floor. Even the smell was reminiscent of the past; coffee somewhere, dust and wet floors; and the sounds were familiar; phones ringing in distant offices, the occasional voice raised in mirth or greeting. He smiled and stood to read the notices tacked to a bulletin board.

At ten minutes before three o'clock several officers entered the front door. He looked up expectantly as they checked in at the desk or turned and disappeared down one of the hallways leading from the front area. His eyes met those of the desk officer and he shook his head. "Not yet," the uniformed young man said, shuffling some papers.

At three fifteen Walt was becoming restless. He stood and watched the man behind the counter answer the telephone. He spoke a few words, made eye contact with Walt and gave him a nod. Hanging up the phone, he said, "Willie's on his way in. They had a last minute call."

Walt returned to the bench. His heart was doing tricks in his chest. Was the answer just minutes away? When a short, stocky officer walked into the area behind the counter and looked his way, Walt stood.

"Lieutenant Kalik?" Willie called.

"Yes."

"Come on back. Hear you want to know about a missing woman." He swung the gate at the end of the counter open and gestured for Walt to follow him.

They were seated at a desk in a crowded squad room where three other officers occupied similar desks. Walt pulled his copy of the article and the mug shot of Lily Rose from his pocket and put them on Willie's desk.

"The Christmas Eve accident." Willie yelled. "You know somethin' about her? Lord, we been wondering if anyone would ever show up."

Walt's spirits soared. After so many stumbling blocks to actually find a positive result in his search brought a sense of triumph. But, he knew it wasn't over…not yet. "I've been looking for her for several weeks now. It sure wasn't an easy trail to follow." Walt related to Willie Schmidt what he had learned about Lily Rose Smith, her background, the child she'd left at a diner and the reason for his search.

Willie shook his head. "Kinda sad," he said. "We thought…well we didn't think anything like that." He heaved a big sigh. "Kinda tarnishes the image, don't it?"

Walt nodded. "It happens. At least we know what happened to her."

"She have any family?"

"Not much that we can find. Just the woman who took the little girl."

"Abandoned her kid." He continued to shake his head. "Hard to believe. At least there's that much then. I knew there was a kid involved," Willie said softly. "Evidence box has a couple of books and a teddy bear. Kid okay?"

"Yes, with the woman. In another state," he moved cautiously. "Can I see the file?"

"I think it's still in the evidence room. Move them out if there's no activity after six months but we were about to give up early on this one, I think. She came out of nowhere. Seemed like no one knew anything about her. Not one response to the newspaper thing. Not even a false lead. No one knew the lady.

"The old file boxes are kept in the tombs, a building down the road. Near enough to go if you have to but it clears up our space here a little." He rose from his chair behind the desk and motioned for Walt to follow him. "My partner's off today. Boy, I wish he was here. He'd love to know we got someone who knows somethin' about this girl. We found her at the accident site, you know."

In the evidence room, Walt looked into the open box and saw the books, teddy bear and a bag containing Lily's clothes and shoes.

"Take it over here. We can spread the stuff out. You want to read through the file?" Willie said, hefting the box and moving toward a long, slightly wobbly metal table.

He spread the things out and handed the manila folder to Walt. "I'll be talking to Steve," he indicated the man behind the screen enclosure.

Walt's fingers lingered for a moment on the teddy bear, then opened the folder. He read the reports, the autopsy report and the actions taken by the Hatter County Sheriff's Department. It was all so routine but nothing of any importance was noted except the result of the fingerprints identifying the body. *No one knew anything about the victim because that's the way she wanted it,* Walt thought. *You did a good job, Lily. But no one will ever really know why you did what you did.*

He took his notebook out and made some notations; the disease was advanced Mesothelioma, the date and time of death, the contents of the evidence box and the place where Lily's body was buried. He stood for a moment just looking at the poor remnants of a life that was no more.

Turning he motioned to Willie who had been watching him as he chatted with the evidence clerk. "Thanks. I've made some notes. I'll report to the woman who is looking for Lily." *Isn't it strange,* he thought, *that although none of us knew this poor girl, we're easy using her first name.*

Willie handed the evidence box back to Steve, thanked him and walked with Walt to the door leading back to the squad room. "So, how's the kid? Okay? Who is she with?"

"She's with…: Walt hesitated. What did he actually know for sure? Not much. "She's in Florida with a distant relative."

"She want the body?"

"I don't think so but I'll have to check and let you know. Apparently there was a rift in the family. I'm guessing at some of this because I never actually saw the woman or the child. It's all been long distance. But, I'm sure she'll be happy to know the end, even if it's pretty sad."

"I'll need to write up something for the file. Let's go back to the squad room, okay?"

"Sure," Walt said, walking next to the officer who seemed almost too kind and laid back to be a Sheriff. "You been on the job long?"

"Twelve years next month. You're retired?"

"Yeah, started out like every officer. Retired from homicide two years ago. Had twenty-five years in."

Willie patted Walt on the back. "Big city is a lot different than out here," he said, pushing the door open and letting Walt precede him into the room. "But we have our cases," he said with a measure of pride.

“I’m sure you do,” Walt said sitting opposite him again. He slid the newspaper article and the mug shot into his notebook and tucked them back into his pocket.

When Willie completed his report he pushed it across the desk for Walt to read. He nodded. “If anything else comes up, which doesn’t seem likely, I’ll be in touch.” He rose and the two officers shook hands. “I’m going to take a look at the grave if that’s okay.”

Willie gave Walt directions to the cemetery and walked with him to the reception area. “Hope everything goes well for the kid. No matter what, it’s not easy losing your mama that young,” he said, watching Walt’s back disappear behind the closing door.

At Hollyhill Cemetery Walt stood at a grave marked with a plaque in the ground where a head stone might be. He looked around the bleak area at the back of the cemetery. Here there were no headstones, just a field of snow, with patches of wind-scarred grass bared by the constant onslaught of wind.

The dirt covering the grave was still bare. He tried to picture the mound settled and covered with grass. A cold wind blew across the headstones and markers. “Well, this is where it ends. Not much of an end, Lily. I hope you’re at peace somewhere,” he murmured, his hands clasped together. He felt his eyes water and blamed the wind, turning and hurrying back to his car. He had to go home. He had to call Madison. *What then?* he thought and for some unknown reason his thoughts immediately went to Jo. He’d call her first.

As Walt drove home he had to force himself to concentrate on the road ahead. His mind insisted on revisiting the day, the ups and downs and the final outcome. He had succeeded in his quest to find Lily Rose, but what now? And why did he feel almost let down? It didn’t make sense.

Is this the result that Madison wanted? Would knowing her mother was dead help the child? And, should she even know at this young age? Well, that part of the equation was out of his hands and he felt a sense of relief at that.

Back in Philadelphia, Walt pulled into the ally behind his apartment building. As he got out of the car he felt tired, exhausted both physically and mentally. "Come on, man, you're not that old," he muttered as he unlocked his back door and entered the kitchen. *One thing, I'm grateful I live on the first floor. Don't know if I could trudge up all those steps to the third or fourth floor apartments,* he thought, going through to the living room and collapsing into his favorite chair. He leaned back and closed his eyes. He needed a few minutes before he called Jo. *And then I have to call Madison.*

He'd had no intention of falling asleep but ten minutes later he jerked upright realizing that was exactly what he had done. Reaching for the telephone he flipped the address gizmo next to the phone open. He dialed Jo's number, glad he'd taken those few minutes to rest. His mind was focused now. He listened to the phone in Jo's office ring but after five rings her answering machine clicked on. "Hi, I'm out on assignment. Doesn't that sound interesting and important? Leave a message and I'll get back to you."

Walt left a message and went into the kitchen. He hadn't eaten since breakfast in the diner this morning—it seemed like a lifetime away, his stomach rumbling on cue. He stared at an array of cans on a shelf in the cupboard, then picked up a can of soup and a package of crackers. He began to make a hold-off-starvation meal. *Maybe Jo can meet me for a real dinner*, he thought pulling the top from the soup can.

CHAPTER THIRTY-ONE

Love at first sight is easy to understand; it's when two people have been looking at each other for a lifetime that it becomes a miracle.

Amy Bloom

"Looks like liquid rubies, doesn't it?" Jo said, twisting the long-stemmed wine glass in one hand.

They were seated in a booth at Ianelli's Restaurant. Earlier, when she'd returned his call and Walt had suggested meeting there, she'd been surprised. "That's kind of upscale, isn't it? What's the occasion?"

"A celebration," he'd replied.

"What are you celebrating?"

"Let me surprise you. Seven-thirty okay?"

"Sure. I'll go home and change. Meet you in the bar?"

"Yeah."

The background music was semi-classical, occasionally featuring a Frank Sinatra or Jerry Vale ballad. Right now Andrea Boccelli sang *Time to Say Goodbye*. "I love that song," Jo said.

"Me too and I don't even know what he's singing."

"He sings it in both Italian and English. That song is kind of sad but he's one of my favorites."

Walt laughed softly. "You like any Irish or Polish singers?"

"I guess, but the Italian brings back memories. My uncles and my father all had great voices. When we got together for holidays they always ended up singing a'capela. I miss my dad." She leaned forward. "You never told me what you're celebrating."

Walt hesitated then sighed. "What *we're* celebrating, Jo. I found Lily Rose Smith today."

The candlelight illuminated the surprise on Jo's face. "You did! Why didn't you say so sooner? Is that what you're celebrating? Have you called Madison?"

"Not yet."

Jo stared across the table at her friend. He seemed tired and saddened. "Why not? I thought you'd be happy that you were successful. Come on, Walt. Madison needs to know right away. I can't believe you didn't call her first."

"Tonight or tomorrow morning's not going to make any difference."

"Tell me," Jo said, leaning back on the soft padded cushions behind her.

"She's dead. Died in an automobile accident in the same snowstorm Madison was stuck in. Died Christmas Eve, probably right after she dropped the kid off. Accident site was about thirty or forty miles from the diner."

Jo studied her companion. "That's it?"

Walt shrugged. "She's buried in a little cemetery up there."

"You saw it?"

He nodded and drained his wine. "Another?" he asked her, signaling the waiter across the room.

"One more with dinner," she said, not taking her eyes from his face. There was something different about Walt. She felt a shiver run up her spine and folded her arms across her chest. "Tell me all about it, okay?"

Walt ordered more wine, telling the waiter to bring the bottle this time. "Yes, sir. Your order should be ready very soon. Everything is prepared fresh," his accent a musical hint at his origins. He nodded and backed away from their booth.

"I went up to the diner where Madison found the little girl. It was a long shot and at first I thought I'd struck out…again. Then one of those quirks that keep policemen sane happened. A woman who was eating there remembered seeing…or thought she'd seen…Lily's picture in the newspaper but it wasn't a sure thing. She said she might be mistaken."

"And had she…had she seen her in the paper?"

"She wasn't sure but I went to the newspaper office and looked through the old issues for the month of January. Figured if it was there it had to be then, seeing as how she disappeared around Christmas."

Walt waited while the waiter opened and poured the wine. "Just a few more minutes," the waiter said with a wave of his hand.

"And you found her picture?" Jo leaned forward, her arms on the table, her fingers laced together to keep them from trembling with excitement.

He nodded. "It was a small article asking for information as to any local contacts for Lily."

"Were there any responses?"

"No, but it listed a contact at the local Sheriff's office so I went there to talk to the officer who had the case. Car went over the side of a mountain in the storm. I read the file, it wasn't much."

"But, you found her, Walt. That's all Madison wanted. What she does now is her business. But, you found her. Aren't you happy? Proud?"

He shrugged. "It was sad, Jo. A sad end to a sad life and she was… alone at the end. I stood there at her grave. It was ugly. There was a little wire basket on a spike stuck into the ground next to the marker. No one will ever put flowers there. No one even cares she's gone."

He looked away and Jo thought she saw tears glisten in his eyes. She reached across the table and took his hand. "You did your job…and a good one. What she was was her choice. What happened to her was beyond your control, or the control of anyone really."

"I know but the things in that box…no identification…a few items, an autopsy report and a police file. There was a teddy bear, for God's sake. It was sad and it showed how alone she really was."

"She had a child she gave up."

"But you don't know why and we won't ever know."

"Do you?"

"Not really. She had a terminal disease, wouldn't have lived very long maybe."

Jo leaned back her hands now in her lap. "There you go then. She made the choice."

The waiter returned with a tray. He placed two steaming plates of pasta in front of them, added side dishes, topped up their water glasses and asked, "Will there be anything else now, Sir?"

"No thanks," Walt said, waiting for him to leave.

"We all make choices, Jo. But, did she really chose to be alone or was it circumstances?"

Jo shrugged. "Circumstances guide us all at times but we still have the choice to either accept them or do something about them. Maybe what she did was…ill-advised."

"She loved the little girl."

"How do you know? She abandoned her." Jo's voice turned cool, unforgiving as she thought of the child being abandoned. "And on Christmas Eve," she added.

Still Walt stared into space, his hands resting idly on the table, the fingers of his right hand around the wine glass.

"Sometimes we choose not to make *any* choices and that might be worse than making the wrong choice."

Jo sighed, a quick breath that burst from her lips, her fork suspended in air above her plate. "You're different tonight, Walt. Philosophical, deep. Can I help?"

Walt forced a grin. "No. I'm just tired…but hungry. Eat," Walt said picking up his spoon and fork.

For several minutes Jo twirled her pasta, tasted the chicken and then realized she was eating alone. Walt just stared at her across the table. "What's wrong? Don't you like your food?"

"Just watching you." He forced a smile. "I don't want to spoil this evening, Jo. I really looked forward to it." He twirled pasta around the tines of his fork. "Best

Italian food in Philly," he said, poking the food into his mouth.

She watched him. "There's something else, isn't there?"

He put the silverware down. "I guess so. Maybe it was the weather…the atmosphere…it was eerie and so damned final. Standing there in that lonely cemetery, the sky gray and the wind blowing like crazy, I realized how alone she was…and how alone a lot of us are."

"You're not really alone, Walt. You have friends…family… me…"

He nodded and sipped his wine. "I have old buddies but we don't get together much anymore and it's…it's not the same. Over a couple of beers, Hank talks about fishing and hunting; George talks about his grandkids. An hour and we've all heard enough." He paused, looked away and then back at her. The flickering candlelight caught the highlights in her hair, pulled back and wound into a coil at the nape of her neck. Her hair was so black the highlights looked like a raven's wing. *God, she's beautiful,* he thought. *What's she doing with an old coot like you?* He smiled. "You're alone too, Jo."

She looked away, his eyes too compelling for the moment. "A choice I made."

He nodded. "You must have had a dozen proposals."

The moment was made lighter by her laughter. "Not exactly dozens. There were a couple. Not the right man, not the right time…who knows. I'm happy with my life."

"I know."

"How do you know?"

"You light up the room when you're in it," he said, keeping his eyes focused on his plate of food. "Eat, it's getting cool." He broke a breadstick in half and offered it to her.

They finished their meal, the waiter shaking his head at the amount of food left on the plates as he removed them. They turned down dessert but stayed to finish the wine. The music was soft, the candlelight adding a nice ambience. Later neither remembered what they talked about. Madison was mentioned but Lily wasn't.

He walked her to where she'd parked her car. It wasn't in the same lot where he'd left his. In the cold night, huddled into their coats they were reluctant to part but they ran out of things to say. He put his arms around her and pulled her to his chest. For several moments they stood next to her car, her head resting on his chest his fingers stroking her back. She raised her face, the street lamp illuminating her features. "You're one good looking lady," Walt said, bending to kiss her. He was surprised when she returned the kiss.

Breaking apart, she pressed the button on her key chain to open the doors. The sound made a sharp intrusion in the quiet night, the headlights blinked, cutting a path in the darkness. "Thanks, Walt. Thanks for everything."

He stood where he was as she slid behind the wheel. He searched for words but they didn't come. Their eyes met and she winked. He smiled. "Call me," she said, pulling the door closed. Walt watched her pull forward and turn onto the quiet street.

"Thank you, Jo," he whispered, watching the taillights until they disappeared.

~ ~ ~

The morning sun was still very low in the sky when Madison tiptoed along the walkway to the top of the stairs. She looked across the pool area to the parking lot and saw her car in a guest spot. The parking space for Unit 310 was empty. Philip had already left. She hugged herself against the morning chill, her robe buttoned, her feet in soft slippers. As soon as the sun rose in the sky she knew the temperature would climb to something more comfortable. For several moments she stood still, staring at the parking lot, then she turned and went back into the condo. Picking up the newspaper, she stepped inside.

Closing the door behind her she leaned against it. Her eyes scanned the framed photographs Philip had leaned against the couch late last night. *They will be perfect in the living room*, she thought, planning to take them over to the house today. *How generous of Philip, but then that's not exactly a surprise, is it?*

The wall clock in the dining area showed the time to be seven-thirty. It seemed so quiet and yet it was no quieter than any other morning since she'd been here. Unless Bitsy was awake, she lived a quiet life. Crossing the carpet to the windows leading to the patio, she pulled the drapes back and slid the door open.

The view was serene; the blue waters of the Gulf still darker than they would be when the sun began to lick the tops of the small waves. She watched birds circling over the beach and saw the palm fronds dance slightly in the soft breeze, which she knew would increase as the day went on. She'd become accustomed to the nuances of Florida's weather. Breezes didn't come up much until ten-thirty in the morning, the soft clouds didn't appear much earlier either and the temperature rose slowly as the sun moved across the sky. *And then there are those spectacular sunsets.*

She went into the kitchen, put the newspaper on the table, and began to make coffee. "Have to remember to change the newspaper delivery next week, too," she murmured, reminding herself to add that to her list.

Waiting for the coffee to drip into the pot below, she sat at the table, her fingers tracing the pattern on the place mat. "Those spectacular sunsets," she whispered, remembering last night. She smiled. *Bitsy sure had fun*, she thought. *And you did too so don't deny it. But,* she cautioned herself, d*on't read too much into it either.*

She poured a mug of coffee, added cream, picked up the newspaper and went out onto the patio. It might be cool for a while but as soon as the sun peaked over the rooftop it would be wonderfully warm. She looked into the clear sky and saw an airplane high above the gulf. It was so high she'd never have seen it if the sun hadn't just winked on the metal body or wings.

Philip's plane? she wondered and then laughed at herself. *As if that wouldn't be the ultimate coincidence.*

She sipped her hot coffee, pulled her knees up and opened the paper. She separated the sections, putting the ones she'd read first on the chair next to her and the rest on the floor. She was just snapping the first section open when she heard the door slide open behind her.

"Grandma?" Bitsy croaked, her voice still sleep-clogged. "Can I come out?"

She turned to see the little girl caught in the narrow space she'd opened, Joanie dangling by one arm. "Only if you get your robe and slippers, okay?"

Bitsy nodded and disappeared. "Well the quiet day is over and the fun is just beginning," she murmured, setting her newspaper aside.

Later, after breakfast and when the beds had been made, Madison was in a quandary. Bitsy wanted to go to the beach; Madison knew she should really work on her manuscript and she also wanted to take the pictures over to the house on Thunder Creek Road. Still something held her back and she dawdled over deciding what to make for dinner, and straightening the food on the pantry shelves. What was she waiting for?

The musical sound of her cell phone brought her up short. Who? She ran from the kitchen to the living room where her phone lay next to her laptop. "Hello?" she gasped.

"Madison, it's Walt Kalik."

"Oh, Walt," Madison said, perching on the edge of the chair, her fingers suddenly icy and stiff.

"I have news," he said, his voice unreadable.

Was it long awaited news? Or just something new. "Yes?"

"I found Lily Rose Smith."

Madison looked up to see where Bitsy was. She was nowhere in sight so she called, "Bitsy?"

"I'm in here, Grandma," Bitsy called from her room. "Do you want me?"

"No, stay there, honey and I'll be in in a few minutes."

She turned her attention to the phone cupped to one ear. "What did you find, Walt?" She heard him sigh.

"I found her…she's dead, Madison. I'm sorry."

Madison choked back her instinct to repeat what Walt had just said. Instead, she stood and walked out onto the patio, drawing the door closed behind her. She leaned against the railing, her eyes on the closed doors. "Tell me what you found…please."

She listened closely as he related the activities of the previous day. He didn't mention that he had already told Jo all this. When he was finished telling her about the grave and the things he'd found in the evidence box, he waited for a response. He heard her deep sigh on the other end of the telephone connection. "Are you okay?" he asked.

"I'm okay. Thank you for finding this out. I'm afraid…"

"It's tough news to give anyone. I've done my share in the past and it just doesn't get any easier."

"I'm sure it doesn't," Madison said, struggling to find words that eluded her. Her mind raced but no words came to her lips.

"I understand. Listen, you think about what I've said. There are a couple of things that you might want to do but I'm not the one to tell you. Maybe now you might want to talk to a lawyer."

"Yes. Maybe. Well, thank you. And, Walt, send me a bill. Jo has my address."

She folded the phone and disconnected the call yet she remained where she stood. She didn't notice the temperature, the breeze, the sun that had slipped over the roof and now warmed the railing she leaned on. She didn't know what to feel, how to react. Wasn't this what she'd expected? Then why did the raw truth seem so devastating? She needed to talk to someone. Who? Lolly? Jo?

She sat in a chair, still facing the window. One thing she didn't want was for Bitsy to hear any of this…not now…she didn't know when but that didn't matter right now. Her fingers trembled as she selected Jo's telephone number.

The traffic on Gulf Drive was steady, but it's muted pace not enough to encroach into her concentration. She listened to the phone ring in Philadelphia, praying that Jo was at her desk; that she would answer. When she heard Jo's voice, she began to cry. "Jo," she wheezed. "Jo…"

"He called you."

"Yes."

"When?"

"I just hung up."

"Where are you?"

"Outside on the patio."

"Where's Bitsy?"

"In her room."

Jo blew a puff of air into the room. "Take it easy. He told me last night."

"Why didn't he call me last night?" Madison's mind rushed back in time. *Last night we were with Philip. Last night was…it wasn't the right time.*

"He thought it was too late in the evening when I saw him. It doesn't matter, does it?"

Madison shook her head as if her friend could see her. "I don't know what to think, what to do. What should I do?" she whined.

"Nothing right now. What did Walt say?"

"He told me what he found. What he did yesterday. He said I might want to talk to an attorney."

"That might be good advice. What about Bitsy?"

Madison hesitated. What about Bitsy? Hadn't she just exchanged major worries from *where is Lily* to *what about Bitsy?*

"I'm almost sorry I know," she whispered.

"No you're not. It's just the shock of the news. There was nothing you could have done that would have changed the results. Lily had made her choice long before you came into the picture. Everyone makes choices during their lifetime. They are personal choices that have nothing to do with anyone else. What matters most now is how you proceed with Bitsy."

"Well, I'm never going to give her up," Madison said, her voice strengthened with conviction.

"Of course not. But, it might be wise to consider legal advice."

"No. That would open it up to speculation. Speculation by someone who didn't…care about her, not like I do."

"Listen, Sisty," Jo said, reverting to the childhood nickname only she and Lolly were allowed to use. "You can't make any decisions about anything right now, you're in shock. Do nothing. When you can think calmly, you can make plans. I'll help you, you know that."

"I wish you were here," Madison couldn't stem the tears or quiet the sobs that caught in her throat. Her eyes constantly scanned the glass doors for signs of Bitsy. Bitsy couldn't see her crying.

"You'll scare Bitsy," Jo said, reading Madison's emotions from afar.

"I know," Madison said, pulling a crumpled tissue from her pocket and dabbing at her eyes and forcing herself to stop crying.

They spoke for several minutes, Jo consoling and Madison stabbing at possibilities that were really all impossibilities.

"Call me whenever you want to talk, day or night, okay?" Jo said when they had talked of everything both could think of and yet not making any inroad on what needed to be done, or when or why. "I'll call you tonight after Bitsy goes to bed. What are you going to do today?"

Madison drew in a deep breath. "I was going to write but it just didn't seem the right time this morning. It was as if I was waiting for something and then Walt called."

"What else were you going to do?"

"Bitsy wanted to go to the beach."

"No, that's major thinking time and you need to do something that won't let you dwell on this all day. What else?"

"We were going over to the Thunder Creek Road…"

"Perfect. Do that and then go to a movie, take Bitsy to an amusement park, surround yourself with people and activities."

"I don't know…"

"Dammit do it. If I were there I'd drag your sorry ass out of that condo so fast your head would spin. Now listen to me. Don't sit there and mope. Bitsy will know something is wrong?"

"Okay," Madison whispered. "Should I call Lolly?"

Jo hesitated then said, "No. You'll just get all upset repeating this and the two of you will cry long distance. Wait a few days. It won't change anything. You'll do that for me?"

"Okay."

"Want me to come down?"

"No…I mean yes, but that's not fair to you." Madison pictured her friend. She would be leaning back in her chair in that messy office, her fingers ripping through her hair like she did when she was nervous or concerned. "You're a good friend, Jo. I know you'd drop everything and come to my rescue, but this is something I'm going to have to get through."

"You can do it."

"I know." She paused, going over some of their conversation. "When did Walt tell you?"

"We had dinner last night at Ianelli's."

"Ianelli's? Well," Madison purred, grateful for the diversion. "That's a pretty fancy place. You have something *you* need to tell *me*?"

"No, and don't go dashing off on a wild-goose chase like that. He wanted somewhere quiet so we could talk…about this stuff."

Madison forced a smile. She was about to make further comment on what she perceived as a new stage in her friend's life when she saw Bitsy at the door.

"Got to go, Jo. Bitsy is coming."

"Dry your eyes and take a deep breath. She's what matters now, right?"

"Right. Bye. I'll talk to you later."

When Bitsy stepped out onto the patio floor she was unprepared for what Madison did.

Stepping forward Madison scooped the child into her arms, crushing her to her body and burying her face in the dark curls, she turned in slow circles on the tiled floor. "I love you, I love you," she whispered.

"Grandma, you're squishing me," Bitsy cried, pushing away.

"Oh, sorry, honey. I…I love you so much," she said, letting the little girl slide down to the floor.

"I love you, too, but you scared me."

"I didn't mean to, sweetheart. I just had to hug you."

Bitsy studied her grandmother. "You look funny," she said, her hands on her hips.

"Funny?" Madison said, brushing her hair back and running the back of her right hand across her eyes.

"Yes. You look like you're crying."

"Oh, that." Madison said, turning away. "It must be those darn old allergies, again."

CHAPTER THIRTY-TWO

The secret of success is constancy to purpose.
Benjamin Disraeli

The evening was cool but wearing slacks and a bulky sweater, Madison was warm and snug sitting on the patio. A glass of white wine rested on the table next to her and her cell phone lay on the lounge chair near her hip.

A clear dark sky was softened with stars; a sliver of moon rested comfortably in the black velvet blanket overhead. She waited for Jo's promised phone call and she reminisced about the day that was coming to an end.

A jumble of emotions, she thought. Shock and doubt after Walt's call; raw emotion as she spoke with Jo and then, taking her friend's advice she and Bitsy had left the condo. They had driven south down the coastal highway further than they'd ever been before. Jo said to get involved, surround themselves with people and activities, but this seemed to be more appropriate for them. *After all*, she thought, *both Bitsy and I are loners to a degree.*

She remembered Bitsy's curiosity as they started off. "Where are we going, Grandma? Another beach? I don't have my bathing suit."

But they only walked on the beach, crossing dunes that seemed to be undisturbed by the feet of others before them, running barefoot in the waves as they caressed the shore. Bitsy gathered shells, her pockets bulging with them until Madison had to call a halt. "Just keep the pretty ones," she cautioned and Bitsy countered with "But, Grandma, they're all pretty."

Once the little girl rushed up a dune, sending sand cascading down behind her. "A flower, Grandma," she called, tearing a long stem with a tiny yellow and white flower from the dune. Madison tucked the drooping flower into a buttonhole in her jacket.

They stopped for lunch at a hot dog stand near a fishing pier, then turned back toward home but still they didn't return to the condo. "Let's go to the Mall," was all Madison had to say to ignite Bitsy's excitement. Shopping was now one of her favorite pastimes.

At the Mall, Madison remembered Jo's advice, 'go to a movie' so she looked at the listings for the multi-screened theater. One rated PG seemed appropriate so they went in and spent an hour and a half in the dark watching a dysfunctional family on vacation in the mountains of Colorado. There were so few attendees it was as if they were at a private showing. Madison savored Bitsy's laughter, her boundless giggles piercing the almost empty interior of the theater. In the dark, with just enough light to see her precious granddaughter's face, she thought about their situation and mentally reviewed her options…her choices, as Jo had suggested.

They ate dinner out and returned to the condo after eight o'clock. Madison bathed the tired little girl, tucked her into her pajamas and knelt by the side of the bed next to Bitsy, listening to her prayers. Bitsy didn't need coaching anymore and the sound of her voice speaking to God brought tears to Madison's eyes every night. Tears of joy, tears of happiness and tonight the tears were a combination of many things, but they didn't include sadness or regret.

She jumped momentarily when the phone rang as even that small sound pierced the quiet. "Hi," she said, cradling the phone to her ear.

"You were waiting for me," Jo laughed

"Out on the patio with the phone by my side."

"How are you? Have to say you sound better than this morning."

"I am and you were right. It was just the initial shock, the end came so abruptly I wasn't ready for it."

"But it was what you expected."

Madison paused a moment. "Yes. Sometimes I felt guilty."

"Guilty?"

"Well, sometimes it seemed as if I wished Lily to be dead but I don't think that was really it. What I felt was resignation that I was almost sure she was and yet needed the confirmation to be able to move on."

Jo settled back against the pillows she'd pushed behind her back. She was in bed, the television on mute, a book by her side." Well all that stuff is over. No more guilt, no more indecision. You'll bc fine, Sisty. You and Bitsy will be fine."

Madison laughed. "I remember when you were angry with me for even keeping her with me temporarily."

"I thought you were nuts. I've since changed my mind." She paused and then added, "You're all Bitsy has and she couldn't have a better family."

Madison's eyes crinkled above her smile. "Thanks. That's what I rationalized this afternoon. We went for a long ride and it was just what I needed."

"No crowds? No movie?"

"No crowds, even though that was your advice. We did go to a movie. Bitsy loved it. I think she's only seen a handful of movies in her life, if that. Last week she went to the library for a children's movie time and she was so excited."

"She's going to have a wonderful life with you."

"I hope so. This evening after I put her to bed I made a list."

Jo laughed. "You and your lists."

"Well, they work."

"What was on your list?"

Madison switched the phone to her other ear. "I listed the facts and the possible problems. The list of facts was larger than the list of problems."

"Tell me." Jo pushed another pillow behind her shoulders.

"Well, first there is virtually no one who will be even looking for Bitsy. Her mother is gone. We know of no other family or even close friends and I think the police have probably no further interest in her."

"There was that hooker Walt interviewed."

"Yeah, Missy and wouldn't she be a good guardian," Madison chuckled. "Then, even if there were family, and there has to be someone somewhere, where would we look? We have absolutely no information on Lily except her nefarious life in Philadelphia dating back four or five years.

"Jo I couldn't part with her now. She *is* my granddaughter. Oh, I know, there will be times when things might come up but I think I can weather those storms. There have to be answers. If I go to a lawyer and confess how I acquired my granddaughter he might suggest making it known to authorities. And then what would happen? Child welfare would step in and take her away," she paused, her throat closing at the very use of those words. "No. She's mine, she's happy and I'll always take care of her…like a grandmother."

Neither spoke for several moments, emotions choking the throats of the two friends thirteen hundred miles apart. Finally Madison said, "I miss you."

"I miss you too. I think I'm going to ask for some time off. I didn't even take all my vacation last year. I could…"

"Oh, Jo, do you think it would be possible?"

"I do and I've already begun making plans. If I ask for two weeks off in February I'll be coming down right after the movers drop your stuff off. I could help you get settled, and then check out that part of the country. I need to be able to picture where you are. It doesn't seem real unless I can do that.

"I've never been to the west coast of Florida. I've been to Miami twice on assignments and once down to the keys. I think I need a break. I've been tied up in your emotional struggles for a while and now there's…"

"Now there's…what?"

Jo didn't answer and Madison felt her pulse surge. "Jo is there something else?"

"Don't get your knickers in a twist," she said, imitating one of her favorite Brit-com characters. "I think… Well…"

"Oh, for Pete's sake. What?" Madison demanded.

"Now don't go dramatizing things. This is not a book you're writing. But, ever since I got Walt involved in this search, he's been on my mind. We've been out a couple of evenings and…"

"Dates!" Madison shouted.

"Wait! Not dates. Don't go getting ahead of yourself…and us. Last night…"

"At Ianelli's," Madison interrupted.

"Yes, at Ianelli's. Well, it was kind of emotional. Walt felt so involved with the people in his search, especially Lily. It was kind of like he knew her and was sorry that her life was what it was. Does that make any sense?"

"I think so. Her tragic life had to make an impression."

"Well, it did and we both felt…I don't know…kind of a bond developing."

"Oh, Jo. I'm so happy for you."

"You're jumping the gun, Sisty. Two dates, and I use that word cautiously, one of them certainly questionable as a date, doesn't make a romance, or anything like it. Let's not get ahead of ourselves, okay?"

"Okay. But you will tell me if anything…"

"I will. But only if you promise the same thing."

"What same thing?"

"You and Philip," Jo said.

They laughed, their giggles reminiscent of times past. When they caught their breath, Madison said, "Oh, that felt good. I miss you so much, Jo."

"I miss you. And I'll let you know about my plans." She paused. "About coming down, I mean."

When Madison flipped the phone closed, she leaned back, a smile on her face. It was going to be okay.

She and Bitsy belonged together. Bitsy needed her and she needed Bitsy…needed her to fill that deep empty hole she'd been denying for so many years. And Jo? Jo was a wonderful woman and Madison never really figured out how she had remained single for so long. It wasn't just her career… *No,* Madison thought, *maybe she's too sensible, too cautious, looking for perfection. Is there anything like perfection*? She silently prayed that whatever happened it was going to be wonderful for her friend. As for her? Well, a love life wasn't on her agenda at all. Philip was a nice friend. She put a firm period at the end of that sentence.

As she picked up her wine glass and closed the doors and drapes for the night she thought about Jo and Walt and smiled. *Maybe, just maybe this time...* she thought. But as she rinsed the glass and tucked it into the dishwasher she remembered Jo's reference to Philip.

She paused in the dim kitchen. She hadn't said anything to Jo about the evening she and Bitsy had spent with Philip. A twinge of guilt passed through her and then she shrugged it off. *Today was too full of other news*, she thought. *I'll tell her about that soon. Not that there's anything to tell.*

~ ~ ~

The heat and humidity in Florida never reached the sweltering, smothering air that blanketed Philip in Belém, Brazil. He looked from his watch to the clock on the terminal wall, adjusting his watch to local time. It was fifteen hours since he'd left Tampa and so far he'd landed in Miami and Sao Paolo before arriving here. He was physically tired but his mind raced with thoughts of tomorrow and the following weeks.

Tomorrow he'd meet with the rest of the crew in Manaus and from that point it could be anything from a puddle jumper airplane to a canoe before he reached his final destination.

He picked up his luggage and equipment and was about to leave the terminal when his eye caught a stand displaying souvenirs and postcards. He randomly selected twelve postcards, purchased the necessary stamps and then left the terminal to hail a taxi for the short trip to his hotel. He'd been here before and knew that Belém was a bustling metropolitan area. His hotel would be luxurious compared to what lay ahead of him and he thought about an elegant meal, served as late as eleven o'clock in the impressive dining room at the hotel; later a good night's sleep and a hot shower, small extravagances he'd thoroughly enjoy before the next leg of his journey.

In his room he lay across the bed for a few minutes. His mind ran forward imagining some of the circumstances he would be facing shortly. This shoot was to capture on film some of the many endangered animals and birds that were facing extinction in the next twenty years. It was exciting and all encompassing. Rarely when he began an adventure such as the one he was facing did he let anything else creep into his mind. He needed total concentration.

"Why, then," he mused, "did I buy twelve postcards?" It was the first time he'd ever done this. His sisters knew that when he was out of the country they wouldn't hear from him until he returned. His forehead wrinkled with incomprehension until the image of Madison came to mind. "Because over the next weeks you'll be sending them to Madison, by mule back, if necessary." He closed his eyes and drifted off to sleep.

CHAPTER THIRTY-THREE

The world is round and the place which may seem like the end may also be the beginning.
Ivy Baker Priest

Madison and Bitsy moved into their home on Thunder Creek Road on February tenth. Carol and Ray McWalters brought them lunch and invited them to dinner that night. They immediately became Aunt Carol and Uncle Ray.

"Now I have a big family," Bitsy said. "Aunt Lolly, Aunt Jo, Aunt Carol, Uncle Phil and Uncle Ray. Wow," she said, ticking off the new members of her family on her fingers; her tanned cheeks puffed out by a huge smile, her eyes sparkling as if they were lit by some inner illumination. "When am I going to see Aunt Lolly?"

"She might fly over sometime later this spring. Probably when Caitlin and Jason are out of school so they can come, too. They are your cousins."

Bitsy blinked rapidly, raising herself to her tiptoes, absorbing this news and these names. "More family," she said, with adult-like resignation.

Madison had to restrain herself because she wanted to pick her granddaughter up and dance around the newly arranged living room. Instead she leaned down and brushed a soft kiss across the little girl's forehead. "We are both very lucky, honey. You have a new family and I have you."

"Well, I have you, too. Grandma." She hesitated and Madison waited for some reference to her mother but none came. She'd noticed that Bitsy rarely made reference to her mother lately. *Surely she can't have forgotten her*, she thought as she watched the puzzled little girl.

But, Bitsy smiled at her and then danced down the hallway to look into her room. A new single bed with a trundle beneath, a bureau with a mirror and a matching desk were attractively arranged on the soft blue carpet. A new three-shelf bookcase stood ready to receive the collection of books Bitsy had already amassed.

Beneath the window, covered by narrow Venetian blinds, was a toy chest. When they were choosing Bitsy's furniture, Madison particularly selected a toy chest of good quality, with a flat top and not the domed one Bitsy preferred. "Later, honey, when you're older we can put a cushion on top of the toy chest and turn it into a nice padded bench with storage beneath. Bitsy's puzzled expression evidenced that she hadn't and couldn't look that far into the future. Nevertheless, she kept returning to the room, circling slowly, running her fingers over the tops of the chest and the bureau and tucking the covers around Joanie who had a position of importance against the pillow shams.

"When we decide on curtains throughout the house, you can choose the ones for your room, okay?" Madison asked, standing in the doorway and watching the child's excitement. She sat on the side of the bed. "Are you happy, Bitsy?" she asked.

"Oh, yes, Grandma." Bitsy ran to her and buried her head in Madison's lap. "This is the best house of all and this is the best room I ever saw." She looked up into Madison's face. "Thank you, Grandma. I love it."

Jo flew down the following week. Bitsy and Madison went to Tampa International Airport to pick Jo up and this was another new and exciting first for Bitsy. She was stunned by the crowds of people, the number of cars in the parking lots, the airplanes that roared off runways and others that glided noisily down to earth. Bitsy puzzled at the hollow-sounding announcements that drifted mysteriously from speakers high above them and she looked around for the source of these voices.

As they waited in the area set aside for Jo's flight, Bitsy sat quietly in one of the plastic chairs facing the walkway. She'd spent some time at the huge windows looking at the airplanes as they stood outside or raced down a distant runway, but she soon came to sit next to Madison.

"Where are they going?" she asked.

"Who?" Madison said, watching the child's awestruck face.

"All those people," Bitsy replied, pointing to the never-ending mass of people passing along the corridor.

"Oh, to lots of places. Some are going away on vacation or business trips or to see friends or family. Some are coming here for vacation. Some of them, like we are, are waiting for their friends to land."

"There are so many people," Bitsy sighed. "How do they all get to the right places?"

Madison laughed. "It's not always easy but eventually they all end up where they belong."

The reunion with Jo was happy, tearful and exciting for all three. On the trip back to Osceola Beach there were few moments of silence in the car.

Jo loved Madison's house. "It's perfect. Who would believe that a house could be made in some factory somewhere and then turn out to be so wonderful. What space, what storage. I'm impressed."

"It makes my apartment in Philadelphia look like a little box, doesn't it?"

"Well, that's a great apartment. Perfect for one person and right downtown. You won't have any problem sub-letting it…or selling it," she said, studying Madison's expression.

Madison just shrugged her shoulders. "Wait until you see the beach. We'll go tomorrow."

"Yea," shouted Bitsy. "I love the beach, Aunt Jo. It's so neat."

Madison laughed. "A word she's learned from her friends at the library."

"A perfectly good word and very appropriate I think," Jo said, ruffling Bitsy's curls.

The time of Jo's visit sped by, filled with trips to the beach, the Mall, shopping for the new house and dining out. Madison took her to the restaurant on the island where Philip had taken her and Bitsy. She related the story and watched Jo's face soften as she read more into the occasion than Madison wanted to admit.

"Don't see things that aren't there," she warned. "He's on assignment. When he comes back…well maybe we'll see him once in a while. That's all I expect, Jo. I'm not looking for anything more." She didn't mention the postcard she'd received early this week.

Then it was time for Jo to return to Philadelphia and Madison and Bitsy were in Tampa International Airport, again. This time it was more familiar to Bitsy and she played the part of a seasoned traveler to the hilt. "Those voices are announcements," she told Aunt Jo. "When are *we* going to go on an airplane, Grandma?" she asked and Jo and Madison laughed.

"Now you've done it. Put the wanderlust into her," Jo said, bending down to whisper to Bitsy. "Tell your grandmother that this summer you want to come to Philadelphia and visit me. But don't come until we have some decent weather."

Bitsy watched her grandmother and Aunt Jo as they spoke softly before Jo had to board the plane. She took Madison's hand after Jo disappeared down the hallway to the airplane. "She'll come back again, Grandma," she said comforting her grandmother when she noticed Madison's eyes glisten with tears.

The next few weeks passed calmly. Bitsy's birth certificate arrived one morning and Madison's heart jumped in her chest. It was almost like getting a title to the child; a piece of paper that proved…*proved what*, she thought, then pushed any negative thoughts from her mind.

Later that morning she and Bitsy visited Collier Country-Day Academy. It was a Wednesday and

Madison met with Christine Delaney, the principal who happened to be in that day. She shook Madison's hand and greeted Bitsy. "I'm usually here all week but this week this is the only day I'm in the office. There's a conference of private school educators in Tampa and all the sessions I signed up for were on Monday, Tuesday, Thursday and Friday. But, first let's take a tour and I can show you our facilities. Most of the classes are in session right now but we won't disturb them if they're working. They're accustomed to us bringing possible new students on a tour."

They moved down broad halls and Madison found that the inside of the building seemed too large for her impression of how big the school was from the outside. Too, there was a long extension that ran out the back, dissecting what she thought were playing fields when they had stopped to look at the school. *That seems like such a long time ago*, Madison thought as they entered the lunchroom.

"We don't call it a cafeteria because it really isn't. Our food is prepared over there in the kitchen but the children all get the same meal every day. We have a nutritionist who plans the meals and exceptions are made only for allergies or other dietary needs," Miss Delaney said. "The older the students get the more they complain but it all works out."

"The room is so cheerful," Madison said, taking in the tables, chairs and open airy atmosphere. "All your rooms are so well planned and comfortable looking. I'm sure it adds to the educational quality."

Miss Delaney smiled. "We are proud of our academic results. We have some wonderful students. Let's go back to the office and we'll go over what might be a plan for your granddaughter, Ms. Millhouse."

Forty-five minutes later, when Madison and Bitsy left, she had a folder full of information and Bitsy had a curious look on her face. Madison watched her in the rearview mirror. "Did you like the school, Bitsy?"

"Yes," she said, "But it wasn't like my daycare."

"Well, this is more like a regular school rather than daycare, honey. You'll learn a lot there. In daycare you were just…taken care of. I don't think you had any lessons, did you? This kind of school prepares you for real school, as you call it."

"At daycare at the church, we sang songs and had story time. Mommy told me my numbers and letters."

Madison waited. Was this an opening she'd feared?—Bitsy mentioning her mother? *Would she ask questions*? *And if she did, how do I handle it*, she thought, staring at Bitsy's image in the mirror. *No, don't panic, Jo and I both decided now was not the time to tell her about her mother's death if at all possible. Later is time enough.*

Bitsy folded her lips in and frowned. "They didn't have a television or blocks or a sandbox," she said. "They didn't have a nap room, either."

Madison laughed. "No, honey. No blocks or sandboxes, but did you see how many books each room had? The older grades have so much equipment and the pre-school area, which is where you would go, had lots of interesting things. A small stage, a piano, lots of books and computers! You won't be taking any naps there."

Bitsy's face brightened. "A computer like yours, Grandma? I could learn how to use a computer?"

"We'll have to think this over. The tuition isn't as much as I thought it might be, for pre-school anyway. As you move up in the grades it gets a bit more because the students have more teachers, but…well, we'll see. Do you think you'd like to go there?"

"Everyday?"

"Yes, during the school year your classes are from eight o'clock until noon, then first and second grade is from eight to two o'clock."

"I think I would miss you, Grandma, if I went every day."

"When you go to real school, honey, you'll have to go every day."

"Oh," Bitsy said. "Well, then I guess it would be good."

Two weeks later, Bitsy was enrolled in Collier Country-Day Academy. Madison took her and came back for her at noon. The first morning it was a toss up as to who was more nervous, Bitsy or Madison but after that first day, Bitsy didn't understand why she couldn't stay longer. "Some of the kids stay all day," she said, her hands clutching some papers, her lips pouting.

"They are the children whose parents work. It's afternoon daycare. You come home so we can do things together."

It was working out just right. Madison was able to finish her thirteenth novel and get it off to Alan for editing and publishing. After that she spent mornings doing housework, talking with Carol and Ray McWalters and doing some volunteer work at the book store in the library one morning a week. She also rushed to the mailbox after the mail carrier had left. Sometimes there was a postcard from Philip. The postcards were carefully worded. No 'I miss you', just interesting things that happened to him in the jungle.

The afternoons were spent with Bitsy, visiting the library, going to the beach and just the ordinary things that a little girl and her grandmother did. They even baked cookies.

When the school term ended in late May, Bitsy was torn between wanting it to continue and being able to sleep late and be with her grandmother. After a few days, she was contented to tag along with Madison. She was happy and Madison reveled in that fact. They kept the school thought alive by making sure that some reading and studying of some sort was done every day.

In June Lolly, Caitlin and Jason flew from California to visit them. Caitlin shared Bitsy's room and the two, despite the great difference in their ages, got along very well. Jason slept on the screened porch in his sleeping bag and begged to go to the beach every day. Madison and Lolly renewed their friendship.

"We're alike in more ways than I realized," Lolly said as she helped Madison prepare dinner in the bright kitchen.

"Well, I never had any reason to be very domestic before. Actually, I love it. And Bitsy is such a pleasant and agreeable child. Oh, she has her moments when things don't go quite the way she'd like them to, but all in all, she's a gem."

"I can see that," Lolly said, peeking into the living room where Bitsy was showing Caitlin her skills on the *GeoSafari* laptop Madison had recently purchased for her. "You'll spoil that child, though, if you aren't careful."

"I'm trying not to but she was so disadvantaged before she came to me. I guess I'm trying to make everything up to her. She's bright. I got very good progress reports from school and she took to that laptop like a duck to water. "

Lolly put her arm around Madison's shoulders. "You're a good grandma, Sisty. I never would have thought you could do it." She hesitated and lowered her voice, "Any more trouble with the past creeping up?"

"No," Madison whispered back. "She rarely asks about her mother. I'm not sure what goes on in that little head but somehow she seems to be able to adapt and move on."

"Kids are like cats," Lolly laughed. "Toss them in the air and they land on their feet. As long as they're warm, fed and cared for. You're doing a fine job."

"I've never been happier," Madison said, swallowing a lump that suddenly jumped into her throat.

"I know...and that makes me happy."

She put the beans she'd been cutting into the colander. "What about your next book?"

Madison turned and leaned against the counter. "You know I think the Detective Bloodworth Mysteries are over."

"Really?" Lolly stared at her sister. "But you are going to continue to write, aren't you?"

"Yes," Madison said with a wide grin. "I've already written two children's stories and sent them to Alan. He, of course, was surprised but he said they were good. He's trying to market them. With the royalties from my other books and the trust Dad left me, as he did you, we'll be okay. And, if push comes to shove, I can always go to work, especially when Bitsy is in school full time. But," Madison said, turning to look out the window, "I take things a bit easier now. I never realized how stressful my life was before Bitsy."

"I think it was pretty stressful right after you…acquired the child."

"That didn't last long. We fell in love right away."

"Speaking of love," Lolly whispered. "What's with Philip and you?"

Madison shook her head. "You and Jo. We're friends, Lolly. He's a nice guy. He and Bitsy get along well. We all do. We go out for dinner once in a while, the three of us, and he's taken us to a couple of museums, down the coast to watch manatees, visited tropical gardens, outings like that. But, don't read love into that equation okay? We're happy just as it is for now."

"For now," Lolly mumbled softly, going into the living room where Bitsy tired to engage them all in a game of Old Maid.

CHAPTER THIRTY-FOUR

Now that you have come, dancing into my life...a guest in a closed room...
Catherine O'Brien

Ten years…

Madison sat at her desk in her studio looking through the window at a pair of cardinals as they splashed in the birdbath in the back yard. The Spanish moss festooning the oak trees was swaying with the gentle spring breeze.

It was Friday afternoon and she'd been working on the latest Grandmother Mary book. She smiled. After the last Detective Bloodworth book, and following a few children's stories geared for very young children, Madison had begun a series of Grandmother Mary books. The popular series began with a simple story directed at older children. The series was about a grandmother, Grandmother Mary, from a small town in the mountains of Pennsylvania who rushed from place to place getting involved in various plots, always including two or three children, always with a message; a message of love, courage, honesty and other virtues. The series had received several literary awards and was much in demand. The one she was writing now had Grandmother Mary in San Francisco. She and three children were trapped in a building following a small earthquake. Madison had spent the afternoon researching California earthquakes.

She stretched her hands over her head, relieving a knot at the nape of her neck, and looked toward the door that led to the porch. It was ajar and she heard the voices of Bitsy and her very best friend, Chelsy. She rose to look out the door into the porch. *How many times have I seen those two hatching schemes*, she thought. *Doing homework and giggling together?* They had been together since the very first day at Collier Academy. Chelsy was Bitsy's best friend, the one she told her secrets to, and the one who shared her dreams and laughed at their escapades. She watched them paging through a fashion magazine, Bitsy's dark curls pressed against Chelsy's shoulder-length blonde hair, so straight it looked as if it had been ironed. *And maybe it has*, she thought.

"Oh, look at that," Chelsy gasped. "I'll bet my mother would never let me wear that!"

She pushed open the door. "You two ready for a snack?" she called.

"What kind of a snack?" Bitsy asked cautiously.

"Well, I was thinking of spinach and raw onions," Madison said, stifling a smile.

"Yuk," they both chorused. "You're kidding, right?" Chelsy asked, her wide smile exposing a mouthful of metal braces.

"How about cookies and iced tea?" Madison asked, stepping into the porch. "Dinner is going to be a little late tonight."

"A snack would be great, Grandma. Can we help?"

"Not this time. I need a break. I'll fix it and then join you for a few minutes before I go back to work, okay? Philip's coming but not until after seven o'clock."

In the kitchen Madison prepared a tray with three glasses of tea she'd brewed earlier, green tea with fresh ginger, one of Bitsy's favorites. She added a plate with some cookies the three of them had made earlier in the week. Chelsy's parents both worked so it was almost a daily occurrence that the girls came home from school together. Chelsy's mother picked her up before six usually. Tonight since it was a weekend, Chelsy was spending the night.

Madison heard their voices.

"Next week's your birthday," Chelsy said, pushing the magazine aside.

"Yeah, fifteen.

"I'm jealous. I won't be fifteen until June."

"It's not that long."

"But your birthday is going to be so fun," Chelsy pouted. "Imagine going to Tampa for the whole day, seeing a play, having your party in a fancy restaurant and staying overnight. Then the amusement park the next day. It's too awesome."

"You're going, too," Bitsy said, poking her friend with one sneakered toe.

"And your whole family is going, too," Chelsy countered. "They're all neat."

"Aunt Jo and Uncle Walt are flying down. Uncle Philip and Grandma. That's all. Aunt Lolly and my cousins can't come until summer."

"Your grandmother is neat."

"I know."

"What happened to your mother?"

"She died a long time ago, in an accident."

"How about your Dad?"

Bitsy shrugged her shoulders.

"My mother told me never to ask you about your parents, but you never talk about them. Everyone has a mother and father."

"I don't. I have Grandma," Bitsy said, her voice strong and confident.

Madison held her breath. Year's ago she'd told Bitsy some of what happened to her mother, leaving out the tawdry past and dwelling on the fact that her mother had been killed in a terrible automobile accident in a snowstorm. Bitsy remembered the storm, remembered waiting for her grandmother.

The memory rushed back to her. "Your Uncle Walt discovered what happened to your Mommy after she left you at the diner," she'd said. "Remember? You were waiting for me when I got there. He said that from the direction your Mommy was traveling when the accident happened, she was probably heading back to be with us."

There had been other questions over the years but nothing that caused any consternation. *Still,* she wondered, *why had Chelsy asked these questions today? Had Bitsy brought up the subject earlier?*

Madison pushed the door open and stepped out into the porch. "Here we are," she said putting the tray on the table. "You serve, honey. You're the hostess with the mostess today."

That night after they'd enjoyed dinner together and then a game of cards, both girls had disappeared into Bitsy's room. Later Madison tiptoed in to turn off the music they'd been listening to; she stood for a moment looking at the two girls then turned and closed the door softly.

Ten years, she thought. *So much has happened. Bitsy was such a little girl, almost a baby; now she's a lovely young woman... fifteen year's old next week. Jo marrying Walt last year after year's of just being a couple and now planning to retire to Florida next year. Lolly and Steve happy empty-nesters, the kids out of college and on their own.* She paused in the hallway. *And, Philip...*She smiled and went out onto the screened porch where he waited for her.

"I was just thinking about all the good things that have happened in my life over the past ten years. Bitsy was so young, now she's a young woman. My life seems to have evolved into something I'd never even dreamed of."

He beckoned for her to join him on the padded wicker couch. "And you get more beautiful year after year. How do you do it?"

She sat next to him, waiting for his arm to circle her, pulling her next to him. "I think you exaggerate, sir," she said, laughing softly.

"Never. Me exaggerate? Impossible. I tell the truth, woman."

They sat in the dark, two candles flickering in a pool of melted wax. Across the wide lawn they could see lights in the McWalters' house. "I think Carol is handling Roy's death very well, don't you?" Madison asked.

"As well as anyone can handle that kind of tragedy. He was ill for a couple of years. That's always difficult for a loved one to watch. I'm glad their daughter-in-law, grandson and her new husband are moving back to help her."

"And I'm glad I purchased this house five years ago. I couldn't face the thought of leaving here. Anyhow, building a special addition for Carol onto the house over there so that they can have the main house and still keep the family together sounded like such a good plan to me."

"She's lucky she has them. She and Roy had such a close marriage."

"I know. I loved them both. They were so kind and helpful when I was adjusting to…"

"To your new life," he whispered, his fingers caressing her arm. "Everyone needs someone to care for."

"I know," she whispered back, turning her head to look into his face.

"Are you happy?" he asked.

"Yes, I am. I love what I do, I love where I live, I love my life."

Philip leaned forward. "I'm happy too. Happy to see you happy. I never thought…"

"Never thought what?"

He rose and paced across the floor, pausing to stare out into the darkness. "I never thought I'd love anyone again."

Madison moved to his side. She remembered years ago when he told her about his wife. Diagnosed with ovarian cancer at the age of thirty-two, he'd watched her die over the next two years. "She just melted away, bit at a time," he'd said, his voice choked with emotion. "Never again," he'd said. "I'll never marry again."

Madison understood. After her long affair with Jim and all the loneliness, the secrecy and the bitterness she'd felt, she swore she would never commit to a man again after she ended that part of her life. Of course, she'd rationalized; having Bitsy in her life changed everything.

She leaned against Philip and felt his arm circle her waist. "I love you," he said. "I've known it for a long time but I was afraid to admit it. Do you think I'm crazy?" He looked down at her upturned face. "Do you think…"

Madison felt her heart swell to enormous proportions within her chest. "I'm not sure what I think Philip. But I do know this. I wouldn't want to live a day without you. Without knowing you'd be here… that I'd see you…"

He turned and pulled her with him back to the couch. "I thought that, too. For a long time I thought that seeing you, being with you and Bitsy was enough, because you're such fun to be with. And Bitsy…" They settled against the cushions again, his arm around her.

"And Bitsy…" she whispered. "That might make a difference, right?"

"To you?"

"No, to you."

She heard him chuckle and even in the darkness she knew what his face looked like, laugh lines deepening, perpetually tanned cheeks puffed out, mouth softened by his grin. He had a nice laugh. "No, not to me. I think I fell in love with Bitsy at the same time I fell in love with you, Madison; maybe I even loved her first, I don't know. I'm a late bloomer, I guess. It took me a long time to realize how stupid I was, how stupid this long distance relationship was. But wherever I was over these past years, I couldn't wait to get back to you."

She snuggled into his side, resting her head on his chest. "I love you, too, Philip. I think I've known it for a long time even though I denied it."

"Why did we both deny it?"

"Because of the past, I guess. Because we were comfortable with each other and neither demanded any more. But now…now that it's out in the open…what do we do?"

Madison was startled when Philip jumped up. "We're going to do something about it. Will you marry me, Madison?" He held his hand out to her.

She put her fingers into his palm and felt him tug her upright. "Will you?" he asked burying his face in her hair, crushing her body to his.

"Yes," she whispered. They stood entwined in the soft breeze. A night bird called softly and another answered. She pulled away and he bent and pressed his lips on her. He'd kissed her before, on the cheek at first and then a soft brushing of his lips over hers at Christmas and on special occasions…like a spectacular sunset on the beach and when Bitsy was out of sight. Those moments seemed to have been snatched from another time, eagerly embraced and just as easily set aside. This kiss stirred them to a passion they had never allowed to form. "What about Bitsy?" she whispered after they had parted but still clung to each other.

"She's getting a grandfather for her birthday," he said, laughing and crushing her to him again.

A word from the author...

I hope you enjoyed reading *A Grandma for Christmas* as much as I loved writing it. If you are interested in any of my other published novels, or would like to send me a review, please contact me. I love hearing from my readers and my email address is listed below! P.S. autographed books make wonderful gifts.

Never Look Back	18.95
Beyond Innocence	17.95
Secrets *	18.95
Echoes **	17.95
Nobody's Child	15.95
Following Daddy	13.50

Florida residents please include 7% Sales tax.
Shipping and Handling $3.00

* Recipient of a National League of American Pen Women literary award - 2005
** Recipient of a Florida Writer's Association literary award –2004

Thank you!
Sunny Serafino – for emails use
sunnyone@strato.net - subject 'books'.